LORD MONTÉ

THE JOURNEY FROM
NOTHING TO THE THRONE

N.D.M.

N.D.M.

LORD MONTÉ

THE JOURNEY FROM NOTHING TO THE THRONE

N.D.M.

Foreword By:
Kim Moore

Pearly Gates Publishing, LLC, Houston, Texas

Lord Monté: The Journey from Nothing to the Throne

Lord Monté:
The Journey from Nothing to the Throne

Print ISBN 13: 978-1-947445-98-7
Digital ISBN 13: 978-1-947445-99-4
Library of Congress Control Number: 2020912320

For information and bulk ordering, contact:
Pearly Gates Publishing, LLC
Angela Edwards, CEO
P.O. Box 62287
Houston, TX 77205
BestSeller@PearlyGatesPublishing.com

DEDICATION

To Dad, Mom, Samuel, Israel, Anna, and Victoria:

You believed in me, cried with me, laughed with me and encouraged me at all the right times.

Thank you.

ACKNOWLEDGMENTS

First, I thank my **Lord and Savior** for the ideas that inspired me to put pen to paper.

To my **Family**: We did it! Most times, I can't believe it myself.

To **Mr. Michael and Mrs. Amber Jones**: Thank you for noticing and blowing wind into my sails. I will be grateful for you forever and ever.

To **Carrie**: I would have put this beautiful work down and quit were it not for you. Thank you for the encouragement.

To **Chelsea Jackson**: Thank you for seeing something in this work's humble beginnings.

To **Mom, Anna, Julia, Mr. Park, and Mrs. Laurie**: I appreciate each of you proofreading my work. Thank you for your time.

The ideas in this book took root at Camp Netimus. I thank the following for all the encouragement, fun, and magical experiences: **Nora, Maya, Ashley, Sierra, Mary, Francis, Paige, Luna, Nina, Sidney, and Natalie.**

A special thank you is being expressed to **all the kind people** who sewed into me to help get my first book published.

Lastly, to **Pearly Gates Publishing and Mrs. Angela**: Thank you for your efforts to make this book as successful and impactful as it can be.

I pray the Lord blesses and keeps you all.
Numbers 6:24-26

FOREWORD

When your teenage daughter says she wants to write a book about "things"—things she shouldn't even know about…dark, the stuff people hate to discuss—I admit I was skeptical. However, she worked diligently to convince me of the following:

If we never go into the dark, we can't give it light.

Someone must go into the worst places to bring others hope.

The best thing I ever did was let her keep writing. As I read this book from cover to cover, I was very inspired and couldn't put it down.

If I could, I would climb into Lord Monté's world. Since I cannot—since **we** cannot—I stand boldly and assuredly when I say to you:

You will come to both love and despise this literary work…but you will not want to stop reading.

For my sake and yours, this Momma is making her daughter write even more!

Kim Moore, Mom of Naomi Moore
Author of *Are All Adults Grown-Ups?*

INTRODUCTION

It is human nature to "judge a book by its cover." We do it almost without thinking—often quicker than we can blink. As a result, we also do not take into account a person's story.

Everyone has a story. Younger people are trying to write theirs, and older people are trying to share their own so that it lives on.

This book was written over the course of three years. Through the early mornings and late nights at the computer, "it" began to materialize for me...this *idea* that has been threaded through the pages. Within, you will find *disturbing* scenes (the kind that no one wants to talk about), *action* scenes (sure to make your hair stand on end), and *heartwarming* scenes (guaranteed to make you smile).

When I find myself judging what I can see of a person (half of the story), I want to catch myself a second after. They deserve that. For example, the wealthy aren't always privileged just because I didn't see the work they put in. Perhaps those who have hit a low point are not incapable, just broken. Whatever the story or circumstance, I do not want to assume. I want to listen so that I can learn.

Stories change, though. I am "here" today and "there" tomorrow. I choose, however, to cling to living hope. That is why I can make the decision to stick with it. I forgive, so I am not bitter. I apologize, so I am not ignorant. I smile, so I am approachable. Depression, bitterness, and ignorance are all choices—meaning I can choose not to fall into them.

As can you.

As can all of us.

If there is anything I desire for my dear readers to pull from this story, it will be the following two things:

1. Be slow to judge, and
2. Be quick to hope.

Although life holds many traumatic moments, the story **must** be told. Just when we are convinced that we are all alone, nobody loves us, and nobody cares, know that there is someone who **always** will…*whether we notice or not.*

His name is
Jesus Christ.

TABLE OF CONTENTS

1: LORD MONTÉ

I killed my parents when I was 12 years old. I wish I could receive all the credit, but my brother abetted me.

I know what you're thinking: **"He's crazy!"** That's hardly the word. I am a man of abstruse judgment – of darker ways and deeper meaning.

Who am I?

I am Lord Monté, III. I bleed from my mouth, curse through my actions, and scar through my gaze. People's reactions to my thinking are unfair and unjust, but so is the world...

My brother killed himself weeks after our parents' deaths. Suicide is such a dreadful thing. The victim's world stops, but yours goes on. I was left without a vital piece of life, all because my brother let our parents' deaths play with him.

What a waste.

The world's inhabitants show no appreciation for anything. They run from death as if they can truly escape it. In the end, we all must pay. Paying sooner is a release from the yoke of debt, which is, as you would agree, a relief.

Are you still following along? Wow. No one has ever listened to me this long.

I'm sure you're still wondering about my parents. Well, don't. I succeeded in giving them the most painful death I've ever given. No worries, since I know that is what you're worried about. A better man would have lessened the pain a bit. I am not a better man.

What is a better man? Is he one who tries harder than the other? What is trying if it amounts to nothing? What is life without death?

Unanswerable questions materialize everywhere in life. However, a true genius can find enough of what the answers are. You see, my parents didn't understand my genius. How many people do you know could pull off a murder at the age of twelve? Probably not many…at least I hope not. I would hate for you to be associated with a murderer.

Despite your assumptions, I am not a murderer. It's this simple:

Murder is predetermined malice. Nothing I do is ever predetermined. As a matter of fact, I don't think about anything until after I've done it.

Unfortunately, though, long travels and freeing the world of what destroyed my life are over for me; I am dead – stabbed through my throat like an animal. I suppose it's what I deserve because a better man would have told my killer what I'd been through…maybe even apologized.

I suffer no regret, and no one should apologize unless they do. Everything I did was done for a reason. Soon, the boy who killed me will understand.

Remember me. There are few who share the genius of me: **Lord Monté.**

2: DUSTIN ELRIC CARPENTER

Hey ho, nobody home;
No eat, nor drink, nor money have.
I none – still, I will be very merry!
Hey ho, nobody home.

Quick, sharp breaths came from Julius' nostrils, maybe even a snort or two. Nothing came from mine. For all appearances, it seemed as if I wasn't even breathing.

My ripped, rugged, jet-black hood and cape covered my face with shadows. Only the wind could rip through, as I slowed in front of my destination.

The Yellow Diary Pub stood cold and still in the darkness of nowhere. Undoubtedly, the roof was falling in, and

I wondered when the slumlord would confess it. Trees hung over it, their limbs resembling human ones stretching out to hide it. The moon didn't even like to shine on it…at least I'd never seen it do so before. The merry laughter from the interior betrayed any façade of solemnity. It was an enjoyable location…an unlikely place to meet in secret.

Before I could pull the reins or whistle, Julius slowed to a halt. I leaned back on my saddle and folded my arms. *"Oh, what a lovely attitude, mate! More of it and the clouds will open and rain sparkles and sunshine, eh?"* He responded with an unrepentant snort. Laughing, I climbed down from the black beast and rapped his side gently with my knuckles. *"Don't worry. You get at least two hours off."* I patted him right on the white speck sporting his nose before tying his head to a post and walking up the stairs to the heavy wooden front doors.

There was an eerie stillness outdoors. I soaked it in, slipped on my mask to cover my mouth, and readjusted my hood. I hoped it was incognito enough to hide my identity. *Can't have anyone recognizing me, can I?*

I finally pushed open the heavy door. With it came a wave of heat from the massive fireplace in the back of the front room. Chairs were strewn about from underneath the tables in a chaotic manner, and either the floor hadn't been swept in weeks, or the occupants of the pub were mistaking it for their plates. There were plenty of people inside, just the way I wanted it to be. I was just another face in the multitude…

"Oi, stranger!" The cry over the laughter came from the heavyset, wide-nosed man behind the bar ahead and to my left. I could tell the mask disturbed him, but his job as the barman compelled him to welcome me. *"Ale or mead for ya lad?"*

I needed to disappear from the room. The easiest way to do so was to act like every other person in it—minus the mask and hood I wasn't pulling off. *"Ale. To the table in the corner there,"* I added as I spotted my friends in the back of the room by the fireplace.

Woodruff was the first to spot me. All smiles, Woodruff is a redhead with a thick beard and even thicker build. He was the only one to stand as I approached the wooden table adorned with mugs full of mead, ale, and beer. Five chairs were occupied, and two were empty, waiting for participants. *"Pleasure seeing you, mate! Ecstatic to hear your secret. Sounds like jolly good fun!"*

I laughed and pulled off my mask before speaking. *"Perhaps it is."*

Egon groaned indifferently and pulled an empty chair from underneath the table. *"You look bloody awful, Dust. Sit."* I nodded in gratitude and almost fell into the seat, tugging off my gloves and warming my bare hands by the fire.

"D-does the king k-know about t-this?" Silas stuttered out.

I stared at each of the five there and then at the last empty seat. *"I thought I sent for you all. Where's Arthur?"*

"Probably on his bum in the mud. His pa's always got him working on something, doesn't he?" Egon made the statement, but it was Woodruff who got a big kick out of it, to Ocean's dismay.

"Guys, Dustin seems serious. Quit jesting," Ocean said. Egon snorted, but she didn't give him another opportunity to speak. *"Silas presented a good question. Does his Majesty—your father—know about us meeting up?"*

I made a show of taking off my boots and turning them upside down to shake out the pebbles. No one spoke, and I found the heavy silence of curiosity to be strangely amusing. If I ever want them to shut up in the future, I'd just tell them I had a secret. Smiling, I answered. *"Not responding to any questions 'til Arthur gets here, mates."* A simultaneous groan slipped from everyone at the table, except for Cederic. I felt the need to egg him on. *"Cederic, you seem quiet. Show these cox combs how to be patient and wait."*

I could have imagined it, but the left side of Cederic's mouth might have lifted ever-so-slightly. *"I'd show them,"* he said in his classic deep voice, *"but I think they don't want to know."*

The bartender, in all his girth, came over to put a mug full of ale down in front of me. I nodded thanks to him, and the simple gesture seemed to make the man relax — maybe forget about my hood and mask. *"Y'sure you lads — oh, and miss — need to be out here this late? Hate for your old man to have to find ya out here acting foolish."* The question was mostly directed at me, the youngest at the table.

"We're fine, sir. Thanks for the ale," Egon said while scratching the tattoo on his right arm. He dismissed the bartender and barely waited for the man to walk out of earshot before asking, *"How do you know Arthur's even coming?"*

A burst of laughter erupted from across the room. No one around the table looked over to see what caused it.

"I'm sure he's coming," Ocean said to Egon. *"I asked him in sparring yesterday."*

Silas shrugged. *"The l-lad's been late before, O-Ocean. Even n-never showed u-up one t-t-time."* He spoke quietly, as if afraid she might actually hear.

Ocean was quick to defend Arthur. *"Arthur wouldn't have stiffed us, knowing how important this talk is."*

Egon must've thought differently. *"But we don't know a buggin' thing, do we? Dustin hasn't told us anything,"* he said. *"Besides, maybe the lad fell off his little Shetland pony, eh?"* Woodruff laughed, and even Silas smiled.

The people from the table to my left kept glancing over at our table. I noticed and thought it was my hood shadowing my face bothering them, but too many eyes moved Cederic's way for me to believe that for long. I soon realized I wasn't the center of their attention; they were looking at Cederic's dark skin. I pointedly returned a burly man's stare, and that put an end to it.

Ocean looked about ready to tell off all the Warriors for their behavior, when the door to the pub opened and in came a gust of cold wind…and Arthur Foreman. Everyone in the pub turned to look, but most immediately lost interest.

Two years my junior and cheeks flushed, he lacked the raw edge to be of any danger to anyone. I noticed, though, that he was quite flustered. His brown curls were amiss on his head. He spotted our group, gave a smile with no meaning behind it, and came towards us.

"Cheers, mates," Arthur greeted. *"Sorry I'm late, but the gaffer had a job or two for me, and who says no to the man? Had to tell him I had a spar with the prince to get him off me! Thought about telling him about this secret meetup, but seeing the whole thing's*

secret, I figured Dust wouldn't take a liking to me divulging him with details about the — "

"For the love of all that's good in the world, sit down, Arthur!" Egon interrupted gruffly, kicking the last unoccupied chair out from under the table.

Arthur jumped and raised a startled brow at the statement and the action. *"Right-o, man. Sorry,"* he said, sitting down.

"You about told the whole pub about our 'secret' meetup, you little bugger!" Woodruff said, laughing.

Arthur blushed deeply and mumbled an apology. Silas grinned. Ocean couldn't hide a smile as well.

Cederic, however, was intrigued. *"Well, we're all here now, Dustin. I'm curious. What about Silas' question? Does your father know about this?"*

I raised a brow. *"As a matter of fact, I have a strict order from him."*

Everyone around the table glanced at each other. Woodruff faltered, but his smile remained. *"Pardon me? This is under your dad's approval? This whole secret meeting…"*

I nodded, confirming this wasn't just another one of my pranks, which I did occasionally do. *"Hear me out, guys. This is important, actually. It's a little mission I think my dad has in mind."*

The statement took the group of Black Warriors by surprise. Arthur was quick to be the most confused of the lot. *"Like a rescue mission?"* he asked.

I glanced around before saying, *"It's not a rescue if you're killing its usurper and taking the kingdom."*

The silence was deafening. I thought for just a moment that I had lost the attention of my audience. Baffled, Egon looked around the pub as if to find someone then returned his attention to me. *"I **do** hope you're kidding, mate. Are we the only ones you called? I have an inkling it would take a lot more than seven soldiers — two of whom, forgive my saying this, Prince Dustin, are too young to have fought in any battle whatsoever."*

"Well," I said with as much confidence as I could muster into the word, *"that's what training's for, isn't it?"*

"You've failed to give us all the details," spoken by the deepest voice in the room, Cederic. *"What is this kingdom?"*

I didn't hesitate. *"Jocund."*

Egon shook his head in irritation. *"Bloody nuisance, this."* Woodruff raised his eyebrows. I even got a reaction from Ocean and Cederic, who both exchanged looks of disbelief and a tiny bit of bewilderment.

"Jocund? The one east of Haestingas? The one rumored to have been taken by Lord Monté?" Arthur's voice had raised a pitch as he'd gone on.

"Yes, that's the bloody one, Arthur!" Egon exploded. Woodruff laughed.

"Yes, you're quite right, Arthur," I confirmed. *"We won't attack aggressively. My father and I agree it is too much hassle to siege. A siege would depend on Lord Monté giving up the kingdom or risk starving his citizens. It seems the man would kill them all before he'd relinquish power, so a siege won't be in our best interest. We do*

not have the ability and the resources to go to war with Jocund. If we could get into the castle quietly and disguised, we might have a chance, indeed. If the Lord Monté and his attendants fall, so will his corruption. Then, we'll take the kingdom of Jocund for us."

Ocean asked the question I'd known was coming and had presumed would have come quicker: *"Why must we take a kingdom we have few ties to…one that's been experiencing famine? For what purpose? If saving them is all you want, then let's do it and then come home."*

I sighed deeply. This was the hardest part; them not knowing. I had been warned not to tell a soul, but maybe it was the most critical part. *"To claim what belongs to me. To steal back what has been stolen from Jocund."*

Everyone, including Arthur, connected the dots—even though they hadn't been spoken…only danced around. The troubling fact was I couldn't tell them the whole truth. I couldn't fully trust them, although they had served my father faithfully for years and fought in wars strongly not in their favor, all for the sake of Sans Défaut—my father's kingdom. After all, if I told them everything, I'd endanger them.

Now, they had a choice, and quite the difficult one. Do they go blindly into a seven-day journey they had no clue as to the intention of the ending? Looking from their standpoint, they were heavily outnumbered.

"What do you guys say?" I asked as casual as I could without choking over my own acting.

Across the room, a drunk man was singing a song about a weary traveler who found rest in a cave. On the other side, a sleepy man who had the chair groaning underneath him snored obnoxiously while falling asleep in his mug of beer.

Woodruff took a swig of ale and tried a smile, stretching his freckles. *"Aye, mate. To a big man like me, Jocund is just a stone's throw away."*

Egon gave him a pinched look but, to my surprise, didn't say anything. Call me foolish, but I couldn't help but ask, *"What about you, Egon? Haven't heard you speak in a while."*

Everyone chuckled. Egon noticed their teasing and rolled his eyes. *"I don't know what to say. The whole idea is absolutely ludicrous!"*

"Ludicrous is e-exactly the word. B-but Prince Dustin has never led us into something we couldn't win before, a-a-and I don't think he would-he would now."

Six pairs of eyes turned to the man who made the statement, but it was the woman at the table who continued.

"I don't like dismissing what I've never even tried. Silas is right. Let's bloody do it or go down trying."

3: ROSETTA KELLINA MABEL

7 reasons to die.
7 reasons to live.
I'm torn by dust and shadows
That never cease to rip.

A question I've pondered persistently is: Is the sky grey or blue? Blue is what I was taught to believe, yet grey is the reality. How do you tell someone the sky is grey if theirs is thickly covered by clouds of hopes and dreams?

Well, you invade their kingdom, and when they complain, you weed them out. You send an order to snatch hopes and dreams away quicker than anything. You send them death.

The only problem with this order was me. I was out of place. Edmund the Harker should've had this deed, not me. Not the innocent clothier…the one who hadn't spoken to the Lord Monté since she's managed to evade her own death.

The chancellor had told the castellan, and the castellan had told me: The Lord Monté had been specific with the instructions he'd given. The Harker would accompany me, but I must be the one to read off the scroll the genuine words of the iniquitous Lord of the kingdom.

I finished my braid, which fell down my back, sighing at my simple frame in the glass staring back at me. My room, defiant of everything crashing around me, was the most peaceful place in the castle. Expensive? No. Spacious? Enough. It was, however, the only place where the horrors of my past couldn't speak to me. It smelled of dust and flowers: dust because I wasn't in my room enough to care, and flowers because a friend was always bringing them into my room. There was only enough space for my bed: a small, wooden one with a deep gash on the left post of the footboard from a foolish but fun night of play with a princess long ago. A brilliant oak wardrobe stood proudly at the right side of the bed, and next to it, the glass I peered into.

I wore a white gown and my bliaut, a deep red. My feet were simply sandaled because they wouldn't be seen — and because I was slightly embarrassed to show up wearing anything fancier with the news I had to tell in the village's main marketplace. I was hesitant to express pity, but I am human, after all. There are things I can't avoid. With one last glare of anger and sadness at the glass mirror, I moved out of my chambers and down a bustling, window-lit, early morning corridor.

Destiny — or maybe knowing her movements and morning schedule as well as I did — led me to run into Lydia Taylor. She was carrying a bucket of clean water she must have gotten from the Ewerer for the castle gardens. She was incredibly jolly and whistled a happy tune. I was circumspect to tell her about the task I was headed to achieve, and frankly, she didn't give me a chance.

"You have no clue what Mack's been up to today! Sending me to fetch all his things, you'd think I was his servant. What a horrid imbecile!" I smiled at her outburst, shoving my concerns to the side for a moment.

Mack was one of the many gardeners privileged to work in the Lord's garden. He'd gotten there maybe a month ago and had taken charge quite like he'd been there all his life. Regrettably, he took a strong disliking to Lydia not long after he arrived, for she was one of the only gardeners who had spoken aloud and against his abrupt self-proclaimed promotion. She had a knack for being the bold one and it had gotten her into trouble more than a few times.

Despite her resentment for the man, her face shown remorse at having insulted him as harshly as she did, and my silence broke her. *"Well, if the man was half a bit more reasonable, I might think him a nicer fellow. He's far too much like me, you know?"*

I laughed and elbowed her gently on the arm. *"He isn't the most pleasant-looking man in the garden. His nose is too crooked. I'd say you have him on that."*

We both giggled and found ourselves nearly running into the castellan, Margery, who was on her way down the corridor. Her red hair was a mess, just like she always seemed to be. *"Rose, did I not just assign you to deliver the Lord's message in the center village?"*

I grew serious. Lydia had a harder time putting a cap on her giggles. *"Yes, my lady,"* I said in a huff.

She cast a disapproving look at Lydia and me. If you ask me, the woman casts a disapproving look at anything shining brightly in a room. *"Then, I'd urge you to do it. Delivering the Lord's messages is a serious matter. I expect it to be delivered in earnest."*

I nodded quickly and mumbled *"Yes"* again before she moved on.

Lydia let out her burst of laughter as we continued down the corridor. *"Margery is frazzled half the time. Makes her mad to see us just getting along."* I bobbed my head slightly in agreement. That's when the important part of Margery's statement made Lydia ask, *"What was the part about the Lord's message? Did you finally knock Edmund off his high horse?"*

"Oh, Edmund's not so bad," I felt compelled to say.

Lydia shook her head. *"Not a bad person at all, only he talks too loud. Shouts all the time, like he's giving a speech with intentions to blow off my ear. I don't know how the lad keeps any secrets…"*

"Lydia," I said in a hushed voice as we took the spiraled steps down to The Great Room. *"I think the Lord has grown tired of the commoners."*

My comment made her stop mid-chuckle. She stared at me like I had just told her the Lord Monté had sentenced them all to death. *"This soon? What does he plan to do?"*

I shook my head from side to side. *"I don't know, Lydia. I don't know what's written on the scroll he wrote. I doubt it's anything good, though."*

*"Well, why isn't Edmund fully in charge of this? Why are you — the **clothier**, of all people — assigned to his job?"*

She asked the same questions I'd been pondering…

"I'll let you know as soon as I return," I said as we entered The Great Room.

She gave me a look as if to say, *"You **better** tell me,"* but managed it gently in a way that only a best friend could. *"Did they bring you a carriage like they do when Edmund goes places?"*

I smiled. *"Yes. It's out there waiting for me. Do you have time to see it?"*

Her eyes immediately told me no. *"Does Mack ever give anyone any time at all?"*

I squeezed her shoulder. *"You'll live. When I get back, you'll start your early morning chitter-chatter again, and everything will go back to normul."*

Lydia gave me a playfully narrowed look. *"I'm not always chitter-chattery in the morning."*

I nodded. *"You're right. When you're not talking, you're still tired."* We exchanged goodbyes as I approached the castle's front gate.

Aldus, the porter (or, more accurately, the terrorizing guard who followed the Lord Monté in his travels), was quick to stop me…as usual. He asked if I had permission to leave the castle. When I handed him the seal with the Lord's name on it, he raised a brow.

Aldus has the darkest skin I had ever seen and an accent even thicker than his arms. He scared me, and it wasn't just his dizzying stature more than it was his friendship with the Lord of the kingdom. Surely, anyone who could befriend the devil had to be one himself. Whatever the truth was, I made sure to keep my conversations brief with him and never look him in the eyes.

"Making friends with the Lord, I see," Aldus said to me after glancing over the paper. He searched and searched for something fake, false, any sign of forgery…

"Not at all," I said. *"The scroll was given to me by the castellan."* I made sure to say it as pointedly as I could so that he knew I had no intention whatsoever of talking to his friend. He seemed amused and looked up at me, making me draw back slightly. His smile made what felt like a cobweb tickle my spine—a cobweb I had created, of course, in my own imagination.

"Of course not. If the Lord ever spoke to you, you wouldn't walk so leisurely whilst delivering his messages, would you?" He said it slowly as if I were hard of hearing, and he wanted to make sure I heard every word. I nodded too quickly, and he laughed. *"Off you go, then."* While I was hurriedly walking to the carriage, he finished, *"And don't think the Lord doesn't have enough spies in the village. Whatever you do for him, you do in haste. Do you hear?"* I didn't turn to answer him. My back stretching the distance between us at a rapid rate was answer enough.

The carriage seats were cushioned, and I felt a twinge of excitement at being in such an expensive thing. I couldn't wait to tell Lydia! At the same time, I felt foolish for being excited after what Aldus told me.

*"Whatever you do for **him**, you do in haste. No time for nonsense and foolishness."*

As the coachmen waited for Edmund to come to the carriage, I couldn't help but reach out, touch the cushions, and imagine myself as a princess on her way to a ball. I could envision the jewels around my neck and the sound of music and laughter as I pulled up to some grand manor with the attendants awaiting my arrival—and only my arrival. The thrilling moment when I stepped out of the carriage…the *"Oohs"* and *"Ahhs"* as I walked into the—

"Daydreaming again, eh?" Edmund shouted from the rectangle of light of the open carriage door.

I jumped, and my cheeks flushed. *"Do you have any idea why I'm here?"*

"Not one bloody clue, sweetie. Glad to have you join me, though." Just as Lydia had mentioned, Edmund had a voice with a volume high enough to shatter glass. Lydia had a joke in which one day, whilst delivering his messages, the man went to talk to someone else and discovered he'd lost the ability to lower his voice. There was no way to know if it was true, but it sounded close enough to me.

"So, what does the message say?" I inquired.

He was climbing in and closing the door when I asked, and he flashed me a look as if I were the stupidest human being in the world. *"I don't read the messages before they must be read to the public. I don't mess with what the Lord Monté assigns to me. If you're smart, you won't either."*

My left ear rang as the carriage pulled off. I nodded, showing him I was exasperated with a raise of my brow and a roll of my eyes. *"I guess I just look stupid today."*

Edmund cast me a wary look. *"Huh?"*

"I seem the victim of getting a lecture every time I open my bloody mouth."

We rode the rest of the way in silence.

<p style="text-align:center">~~~~~~~~~~</p>

"This, my friends, is the decree of the Lord Monté: For all those who grumble about your current situation, fear your next one. For the Lord of the land has grown tired of such maddening stillness and is looking for a half-pint of enjoyment." The wording used in the speech made the crowd buzz. I could already sense the tension. *"It has come to my attention that the kingdom of Jocund is enduring a relentless famine which has deprived the land of the amount of food necessary to feed the people. So, it is only fitting that we lower the number of our population as the food runs dry, until it has passed us, and we can return to the normality of living."*

A couple of gasps flowed through the crowd. Blanched faces stared back at me. One powerfully built man cursed aloud from the back of the crowd.

I continued.

"From tomorrow night and forward, one person from each family — able or not able — will join a brutal game of survival, with weapons of my choice in a time period of my choice. When the time is up, and the bell is rung, those who remain standing will receive a reasonable portion of food for four days…until the next Battle of Bloodshed can be held."

I quickly scanned the rest of the decree with my eyes. *How could any of this be good news?*

"As these words were written, a clearing was made in the Woods of Division for this purpose. If the bell is rung after the chosen time period and no one has fallen due to the mercy of the people of Jocund, everyone chosen for the Battle of Bloodshed will die where they stand."

The shock electrified the atmosphere, and, for some reason, I became acutely aware of everything around me—the dust which clung to my sandals…the small amount of dirt irritating the skin under my fingernails. Strange things to notice at the moment, but I knew why I felt them. For some unfair reason, simply because I had a job in the castle, I was above this decree. I would continue to have plenty of meat, milk, cheese, and wine at my disposal. *But these people…*

I kicked myself, forcing my heart to harden. It was their own bloody fault for whining, wasn't it? It had nothing to do with me, so why should I feel guilty?

*"Hunt or be hunted; kill or be **killed**."* That last word burned on my tongue like acid. I'd grown to like the taste of acid…when it was pouring on someone else. Even it seemed like a victory in these times, but I didn't enjoy the faces of the peasants as theirs bore into mine.

The stunned silence could only last so long before it changed into bitter words of absolute chaos. I quickly stepped away from the crowd, as insults already being slung at me from within the mass slapped home. I gritted my teeth but felt no catharsis in the action. The insults annoyed me almost as much as the pity I felt for them.

I nodded towards Edmund, indicating to hurry us off. He raised a brow. *"They want **your** neck strung and wrung on a rope almost as much as they want the Lord Monté's,"* he smugly stated.

I stuck up my chin in stubborn defiance of my breaking heart and readjusted my left bliaut. *"If they aren't careful to respect the Lord Monté, it'll be **their** necks."* My voice was sincere.

I'd just finished the sentence when there was a movement to the right of me. I tensed—winced, even—expecting a blow from anyone in the mass irate enough to want to strike me, but the guard who'd been sent with us (I didn't bother to ask his name) stopped the intruder before he could reach me. I was surprised to turn and see the guard twisting the ear of a boy who was, at the most, 11 years old but squealed in pain like he was a two-year-old girl.

"Ow, ow! Please stop! I wasn't doing anything wrong!" he pleaded, trying to reach his throbbing ear with his hand, to no avail.

The guard had an iron grip and chuckled as if the boy being in pain was a birthday present. He twisted the boy's ear farther. *"You don't sneak up on a noblewoman, you twit! Do you want me to teach you a lesson?"*

The boy was near tears. ***"No!"*** he cried.

I'd seen enough. *"Let the boy go, for God's sake!"* My irritation earned a raised brow from Edmund and an annoyed look from the guard, but it served to have the boy's ear released immediately. I couldn't say I wanted to hear what the boy had to say, but he hadn't hurt me at all. Being punished for nothing is useless discipline. Watching it made me sick.

"Thank you, my lady," the boy said. His gratitude at the person who'd just assured a family member of his would die within the next week made me sicker.

"I wouldn't go thanking the likes of me, boy. ***See if you're thanking me in a couple of weeks****,"* I said harshly. His eyes filled with tears, and I turned away quickly so that he didn't see me bite my lip to keep it from trembling whilst I walked away.

4: DUSTIN ELRIC CARPENTER

Friends come; friends go.
Round and round, and then their ghosts,
But two or three, you hold them close;
Never ever let them go.

Traveling is no banquet. Preparing teetered on being even worse. Keeping the whole thing secret? Well, it's utterly strenuous! Poor Arthur must've had the hardest time. He could barely keep our secret meeting under the dirt, and now, a secret journey. The boy was practically hysterical with trying to hold the words in. I doubt, however, that he'd risk the wrath of his friends or, more accurately, Egon—the one who seemed well aware of Arthur's struggle and made sure to tell him he wasn't coming if he spilled.

The only other being who was in as strong a disposition as Arthur was Julius, only his was quite the contrary. I knew it as soon as he eyed me carrying my canteen and luggage and then hoisting it onto his back. His eyes seemed to say, *"What? You think this secret journey flew over my head, Dust?"* I stroked his mane and clicked my tongue. *"You're too smart,"* I told him. He didn't seem to appreciate my flattery.

As we strode along the road in Precursory Woods on the way to Ocean's favorite waterfall where she decided we should meet, Julius made sure I felt every bump or ditch in the road, to which I humorously said, *"You just aren't as quick as you used to be, Julius. You used to be able to miss those ruts."* That only made him angrier.

I loved to write while riding Julius, although my handwriting wasn't the brightest one around. The potholes made the words on the yellow paper almost indecipherable — but I wouldn't give Julius the pleasure of knowing that. This letter, though, was quite the important one. I didn't want the receiver to think of my writing as unattractive or me as disagreeable, so I wrote slowly and thoughtfully, trying not to breathe too hard. Little good that did…

Julius' neigh caught my attention. I glanced up to find we were at our destination. Cederic was riding towards me, apparently the only one here at the moment.

I put my ink, feather, and letter away before he reached me. I didn't want to be in the position to lie to him about its contents.

"Writing again, Dust?"

"It's funny; I can't stop these days. Anybody else here yet, man?"

Cederic lifted a dark brown on a darker face. There was humor in his deep voice, which sounded almost like a hum. *"It would seem we're the only ones here on time."*

"Well, what do you bloody know?" I tensed and turned at the voice to see Egon creeping up slowly on his mustang. *"When does Dust ever show up on time?"*

"Don't forget who you're speaking to, Egon," I jokingly reminded him.

"Oh, yeah. I almost forgot."

Cederic shook his head in faint amusement as Egon joined our ever-growing circle. *"It amazes me how Ocean can find such peace in this place."*

Cederic made a low sound in his throat, speaking his disapproval without opening his mouth. *"I don't know. If you are looking for peace, nature is the best place to find it."*

Egon grunted but couldn't disagree with the statement.

I smiled. *"Seeing she likes it so much, we might as well knock her into the water when she gets here, eh?"* Both men chuckled at the thought. It would be a darned good joke — one which would earn us a month's worth of scorn from the victim. Somehow, it made it all the more appealing…because that's just how a prank was.

"So, I know whatever this mission's about is top secret," Egon mockingly said to me, *"but may I ask: Do you have some grudge with the Lord Monté?"*

"None of the sort, actually."

"Good. It's not my intention to be decapitated by the Lord for revenge. We are seizing the castle, correct?"

"It's as you say."

Egon blew out of his nose in a huff of exasperation. *"Bloody crazy, this whole thing…"* The approaching hooves of two horses drowned his mumble. Their riders, Ocean and Arthur, were smiling and moving towards them.

"About time you got here! Either of you seen Silas or Woodruff?" Egon called.

Arthur grinned as they approached the still group, his thoroughbred thumping him along while Ocean's shire horse, Daisy, walked as smoothly as her rider. *"Woodruff is behind Silas, but he's bound to pass the lad. Silas is too busy reading his eyes out to move any quicker."*

"They take their time, don't they?" Egon snapped.

I had to hold in a laugh at the statement, considering it had been mere minutes before when Egon himself had arrived. *"Have you studied this waterfall, Ocean?"* I asked, setting my plan into action immediately.

She raised a quizzical brow. *"Studied it? I suppose. It's my favorite place in the Precursory Woods."*

"Oh. Then you would know it's an overhanging waterfall."

"No, it's not."

"Is, too! Here. I'll show you," I said, sliding off my horse. I caught the twinkle in Cederic's eye and the smirk in Egon's as I threw my leg over and stepped down from Julius.

Ocean climbed down off her horse, but her face showed disbelief. She followed me around to the side of the base of the waterfall, closer to the bank.

"See?" I said, pointing to the place behind the waterfall. Of course, there was no space, but I needed Ocean to peer out at the waterfall to push her into the flat water in front of us.

"Where?" she asked from beside me. I extended my pointer finger more, making her look harder.

Suddenly, I felt something push **my** back. The momentum of my extended arm and the force from behind me catapulted me into the water. I fell on my side, and water splashed up on the right side of my face. Disoriented, I got my hands underneath me enough to twist and sit up. Shaking the water from my face like a dog, I yelled, ***"What the he—"*** After the initial fall and a moment to breathe, I realized what happened.

"The next time you are planning to push me into the water, do so quietly," Ocean—the reason I was on my backside in the water—said, winking at me.

I grinned sheepishly. Before I knew it, I was laughing from where I sat in the water. Ocean smiled. I looked at Ocean's hand offering to pull me out of the water, almost circumspect to accept any help from her. With the wind biting at her flushed skin in the early morning and whipping her short boy cut around like a vortex, there was no sign of further friendly animosity, so I took it.

Ocean—the only female I had called to be a part of the group—I'd handpicked a fortnight ago and was a great addition to the team. She kept the boys straight when they got too unruly. I felt we would need it, especially down the road when things grew tougher. She had, however, insisted on Arthur coming. I think everyone was a bit skeptical of what would come of his presence. Arthur had a record of freezing at infamous moments, but Ocean was quick to defend him, just as she did everyone.

"Traitors," I said to Cederic and Egon as soon as I was out of the water and walking towards the cluster of horses. They'd been laughing the entire time. *"Turned on me as soon as the tides changed, didn't you?"*

*"Well, **we** didn't want to be thrown in the water, Dust. Some of us learn quicker than others,"* Egon pointed out. I smiled.

Woodruff came bounding in quicker than any of them had. *"Silas is right behind me. Maybe we should… **Holy long johns, Dust!** You've been in for a swim, then?"*

Well, that set off everyone laughing again. I gave him a pinched look for bringing it up, and he laughed, sensing he'd said something witty concerning the situation before he'd rode up.

"Everyone brought food?" I asked, partly because we needed to get serious and partly because I was thinking more and more that they were running the joke into the ground.

"Yep. Mum thinks this is a crucial trip concerning training, so I'd better come back," Arthur quickly stated.

"Yep. You'd better do it, bugger!" Egon said to Arthur with him in his left arm, covered in crude brands and tattoos he'd gotten years ago. The strike didn't do much damage to the man.

"Did I m-m-miss something?" Silas said, rounding the bend in the road and moving slowly towards them.

Ocean, Arthur, and Woodruff laughed at the question. Silas had a puzzled look as he reached them, which bunched the skin on his face and made his buzz cut hairline lift higher.

Woodruff took the aqua blue book from Silas' hands and read the title aloud: *"'The Troubling Habit of Sea Monsters.' Where did you find this?"*

"Old Noll who r-runs the village library gave it to m-me. It's actually quite good."

Egon raised a brow full of brown hair. *"If it has mermaids in it…"*

Silas perked up, sitting up straighter on his horse. *"It does! Three t-t-to be exact, actually!"*

*"Yup, it's probably horrible. Dust, how **do** you put up with this bloody man?"*

I grabbed the pommel and hoisted myself up and onto Julius. He groaned underneath me as if I were the heaviest person in the world. I gave him a sentimental pat on the side before I answered Egon. *"I ride out in front of him,"* as the others whistled their horses after me. I said the rest, barely turning my head and calling back over my shoulder. *"And I let the man read."*

The Black Warriors were in a state of doubt—at least I'd convinced myself of it as we trotted down the road in Precursory Woods. The way they were looking around and up into the trees was an obvious statement of their uncertainty.

Precursory Woods was known for peculiar things the deeper in you went. Everyone in the kingdom of Sans Défaut had grown up listening to the creepy stories. I almost wanted to laugh away the haunted vacancy in my own heart, but I was afraid if I shrugged it off, I'd regret it later. Indeed, I already doubted I'd put too much trust in the Warriors — and their trust in me.

~~~~~~~~~~

I recall my last private conversation with my father…

The room was large, with 15 windows spreading down to the end of it. It had tan colored walls, white molding, an ornate design coating the ceiling above, and four chandeliers stretching across.

I sat on a sofa in the middle of it all.

"Father!" I stood as he entered, erect and giving the king the respect he deserved.

"Elric," he said, smiling and dismissing the servants who'd opened the double-doors for him. *"You called for them?"* he asked after they'd left. The curl in his hair remained, but the grey was beginning to take over.

"Yes, I meet with them in four days," I said — referring, of course, to the Warriors I'd selected.

He nodded, taking a seat across from my sofa. He motioned for me to sit, but I declined. He smiled at this. His smile had always been tight and heartwarming. Tight smiles were ones you could trust. Liars never bothered to smile so strongly or as hard as they could. *"You're nervous,"* he said. *"The days before I traveled here years ago, I couldn't sit down hardly. However, these are much graver circumstances, aren't they?"*
~~~~~~~~~~

"It must be done," was all I said. I wouldn't doubt—not for a minute in front of my father, who I owed so much.

"You know you can't tell them," he said after a bit of silence.

I paled, knowing full well he was speaking of my company. *"Do you doubt their loyalty, father?"*

*"Do **you**?"* The sunlight from the windows struck his eyes, giving them even more questions.

"I'd give my life for any one of them. Likewise, I am sure they'd give their lives for me," I said confidently and quickly.

He nodded. He'd **wanted** to hear this from me. *"Then, I'm sure you cannot tell them. Information endangers whoever is burdened with its knowledge. We wouldn't want them in any more danger."*

I dropped onto the sofa across from him, my legs too weak to stand any longer. *"How am I supposed to convince them to do this...this **venture**...if they don't even know why we're doing it?"* I wasn't whining. Rather, I was exasperated with the complications. I spoke in a low voice.

"If they are as loyal as you say they are, I do not think you will have a problem, Elric."

"I hope it is so."

The king glanced over at me again and then took his own turn talking in a low voice. *"You cannot speak to her, either."*

"Yes, I know."

*"Not without endangering everything — Jocund, you, the Warriors...**her.**" He sighed. "This is very important."*

"I know how important it is. I know how important she is to me. I will not attempt to contact her."

The room was still.

After a moment, my father asked, *"You're going to write her, aren't you?"*

I raised a surprised brow. *"I never said that."*

"Nor are you sure of it now. Your love for her has grown immensely, and your amusement for writing has not wavered since you were a child. I do not think this is a coincidence." Often times, my father could read me better than I could myself, so I didn't deny it. *"How will you contact her?"*

"Pigeon messaging, I suppose."

He shook his head. *"Why on **earth** did I teach you pigeon messaging?"*

"For this very moment."

He stood. *"Just be careful, Elric. You are not alone this time on one of your expeditions. You are the **leader** now. Do not send your men where you would not go by yourself."*

I stood. *"Thank you, father."*

There were no mentions that this might be the last time I spoke to him in a private conference. He did, however, embrace me, like when I was a boy.

Strangely, I wished there were ways to go back in time. I would have stayed by my father a bit longer.

After that day, he'd referred to me as nothing else but Prince Dustin.

~~~~~~~~~~

I used the excuse of "relieving myself" to get away from the group. By myself but equipped with a signal Cederic said we should have if we were in trouble, I quietly whistled a tune I'd learned as a child into the open…a song only **one** creature could understand the deeper meaning of.

Such was the case now.

Seven pigeons flew down to meet me. They cooed and cawed yet stood still because the song had told them what I wanted. Having slid all my papers into cylinders, I attached them to all seven pigeons while they stood, bored and itching for the long journey they had ahead of them. I stroked one of their backs, and he just tilted his head to stare at me. Laughing, I told them the location where I wanted them delivered and whistled them off.

Years ago, my dad had taught me the secret. I'm glad it somehow paid off.
~~~~~~~~~~

5: ANONYMOUS

Be careful with your fists;
They can make a bruise.
But be careful with your words,
For they can make them, too.

I felt the slap on my cheek, and it burned. I knew what was coming next, but my body wasn't prepared for it. Another blow sent me sprawling back onto my bum.

"You stupid, stupid boy! I swear: You're never gonna get anything through your bloody head!" the man I call my 'Pa' roared above me.

I'll tell you this: Friends never understand what *"My Pa will be angry if I'm late"* means. To **them**, it could mean a scolding or spanking on their backsides. Me? I'm different—or, rather, my dad is different. I get The Fork.

Laugh if you want, but in my situation, you'll see that The Fork is no laughing matter.

He lifted me from the ground by my grimy shirt and brought my face close to his. His mouth was a stinky cavern. I knew better than to wrinkle my nose at the horridly sharp smell of tobacco from the pipe hanging loosely from the side of his mouth. I didn't dare close my eyes, either. Any slight movement from my part might start him off in another unreasonable rage.

"Where have you been, you stupid boy?!" He shook me so hard, my teeth clattered. My response wouldn't matter. If I lied, he'd beat me; if I told him the truth (*"Cecily didn't know the meaning of 'My pa gets mad if I get home late'"*), he'd beat me. It's best I just keep my pleasures to myself. My one striking force was my secrets.

I looked back at the hard-nosed man and said, *"I ain't been doing nothing."*

I'd barely finished that short sentence when he slammed me against the wall. Something on the panel above our cooking pot cut me in the back of my head, and I felt the cool blood fill the gash and dribble into my hair. My Pa let me go, and I curled into a fetal position on the floor next to the cooking pot, knowing The Fork would come next.

I held back the tears of pain by biting my lip as hard as I could, but I couldn't stop my body from trembling—from fear or forebode, I didn't know…but it was a violent shaking. My Pa didn't notice. He had a way of only noticing himself, his own problems, and other people's faults, but never their pleas for forgiveness.

I made a whacked and desperate attempt to stop my trembling by counting aloud, but it didn't seem to work 'cause I kept gritting my teeth. I only made it to the count of four, when my Pa swept me up roughly, holding The Fork in his right hand. I saw it, and my body screamed against it.

Is it possible to be more afraid of something physically than mentally?

Here, in our small home, it seemed to be the case because, in my head, I couldn't help but say, *"Just another one to add to the pile."* It's funny to me because my body was convulsing against my will at the excruciating **idea** of it.

"No, no, no! Please, no!" I screamed, almost indecipherably. I tried to kick him with my worn-out shoes, but he was too strong. As usual, he won the battle as he placed the horrid, hot fork against the raw and sensitive skin behind my ear. I let a scream tear through my throat. It didn't even sound **human**. As a matter of fact, if I hadn't still had the searing metal on my skin to remind myself of the pain I was experiencing, I wouldn't have recognized my own voice. It was a deep, guttural scream that did little to persuade my Pa that I'd had enough. Not even the smell of my burning flesh did that.

He lifted The Fork from my ear and shoved me across the room. He then overturned a table and said something I'd heard him say a hundred times but wasn't allowed to repeat. His anger didn't replete, so he came at me again…and I curled up again. Suddenly, a voice took to the air before he could kick me in my ribs.

*"Ubel, you shut up, now! Mallory's sleeping, and you're giving me a bloody headache, you **fool**!"* my Ma said from across the room where she'd been sitting and staring at nothing before waking up like she'd been in another reality. Her statement was

a bold one, considering my Pa was in an incredibly dark mood. She was less heroic when noticing the jug of ale she held and the sluggish way she swayed.

My Pa, of course, was not impressed. He closed in on my Ma like he'd done to me seconds ago and backhanded her. ***"Don't ever speak to me like that, woman!"*** he bellowed.

As cruel as it sounds, I was grateful for her distraction. I scrambled up—nearly losing my footing—and ran out the door. My dad would be angry when he turned and found me gone, but if he couldn't find me, he couldn't beat me…and I had a couple of hiding places.

"Mallory's sleeping." What a **hilarious** statement! Did she really think her other son could sleep through that? My brother was much more resilient than I, but even he couldn't stand the booming, the shouting, the ***stupidity***…

The place behind my ear, where years of fork brands resided, ached. It still felt like he was holding the metal instrument there. The newly-placed brand had almost made me forget about the gash in the back of my head.

Almost.

I don't know if other people have fathers like mine, but when he beats you before you can barely walk, you quickly learn you cannot run to friends for help and refuge. Those are, after all, the places my dad checks first.

The other things I've learned are he won't search for long, and that he doesn't beat me because he's concerned for me as much as he does just to pacify his dark mood — something he can't do while scrounging around for his son. After half an hour or so, he gives up, returns home, and threatens my Ma again until his anger is spent. Then, he'll go to bed. No matter how much my Ma says she loves him, she won't go in the room to sleep beside him. She chooses to curl up on the cold floor next to the fire and sleep.

My Ma never admits our family is obviously dysfunctional. She talks all day of loving my Pa, all while she drinks away her true sorrows from a jug of beer, mead, or ale. If ever Mallory or I speak of reality, it sets her off in a bitter rage that's almost worse than my Pa's.

She's never touched The Fork. The Closet is where we go when she reaches her full capacity. Oh, the pain of The Closet. She'd say, *"For your own good."*

I laughed dryly on the way to my hiding place and shook my head.

Mallory was better than me. He would speak all day of how horrible our Pa was, just to spite Ma. Boy, did he get his hide tanned for it, but at least he'd had the courage to speak the truth. I just nodded and barely spoke at all. I listened to the lunacy, hoping I'd have a day without a trip to The Closet, a moment without The Fork, or an hour without a bruise. Nothing hurt Mallory, though. Not The Closet, nor The Fork. The boy was made of steel, and I was made of glass. I wondered why it was so…

Even now, as I walked alone in the dim light of the evening, tears slid down my cheeks—unbidden and uncontrollable. My nose ran just as badly, and I sniffed like an utter fool, over and over and over.

In the depths of my large trouser pocket, my favorite journal slapped my side. It provided a steady rhythm I spoke aloud to console myself. *"Pap. Mmm. Pap. Mmm. Pap,"* I said through a knot, shaking my voice. *"Slapping journal. Slap, slap, slap."* I laughed at myself and, as strange as it sounds, I felt much better after the little chant. It was as if the world was worth living for. So, I said it again. Then, again. I said it until the tears came from the deepest laughter I'd felt in weeks. By then, the snot dribbling down my top lip had nothing to do with my family, but rather the wonderful cold and the sting of laughing too hard.

That's when I approached Creepy Maggy's cottage. It was a lonely place and far too still. The cobwebs made it seem haunted. The dark colors that Creepy Maggy had decorated it with only made it appear even more evil, but I knew better.

Mallory and I had walked the rooms of the cottage before. No one lived there. It just made strangely creepy sounds. Both of our assumptions were that maybe some grown-up who didn't want his child hanging out in an *old, creepy cottage* sent the message of a spooky woman living there, and it "stuck." Unfortunately for whoever the grown-up was, my favorite hiding spot was in her front yard: the biggest climbing tree in all of Souffrance. Nobody wanted to touch it. Lucky me.

With a habitual glance around, I placed a steady foot on the first limb and continued the climb 'til I'd gotten a third of the way up. Sitting with my backside on a particularly strong branch, I reached into the folds of my trousers and pulled out my journal and pen. Before I could even get my ink ready, words came to me…as they always do.

> *"The boy got beat again and again,*
> *Until his mother intervened.*
> *Not because she cared at all,*
> *But because the noise was giving her a headache.*
> *As usual, people only care when they themselves are involved.*
> *Tell me if I am wrong.*

The world is corrupted;
Opinions, bias,
Bruised, broken, lost, and gutted.
Tell me if I'm wrong, though I know I'm not.
Now, tell me if a boy of 12 years
is supposed to know this much."

I stared at the words and wondered if anyone could answer them. I would like to meet the person who could. I would have tons of other questions prepared. I wondered if they could answer every one of them. Not likely, but I hoped they could. I hoped I'd meet them soon. I needed something to pass the time…to get my mind off the parents I had, the life they lived…**everything**.

Mallory steamed in it. I had grown to assume he never stopped thinking about it. Even while out there playing with Cecilly and me, he seemed to think about it. His face pinched with the strain of it. Thinking and thinking and thinking… Why did he think so much? Maybe that's what made him so strong. Mallory was a giant—the giant I wanted to be. Why couldn't I be like that…like him?

Groaning at myself, I put the pen to work again against the page. Its tail end wiggled quite madly, as if it wanted to get the words out just as much as my heart did. When I was finished, I lifted the page closer to my face so I could read it, just as the last bit of sunlight was slipping away.

"It would seem I have a rather hard time
Understanding why life can't be better than this.
Every time I think I have a hold on it,
It slips from my grasp again.
I don't want to have to do the Big, Bad Thing.
I won't, I won't, I won't!
But sometimes, I—"

"Hey, are you up there?" I heard someone whisper harshly from below. I recognized the voice immediately as belonging to my brother. He was the only one who knew our secret hiding place, after all. Not even Cecilly knew about it, and she knew just about everything — except for our parents' rages and the tree.

"Come on up," I told him. I then went back to scribbling on my paper. The tree shook with the effort of my brother's weight pulling his way up. I didn't look down. I wanted to finish my sentence.

"What are you writing?"

I looked up and smiled. *"About Archie, as usual."*

Mallory wrinkled his nose in an unnatural way. *"Why don't you just admit Archie is **you**?"*

I refused to be offended by my brother and just shook my head. *"It's not."*

He shrugged his head in frustration, but he didn't push. Instead, he took the journal from my hands and read the words written there, with a look suggesting he didn't agree with me having written any of it.

*"Why do you write in a **journal**? Isn't it a little childish?"*

*"Weren't you **sleeping**?"* I asked, snatching back my journal.

He sighed. *"Do you think anyone can sleep through Ubel and Mum's lunatic shouting? Or your bloody cries? You think I can sleep through that?"* He seemed serious, so I took him seriously.

"No, Mallory. I don't. In case you haven't noticed, your protesting isn't doing nothing but getting you into more trouble." I felt much bolder before I said that than after, but Mallory didn't even blink at the statement. He never does.

"Then why don't we just do it?"

"You mean the Big, Bad Thing?" I asked.

He gave me an exasperated look. *"It isn't **bad**. It's what we **have** to do. Okay? You're looking at this all wrong."*

*"Wrong? This thing you want me to **do** is wrong. It's just as bad as what they do to us. No. Worse. Much worse."* I looked at him incredulously.

"Fine. Obviously, you haven't seen enough yet. You're scared, aren't you? You've always been scared – "

Before he could finish his sentence, I started climbing down the tree. He grabbed my arm so I couldn't step down to the next limb. I would've pulled away, but I caught the look in his eyes and found he was hiding something behind his dark mood.

"Listen," he said. I caught a tremor in his voice I'd never heard before. *"I can't do this anymore, okay? I can't. We don't have to. I just…need you to help me."* In no time at all, the tremor was gone. The next statement sounded like the Mallory I knew. *"So, get over yourself, okay?"*

I jerked from his grasp and scrambled down from the tree. I took off in the direction of home, knowing I couldn't go there. The tears came back, fresh and hot. I'd never been one who could control them. This time, however, I willed them away and let the anger stay. It was like a furnace being kindled deep inside of me.

Mallory had never told me he "needed me" before. Now that he had, it was a shame I felt compelled to shut him out.

6: ROSETTA KELLINA MABEL

In the Spring, things come alive.
In the Summer, they thrive.
In the Fall, they start to die,
And in the Winter, they hide…
Until the cycle repeats itself
And leaves me wondering why —
Why do things die?

Even more disturbing than the news I'd delivered was the sound of men working and a saw cutting through bare wood, over and over again. It sounded like a death sentence being chanted into the air, robbing it of joy.

The kingdom of Jocund was in an uproar. Lord Monté was the Most Wanted man for miles. There had even been reports of suicides, although granted, not many. Most men felt inclined to be the one to fight for their family. The suicides reported were typically from families who had no male figure old enough or strong enough to fight.

Still, the thought disturbed me. *The cowardice of it all...* I didn't know, however, if one so detached from the situation should care so much. All my mixed emotions were giving me a headache. Agitated, I walked through the big archway and onto my private terrace. I gripped the terrace's guard wall and looked up into the sky.

Everything dies and turns to dust at some point. Even nature has its cycle: Spring, Summer, Fall, Winter. Animals didn't care. Birds were above all the trouble...above all the cries...above death. They chose if they wanted to look down or not and address the issues humans faced. Somehow, I felt jealous. Then, I was embarrassed because I envied an animal.

Was I so low?

The creaking sound of my room door opening caused me to turn and see Wilmot coming in and through the open archway separating us, though we could see each other quite easily. Wilmot was unknown to most. He was actually an elderly janitor, but everyone sent him on errands so much, you would've thought he was a Harker. The poor guy was too insecure in himself to tell anybody no, so the cycle just kept going around and around. He was probably going to lose his job. Oh, the joys of life.

"Wilmot!" I exclaimed happily, as if I hadn't just been gripping the guard wall. *"It's good to see you!"*

He removed his dirty cap and nodded like he was mute.

It was like talking to a 12-year-old boy. *"So… Who sent you?"* I asked.

He ran a hand through his greasy, blonde hair with specks of grey. *"Uh…Margery…But you know, I've quite forgotten what she told me to tell you…"*

I walked towards him and touched his shoulder in a consoling manner. *"That's alright. Fortunately, as the circumstances are, I already know what she wants to bloody tell me."*

Wilmot—possibly the meekest person I know—was alarmed at my language. *"Miss Mabel, if you don't mind my asking: What message did she want to deliver?"*

Without answering, I started to gather my things: needle, thread, and pins. I hastily shoved them into a bag, as Wilmot stood bewildered in front of the door. When I was finished, I turned to face him and, while exhaling, said, *"I'm supposed to be down at the factory."* It's as if the statement made Wilmot look around and notice his surroundings—meaning he noticed my body shivering and shaking from anxiety. To my great annoyance, though, he made a comment about it. I guess it **was** the polite thing to do.

"Miss Mabel, are you alright?"

I grabbed my bedside cabinet to steady myself and answered bluntly. *"No, but if I told Margery that, do you think I'd receive any sort of break?"*

Wilmot's face was sad. I felt bad for being so honest. All he said was, *"I suppose not."* He then offered to help me from my room to the factory. When I rejected his offer, he reluctantly stepped out of the room.

There was a moment of complete silence. I embraced it, closing my eyes and leaning my head back. Then, it was over as quickly as it had come. My shaking had calmed a little, so I was able to let go of the cabinet and make my way to the door.

The corridor outside was mostly empty. Everyone was off following their daily schedule—everyone except me. I still felt like quite the idiot for not feeling up to returning to the factory after delivering the message. I had almost cried for the children who would be without a father in a week.

For Lord Monté's Battle of Bloodshed to work, someone had to die. Who knew? If the famine didn't stop and continued for another month or so, everyone could die. It was possible the Battle of Bloodshed would run out of material.

I shuddered. *Material.* How come even I looked at them as something other than human beings? *Maybe the Lord has a spell on everyone in the castle. Maybe I have grown conceited and selfish in the years of the Lord's reign.*

The latter terrified me.

Walking down the corridors a little faster, I took the flight of stairs at the bottom level. Instead of going left into the Great Room, I kept straight and rounded a turn through two rugged doors into the factory. The atmosphere was alive. Even the air danced in delight. The factory, though not a huge room, was full of people. In truth, there were merely three people, but I was proud of the factory about as much as Lydia was proud of her garden.

Héloise noticed me first and waved, which caused Kip and Faye to turn and smile. I smiled back, sent a prayer to whoever was listening to stop the last bit of my shaking, and walked towards Faye, who was using the loom. I noticed she was a bit frustrated at it, to which made me say, *"Faye, take a break. I'll work the loom while you're gone."*

She looked a bit relieved, but she added, *"Are you sure?"* It appeared almost as a second thought.

I laughed. *"Yes, and if Margery tells you off, tell her, 'People take breaks. It's simply human nature.'"*

"And get sent to cleaning the garderobe? I think not, lass."

I felt delirious. I almost didn't even hear myself say, *"Oh, please. By all means, tell her who made you say that. Let's see what she'll do."*

By now, Héloise had overheard me and came over to say, *"What's gotten into you, Rose?"*

Faye shook her head, turned, and left. She tried to hide the smile that appeared on her face. I had sat down in her chair and crossed my right leg over my left in the most elegant way possible.

"If the commoners must die for no reason, what's there to stop me from losing my life in the same manner? Better everyone bloody dies on break than working." I said.

Héloise giggled at me, and Kip gave me a narrowed look. *"That's the first time you've ever talked in such a compassionate tone when the commoners are in the same sentence,"* Kip observed.

"Well, I'm not overly fond of the murder of women," I replied.

"Women?" Héloise asked anxiously. *"I thought it was only men who would participate in — "*

"The contrary," Kip interrupted. *"**Children** might end up fighting for food in the end."*

Héloise's expression was full of shock. I couldn't help but be slightly irritated she didn't know this already. *"The **end**? What does **that** mean?"*

I couldn't stop myself. *"When the Lord runs out of bloody material!"*

*"**Rose!**"* Héloise said in dismay. *"Stop saying that **word**!"*

I was in the mood to be difficult. Kip seemed to notice, but Héloise had never been even a tad attentive. *"Bloody, bloody, bloody,"* I repeatedly said, making Héloise's jaw drop.

*"Rose, you are being **ridiculous**!"*

"Am I?" I asked, just as Lydia came in, holding a basket full of flowers.

"Goodness me! I've never been so happy to see you in my entire life, Lydia. What's gotten into your friend? She's speakin' 'bout as recklessly as James the Blacksmith does to Héloise when he's in one of his romantic moods," Kip said with a smirk. Héloise let out her trademark giggle and sent a pleading look to Kip, but everyone knew she enjoyed talking about her lover as much as he loved talking about her.

Lydia looked at me, saw the expression on my face, and, while setting the basket of flowers (surely, for us to use for dyes) on one of the two tables, said, *"Oh, she's just venting. So's all the village. You should see 'em out there. Angrier than Aldus when he catches someone trying to sneak in or out of the castle!"*

"They shouldn't have provoked the Lord and gotten themselves into knee-deep mud," Kip said.

I sighed. *"I doubt it would've helped. The horrid man stole our entire village. If you ask me, the fool's just out for blood."*

*"Rose! Am **I** to be beheaded for **your** inability to shut up?"* Héloise asked, glancing around to make sure no one but the group there had heard my statement — although it was obvious, we were the only ones in the room.

*"**Shut up?** I've been shutting up all day! It's about time somebody said something…"*

"Well, for the sake of all of us, would you 'say something' in your own quarters?" Kip replied. Lydia and Héloise laughed, removing some of the tension in the room from the dreaded 'message.'

"Oh, hush. You all wish you were as free as I am," I said.

"If everyone in the castle got away with as much as you, we could possibly revolt," Kip stated with a raised brow.

I rolled my eyes. *"Quit whining and sew."* My statement was backed up further by the sound of footsteps near the door, causing the girls to scatter like rabbits to their sewing instruments. Lydia turned to leave.

The man on the other side of the door was Chancellor Kenneth — a person I wasn't particularly happy to see, but Lydia was. She thought Chancellor Kenneth regarded me with much more admiration than was appropriate for an acquaintance or a friend.

"Chancellor Kenneth. It's good to see you," Lydia said happily.

"Mutual feelings for you, Miss Taylor," he replied. His eyes caught mine and locked there. I made sure not to shift and looked him in the eyes most confidently. *"Good afternoon, Miss Mabel. I trust sewing is going well?"* he asked.

"As well as it can," I said smartly. My answer was, perhaps, colder than Lydia liked.

She interceded to make sense of my bluntness. *"Rosetta had to deliver the Lord's message earlier. It is grave — the remnants of it — so, as you can see, her mood reflects that."*

Kenneth's gaze never left me. *"I heard. May I ask why the clothier was sent in the Harker's stead?"*

"Rose was never told wh — "

I cut Lydia off. *"I thought if anyone knew, it would be **you**...seeing you are close friends to the Lord of the kingdom and all."*

Kenneth glanced back and forth at both Lydia and me until finally settling his gaze on me. *"The Lord didn't tell me about the message nor the deliverer. If so, I would have begged him not to put you through such terrible truth. On the contrary, I had no clue what the message contained and assumed Edmund would have been the one to handle it. My apologies."*

Lydia, tired of trying to cover up my rudeness, shot me a look that propelled me to say, *"You're forgiven."*

From across the small room, Héloise called to Kenneth, *"Is James doing okay? I know sometimes things get really busy for him..."*

No one bought the excuse.

"'Busy' is quite the understatement; for now, the Battle of Bloodshed is being held. The Lord wants the best armor for the best contest."

"Oh, what a horrid name for it." Héloise shivered.

"The Lord thinks it is perfect," Kenneth said pointedly.

I couldn't take his defensive tone. In my own exasperated one, I said, *"Must you tell us what the Lord thinks?"* It came out a little harsher than I meant it. I was mad at myself for being so angry at the Lord Monté that I would let it out on Kenneth so directly.

*"It's his **job** to be with him every day, Rose."* Lydia defended him, furthering my irritation.

Kenneth, ever polite, answered, *"Yes, but it's quite unnecessary for me to speak of it continually. I must beg your forgiveness yet again."*

"I'm afraid you would be begging forever. Rose is just in one of those moods," Héloise stated.

For the first time since he came in, Kenneth laughed. *"Yes, it's wonderfully dreadful, isn't it?"*

At that statement, I couldn't help but laugh. I cursed inwardly for doing so because it seemed to bring Kenneth great delight.

"I meant to tell you: The Lord has required all of us to attend the Battle tomorrow night. I wouldn't bring up the Lord again if this topic hadn't been what I came here for," he stated.

*"**All** of us?"* Lydia asked. *"I thought it was just the nobility."*

I forced a laugh. *"No. Inviting nobility strictly would be too sensible for him."*

Kenneth cast me a funny look, somewhere between agreeing with and disapproving of my statement. He stared at me for a second, then tore his eyes away to answer Lydia's question. *"I think the Lord wants to prove a point to us."*

*"What **point**?"* Lydia asked in irritation.

Kenneth said the next few words like he was sure of it. *"I am not permitted to say. I'm not even fully sure I understand him."*

Kip called from across the room. *"Rose, Lady Joan needs to be fitted in her quarters."*

As I stood, Kenneth said, *"I'll escort you."*

Without hesitation, I replied, "Thank you, but I think I'm quite capable of going on my own." I left the room without checking to see what the reaction to my refusal looked like.

~~~~~~~~~~

I'd never been more exhausted than after this day of work, mostly because I knew what tomorrow would hold. It wasn't comforting.

Most evenings, I would stand on my balcony for an hour. Not for any specific reason, but sometimes, I just needed the breeze. In the mornings, I would watch the birds and wish I were one of them. Tonight, though, I threw myself on my bed, placed my pillow over my head, and was asleep in minutes.
~~~~~~~~~~

It was the unique sound of birds that woke me from my slumber. It was too late for birds to be out and about. Why were they so close to my balcony? When I'd taken the time to wipe the sleepiness from my eyes, I saw there were at least seven of them on the guard wall to my balcony, staring at me intensely as if they had a point to make. *"Not now. I'm sleepy,"* I mumbled.

Just as I closed my eyes again, I was startled upright by the loudest 'squawk' I'd heard in my life. Throwing my blanket off of me, I stood too quickly, stumbled, regained my balance, and walked to the balcony where the birds sat waiting. *"I don't want company now. Come back in the morning, please."* I shooed one away, but to my great annoyance, it flew eight feet in the air and then came back down to rest on the guard wall. I cried out in frustration. I tried shooing them away again, only to watch three do the same as the first. Their blurry figures came to rest on the guard wall again.

Exhausted, I turned and slid my back down the guard wall until I was sitting with my back against it. Sighing, I put my hands out, palms up, and stared at them. Normally, the torches on the ends of my balcony gave away flickers of light, but I hadn't lit them tonight. I hadn't done anything. I just wanted to sleep…to rest…to not worry about anythi—

The flapping of wings made me jump. Suddenly, a bird was in my hands, still and calm. It was so calm, it made me actually pay attention to what was in the bird's talons. *A cylinder?* I took it from his talons, and he squawked a thanks before flying back to the guard wall to await a response.

Revived, I stood and glanced at all the birds. In the dark—and still half asleep—I hadn't noticed. I now knew what I was looking for, as each had a cylinder on them. They were all, in fact, messenger pigeons and here for only one purpose.

Who would send me a message, though? The only real relationships I had were all in the castle. Lydia would've just snuck up here. She'd done that more than once. Kip, Faye, and Héloise were far too ignorant to know how to summon messenger pigeons. Could it perhaps be Chancellor Kenneth? I hoped not. I knew it was foolish, but I desperately hoped it was from some peasant in the village who'd felt the need to give me company…something **different**.

I felt renewed energy in my bones as I took the cylinders from all of them and laid them all out on the floor of the ledge. I opened each one and organized the papers until the message made sense. Then, I attempted to read it, but got stumped at the first word:

Ro,

The only people who **ever** called me Ro were my parents, and they'd died in the Lord's Theft. Could this mean…?

I continued reading.

I'm coming for you. Don't ever doubt that. The road only gets rougher from here, I understand. But it won't stop me. My company and I are stronger than we've ever been. I've prepared for this for years, and now, the journey has started. It won't be long.
I wish it were easier. That I could swear to you. Frankly, there's nothing I can say or do to get you to believe me. I know this.
I've known it.
However, if you could learn to trust me, we can use this correspondence to get to know one another better. (I remembered in a moment of brilliance that you knew pigeon messaging!) I am sort of happy about it. Otherwise, my arrival there would have been rather surprising.

Forgive me. I am excited, but it's only because I've waited so long to
speak to you. My hands shake (can you tell?) as I write these words.
Mostly because I'm not supposed to be writing to you at all yet,
I couldn't wait.
It is a shame you do not know me, but you will soon.
I'm coming for you, Ro. I'm coming.

With love, your One and Only

Funny… I was out of breath when I finished, even though I hadn't read the words aloud.

My heart stammered because none of this made sense. As far as I knew, I didn't have a 'One and Only.' I knew no one outside of the castle. What a bold statement he made! How did he know he was my 'One and Only' anyway? It was strange how my reaction was far from irritated. Instead, I was intrigued. Who would know me enough to want to come for me? **What did that even mean?** My head buzzed, and the words almost frightened me. Still, I wanted another letter. I wanted to keep talking to him.

I ran into my room to grab my ink and paper, eager to write him back. I thought of what to say for ten minutes and scribbled words for five. My hands trembled as I tried desperately to make my letters clear and precise.

When I finished, I rolled up the papers and slid them into four cylinders. It took me a while to get them in the pigeons' talons because my hands were shaking profusely. When I was finally done, I was grateful I knew how to speak to the pigeons. Then, it hit me: I didn't know where to tell them to go! I didn't know from where the letter had come!

I felt like bursting into tears for some odd reason. The birds stared at me with a look of pity, then flew away with words I knew would never reach the mysterious writer of the letter.

In despair, I walked slowly back to my bed, more tired than I'd been before.

7: DUSTIN ELRIC CARPENTER

Away from home, you never know
What you're going to find.
You expect the worst, hope nothing lurks;
Hope is most certainly never right.

Everyone seemed to settle into the fact that we were closing in on the stairs, and the journey was beginning. Granted, we were on a higher alert than we'd been in weeks. Even I was jumpy, but we all agreed that getting down the stairs before the end of the night was a priority of safety, so we trudged on at a decent pace. It was rounding up to the end of the day. The sun was half-set on the western sky, and dust clung to my cloak, weighing me down.

I let my mind drift to more pleasant things, like my letters. I wondered if they'd reached their destination. I wondered what her reaction was like. Was she excited? Nervous? Scared? I had been rather undignified in my writing, even foolish at times. I tended to do it often when I was exhilarated. What a fool I must have appeared to be!

What if she loved it, though? What if she spun around and around with the letters at her breast, only to fall out on her bed in pure joy? I grinned at the thought, somewhat sheepishly. Darn my luck; it was Ocean who'd been riding beside me who noticed.

"Don't you dare say anything," I said.

She laughed. *"I wasn't going to. I mean, until you told me not to…"* I rolled my eyes, and she continued. *"I haven't seen you blush so sharply since Egon set you up with the girl from Semper Fidelis."*

"That's because I had explained to him in great detail that I had no feelings whatsoever for the girl. He made it his pointed mission to make me miserable."

"As he always does." Ocean laughed, and in unison, we both turned to look at Egon, who noticed our stares and gave his trademark smirk. *"Just can't get enough of me, can you, Ocean?"*

Ocean raised a brow. *"There is a level of disgusting which makes you gawk, isn't there?"*

Silas looked up from his book at her remark and glanced at her. *"I do hope you'll learn to k-keep some of your w-w-wit to y-yourself, Ocean. It can b-b-be quite offensive."*

Woodruff—who'd been laughing at the conversation the entire time—chimed in with, *"Only to the softhearted, my dear Silas."*

"And you are one of those bloody people," Egon muttered lowly, maybe so Silas wouldn't hear.

Ocean laughed again. *"A soft heart is a remarkable trait. I'll try not to offend it."* At that, she turned back towards the road on her saddle.

The men eyed one another, I included. Silas, embarrassed, went back to reading his book, so as to avoid showing it too much. Arthur, however, couldn't stop blushing for Silas, which made Woodruff drown the silence with his boisterous laughter.

"If I were buggin' stupid, I'd think your face was always such a shade, Silas—and what a pretty color it is!" Woodruff laughed even harder. Arthur gave him a pinched look of disdain, which proved to tickle Woodruff more.

"When did a soft heart get you a woman?" Egon asked quietly, so as not to let Ocean hear.

"Forever," Cederic answered. *"Just most of the time, the woman softens the man's heart. Silas has already done the work, the little bugger."*

Egon grumbled at that, which made me laugh along with Woodruff. It was then that Ocean called to the group, *"Boys…stairs."*

I looked ahead to where the earth seemed to stop abruptly to a steep drop where someone had built a set of precarious stone stairs, looking in all honesty like they truly wished to fall apart…without **any** weight on them.

I heard Arthur's voice behind me. *"You're sure there's no other way?"*

I knew the question was directed at me and prepared to answer, but Egon interrupted. I let him speak.

*"You're asking **now**? After we've trotted all the way here, mate?"*

Woodruff slid off his horse, Gibard, and walked towards the edge of the lookdown. *"Well, I can be your test guy."* Everyone laughed. Woodruff was, in fact, the heaviest man there.

I shook my head. *"No. Woodruff's far too valuable. I think Cederic's worth a try."*

"May I remind you," his deep voice cut in with a hint of a smile in it, *"that if you throw the only bit of brains over the edge, you'll all go stumbling off at some point."*

"Good point," I said. *"Woodruff?"*

On cue, Woodruff cautiously tried the first step. The rock underneath him held up. Farther down the drop, another stone step loosened and fell to a cracking death at the bottom.

"Jolly good!" Woodruff said humorously.

"Not at all. It's the way my body's gonna sound when it hits the ground," Arthur said with concern.

Egon snickered. *"Hopefully, it won't sound so hollow."*

Ocean gave Egon a look that suggested she disapproved of the statement and managed the sweet words Arthur needed to tweak his courageous inner spirit. *"You're the lightest out of all of us. You'll be okay. With seven of us here, you'll have an arm to grab if you slip."*

"Right," Arthur said to himself, his brows knitted together in determination. *"I'll walk in front of Woodruff, then."*

"Who wants to walk behind him? By raise of hand..." Everybody was quiet, which made me laugh. *"Woodruff, you're in the back by unanimous decision."*

"Can't say I'm surprised," he said with a laugh.

As we were forming a strategic line, I saw it. Something—no, **someone**—was behind the brush and trees...watching. They didn't move, even though they must've seen me staring hard at the shape. That meant both he and I knew I couldn't make out any detail other than a dark shadow. I had to walk over there to investigate further. Since the man hadn't run, he must have something or someone backing him up, which made him unafraid. I decided against walking over there. I was pretty sure the man hadn't been following us the entire time. At most, he heard us goofing around, so for now, he'd have to keep following us.

"Let's start down," I instructed, cutting into the Black Warriors' chatter. They caught my tone and straightened up.

"Aye, mate," Woodruff said.

Silas, who'd decided to be the first in line, started down.

Everyone agreed I would be safer in the middle of the line. They actually persisted that's where I should fill in. I did so, but not before looking over my shoulder one last time at the figure still kneeling and watching our group.

Egon noticed the gesture and smartly didn't follow my gaze. Instead, he quietly asked me, *"What's going on?"*

Whispering to him without looking back, I replied, *"Someone's watching us back in the brush over there. I'm sure in the next couple of days, we'll figure out who it is."*

*"Just know, if he lays a finger on you, Hell's fire and despair will be a bloody **picnic** for him."*

The stairs were one of the only places in the world where losing your footing was a fatal mistake. Somehow, however, I was more concerned about the horses falling than us. We made sure we walked with the horses in front of us to detect a loose stone. When one was located, we'd step past it—along with our animal—and move on. I held Julius' reign tightly in my hand, for reasons I didn't dare repeat to myself.

To keep Arthur from panicking too much, Ocean, who was in front of me, would call up to him occasionally. *"Looking good up there, Arthur?"*

Arthur, who was behind Silas, would call back, *"At our current pace, should be about an hour now."* That back-and-forth continued, updated maybe every ten minutes. It was Ocean's way of assuring everyone they'd make it down the steep drop unscathed.

When the sun had set, and only the stars were out, our pace slowed. It was too dark to keep up our former time.

Egon, who was behind his horse and me, of course, let out a whisper everyone heard. *"Do I see a buggin' light down there?"*

Everyone turned to look after he asked the question. At the same time, we all heard a loose stone break. Thane, Cederic's horse, let out a strangled cry as more stones broke, and he slipped. Cederic was a strong man, but Thane was a big horse. The animal jerked him off his feet with a grunt and slid him down the edge of the stairs. Cederic wouldn't let go of the rope.

Woodruff, trailing the line, caught hold of Cederic's left arm — the one that wasn't gripping the rope. ***"Let go! The weight of Thane will rip your bloody arm off!"*** he pleaded.

Everything was happening so fast. I hesitated, then moved forward. Egon, older and quicker, got to him first. I realized I was too far to reach them in time. I moved forward anyway, up several stairs…

Egon and Woodruff grabbed Cederic's left arm but didn't pull him up, afraid they would tear his arm in half. Ocean cried out, saying he needed to let go of Thane, but he didn't listen. There was a split second when I thought Cederic wasn't going to let go and that he would either go plunging into the depths along with Woodruff and Egon, or something in his arm would give, and Thane would fall.

He chose to let go.

With the horse out of the equation, Egon and Woodruff pulled him up in no time at all onto some steps quivering underneath the three men. The steps held.

When I finally reached the three, I asked, *"How's his arm?"*

"I don't think he broke it," Arthur said from behind me. His voice seemed to move closer and closer to where I crouched beside Cederic.

"Everybody stay spread out! I don't want the stairs to collapse," I called out. Arthur's footsteps stopped.

"Is his arm okay?" Ocean asked, with genuine concern in her tone.

"Sorry, mate. Thane is gone," Woodruff said solemnly.

"Nothing he could do about it," Egon was quick to say. *"Beast was too heavy for any of us. Lucky he didn't – "*

"Break his arm? Hold that thought," I cut in. Adjusting the sleeve of the man's cloak and tunic, I touched his dark-skinned shoulder. It was fine. Nothing was out of place or swelling. I let out a sigh of relief, then shifted to comforting Cederic.

A Warrior's horse was given to him young. There was a deep bond between the Warrior and the beast. I knew exactly what had been going through his head when he'd chosen to let Thane go. His health — and the rest of the Warriors' — was more important to the prince's journey…more important to the purpose. He had so much faith in me, it almost hurt.

Cederic hadn't said a word since we pulled him up. He only rubbed his shoulder while in a sitting position and gritted his teeth. Concerned for him, I looked him in the eyes sincerely, knowing he'd lost a strong bond with a horse he loved. My own horse, Julius, was just a horse, too, but we'd been through so much together, it was hard not to consider him a close friend.

"Thank you," I said, then paused. *"I am so sorry."*

~~~~~~~~~~

The Black Warriors consist of a select few in Sans Défaut. They were special warriors who mastered only one weapon, trained to wield their weapon better than any foe or ally who dared to wield the same. As much as they were taught how to use it, they were also taught how to prevent it from being taken away from them.

This weapon had a name: **Requisite.**

I'm sure you are wondering whether my father approved of me befriending six Black Warriors. I couldn't tell you if he did, for he never spoke to me about it. Neither did I address it. It was the whim of fate, a gentle whisper that led me to the new and right. It seems it always leads me into things such as this. It's a nuisance, I assure you; a darn good one.

~~~~~~~~~~

There were several trips and stumbles after Cederic's near-fall and Thanes' demise. I couldn't help but glance up to see if the person who'd been watching us was trailing us down the stairs, but I didn't see them. It left me wondering if they had given up, figuring they'd be way behind waiting for us to complete the full staircase and surely spotted if they came down too early.

"I say, it should be about five minutes now, mates," Arthur announced excitedly, making sure both feet touched every step so as not to go too fast. Little good it was doing…

Cederic still seemed to be in pain, but he hadn't said a word. He wasn't a talker in general, but this silence was something else. I could see Ocean was as concerned for him as I was, but the only thing we could do was continue trudging down the stairs and rehearse what could be addressed when we reached the bottom.

I heard Woodruff hum happily from way behind me. He then said, with a stash of energy I envied, *"How about a game, you fools?"*

"How about the one called 'Shut Your Mouth'?" Egon suggested.

Woodruff whistled. *"Oh, well. You're a jolly soul, aren't you? I bet you do a happy dance when you get up in the morning,"* he teased.

I didn't hear anything in response and didn't look back, but I could guess Egon was shooting Woodruff a much-deserved dirty look. The image made me laugh.

"Ah, what are you laughing at, Prince Dustin?" Woodruff asked, seeking to tease someone else. *"You're not permitted to laugh at these corny jokes; only the eccentric ones."*

"Woodruff!" Ocean called back in dismay.

The Black Warriors had stopped treating me like my rank demands a long time ago — not because of the group's lack of manners, but because I insisted we treat each other like common friends. It seemed better that way. Sometimes, though, they did get carried away. Was it bad that I loved it when they did?

"Time for me to hush up," Woodruff stated, still laughing. *"Mom is on to me!"*

"You boys are ridiculous," she said.

"Why did you say 'boys,' Ocean? I hadn't said a word," Egon pouted.

"Quite unnatural that," I chimed in. I felt Egon's piercing eyes drilling a hole in my back.

"I hate to b-break up this infatuating back and f-forth, b-b-but if we all d-don't shut up, Ocean might throw us all over the l-ledge."

As if the stairs heard the statement, a stone behind me loosened and fell. It wasn't 'til I flipped my head around that I saw Egon had barely managed not to slip down the vacancy. As close as they were together, he most likely wouldn't have died, but getting trapped between them may have caused serious injuries. Cederic helped him get to a more stable step, and Egon grunted his thanks.

It only took a moment for Woodruff to think of a new joke, with not much thought given to the atmosphere in which he spoke. *"I'm sure she wouldn't throw 'Mister Softhearted' over the edge, but I think Egon might be less fortunate."*

Arthur laughed, and Egon gave him a what's-so-funny smirk, which made me laugh. *"Woodruff's right,"* I said. *"Let's play a game. How about stone-throwing? Unless, of course, one of you is afraid you throw like a girl."*

Because of the irony of the statement, everyone turned to see Ocean's reaction. She rolled her eyes and stated, *"It's not an insult to tell a woman she throws like a girl. It's simply normal. If a woman can outthrow a man, however, it's actually embarrassing."*

There was a pause.

"*Well, then. Your statement is fairly hard to oppose,*" I said, then continued with a grin on my face.

"*You admitted we were the physically stronger sex. Since it is, in fact, the case, we should stop our bragging, huh?*"

"*Yes, because how **far** can the physical get you?*" Ocean teased.

"*I can hold a whole barrel's worth of ale in my gut. Who wants to go farther than that?*" Woodruff said with a grin. His shallow response was strangely hilarious. A couple of us got a good kick out of it.

Ocean actually threw her stone farther than two of the Warriors, but I wouldn't dare embarrass them by listing their names.

8: ROSETTA KELLINA MABEL

Letters of love.
Letters of mischief.
Letters of war.
Letters of decrees.
They hide around, not to be found,
Then bury you in your sleep.

After the letter, I was buzzing yet a bit disappointed I couldn't communicate with the mysterious man. Surely, *surely,* he'd write again… A silly notion, I suppose, but those are mostly what we cling to when things get stuck.

I could only dream, and Lydia caught on to it quickly.

The following day, she was bringing flowers for the clothes dye into the factory and gave me a look I knew well. It was one that said, **"What's got you all blushing and fluttering your eyelashes?"**

"Spill it," she playfully demanded as she set the basket on the worktable.

I stood from my stool by the loom and examined my work. The dress, with its substantial width, should fit Lady Joan perfectly. That lady had more fat than sense. At least she gave me a lot of fabric to work with. *"Spill what?"* I innocently asked, laying the dress on the table to examine it further. The blue would complement the woman's skin tone, which was good since she had a shape the dress couldn't compliment, no matter how hard I tried.

I felt Lydia's fingers bite into my bare shoulder — the result of my wearing an off-the-shoulder wool dress and sash. She twisted me around and pushed my back against the table, holding both of my shoulders but not shaking them. *"You know you can't get around it. Tell me. Is it Kenneth?"*

Genuinely repulsed at the idea, I pushed her off and laughed. *"Gosh, Lydia! You know me too well."*

"Must I **guess***?"*

It hadn't occurred to me, but for some reason, I liked the idea. *"Yes, please guess."*

"Well, I'm not going to do it with you laughing at me!"

I continued laughing and then let out a sigh, struggling with my own thoughts. I'd never had any reason to hide anything from Lydia, and there was no reason to start now.

Strange emotions told me to keep what I was doing on dinner break to myself. I'd tell her about the letter, but not what I planned to do today. I wouldn't tell her about the trip to the library…

"If you want to know," I started, holding in a smile, *"you have to convince Mack to give you a break and come to my chambers in an hour, after dinner."*

"Done," she said confidently. *"What else do you want me to do, Lady Rosetta Kellina? Would you like me to stop by the kitchen to get you some meat while I'm headed to your room?"*

"Not necessary," I said pointedly at her joke. *"Just don't tell a soul you're meeting with me. Once I tell you this, do not tell a soul what I said…"*

~~~~~~~~~~

On most occasions, one would sit in the Great Room during dinner and converse with fellow workers who slaved away in the castle. Usually, you talked to someone who was in your field of work, such as Faye, Kip, and Héloise. For the most part, I would comply. I would listen to the three go on and on, gossiping away, all while Lydia and I would communicate with varying expressions from two different sides of the room.

Kenneth would often come to my table, even though he was only one table away and could hear every bloody word we were saying. Lydia said I should be flattered the Chancellor — and such a handsome one — would want to hear what I had to say! Indeed, he was handsome. He also seemed to think it qualified him for any lady he set his whim on in the castle. As far as I was concerned, a sorcerer couldn't cast a spell strong enough to make me fall in love with that piece of garbage with
~~~~~~~~~~

the gorgeous green eyes. In fact, Kenneth was one of the reasons I'd decided to take my secret trip now and skip dinner.

As well, all the other workers were too complicated. They liked strange machines and lime burning and hunting. Me? I just liked the birds, sewing, and spinning wool. They were the things I loved. Simple, calm, and far from terribly daring. I always got a headache from listening to those other workers talk about what they liked, what they did, or who their families are. Who cares? They'll all be dead in the next couple of months.

Did everyone think the Battle of Bloodshed contest happening tonight was just a silly contest—one that didn't affect them? It was a bloody sign! They were all doomed!

Then again, I was getting used to that fact, too.

Deep in my own thoughts, I darted down the halls, trying my best to slow down and give my best nonchalant look when someone passed me by. A month ago, I noticed no one was ever in the libraries during dinner. Dusters took the time to dust the nobles' bedrooms. Janitors cleaned the garderobes. Workers munched on good food in the Great Room, while the cooks shouted red-faced orders in the kitchen.

No one was **ever** in the libraries during dinner—the exact place I was going. I had to figure out how to tell the birds where to go. Besides that, life was dragging. Thoughts of the mysterious letter were starting to monopolize everything passing through my head. I couldn't forget it, no matter how hard I tried.

I climbed the two floors up in the staircase closest to the front of the castle. One of the Arming Squires passed me. I think his name is Ivan. He's the grouchy one. The man not only had one of the worst jobs in the castle, which required him to basically be a servant to whatever assigned knight, but it also required him to clean the blood and urine from the knight's armor when he was done in battle. Ivan's assigned knight was one of the vainest, selfish people in the kingdom. As far as we knew, the man was mean enough to get blood on his armor on purpose.

Ivan gave me a pinched look as he passed me, which was his way of saying hello, I suppose.

"Ivan." I nodded a greeting to him that he ignored. I continued up and down another corridor into the massive castle library in the East wing. I'd only been in the library once before. I liked books well enough, but I never felt up to going upstairs to get any, even though the workers were allowed to borrow books.

It's funny to me that I seemed to always straddle the fence. I was somewhere between being one of the nobles under the Lord Monté, and just 'one of the workers.' I knew most of the nobles but worked for a majority of them by making their clothes. I didn't know the Lord personally, while most of the "official" nobles did.

None of that mattered now. None of the filthy nobles received a letter from pigeon messengers. It was rare to find anyone who knew how to communicate with the birds. It was mostly a source of fantasy now—something historically interesting that never happened anymore.

My father had taught me a long time ago, before the Theft…before everything.

The pigeons on my balcony had flown away last night. I prayed they knew where to go. I, however, wasn't one to sit idle. I knew if they did return, I needed to remember some of the stuff about pigeon communication I had long ago forgotten. Surely, there was a book on the subject.

I moved through the big room, reading the labels on the walls next to the floor-to-ceiling racks of books. There were books on *etiquette, speech, writing,* and *reading*. Finally, I stumbled upon where I thought the books about pigeon communication would most certainly be: **Myths**, the funny label read. I booked it over towards that section and started my search. I quickly realized it was going to take me too long. The ceilings were nearly 15 feet in the air, with two ladders covering the whole section. The search could take me days to complete, considering I was working through most of them and could only search during break time. Plus, at some point every day, I'd have to eat. I couldn't starve myself. The whole endeavor could possibly take **weeks**, depending on how hard I worked on it. By then, I could've been sent another bloody letter!

I ignored every one of those negative thoughts, including the ones that assumed the book was on the top shelf or the last one I checked. Maybe. Maybe not. Perhaps it was in one of the first rows. Who knew? With that, I pulled books out of the shelf and examined the titles.

Title after title after title…

Dust fell on me, causing me to sneeze from breathing in too much of it, but I kept looking. I jerked out a tattered red book to examine the title, but I couldn't find it. The side of the book where the title was typically printed didn't say anything. I went to shove the book back on the shelf immediately. My body had gotten used to the rhythm of repetition. It then hit me that the strange book was leather and worn, looking more like a journal than a book belonging to the library. I tugged it back out again, interested in its contents, and flipped the first page open.

Story of Archie Cockburn
To whosoever reads the following words,
Listen closely.

Were personal journals supposed to be in the library, open to anyone who cared or was curious enough to venture in?

I know I should've snagged it, tucked it away in my dress, and read it later. However, I was captivated. Without thinking of what could happen if someone spotted me, I opened the journal and read the first five pages.

It was interesting to watch the boy, Archie, grow from ages nine, ten, eleven, to twelve. The story became very disturbing, though. It told the tale of a boy being abused by his parents. I certainly should've put the book back on the shelf or at least hid it in my dress pocket, but I didn't. I continued to stubbornly read on…past the boy writing in the tree…past his brother's persuasion.

I then came face-to-face with the Big, Bad Thing.

9: ANONYMOUS

Pain leads to sorrow.
Sorrow can lead to bitterness.
Bitterness leads to anger.
And anger can lead to sin.

Funny how such a happy day can be misleading. I'd played with Cecilly from noon to near dusk. We'd played our own aggressive version of horseshoes, and Cecilly bailed out on most of it, laughing and giggling while she watched me wrestle some invisible opponent. With dusty shoes and muddy clothes, I told her I had to go home.

Cecilly gave me a pouting face and said, *"You always got to go home."*

That was a perfectly normal response to my statement, seeing as it was her response every day. So, like every other day, I told her, *"I know, but my Pa and Ma don't like it when I'm late."*

"Are you sure you can't spare just a couple more minutes, Archie? I wanna show you something," she said, using her own nickname for me that she'd chosen when we had just become friends.

I rolled my eyes. *"God, Cecilly. I don't have time to stay. Besides, anything you show me now will be just as good tomorrow."*

She observed my look of uncertainty and tugged on my arm. *"Come on,"* she whined.

I started to walk away with her. I'd never been able to resist her. I glanced back at the spot I'd been rooted to for just a second and then looked back at Cecilly. *"Hey, where are we going?"*

"Just come on. You'll see."

We walked into the woods, next to Cecil's house. We then stepped over logs that started to blend with their environment and trudged our way through creeks and muddy moss. What's funny was it all led to a cave that was tucked neatly between two boulders at the foot of a rather large hill.

I shrugged. *"A **cave**?"* She looked at me, and her enthusiasm made my palms sweaty. *"Cecil, what's in there?"* I asked warily.

Cecilly, with her pretty blue eyes and unruly blonde hair, tugged my arm. When that failed, she grabbed my hand. *"Come on. You've got to go **inside** if you want to see the surprise. You're not getting cold feet, are you?"*

Maybe it was because she was grabbing my hand or a hitch in my testosterone, but I shook my head quickly as ever and spoke words I didn't hear myself. *"Of course not. What's this you wanna show me?"*

And just like that, I was walking into a mouth of darkness, holding Cecilly's hand.

I'd never held her hand before and was embarrassed by how sweaty my palms were. *"Did you bring a light?"* I whispered. I don't know why I whispered, but I remember being afraid my voice would echo and wake the dead.

"Shh. Would you stop asking questions and just walk?"

Easier said than done. I scooted forward — one foot, then another, then another. It felt like we were walking forever. Cecilly pulled my arm, so we turned at a dead end and…

I paused. There was light down this way, coming from crude torches sloppily nailed to the cave's old moss-ridden stone and dirt walls. They lined both sides of the tunnel walls heading back for maybe 12 feet to another dead end. At the end of the dimly-lit tunnel, I could now see a small pool that was about 25 feet round. There were no torches back there, and I realized the sharp things hanging above the pool were white crystals — so white in the pressing darkness, they lit up the back of the tunnel.

I was stunned! It was a remarkable spot. My jaw hung limp and left me looking like the stupidest person in the entire world.

"What do you think?" I barely heard Cecil ask.

*"I mean, it's…so…**beautiful**,"* I said in a huff. I was out of breath for no reason.

I nearly blushed when Cecilly laughed at me. *"You're funny, Archie,"* which she quickly followed with, ***"Race you!"*** I forgot all about her laughter and tore after her, running toward the pool and overtaking her halfway there. I jumped in three full seconds before her. She jumped in after, and not even a second after she came up for air, I made sure to splash her face with water and then duck underneath the wet surface to prevent a revengeful splash from hitting me.

The neat thing about water is that it forces you to slow down. To think. To live.

I heard Cecil call my name. Her laughter is somehow the most beautiful thing I'd ever heard. I remembered at this moment why I was still alive: *For this.* Joy and love and laughter. For water and caves, and girls and crystals. For woods and surprises and blushing.

That's what life was full of — not beatings, burnt flesh, and musty, dusty closets.

I burst out from under the water, grabbed Cecilly by the shoulders, and shook her 'til her teeth clattered. *"This is **awesome**! We've got to hang out here every day! You, me, and Mallory. **All of us!**"*

Cecilly grinned. *"I know! I couldn't believe it when we stumbled across this the other day. It was really dark and scary, so I hung the torches."*

"You hung the torches? That's amazing! I love it!" I finally stopped my rant for a second to think. *"Why didn't you wait 'til Mallory could come?"*

Cecil got all shy when I asked that question. *"I have chores all week that my Pa wants me to finish up, but he told me if I promised to do them when I finished playing, I could hang outside first. Geoff is visiting this week. He's had such important work in Sans Défaut, we never see him. I'm happy he's coming, but because of him, I wouldn't have gotten another chance to show you this."*

I felt a knot growing in my chest. **Why couldn't my Pa be like that? What made Cecil more deserving than me?**

Remembering my Pa, my mood darkened. *"I gotta go, Cecil."* Climbing out of the pool, I realized my Ma would be furious when she saw my shirt and trousers were wet.

Cecil made me forget them. Cecil was gonna get me in trouble.

"You can't stay a little longer? I am sure your Pa wouldn't mind."

It occurred to me then—quite suddenly—a fact I'd known but never acknowledged: I didn't know how to handle Cecil.

"No. I can't. I'll see you tomorrow."

Cecil climbed out of the pool and hurried to catch up with me. ***"Wait!"*** she called.

In my flash of anger, I didn't turn around or slow, knowing full well I was moving too fast for her. I was, in fact, the fastest in our friend circle…and it was dark in the cave—darker still when I rounded the corner.

I heard her trip and fall to the ground, hard. That was enough to make me turn around. I saw where there was a broken crystal lying on the ground and saw how she tripped over it. Hurrying to her, I knelt beside her and offered my hand. *"You okay?"* I hadn't meant for her to get hurt. I saw through the faintest of light the tears in her eyes from tweaking her ankle, which made me feel even worse. *"Let me help you up."* She used my weight to stand.

"I think I'm okay," she said shakily. Without putting a lot of weight on her left leg, she dusted herself off.

I stood next to her—stupid, awkward, and staring straight ahead of me into nothingness. When I felt her lips touch my cheek, I grew stiff. As she pulled away, my thoughts returned. **That** was why she really hadn't cared for Mallory being here with us. Not the cave, the pool, and the crystals. She'd **planned** to kiss me. I felt color rush through my cheeks, but she didn't let me speak. As usual, she had it all figured out already.

"Sorry about whatever I said," she said softly. *"If you need to be alone, I can go home. Do you know your way out of here?"*

Her words weren't making sense. All I could let out was, *"Yeah."*

Then, she was gone—walking further ahead into the darkness towards the entrance of the cave.

I stood there for a while, mentally kicking myself. What's worse was that I **didn't** know my way out of the tunnel. I spent about half an hour wandering through the cave before I spotted daylight and embraced fresh air.

~~~~~~~~~~
~~~~~~~~~~

Ma was not one to be trifled with. I suppose I should've thought of that before plunging into a pool with my clothes on, soaking my trousers through.

I am now getting my ear twisted while trying not to squeal because I had to hold my breath to prevent inhaling the rank stench of ale on **her** breath. Mallory wasn't home yet. I wish he'd been here. He would've stood up for me.

*"You're a stupid, **stupid** boy! Look at your clothes; muddy and wet! Can't you take care of **anything**? Don't you care for **anyone** else?"*

I was in no position to answer those questions. Nor could I hear them clearly. My world was going black. I needed to breathe, but I knew if I could endure for a couple more seconds, she'd throw me in The Closet, and I could suck in the precious air I desperately needed.

As she clutched the collar of my shirt and dragged me along, we moved towards it. I shifted, and she slapped me. While looking down at me in anger, she noticed the bulge in my trousers pocket.

*"What's **that**?"* Her yellow teeth settled slightly apart.

My heart stopped. *Throw me in The Closet, punch me, slap me, burn me, but don't touch my journal. It's all I have.*

"It's nothing. I swear," I said instinctively. I immediately realized it was the wrong thing to say.

She grabbed my hair and yanked it hard. I tightened and sucked air through my teeth as she pulled the journal from my pocket. I screamed for her to put it back and she hit me again with more force, sending me falling to ground on my hands and knees.

"The Story of Archie Cockburn?" my mother read aloud. *"You're such a stupid, little boy. Whatever possessed you to* **write***? No one in our family can write. Maybe that's what's made you ridiculous,"* she cackled.

I couldn't behave this time. I refused to hold it all in like I usually could. The woman I hated most in the world was holding the only thing keeping me going. I felt hysterical. *"I'm a writer. It's who I am! I swear I'll write forever and ever! You can't stop me from doing that. You* **can't***!"*

My Ma raised a brow at my outburst, then grew angry — so angry, she convulsed with it. *"You* **foolish** *boy! You'll never be anything, do you hear? This journal is just another object of evidence of how useless you are!"*

Tears were in my eyes. It was the first time in years I'd cried in front of one of my parents. I made it a point never to give them the pleasure. Now, however, I couldn't stop them from falling.

"I'm going to write about **you** *one day,"* I protessed. I marveled at how calm my voice was; just a slight quaver. It was the first time in my life I'd actually felt proud of myself. *"I'm gonna write about how you treated me. They'll get me out of this crazy place. People are gonna read my stories all the way to Sans Défaut. Just watch, Ma. Just watch."*

From where I was on the floor, I remained in a fetal position. She kicked me — kicking until my ribs were so bruised, I couldn't inhale without stabs of pain. She'd gotten my head once or twice, too. The world was spinning. *"Stop,"* I said brokenly, causing her to laugh…a sound that made me cringe.

*"Stop? **Stop?** Your father will hear about this! I'll make him beat you until you can't walk! You'll never see those stupid friends again, either. How does that sound?"*

I was in so much pain, I didn't answer. When she started walking towards the fire where the kettle hung, I stood — despite the pain — knowing what she was preparing to do but trying to prevent it. *"Ma, please. No,"* I said weakly. *"Please let me have this one thing. Please."* I felt helpless. As she got closer to the fire, I felt even more hysterical.

I took off after her in a sudden surge of energy I never knew I possessed and tackled her from behind. We went to the ground — legs, arms, and elbows entangled. I bit my Ma's arms like a complete lunatic, and managed to grab hold of my journal, yanking it from her hands. I must've looked like an absolute madman. Most certainly, I felt like one. I couldn't block the elbow coming for my eye that she sent while we were wrestling on the ground, though. If I had a couple more years on me, I'm sure I could've beaten her, but she was stronger than I. After that first blow, more rained in. She tore the journal from my grasp and threw it into the fire.

I scrambled after it. Maybe if I could get to it in time…

My Ma was too quick. She pulled me up off the ground, drug me to The Closet, and shoved me in. I tried to fight and push my way out but only succeeded in getting my fingers slammed between the door. Had there been a light in The Closet, I would've noticed my fingers went completely black and were swollen, but there was not a speck of light in this space. All I could do was suck them to make the pain at least bearable while awaiting my sentence.

Boredom was hard to get around. It crept up slowly, like the spider on the ceiling. I thought about eating that spider once.

Hour after hour after hour after hour…

I wanted to kill myself but didn't know how. I'm sure I could've figured out something, but while I was in The Closet, all I could think about was Cecilly and our moment in the cave. *Life wasn't supposed to be like this,* I would think. *As soon as I get out of here, I am going to fix it.*

I wanted to make sure my parents remembered me — to make sure they hadn't forgotten they'd locked a son in The Closet who was now dying of starvation. I didn't want to shout or scream like a baby, though. Doing that would make them prouder of themselves than I'm sure they already were.

So, I sang. It hurt to do so because my lips were dry and cracked. They would bleed when I stretched them, but I sang my heart out anyway.

I remained in The Closet for three days. No food. No water. No sunlight. Nothing to treat my battle wounds from trying to save my journal. I threw up once and halfway through the second day, I had to pee so bad, I did so on the closet floor. There wasn't enough room to get around the urine and vomit, so I had to contend with my living conditions. The Closet wasn't long enough for me to fully extend while laying down, so I cramped a lot. Usually, I could get the cramp out and gritted my teeth against the pain. On the third day, I got dizzy…a lot.

I slept in my own puke and urine, and my nose always stung from the stench. The only time I could escape it was in my dreams. Those were pleasant. Thank God, my parents couldn't touch those.

Sleeping was the only way to escape the horror of my life and where I was. Sometimes, I would pretend I was a character in a story, much like the ones I read. All this wasn't happening to me. I was a great person in a different story, living a different life.

If you're wondering, I did cry. I cried a lot. Little sniffles here and there. I didn't allow myself to cry too much. Crying is what children do, and I was no longer a child.

I spent considerable time contemplating what I was going to do to fix everything—not only my whole situation but Mallory's, too. My thoughts grew dark, like the color inside The Closet. It grew darker still when I spoke. I cursed my Pa and Ma like I'd never done before. For once, I felt like Mallory. I was standing up for something…for myself. I was being strong.

At noon on the third day, The Closet's door creaked open and light I had dreamed of crept in. I squinted my eyes and tensed, expecting Pa or Ma to violently jerk me from The Closet and scold me once more. I braced for the onslaught, but when my eyes adjusted, I realized it was Mallory. He held a finger to his lips, signaling me to be quiet, then beckoned for me to step out.

I stood and then gritted my teeth as my right leg locked, causing me to stumble. Mallory caught me and helped me to our bedroom, making sure the door shut after me. We climbed down the ladder that led to where our cots lay. Descending the ladder was very difficult for me. My legs kept locking, and I dreaded the time when I'd have to ascend it. Once at the bottom, I laid on my cot and stretched fully for the first time in three days.

Mallory just looked at me. *"They weren't gonna get you out of there 'til tomorrow afternoon."*

I paused and spoke for the first time in a full day. My dry lips told me not to, but I didn't listen. *"So, you got me out of there a full day early. Good."* I surprised myself with how composed I sounded, especially after having been locked away in The Closet and starving just a second ago. Mallory raised a thick, brown brow. I told him what I never thought I'd say:

"I'm ready to do it if you are."

Mallory immediately knew what I was referring to and walked over to our creaking floorboard, pulling it up. We'd used that place to store things we didn't want our parents to see for years. *If only my journal had been in there instead of my pocket…*

Mallory pulled out something I'd never seen him put in there before. Shiny and sharp, the sword was five feet long, including the handle. It was bigger than any knife I'd ever seen.

I gawked at it. *"Where'd you get that, might I ask?"*

"Stole it from Jackie's house. What do you think? Big enough to kill someone, Archie?"

My eyes darkened. *"Big enough to kill **two** someones,"* I whispered.

Mallory gave me his dinner. I needed strength for the big night. I wasn't 100% when the sun went down, but I felt better than I had in days — three, to be exact.

Hiding me throughout the rest of the day had been a challenge. I heard Mallory getting a beating once and wanted to run up and help him but knew I couldn't. Everything had to be perfect. My parents couldn't know I was no longer in The Closet.

It was apparent Mallory had thought this plan through for years, although he had to make adjustments because of our current situation. It would only do us good if things went wrong, and our parents thought Mallory was the only one in on it. I could then catch them off guard. Surprise is always good when you are at a disadvantage.

Well, disadvantaged we most certainly were, but we were also enraged. For abused hearts such as ours, rage was something to feed our needs.

I'm sure you would think I knew the dirty details of that night. To be honest, I can hardly remember it. Those kinds of things move in blurry motions, I think. I remember emotions and images, but little else.

For the curious, I will tell you what I recall happened four days ago when we pulled off the Big, Bad Thing.

~~~~~~~~~~

My Pa snored like a pig when he laid on his back. He was in that position when Mallory and I snuck in.

I remember we'd decided to get Pa first, even though we passed by Ma to get to him. (I mentioned before that Ma did not sleep with my Pa.) If we failed and only killed one parent, we'd rather it be Pa than Ma. We could probably overpower Ma if we both tried together, but Pa was as broad and strong as he was cruel. Better to kill him first.
~~~~~~~~~~

We snuck in with our five-foot-long sword. Mallory held it. Seeing **he** stole it, he could probably use it better than I.

Pa had knives next to his bed. *Did he suspect that one day, we'd try to kill him?* In the end, his own snoring prevented him from hearing us sneak up for the kill.

I could hardly breathe as I saw Pa cough up blood after Mallory had cut his neck open. What a revengeful moment it was. How could we have known, though, that it would be so noisy? Pa coughed for close to half a minute before he lost consciousness. By then, the ruckus had woken our sleeping mother from the dead, and she came bounding in to see what was wrong with the man. She gasped when she saw Pa's neck.

I hid behind something. Just what, I cannot remember. Ma came running in without seeing me. Despite Mallory being two years older than I, Ma still managed to rip the sword away, and it clattered to the floor. I ran from behind whatever it had been, picked it up, and stabbed Ma in the back.

Guess what I did after we'd killed our parents? After my wave of **bravery**?

I cried.

Mallory scorned me later for doing so, but yep: I cried.

For once, I accepted this was, in fact, my life. We just murdered our parents — ones who never loved me. Parents I couldn't get back.

What is a stronger word for regret? Remorse? Grief? None of those described what I truly felt. I couldn't breathe or speak. I heaved sobs I couldn't swallow or hold back. As stupid as it sounds, I wanted my parents back not even a second after we killed them.

10: ROSETTA KELLINA MABEL

Confidence and arrogance are two completely different things.
It all begins at where you sit and when you choose to spring.
A joke is only funny when one doesn't have to explain.
In the same way, if you must tell us, you are confident,
and your effort is in vain.

My heart was like a hammer that somehow ended up in my throat. Poor boy, I thought as I lifted and turned the next page to see if —

"I had no idea you liked to read." The voice belonged to Chancellor Kenneth. He stood in the large archway separating the outside hall from the library.

I shoved the book into the folds of my dress and smiled at him nervously, instantly regretting the friendly action because he stepped forward.

"You never told me you were interested in the myths," he pried.

I dropped my head, dismayed at his interest, and disgusted he had climbed two flights of stairs to come looking for me. *"You never asked, my lord."*

"Kenneth," he said, breaking into a smile. *"I dread being called **my lord**, actually."*

I dreaded that now, I'd have to remember to use his name. *"I suppose it can get rather annoying."* Bloody murder! **Did I just sympathize with the man?!** He took another casual step forward. I was running out of steps before we'd actually be engaged in conversation.

*"Forgive me…Kenneth. Dinner is almost over, and I **must** get back to the factory."* I picked up a book I had placed on the ground to put it back on the shelf. When I turned, he was right next to me, helping me push the book in.

"What have you been up to that's keeping you so busy, Rosetta?" His eyes were so intense, I had to look away. I was sure he was on to me. Did he know about the birds? The letter? The journal? It would seem in just a day and a half, I had tons of secrets—none I could tell the Lord Monté's Chancellor, even if I **did** like him.

My body started to shake. I willed him not to notice and shook my head for a few seconds before any words came out. *"I beg your pardon, Kenneth. I have no earthly idea what you're talking about."*

I attempted to step past him, but he roughly grabbed me by the arm. When he loosened his grip, he stated, *"You're shaking…"* There was concern in his tone.

I wanted to curse. Instead, I replied, *"I'm concerned about the contest tonight. I can, in fact, watch a man go down if he is fighting for a real cause. However, a man shouldn't have to fight for food."* I felt my eyes begin to tear up and wanted to curse myself—even moreso when I completed my thought. With a quiver in my voice, I said, *"A man shouldn't have to risk his life for such basic needs."*

"I agree," Kenneth said quickly. It disturbed me how bent he was on gaining my approval rather than those of the suffering peasants.

Chancellor Kenneth would stand by Lord Monté's side tonight and do absolutely nothing. That was enough for me to see the man had little care for anyone else. He would never put his own rank or life on the line and was as selfish as I was stubborn.

"Then, tell him so," I begged. If I was going to have to bear Kenneth's interest, I might as well use it to change Lord Monté's bloody system.

"Tell who?" he asked.

"Lord Monté. You see him all the time. You must have some influence on how he thinks and how he—"

"Shhh!" Kenneth put his hand over my mouth and glanced around, even though no one was in the library. The only way anyone could have heard was if they passed by in the corridor at the precise moment and overheard me. ***"The Lord is not one to change his mind off of whim,"*** he whispered fiercely.

With his one hand still over my mouth, he grabbed my arm with the other. *"He thinks. He studies. Then, he decides. I have no control or influence over anything he does."*

I wanted him to let me go, the darn fool. I wanted him to never speak to me again and to leave me alone. Still, I was happy I'd diverted the subject of books. It made my shaking seize for a moment, and I pulled away from him. ***"If you have no control over anything, then what have you accomplished? It is suddenly alright to have the rank of Chancellor and the attitude of an Arming Squire?"*** I asked venomously.

Kenneth did not like my questioning him at all. I saw his eyebrows raise and then lower in anger. *"Is **that** how you feel about me?"* he spat.

At this point, I was angry, too. Angry at him for not taking me seriously. *"I never said I felt any way about you, Kenneth. You yourself said you have **no control** over what goes on in this bloody castle. Did you think for a second you had control over me?"* I boldly countered.

I had never seen Kenneth's face turn so red in my life. *"You forget who you're speaking to, Rosetta. I didn't come here to be spurned and lectured as if I were speaking to my mother!"* His lowered brows made the statement even sharper, but I didn't let it stop there.

"Then what did you come here for? I am entitled to saying yes or no, am I not? Or are you able to take this liberty away from me as well?"

Kenneth scoffed. *"I would never take it away from you. I love you. Have I not been clear?"*

If I'd known there was going to be a moment of professed love in the library today, I would've avoided it and never gone in. Now, however, I was here and had to make a decision. I suppose the decisions made without thinking too much are often more honest.

"Yes. You've been clearer than you should've been."

There was a moment of silence when both of us were catching our breath and calming our wits to figure out if what we said had been rather wrong or rather right. When a voice came from the archway, it was Lydia's.

"Rose." She paused when she saw us.

I took advantage of the opportunity to break free and walked over to her. *"It's time for me to get back to work, Chancellor,"* I called back to the man. *"I do hope you understand."* We left the library and didn't say a word to each other until we had gotten to the stairs.

"I wish to never go in the library again."

"Nor I listen in on conversations from a corridor."

I glanced at her sharply as we walked down the steps. ***"You heard?"***

"Every *word. I followed him upstairs. You were rather harsh to him, but he was acting like a dunce."*

"A levereter is more like it…"

"He went about things horribly wrong, I think," Lydia said observably.

"I swear, he wouldn't understand the word 'no' if I tattooed it on my cursed lips!"

*"You **were** harsh to him, Rose. Telling him he acted like an Arming Squire? Mocking his character the way you did?"*

"I did not mock his character." I denied her claim sharply. I thought I behaved pointedly but not harshly.

"Yes, you did — and you're going to be a lady and apologize to him for it later."

I stopped walking, and Lydia kept going. I said the word more to the back of her head. **"Apologize?"** I caught up with her.

"Just because the man acted pinched and selfish and said the wrong things at the wrong time, it doesn't mean you don't need to act like a lady."

Now, it was my turn to feel as if I were bickering with my mother. *"Lydia, if I go back to him, he's going to think I changed my mind and that I love him. I **haven't** changed my mind. I still hate his guts, just the same as I did this morning."*

"Then you need to do it with someone else nearby. He'd be too embarrassed to keep going."

*"What if I don't want to apologize? When did his opinion **ever** matter to me?"*

"It matters starting now, Rose. I swear, if someone didn't make you care, you'd never get around to it." She stopped and glanced around warily. *"Now, about the secret…"*

~~~~~~~~~~
~~~~~~~~~~

I think Lydia liked the idea of someone sending me love letters. Maybe she thought it would settle me down a bit. *I honestly doubted it would, but it did give me something to think about.* She practically bounced on the edge of my bed with excitement as she read it. I watched her, holding back a laugh.

"Your one and only," Lydia said as she finished reading. She squealed. *"He called you his one and only! This is so **exciting**!"*

I shushed her, scared someone would hear her from the other side of the door. *"I know!"* I half-whispered. *"I couldn't even **breathe** after I read it!"*

"You said birds delivered it?"

"Yes. I was sleeping when it happened, actually. I was quite surprised when they flew onto my balcony."

"Has he sent any others?"

I sighed. *"I'm afraid not. I wish he would. I so desperately wish he would…"* I glanced toward the ceiling and then down and through the archway leading out to the balcony.

Lydia laughed at me. *"You're in **love**,"* she teased.

I rolled my eyes and smiled. *"Yes, in love with someone I've never seen or even know."*

"Well, how do you know it, Rose?" Lydia jumped from the bed and took my hands in excitement. *"Maybe this man knew you from long ago. Maybe he's an old lover you can't remember."*

I hushed her. *"Well, if all of this is true, how long will this romance last? He mentioned he has a company. Why would he need a company to save me? What if he's coming against the Lord Monté? He'll* **die***, Lydia. He'll die before I even know who he is!"*

Lydia rolled her eyes at me. *"I think you're* **thinking** *too much. He called you Ro, and he's coming to save you. That's all I heard."*

I sighed and laid back on the bed. *"I wonder if he'll give me his name,"* I said, realizing my words were slurred like some love-struck drunk.

Lydia laughed at me again, but this time, I didn't mind. *"Well, considering you think he's a knight in shining armor who's been training for years in* **secret** *to kill the Lord Monté just for his one and only, I don't think so."*

11: DUSTIN ELRIC CARPENTER

*Who you trust is as important
As life or death itself.
A food can lead you to all sorts of mess;
A saint can lead you to rest.*

It felt good to step on solid ground that didn't budge when I shifted or turned. It also felt foreign, like when I have ridden my horse for hours on end, then tried to stand on my own two legs.

It hadn't taken us long to remember the bit of light Egon had seen while taking our dangerous trip down the stairs. We were wary even to pass it, but it was a waste of time to venture sideways. Time was of little quantity at the moment.

"It never felt so good to stand on some grass!" Arthur exclaimed.

I laughed. *"Aye. Let's set up camp here, then."*

"A-are we sure that's safe? This is P-p-precursory Woods — a place we've been warned countless times is enchanted a-and h-h-haunted."

Egon snorted. *"Only for people who read stories about mermaids and believe in ghosts, Silas."*

Ocean rolled her eyes and removed her boots and socks so her bare feet could touch the grass. *"These woods **are** enchanted, Egon. How else do you explain all the stories?"*

"That, my dear Ocean, is just bad luck."

I laughed. *"Well, then. If being swallowed by monsters is just bad luck, we all should surely watch our step."*

Woodruff laughed at that, but Silas remained on edge. *"D-don't you think we're taking th-th-things too l-lightly?"*

I removed my own boots and socks, wiggling my toes to stretch them. I then sat next to Ocean. *"Ocean can double-check Cederic's arm while we go get wood for a fire. When we get back, you, Silas, can take first watch."*

Egon laughed, pointing at Silas' face. Ocean smiled as well. *"I'll relieve Silas,"* she said, volunteering to keep watch after him. Egon volunteered after her, then so on, until everyone had a watch time. We made sure to tie up the horses.

Silas didn't seem the least bit happy to be on first watch. As we took off through the woods looking for good fire material—leaving Ocean and Cederic behind—he replied to Egon's earlier comment. *"I don't r-read books about mermaids, a-a-anyway. Sometimes, th-they happen to be in the book."*

Egon made a deep noise in his throat, suggesting he didn't believe Silas. *"Yes, just like kisses seem to pop up in a romance story, and you never know they're coming."* A smirk formed on Egon's face.

That caused Silas to blush, which set Woodruff off laughing heartily again.

I saw some good fire-burning wood on the ground and picked it up. *"Now, cut it out. You know what Ocean would think of us teasing Mr. Devereux."*

"Aye," Arthur said seriously. *"What'd ya think about that?"* I guess we all knew Arthur was speaking of Ocean's comment earlier this morning about Silas.

"You're too young to understand these things," Egon stated.

Arthur shot him a scoff and a half. "What does being old have to do with it?"

Woodruff, Egon, and even Silas thought the question was funny. Me, being only two years older than Arthur, wondered the same. I silently hoped Ro wouldn't think I was too young to know about love. Or worse, **she** was too young. I felt ready.

The thought of Ro made me look toward the skies and pause. She hadn't answered my letter. Then again, there wasn't exactly a certain chance she knew pigeon-speaking or pigeon-communication. I was, however, itching to send another letter.

Itching to speak to her. Itching to see her… I was just plain itchy all over when I thought of her.

Funny how you could love someone you'd only met once. It was a strange feeling. Like a good friend who lived three kingdoms over, you never questioned if they'd changed, even though you barely ever see them. A whisper fills the gap between you, telling the other not to worry.

Love was a choice. That was all there was to love, and a young person could understand if they tried hard enough.

My happy thoughts were interrupted by Egon, whose hands were full as he stated, *"This ought to be enough firewood, don't you think?"*

Silas nodded the affirmative. *"L-let's get back to c-c-camp, then."*

As we walked back, I tried desperately to stifle three yawns tickling my chest. Somehow, stifling them made me even sleepier. I suddenly felt the pain from a rash growing on the inside of my leg from riding. I just gritted my teeth and told the pains and exhaustion to go away. I'd get my sleep soon enough. Plus, we were too early on the journey for my body to grow weak. If I coddled it, it surely would fail me.

When we arrived back at our newly-claimed camp, Cederic seemed tended to and was lying on his cot that was laid neatly on the ground.

Ocean was feeding the horses 20 feet away and singing a well-known tune from Sans Défaut called "Just Another Broken Dagger." She had a sweet voice and sung a lot back home. Here in the woods, as all the men made the fire and finally laid out our cots, her singing seemed to do more than it did at home. It comforted me and gave me some peace as I laid down and began counting the stars. The light of the fire licked my cheek and gave me warmth. I fell asleep somewhere between the seventh chorus and the eighth verse, with the words reverberating in my skull:

> *Yes, I broke the rivers with knitted hands*
> *And made the mountains haggard.*
> *I killed the wind again, with just another broken dagger.*

~~~~~~~~~~~

It was on Ocean's watch-duty when I heard her scream. I snapped awake to the horror of the sound. **Something** was wrestling Ocean on the ground next to my cot. I sat up fully and grabbed the handle of my sword, jerking it from the sheath. However, I couldn't swing without risking hurting Ocean in the process.

On cue, though, she flung whatever it was off her. It tumbled and rolled a few feet away before running back at her on all fours. Saliva dripped from its chin; its eyes were crazed and white. The skin of the thing was hard to look at, as it was wrinkled, shrunken, and yellow. Was it *rotting*? That word might suit it better. The hair consisted of several black spiderweb-thin strands that were seemingly rotting, too.

Arthur must have awoken as well because from behind me, three arrows zipped past me. They came so rapidly, they nearly blended as one. All three hit their target soundly in the chest, which got the thing to growl, but it kept advancing.

Ocean was trained to use what they call a "swallow." It was a double-edged sword that **thing** must've knocked from her hands. On her knees now and weaponless, her swallow too
~~~~~~~~~~~

far away, she punched the thing hard in the jaw. It snarled and went for her again.

I jumped in front, stabbed the thing in the abdomen just in time, and pulled out my sword. Breathing heavily, I watched it shake and got ready for it to fall and die, but instead, it lunged at me, knocking over both me and Ocean, who stood behind me. I was on top of Ocean now, and the thing was on top of me. I still gripped my sword firmly. It tried to bite my shoulder, but it was being lifted and then hoisted across the campsite by my dear friend (and even dearer friend now), Woodruff. I quickly scrambled up, and Ocean did the same as she grabbed her swallow.

If three rather large arrows **and** a stab (the wound pierced the thing almost all the way through) had not put it out of its misery, the group was probably in for a battle.

Cederic, whose Requisite was called a "shuriken" — most commonly known as Throwing Stars — threw one impossibly accurate weapon at the thing, which hit and stuck into its throat. It gasped, pulled the shuriken from its throat, threw it away, and kept growling.

"Uh…" Arthur said, stepping back a bit.

Egon gripped his staff and narrowed his eyes at the thing. *"Bloody fool should've died by Dustin's sword. Now, it's gonna get less mercy than the devil himself could give!"* That statement had Egon written all over it. Even though the thing looked unable to be communicated with, it turned its attention to Egon and went for him next.

Egon flipped his staff in a vertical-related motion and cracked it on the thing's skull. It pulled back. Two more arrows sunk into the thing's back, and it turned towards Arthur, opening its mouth wide.

On a monster such as this, one would expect to see pointy fangs in their mouth and razor-sharp claws on their feet. Instead, we saw gabby gums that seemingly had lost their teeth years upon years ago. Its so-called nails were beyond even the nastiest stage of yellow.

This thing scared me more than any monster could. This **thing** was human, but just how human could it be? What had happened to it?

Suddenly, it released the strangest sound I'd ever heard. It was something between a screech and a croak. It then jumped at poor Arthur, who had never been in a battle. His knees knocked together as rapidly as his teeth clattered.

"Arthur!" Ocean screamed to warn him, but it was too late. The thing—the human—was on Arthur's head, scratching and scratching. He stumbled back, screamed, and fell. He rolled about like a madman, trying to get the thing off.

Woodruff was the first to reach Arthur. He kicked the stupid thing four times in its side before it rolled off Arthur's head and onto the ground. Arthur jerked away from it, just as it got its feet underneath to lunge at him yet again. Unfortunately for the thing, it didn't notice Woodruff coming down with his Requisite. The ax went straight through the thing's neck. The head, now dismembered from the body, rolled several times before coming to rest.

All was still, except for the Black Warriors' rugged breathing.

*"Bloody Hell! What was **that**?"* Woodruff asked no one in particular.

No one could answer his question. No one had the time. Every one of us heard something moving in the woods, and we gripped our weapons tighter. It got louder, and I distinguished the sound as coming from near where Cederic stood, on the other side of the fire. He must've noticed, too, because his brow furrowed. He slowly grabbed a shuriken from a leather bag beside his cot and made ready to fling it at whatever came from the bushes and trees.

As if on cue, the new threat came bursting from the tree line. Every one of the Black Warriors nearly struck it before we realized it was a human. Arthur did let an arrow fly, but he turned slightly at the last second, so it thumped into a tree rather than the grinning man who stood before us.

The man had no idea how lucky he was to still be alive.

"Hi!" he shouted, making us all jump. Arthur, who'd already nocked another arrow on a string, almost released one again. *"Follow me!"* he instructed. Just as quickly as he appeared, he was gone into the shrubbery.

We all gave each other a glance. No one moved. After fighting the thing we'd just encountered, none of us wanted to walk into more trouble.

The man returned, frowning—not in a creepy way, but more like he was disappointed in us at being reluctant to simply do as he said: follow him.

"Look, the Gummy is gonna wake back up again. Do ya wanna be around for that, eh?" The man's eyes squinted as if he were trying to read our reactions. He had a terribly scrubby beard

and an eye that refused to open. His hair was even redder than Woodruff's, and he wore a furry brown coat over a black tunic and grey tights. His tunic was unbuttoned near the top, revealing a surprising amount of even scrubbier red chest hair.

I hesitated, then spoke. *"Sir, we cut off its head…"* I said, although rather uncertainly.

The scrubby man laughed. *"Ya wanna stick around and see if it happens, **ja**?"*

I narrowed my eyes back at the man and tried to read **him**. Justifiably so, I was hesitant to lead my group of Warriors into an unknown danger.

"Excuse me, sir," Arthur said quietly. His head was still bleeding from the dozens of scratches he received from the thing. *"Who are you?"*

*"Why it matters, I have no idea. I am Endres Kraus, I believe. Nobody knows their true name out here. **Now**, are we ready? I've got food and wasser. It isn't safe out here."*

I sighed and nodded for my friends to follow the strange man. Again, he took off into the woods, and we followed him…albeit questioningly.

It seemed stupid, I know, to follow a stranger into the woods. However, if he was telling the truth about the Gummy (as he called it) waking up, I didn't want to be around to see it.

So as to convince myself, I **also** thought the Black Warriors were great company to be with when in danger. Unless the man had a hidden army somewhere, we were in pretty good shape.

Woodruff nudged me from my right and whispered in my ear, *"Don't you worry, prince. If this mate's up to no good, we'll put a weapon through him quicker than he can spring."* As if confirming my thoughts, that statement put me at ease—at least as at ease as I could be after a crazed man attacked us in our sleep…

A tiny branch rubbed against my gloved forearm. I looked at the back of the man's head. Endres, he'd said. He seemed wild, but he looked sane enough. He was nothing like the thing that attacked the group not long ago. I whispered a *"Hey"* to Egon, who was on my left, gripping his staff and constantly looking around as we moved. He turned at my call and raised a brow. *"Egon, do you think he's the one who followed us?"*

Egon looked ahead at the man and gruffly whispered back. *"That'd be a mite creepy, but I suppose it's logical. Mr. Gummy back there didn't seem sane enough to hide behind a tree."*

Mr. Gummy hadn't been sane at all, I thought.

Ocean cleared her throat from behind me, and I turned. *"You men have any idea where he might be taking us?"*

"I thought the woman here would know," Woodruff said, smiling.

"Not now," Egon barked. *"Bloody man might be listening. Best to get back to silence and just stay alert."*

"I can hear ya, mädchen und jungen. Not much gets past me."

I wasn't sure what all of that meant, but I cleared my throat and addressed what I knew. *"You were listening to us?*

You know you're not doing a grand old job at making us relax, don't you?"

He laughed. *"Nein, I suppose. It wasn't my goal to relax ya. Couldn't be responsible for your nerves if I wanted to be."* He then began to whistle a tune and walked a little faster with a bigger spring in his step.

I wrinkled my nose, and Woodruff chuckled. *"Is it bad that I like this guy?"* he asked.

Crickets chirped a sort of song, and my ears—already anxious and highly on-edge—heard them at an ear-piercing volume. Add in the crunch of every boot to dirt and the quiet *"shh"* sound of leaves against passing shoulders, and we had a full symphony.

Egon responded to Woodruff, not bothering to whisper anymore. *"No. Frankly, he's about as big a **nuisance** as you. If you didn't like the man, I'd be terribly shocked."*

I forced a laugh, but my mind was otherwise occupied. *Had the creature heard our accusation claiming it followed us? Surely, it hadn't followed us but for so long…*

Circumspect, I asked the man ahead, *"Well, then. If you mean no harm, tell us why you were following us?"* I made sure to sound as decided as possible. If it was, in fact, true, he'd been the one spying on us and wouldn't lie about it.

The strange man just laughed, not even bothering to turn around at the accusation. *"I am not your watcher, but I'm sure the lad would be thrilled ya thought it was me."*

"The 'lad,' you say?" Arthur spoke up.

All the Black Warriors fell quiet, further enhancing the sounds of nature. Well, at least to my ears.

"Aye, lad, knabe, bursche. Knew him a long time ago. Used to be a good freund — forgive me, friend. That was before he lost his marbles…"

"Uh-huh," Egon grunted, making it obvious he didn't believe him and that the rest of us shouldn't, either.

I think the rest of us were just as conscious of the unknown when it came to this man, but there was no harm in asking questions.

"Could he p-perhaps b-b-be the monster we just cut the head off o-of back th-th-there?" Silas' stuttering always got worse when he was on edge.

"Heavens, no. But if ya took it from him, those are his kinder — ahem, *children."*

"That ugly, ol' thing?!" Egon exclaimed in disgust. Ocean punched his arm at the bluntness of his statement.

"There are more?" Ocean inquired.

The man let out a sound like a 'tsk' and shook his head, looking back at them and grinning. *"Questions, questions. Fragen, fragen. Suppose you'll have to pay up, then."*

"Pay up?" Egon asked, a hint of irritation in his tone. If the man were too much like Woodruff, then he would most certainly hate him, too. *"What do you mean, old man?"*

With the same grin, the man turned. This time, he sported one raised brow. *"Well, ya don't expect me to keep* *answering questions for **free**, do ya?"* Egon snorted, which just made the man laugh harder. *"Getting a bit of coin from people these days is onerous. I suppose if I was more gut aussehend — physically appealing — I would rub off on people better…"*

Ocean must've felt bad about Egon's behavior. *"We're traveling a long ways. Forgive us, as we're hesitant to accept assistance. The stories of Precursory Woods aren't amusing."*

"Aye, terrible. I've heard a terrible few. You're traveling through it, nonetheless. Either you're complete idiots, or you've got something going for you that one wouldn't notice from mere observation." He twisted his body around and glared at us fully out of his one eye. In his raspy voice, he said, *"Tell me: Are you sieben-seven — the Black Warriors from Sans Défaut, the great kingdom of the East?"*

The man was reacting too calmly to this news for me to be comfortable. *"What makes you think so?"*

"I can tell by the way ya walk. The way ya laugh."

The silence that followed was thick.

*"Nein. I'm only kidding. Do easterners not have a good ear for jokes anymore? Nein, nein, nein. I saw ya fight the Gummy and noticed how comfortable ya all looked with those rather strange weapons. What could they be if not your **Requisites**? Who could you be if not **Black Warriors**?"* He turned back around and started walking again, continuing to whistle an unfamiliar merry-tuned song.

I believe we all remained silent after that because it seemed safer not to let the man speak or hear us doing so. I felt everyone's tension, felt responsible for it, even…

"A-ha! Here we are. Willkommen in meinem Zuhause!"

We broke free from the forest's trees and shrubbery into a clearing revealing a cottage. I couldn't believe what I saw: a place of splendor amid the Precursory Woods! It was built on a rock foundation and had wooden shutters, a beautiful garden, and fully-functioning well next to it. Never in my lifetime would I have believed something so amazing could be found in these woods.

Endres took the front stairs two at a time. He turned and flashed a grin at the seven of us as we gaped at the home like a bunch of fools. Our hands never left our weapons, however. It didn't seem to bother him. *"Come in, come in! Warm yourselves by the fire! Triff meine familie!"*

I moved forward first, but the Warriors stopped me. Almost in unison, they said, *"You stay between us at all times, prince. That's an order."* To be honest, I'd grown not to be annoyed by their overprotectiveness. They believed I could protect myself, but in the end, they made sure I didn't have to.

"Fine. Everyone keep a lookout. We could be stepping into a trap, but I think it's well worth the risk if we find an ally."

Egon glanced at Endres, who was still grinning on the porch. He then turned to me and whispered, *"What fool would attack six Black Warriors? Frankly, he doesn't even know you're not one."*

I nodded. *"It'd be a dangerous move. Then again, we don't know what the man's hiding in this house of his, so be ready."*

The seven of us moved up the stairs, one at a time. I noticed the wooden sign hanging by a red thread on the door, stating:

"The Remnant"

Warily, we gripped our weapons, ready to attack anything as we stepped into the cottage. Endres closed the door behind us and shot a grin and wink our way. A wave of heat nearly swallowed my face when I entered. Half-expecting to see an army of Gummies, I braced my body for any kind of sudden impact.

What met me, however, was the smell of delicious meat, a large candle-lit foyer, and three simultaneous shouts proclaiming, *"Papa!"* That was, of course, followed by the pattering of feet coming straight towards me.

Out of all the things I had braced for, I wasn't prepared for this. Caught off guard, I dropped my sword slightly. All three of the children ran right past me and slammed into the waiting arms of Endres Kraus. He laughed while ruffling their hair. *"You all should be in bed, my mäuschen."* The two little boys with rugged, strawberry-blonde hair and big blue eyes, and one little girl with the same color hair and greenish-blue eyes, giggled. Endres joined in their laughter, his being much louder and deeper than theirs.

I think all the Black Warriors felt the same as I: utterly dumbfounded. I suppose the Gummy had knocked the sense out of us. Of course, Endres wasn't a murderer who lived in the woods by himself, leading people to his home where he held a secret army. Not everything was blown out of proportion.

I rested my hand and stopped gripping the sword handle that protruded from its sheath. Still, I didn't drop my hand completely…

"Now," Endres said, standing and picking up his little girl who looked the youngest and letting his boys, who were no older than six, follow him. *"Where's my Häschen?"*

I wasn't sure what the statement meant, but right after it was spoken, a woman came from what I would assume was the kitchen, closed off from the foyer by one wall.

The woman who stepped out had blonde hair all in one thick braid that fell to the end of her back. She smiled at Endres. Surely, she must've been ten years my senior, if not more. She glanced at the Black Warriors and me. *"These must be the people you spoke of, Endres."* Her eyes rested on Arthur. *"So **young**."* Upon further examination of Arthur's pained expression, she frowned. *"Come. Your face looks repulsive."* She signaled for him to come into the kitchen with her. He started to follow and then glanced at me in question. I nodded my consent, and he followed her out of our sight.

Endres went to walk ahead of us, and I grabbed his arm—the left one, for the other was holding a child. It was heavily muscled. *"I have questions needing answers. Why did you bring us here, and what was that...**THING** back there?"*

He nodded. *"Come into the kitchen, then. My Häschen has prepared a **fest**!"* I raised a brow in confusion, and he grinned. *"A meal."* As he walked away, he called over his shoulder, *"Don't worry, my friend. You are safe here."*

I wanted to trust him. Surely, the man wouldn't do anything rash with his children present. I sighed and followed him into the kitchen. The Black Warriors continued to surround and protect me.

The kitchen was fairly large, even though by comparison, the smallest castle kitchen in Sans Défaut tripled its size. Still, here in Precursory Woods, the kitchen must've been quite the luxury. It had the usual dirt floors, and the walls were made of stone and brick. High ceilings and a handful and a half of windows made me think it was a wonderful place to be in the mornings when the sunlight sprinkled in. There was a thick wooden table for dining a little ways from the cooking area, and a pot with something pleasant simmering in it was over a small fire.

Just a couple feet from the wooden table was a stool. Arthur sat quietly on it, while the woman Endres called *Häschen* (which I assumed meant 'wife') smothered him with a cream I wasn't familiar with. Arthur always squirmed when Ocean tended to him, yet there he sat — perfectly still. If this woman already had him bent into shape, I wished we had met her sooner.

"Tonis, Bruno," the woman called as she continued to rub cream above Arthur's eyebrow. The little boys perked up. *"Would you get the bowls, please? Ilse, would you get the spoons?"*

Endres placed Ilse, his girl, on the ground, and she quickly ran off to get the spoons. The boys were in front of her, gathering the bowls.

Egon, wary, looked around. *"A bit late to be cooking supper, don't you think?"*

"Well, I noticed the seven of you were out and about and figured you'd be hungry. Had my Häschen fix a late supper for you."

Egon narrowed his eyes at him. *"Yeah? What does Häschen mean, then?"*

Endres threw his head back and roared with laughter. His wife had to answer the question for him and did so with a smile. *"My given name is Dagny. Häschen means bunny. He's been calling me that long before we were wed."*

Endres rubbed tears from his eyes, then pointed and shook his finger at a squirming Egon. *"You are a cautious fellow, my friend. Can't say I blame you."*

Egon muttered, bearded cheeks red. *"Haven't told us a bloody thing…"*

Endres caught it. *"Well, sit down, my friend, and I will."* He gestured to the chairs around the table. Egon huffed down into a seat, embarrassed. The rest of us—except Arthur, who was still being tended to—found a seat as well.

The bowls were set on the table, spoons beside them.

Dagny finished prodding at Arthur's poor face and began pouring some kind of stew into our bowls. I could make out fish and some red sauce. It smelt **good**. No. Not good; *delicious*!

Egon went to pick up his spoon just as Endres began to pray. He blushed and set it down. I nearly spit, trying to hold in my laughter. I heard Woodruff, Silas, and Arthur snicker.

After Endres said, *"Amen,"* he shot us all disapproving looks for laughing during prayer. I felt like a child and wanted to tattle-tale on the culprits. Instead, I picked up my spoon and sipped a little bit. Good; there was no poison. I'd been trained to know how it tasted. I sipped some more. It truly tasted good. I put my spoon down when I realized my companions sounded like noisy dogs. Endres was grinning at them. I cleared my throat to drag his attention away from my friends.

"Excuse me, sir. You promised answers to questions..."

*"For a **price**."*

I blinked.

"No, I'm just kidding, man!" he said, laughing. *"Heiliger strohsack, you looked so taken aback!"* The children giggled.

I forced a laugh. *"I suppose I was."*

He banged the table and wiped his eyes. *"Ja, you silly boy. I did promise. I haven't forgotten. What frage needs answering?"*

I paused, trying to understand his sentence, and then continued. *"Who is the 'lad' you spoke of on the way here — the one you said would consider the **thing** back there as one of his own children?"*

"Conrad, you mean?"

Dagny paused her spoon-to-mouth motion and gave Endres a scornful look. *"Endres, not with the children at the table..."*

"Nonsense. They won't understand a whit." Endres winked at her then continued. *"Nein. Conrad's just a silly psycho. It's his Gummies you ought to be fürchte and wary of."*

"Yes. You did mention there were more of them. How many?"

Endres shrugged. *"Don't know. No one does. We only know he calls them Reapers."*

I felt Arthur, who sat next to me, shiver. I felt like doing so, too, but ignored my worry for another question. *"Why do you live out here, then? Especially with psychos like Conrad out there."*

Endres glanced at me curiously, as if I should already know the answer. *"Conrad and his Gummies can't hurt me. It is all written in The Law."*

"'The Law'?" Arthur spoke up for me. *"Come again?"*

Endres shook his head in obvious disappointment. *"Don't they teach you this back in Sans Défaut?"*

We were all silent, which was answer enough.

"The Law is the product of keeping Precursory Woods in check. It is a book of rules so that the woods don't get too rambunctious."

Egon snorted. *"Funny. We couldn't tell you had those."*

Endres raised a brow at him. *"It's the woods. We can't control bug bites and animals. However, my friend informed me you had trouble at the stairs."*

"The stairs?" I asked. *"Maybe a little."*

Endres laughed at that. *"Ja, must've been ugly. The stairs strategically choose when to break. I will have to scold them for that."*

"Hold on." It was Cederic's deep voice that filled the room next. It was also the first time he'd spoken since his horse, Thane, had fallen to his death. I was happy to see the man had recovered. *"How did you know about the stairs? A friend, you said?"*

Endres nodded from where he sat at the end of the table. *"Ja, a **friend**. I won't share his name here, though."* That comment made the Black Warriors look around the table. *"He's another watcher,"* Endres continued, *"the one you **didn't** spot at the stairs."* He said the last bit to me.

"So, where is he now?" Woodruff asked.

Endres shook his head and squinted at Woodruff with his one good eye. *"Nobody knows."*

I swallowed my food, deciding for the first time since our arrival that I might be able to trust this guy. All of this effort would have been an unlikely way to trick someone. Let them meet your family, cook them food, save them from having to fight a Reaper twice…

Yes, **highly** unlikely.

Arthur went to open his mouth again, but Endres put up his hand, suggesting he not speak. *"I have answered questions. Now, a question for you."*

I raised a brow.

"Where are you lot headin' off to?"

I leaned back in my chair and rubbed my hands on my trousers. *"Now, that's a question I can't answer, mate,"* I replied warily. *"I'm sure you understand."*

Endres' normally pleasant face frowned as he knitted his brows together. *"But I don't. You seven have tromped through my forest without warning, causing me great troubles as I've tried to* *figure out who you are. At first, I thought **you**, my friend,"* he stated as he glanced at me, *"were a Black Warrior, along with the other six. I was wrong. I recognize your face."*

It was probably not the most auspicious timing for that statement. After all, I heard a lot of Black Warriors shift to grab their weapons.

Ocean spoke up, her voice tense. *"Specify,"* she said slowly.

Endres squinted his eye and pointed a finger at me. *"You're, in fact, the Prince of Sans Défaut, aren't you?"*

Well, that was all Egon could stand. He stood, sliding his chair back from underneath him. He was two chairs down from the end of the table and flipped his staff around in a blurring motion, stopping inches from Endres' throat.

Dagny screamed and covered her mouth, which made the children scream, too. **"What on earth...?**

Egon eyed Endres sharply. *"I am led to ask what game you're playing, sir, for I won't loiter here any longer! How do you know these bloody things?! Lay a hand on my prince, and I will slam this staff into your throat and crush your larynx!"*

Endres paused, then smiled. I noted he didn't move. He was well aware of the capabilities of a Black Warrior. He needed no warning.

"Speak!" Egon shouted, waving his staff even closer.

The little girl, Ilse, sniffed from across the table. The boys' mouths hung wide open. Dagny was visibly shaking, her arm held tightly around her daughter.

"That's enough!" I shouted, wondering why I hadn't done so sooner. *"Egon, but your staff away!"*

Egon lowered his quarterstaff but did not put it away.

Laughing to himself, Endres calmly said, *"I was going to say that I am friends with your father, Dustin. **Good** friends."*

I lowered my brows, hesitant to believe him. Then, I remembered something…a dinner of some kind back in Sans Défaut years back. I recalled the scent of candles and sitting in a plush red chair as my feet dangled, which were nearly a foot-and-a-half above the wood and special red rug. My father was speaking to an ambassador of his…

~~~~~~~~~~

"Tell him to set up an outpost in Precursory. Should be enough adventure for the man." My dad had laughed at that.

The ambassador nodded. *"I will send your wishes to Kraus."*

Endres *Kraus*. I thought to myself, *I've been a buggin' fool!*

~~~~~~~~~~

Back in the present, I nodded. *"I recall your name, man. My father spoke of you."*

The Black Warriors seemed to let out a sigh of relief. The tension in the air fell away.

Endres tipped his chair back and grinned at the Warriors and me. *"If I was a gambling man, I'd say you seven are the most overly-protective people in the world. That's good."* He leaned forward. ***"You'll need to be."***

Later, I sat with Endres next to their fireplace. He smoked a pipe; I wrote to my father. There was nothing but the flickering firelight against Endres' rocker and my hair as I sat on a sofa across from him.

"Endres?" I decided now was the time to ask what had been preying on my mind for a while now. It had been suggested, not stated, and I wanted to just get it out in the open.

"Ja?" he replied, looking up at me.

*"My father… You **knew** him?"*

He nodded affirmatively.

"So, you know where we're going?"

He pulled the pipe from his mouth slowly and sent smoke into the air. *"I have an **idea**."*

*"What is your **idea**?"*

"Jocund. Your aunt's. Maybe more."

I let out a sigh. It was a relief to have someone who knew everything. Despite his vague answers, I knew he had a better idea than my company did.

"I don't know if I can do this," I admitted.

"Do what?" Endres looked at me, curiously.

"This... This journey. This mission. It's..." I breathed deeply, despairing at my own weakness, looking down at my palms. *"It's too late to say, 'I'm not ready.' Yet, I didn't feel this way when I left. I..."* My voice broke, but I had to tell **someone**. *"I feel like a captain before he steps onto his ship. He thinks he has everything under control. The waves. His heart. Then, he climbs on board and sets sail. Then, when he's surrounded by blue, and there's no way out but to push through a storm that roars upon him, the waves and winds decide to rage. A moment of realization hits the captain: He's going to die out there."* I stopped abruptly before finishing my thoughts. *"I'm going to die out here, Endres. This is all **hopeless**."* I felt a bit better. At the same time, I also felt more vulnerable and weaker.

"Hmm... You're very intense, aren't you?" he asked, staring intently.

*"Is that **all** you have to say?"*

"Nein. I'm sure more will come to me."

"Kraus," I warned dryly. I was in no mood for his teasing.

He put up one finger and shut me up when he said, *"Wisdom comes with **silence, reflection,** and **prayer.**"*

We sat in complete silence for the next half an hour. Meanwhile, I began to feel miserable. All my "opening up to him" and delicate honesty had been for naught, leading me to feel a bit deflated—as if someone had squeezed the air out of me. I was just leaving to retire to my room for the night when Kraus caught hold of my arm as I passed his chair.

He looked up at me, his brows etched together. *"I haven't been on this earth half as long as some, Junge. There are, however, some things I'd like to believe I know. I've seen people — weak people,* *inadequate people — **stare** at death long enough to make it squirm. I've seen it move out of their way long enough for them to go by. I've seen, by some power, a storm **be still**. The mission accomplished. The journey made. So, don't ever say anything is hopeless. Hopeless is when you hope less than you should, not when hope is absent."*

I stepped away from him because his eyes were intense, but we didn't break eye contact. Not for a moment. I breathed deeply through my nose, suddenly realizing I hadn't been breathing at all while he spoke. I then retired to my room.

12: ROSETTA KELLINA MABEL

Take a sword, raised in the air;
Swing it down, lose your head
So flippantly, without care.
Love often comes from a Battle of Bloodshed.

The energy was disturbing. How could people be so happy to watch others die? How could they laugh like it was only a game?

What fools they appeared to be… What **fools.**

My palms were sweaty, and my head was aching. The fighters hadn't even been introduced, and I already wanted out more than I wanted Kenneth to stop staring at me from where he stood beside the Lord's wooden throne that sat atop a large stone podium.

The place was made up like a show of some sort. Chairs moved up like stairs circling an open space, which would soon be the center of attention. On the right side of the stone podium were the hungry nobles—or, rather, good friends or fools wishing to seek an alliance with the monster. They all ate and lounged like idiots, laughing and drinking from wineskins their personal attendants brought to them.

On the left side of the podium were servants—anyone employed for work in the castle. That side seemed less energetic. I reckon they felt lost and confused. I supposed none of them were wringing their hands quite like I was.

There was no room for the peasant villagers to watch the show, although it was **their** family and friends who would be slaughtered. Most waited outside of the circle listening for a mention of the name of their loved ones. A couple of moments ago, a soldier had been sent to shut up a woman's wailing outside the Battle of Bloodshed's circle because her cries were disturbing the nobles.

I hadn't heard any wailing in the last few minutes…

I had seen the Lord Monté only once before this, and it was years ago. He seemed even more mysterious and terrifying now. He sat straight-backed in his chair, wearing his armored boots and gloves. A grey cape and hood masked anything above the tip of his nose from view. The one time I saw him, he wore a cape. Was he ever seen not wearing one? I watched and noticed the man barely moved. The only thing that appeared to do anything was his mouth—two thin lines of lips as red as strawberries…lips which had turned up on the ends in the slightest smile whenever he found something amusing. When he smiled, I could never tell what made him do so.

Perhaps it's demons in his head, I thought. *The man seemed evil enough to have a whole legion of those.*

"Hear ye, hear ye." Edmund's bold voice cut through the noble's chatter and brought silence. He stood a good 12 feet or more to the side of the Lord Monté, face cut off from view by a large paper. It measured from the top of his head to his belly, making it appear as if two legs stuck out from the bottom of the paper. *"These are the words of the Lord of this land – your Savior and King; your God. We mustn't weep over blessings. Your families' deaths will be your survival. A blessing in disguise. Something you should smile about."* He paused. *"The blood spilled today will be a sacrifice to the gods of the sky, to open up and give us rain, and spare us this famine. For now, we mustn't worry, but rejoice…"*

The silence was thick.

Edmund lowered the paper, saying the final words without reading them. *"As long as your Savior lives, the walls of the kingdom of Jocund will stand."*

The silence held for several seconds before someone on the nobles' side of the circle raised a fist and screamed, ***"Long live the Savior! Long live the Savior!"*** It didn't take long for that whole side to join in on the chant. Soon, it felt like a drumbeat no one could ignore.

The employees on the right side also took up the chant. I suppose it was done to save our necks from death in the long run.

The chant stuck in my throat, and I couldn't say them. I felt naked not raising my fist with the rest, but something stopped me. As crazy as this sounds, I felt the gaze of someone on the podium. I assumed it was Kenneth, but this gaze burned me straight through, so I looked up to address it.

The Lord hadn't appeared to move his body. Only his chin had turned slightly in my direction…and stayed there.

He's staring at me, I thought.

My good sense countered that thought. *Nonsense! He could be staring at anybody!*

Still, I **felt** it. I **knew**. All of a sudden, I couldn't ignore it.

Raising a shaking fist, I recited the words through my teeth and closed my eyes. I felt his gaze long after the chant had quieted. Or, at least I thought I did. I let out air I didn't know I was holding in. Lydia, beside me, heard the release and gave my arm a gentle squeeze.

Edmund started reading colors off the list, representing the insignias on the men's helmets. I barely heard him. The flush of blood in my ears was deafening. The roar of cheers and boos grew into background noise as people entered the center, holding steel weapons and looking uncertain. Most of them didn't know how to handle a sword. After all, peasants only used slings, staffs, and an occasional crude bow and arrow. Anything steel threw them off like formal dress wear.

As far as the echoing boos, the nobles would boo anyone who wasn't "good betting material." They'd all placed their bets earlier in the day, and nobody betted on women and old men. Those warriors—as brave as they were—were not favored whatsoever with this crowd…

I stared at the middle of the circle, trying not to focus on anything in particular. When the boos grew loud, I saw a scrawny, little thing make his way into the circle.

My lips parted, and my throat closed.

It was the boy I had addressed and scorned yesterday morning after reading the letter the Lord had written; the boy who'd gotten his ear twisted. I let out a tiny scream that was drowned by the boos. He wore a helmet far too big for his head and boots too large for him, as well. Apparently, a child who was favored to last no more than five seconds in any fight wasn't important enough to get armor forged in his size. With what he wore, he was going to have a hard time seeing and moving in that oversized gear.

I dry-heaved. Fortunately, it was dry 'cause had it not been, there would've been a mess on the man in front of me. Probably would've landed all in his hair. I didn't fancy cleaning it up, either. I had unintentionally starved myself today. I hadn't felt up to dinner, knowing what was to happen after.

All day, I had pitied myself for being forced to watch this horrid "show." *What about the people who'd had to fight in it?* If I **pitied** myself, they likely wanted to **bury** themselves in a hole somewhere.

I watched as the boy lined up with the rest. There were two tall men on either side of him. He glanced at both and stood as straight as he could.

The man on his left who wore a purple insignia on his helmet pushed the boy's head down in a mocking fashion. When the boy struggled free, the soldier spat on him and said something. The boy said nothing.

Two more names were called. The man with the purple insignia pretended he was shuffling sideways to give more room and purposely pushed the boy to the ground. The crowd laughed.

I gritted my teeth.

The man on the boy's right who wore an orange insignia stepped between the boy and the purple insignia soldier. He shoved the purple soldier in the chest so hard, he nearly fell over. After they were separated, the last names were read off the scroll.

I remembered then where I'd seen the man wearing the orange insignia before. I recalled him cursing loudly while I read the letter in the square. He'd stood in the back, crossing his arms the entire time. I felt an immediate like for him for defending the boy from the man in the purple insignia. I had an immediate dislike for the latter.

*"That man is **cruel**," Lydia whispered from beside me. "That boy's gonna have a hard enough time fighting all those men. Why make it worse? If I were out there, I'd stand him up and stab him straight through."*

The participants—rather, unwilling participants—took their positions in the circle. In total, there were maybe over 150 fighters. A hush fell over the crowd.

The Lord Monté spoke something to Kenneth that no one could make out. The Chancellor leaned over and grabbed the clapper. To further the suspense, he hesitated before pushing the clapper against the bell, causing it to sound.

There was immediate movement on the sand in the circle, yet somehow, it was still hesitant. The **only** eager person was the purple insignia man. He took off after the man closest to him—a man in his mid-60s wearing a green insignia who was caught off guard and tried to raise his sword in defense. In two swings, the elderly man was down. The first one knocked the sword from his hands, and the second sliced through his throat. Blood sprayed onto the purple insignia man's chest. The crowd roared at the sight of the first kill.

I felt nauseated.

Lydia must've had similar feelings. She squeezed my arm so hard, I wondered if the blood would stop flowing into my hand and it'd go numb.

The little boy spun around, seeking someone to kill, barely keeping his sword from dragging in the sand. It was clearly too big for him to handle. To my irritation and intense dismay, the purple insignia solder noticed the boy and headed toward him, all while the nobles screamed their approval. They took up his name like a drumbeat:

"Purple! Purple! Purple!"

*Why strive to kill a **boy**? What did it **prove**?* I thought angrily.

The orange insignia soldier had just killed a blue insignia soldier—a man who was maybe a few years older than he. As the man died, he held his hand but made sure to remain alert. When the man died, he took notice of the crowd's praise. He then spotted the purple soldier slicing a poor woman down and then making a beeline for the boy who couldn't see through his too-large helmet and was basically just swinging at air. The orange soldier bounded towards the boy, and I cursed when I realized he wasn't going to reach him in time. Four more strides, and the purple soldier would reach the boy. The orange soldier needed at least eight…

Call it a miracle, but the boy saw the purple soldier coming and started to swing madly in his direction. When the man reached him, he couldn't just cut him down. He slammed his sword against the boy's, throwing the boy's sword to the side. He then swung to slice straight through the boy's abdomen. The boy moved back remarkably quickly. I couldn't figure out how he saw the blow coming. Still, it nicked him just enough to send him crashing to the ground. The purple soldier couldn't finish the boy because the orange soldier had reached him—and purple wasn't ready.

The crowd was louder now than it had been before. They were truly enjoying this little show—the same "show" that was causing **me** to shake. This was not **"entertainment."**

If the boy hadn't moved in time, he would be dead right now. I shuddered at the thought…

The orange soldier kicked his foe in the side, sending him sprawling into the sand. Somehow, through the gaps between the crowd's head and the soldier's helmet, I was able to read the lips of the orange soldier as he spoke to the purple one:

"Stay down, or I swear I will…"

I didn't catch the rest of the threat. I didn't have to. The purple soldier stood, and the orange soldier shook his head in what can only be described as great irritation. I clenched my hands at my sides and bit my lip, the latter being an action I always scolded myself for doing. The purple soldier went for the orange one and, before I knew it, their swords were locked. There were, of course, other battles going on around this one, but none interested the crowd as much as the purple-orange squabble. The two men fighting were in their mid-20s, while the rest were mostly built of "less blood-pumping material."

Swords clanked and rang in the evening air. The torches on the podium and around the circle lit the space, giving it an eerie feeling. A frightening feeling.

The purple soldier was wilder in his fighting style. Smart, but wild. On the other hand, the orange soldier was poised, moved his feet without losing his stance, and made the purple man come to him, rather than making lunged attempts at his enemy's body.

It made me wonder if the orange soldier had ever handled a sword before. He definitely looked more comfortable with it, although he did seem to favor his left leg and never used his left hand to hold the sword.

The purple soldier, in all his glory, didn't seem to notice his opponent's tendencies and swung like a drunken blind man. It didn't take long for the crowd to see who was the one influencing their duel. The matchup lost its favor with the crowd, and they began to boo, signifying the orange soldier needed to go ahead and end this.

Personally, I don't think the orange soldier wanted to kill the purple one. He got the perfect excuse not to do so when the boy stood and tried to join the fight. He kept signaling for the boy to stay down in the sand, but either the boy wasn't listening, or he couldn't see him. The latter was starting to make more sense than the former. I felt a pain in my heart when the man turned to address the boy and barely got around in time to block the purple soldier's blow. He wasn't ready when the man disengaged and threw an elbow. The orange soldier went stumbling back and lost his footing. The purple fighter advanced…

With the orange soldier caught off guard, surely, he would die this time. He tried to regain his footing, but everyone knew it was too late. The purple soldier had reached him.

The bell rung.

The sand was drenched with blood and bodies, but two in particular who should've died were still standing.

I let out a sigh of relief and fell into my chair. I no longer cared about what Edmund was going to say.

A slew of questions entered my mind.

How had the boy survived with only a gash in his stomach?

How had the orange soldier avoided being stabbed there on the sand?

Why did the Lord stop the fight at that precise moment?

Did the Lord feel pity for the boy and the orange soldier?

Could *the Lord even feel pity?*

The smell of blood drifted into the stands. It smelt of sour copper. The stench tore my stomach to pieces. I broke free from Lydia's hold, shoved my way down the line, and left.

Outside of the circled area was no better. An older woman who'd been weeping on the ground grabbed the hem of my dress and cried out, ***"Did you see my dear Eric? Did he survive?"***

I was torn between my disgust for the "show" and deep, unnerving sadness. *"I cannot tell without the color of his insignia,"* I replied, trying to press forward.

She grabbed another fistful of my dress hem and stated with desperation, *"Green. He wore green. Did you see him? Please, tell me…"*

I closed my eyes. Sadly, she spoke of the first man to have died. The soldier wearing the purple insignia had cut him down at the start. The way the crowd had cheered… I shook my head as if I didn't know the answer and pulled away. I did not want to answer something so difficult to say. However, my hesitance must've been answer enough, for the woman wailed and curled up on the ground.

Someone to my left roughly grabbed my arm and demanded to know if his brother had died.

I had to push my way out of the riot forcibly.

In their haste to catch me, someone else tore my left sleeve. The right sleeve was the only thing holding up my dress.

Once free from the riotous area, I ran deeper into the Woods of Division until I could barely hear Edmund reading off his stupid scroll. When I finally stopped running, I vomited once, and then twice. I dry-heaved for what felt like minutes on end until my sides ached, and I shook. At some point, I had fallen to my knees in the dirt, ruining my dress. I told myself it was okay. The boy hadn't died. The orange soldier had lived.

Still, many had… I pushed the horrid thought away.

What was to become of the green soldier's wife? Would she, too, die some gruesome death eventually, playing as "entertainment" to some noble wretches?

What was to become of the boy and the orange soldier? How could the boy possibly last another round?

I grabbed the dirt in front of me to keep from gagging again. Tears blurred my vision. I didn't want to think about the Battle anymore. I tried to think about the letter, but even **it** seemed like a pile of ash now. Life played cruel games. The letter was just another. I sat in that spot for minute after minute, hugging myself in the dirt and cold. I tried thinking of nothing. Blackness. Blank.

I heard voices and froze.

"Sticking your nose in everything, Ferrando. Lucky you are still alive." The voices were a-ways off and seemed to be stationary.

I stood and moved towards them slowly, all the while listening to the voices.

*"Lucky **you're** still alive!"* The voice came from a young boy.

I recognized it to be the boy from the fight — the one I'd "met" at the Lord's Decree. Had I stumbled upon the soldiers' station behind the podium? *They must be putting up their weapons,* I thought. Just as I thought it, the station came into view. There were eight stations of about 25 people. Most of them wanted to steer clear of the squabble between the three.

Ferrando. I saw the boy sitting with his arms crossed defiantly as he tried to ignore the gash in his stomach, even though he wore the pain on his face like a trophy. His blonde hair was so dirty, it was practically brown. He did his best to focus his scowling at the purple insignia soldier.

The purple soldier was seated on a bench as he held his helmet against his hip. He had light blonde, neck-length hair, and a terribly crooked nose.

The orange soldier dangerously had his back to the two. He was too busy removing his Brigandane body armor to notice or listen to either of them. His skin was tanned, and he had a thin beard with black hair that was cropped short, as required for battle. His arms were thick and defined. He looked nothing like the hero he had seemed to be while wearing his armor. As a matter of fact, he looked downright **tired**.

I made sure to remain well hidden in the darkness of the forest.

*"Shut up, **boy**,"* the purple soldier sneered. *"You need to learn not to run your mouth."*

"My name is Peter," he said, annoyed.

Peter? *Then which one of them was Ferrundo?*

The purple soldier seemed sick of him. *"Was your father too weak to fight, or did he commit suicide before the Battle like a coward?"*

Peter's face turned red hot with anger. I wondered if he would attack the man despite his gash. Before anything could progress, the orange soldier stepped in. His armor off, he wore a simple tunic and belt with boots that were worn and tearing.

"*Both of you, stop. You acted like a darn **fool** out there, Merek,*" he said to the blonde-haired man.

Merek—the purple soldier—started to take off his armor as well, starting with the shoulder piece called a pauldron. "*The Lord has given me a chance to be famous. Did you hear them shouting my name?*"

Peter scoffed. "*I heard them shouting a **color**—the one they had bid on. They don't **care**.*"

This is a new side of Peter, I thought.

His comment earned him a sneer.

"*Besides,*" Peter continued, "*I don't know what they were screaming about anyway. You didn't kill me. **I'm still here!**"

Peter was brave to speak the way he did. Didn't he know that when they met again, he had no chance?

"*Give me a second chance,*" Merek said as he leaned forward. "*I'm gonna put a sword through your neck and throw your head to one of those pretty noble wenches.*"

The boy didn't even shiver. "*And pray she doesn't throw it back at you.*"

Merek stood, and the man I now assumed was Ferrando shoved him back into a sitting position. "*Boy, shut up. I'm trying to save your neck!*" When he turned to Merek, he threateningly said, "*As for **you**, I'd be extra careful on who I preyed on in the Battle. Watch your back, or I'll put a sword through it.*"

I wanted to curse Lord Monté for pitting the people of Jocund against themselves. It wasn't right. I shook my head in frustration and then froze when I realized Ferrando was coming towards me. He hadn't seen me because he was looking down at the ground for something, but I knew if he kept heading my way, he would discover me crouched behind a tree in a dirty green dress. Embarrassed, I scrambled backward — which would've been fine had I not stepped on a branch. Its breaking sounded much louder than it actually was, owing to the fact of the circumstances.

Ferrando moved quickly towards me, grabbing me just as I turned to run off. His hand felt like iron. The shock and abruptness of his touch made me faint.

I woke back up a minute later to Ferrando carrying me to the stationed area. I gasped, remembering what happened. Ferrando frowned down at me through his beard.

"I didn't mean to scare you, my lady. Forgive me. I thought you were one of the Lord's spies." The use of 'my lady' meant he recognized the more expensive dress and assumed I either worked in the castle or was a noble.

"Put me down," I said dryly.

He nodded and proceeded to pretend to drop me accidentally. Instinctively, my hands went around his neck. I clung to him like an idiot, which made the man laugh. He had a deep laugh that rumbled in his chest.

My hands shook from nervousness. I narrowed my eyes at him and asked, *"Do you mean to be **funny**?"*

"Oh, wasn't it?" he said, amused. *"You're right. It would've been funnier had I dropped you in the dirt, **messenger**."* He said that last word in a tone dripping with accusation.

"Who's that?" Peter asked, which made Merek look up. He raised his brows high. Peter peered at me as Ferrando sat me down. His eyes softened when I had expected them to harden. *"Oh, I remember you. From the decree yesterday morning. I got my ear twisted over you. You tried to look tough, but you bit your lip as soon as you turned away."*

I flushed. *"Look, I didn't come out here to be publicly told off by a couple of peasants."* That came out harsher than I meant. It seemed everything I said these days did. Was I just **rude**?

Ferrando walked away from my side and went to where he had laid his armor. He sat down on the bench.

"Then what did you come out here for, beautiful?" Merek asked.

I gritted my teeth. *"Do you think those of us in the castle **like** the Battle of Bloodshed?"*

"With your attitude, I wouldn't put it past you," Ferrando muttered.

*"**Attitude?** You grabbed me and picked me up like a savage brute!"*

*"And **you** were listening to our conversation like a nosy noblewoman!"* he countered.

Merek snorted and spoke before I could. *"Noblewomen have always been nosy. They're only good for looking at, I swear it."*

That statement made me want to make his nose even more crooked. *"They're good at getting people **hung**, too,"* I spat.

He sneered.

"Besides, I am not a noblewoman."

"So? Your job makes you better than the peasants on the street, even though you were a peasant by birth, doesn't it?" Ferrando shook his head in disgust and turned to make sure his armor was put away properly. *"What happened to your sleeve, by the way? Too many drunks seated around you?"* he called over his shoulder.

I realized then that I liked Ferrando way better with his helmet on—when he couldn't talk too much, and he appeared to be the hero of a story. *"Someone outside the fighting circle wanted to know if a family member of theirs had died. My sleeve ripped when it was grabbed."*

Ferrando turned slightly. *"Violent, huh? Violence is different when you're in the middle of it and not watching, isn't it?"*

I was already annoyed with him, so I raised a brow and chose not to say anything in defense.

Peter squinted his eyes at me and asked, *"What's it like in the castle?"*

"Bloody fools and work. That's all it is, boy," Merek said.

I shot Merek a dark look and then asked the boy, *"Where's your family?"*

He flinched. Funny how such an honest question would make him do so. *"My Pa died when I was young. My younger brothers both died three weeks ago of starvation. My Mum's about to go with them. I'll take her food tonight, though. She might be too close to death now for saving."* He paused. *"She did not know about the decree, nor me going to fight. She's too sick. Better I than her."*

I felt deep sorrow for Peter but was hesitant to share it.

Merek snorted…again—something he seemed to do a lot. *"Better for whom, boy? You won't survive the next round, remember?"*

I gritted my teeth again. *"Why were you so desperate to kill the boy? He's nowhere close to being a real match for you."*

He grinned, revealing a missing front tooth. *"Glad to know you were watching me so closely. It seemed I was the center of attention!"*

*"Is that **all** you care about?"* I snapped.

Ferrando turned around. *"Yeah. Where some people might care only about their rank, others care about fame and fortune."* Everything he said dripped of accusations and bitterness towards me.

*"I don't care about my bloody rank – **Ferrando**, was it?"* He looked at me hard, then turned back around.

"Mighty big word for a small runt like you," Merek said, referring to my language. I cursed at him, and he raised his eyebrows. *"Well, she was right about not being a noblewoman. No feminine manners at all there."*

"My manners are shown to people I care about," I said as my irritation grew.

*"Do people like you care about **anybody**?"* Ferrando asked. He must've seen me flinch, for his eyes shown a hint of guilt for saying such a thing. I wondered why he reacted that way, especially when it had been his mission to provoke me to be irrational only moments ago.

"I care enough," I said through my teeth.

Why was I speaking to these three? Why did I care about their opinions?

Because I'm an actual human being, not an immovable rock, some part of me thought. For whatever reason, I chose to ask another question.

"Did the Lord not send anyone to tend to your cut?" I asked Peter. His face was flushed white from the loss of blood.

"I am friends with his Mum," Ferrando stepped in. *"I will see to it."*

"Nonsense," I said, feeling the need to appear kinder. *"He may come to the castle with me. There are plenty of physicians who can take care of something like that."*

Peter's eye lit up. ***"Really?"***

Ferrando cut in quickly. *"He doesn't need physicians."* He spoke rather bluntly and rudely, so he added, *"But thank you."*

Peter turned to him from where he sat, his gaze seemingly drilling a hole through the man. *"Ferrando, you can't keep me from going to the castle!"*

"Your Mum told me to keep you out of trouble..." he said bleakly.

Peter shrugged and stood with a wince. *"Well, seeing as she's not feeling well, I will go to the castle. I want to see the inside of it."* He paused. *"I promise if I see the Lord, I will plunge my sword into him – **thoroughly**."*

Merek snorted…again.

Ferrando shrugged and sighed. *"Well, I suppose that's it, then."*

As the boy came towards me, I gave him as comforting a smile as I could manage. *"You can come with us."* I directed my offer quite pointedly to Ferrando, and Merek grinned at me.

Ferrando shook his head quickly. *"I think not. Castles aren't for peasants like me. They're for guards, nobles, and ranks."* He looked at Peter and said, *"You come straight to the village once they patch you up, you hear?"* Without waiting for a reply, he turned and went back to work, putting his armor away in a large bin.

Sighing, I turned and walked back to find Lydia with Peter at my side. As we walked, I wondered if Ferrando was right. If peasants weren't for castles, what even was I? I had spent my entire life around the likes of everyone…

13: DUSTIN ELRIC CARPENTER

Danger makes the winter blow,
Softer still, softer still,
Waiting for a single flake to kill.

It was this night the pigeons returned. They came to my room through a window in Endres' house that illuminated my room with moonlight.

My heart wanted me to open the cylinders to retrieve the letter from within. I accomplished that task but fell asleep while sorting them out. I awakened later in the night and finished sorting the papers. I read the whole thing twice before grinning.

~~~~~~~~~~
~~~~~~~~~~

N.D.M.

I dare say it is a shame I do not know you!
You spoke of me quite fondly in your letter, but I have no memory
of anyone who may fit your identity.
Indeed, your handwriting is quite loathsome when you are shaking,
I would agree.
But I can forgive you for that, seeing I just made your acquaintance.
You must know I am wondering a million things.
Who are you? How do you know my name?
When should I expect you?
But there is one thing I do not understand, despite my trying:
Why are you coming for me at all?
I am not even sure if you are a real person out there in the world
writing to me or just a prank from one of the Arming Squires.
So, if this is to be secret and I am to get to know you,
I must know something first:
Why on earth are you coming for me?
My job, my work, my life is here in Jocund —
a place where no one can get in or get out.
I do not wish to sound frank, but if you wish to stay free,
do not come for me.
The famine will kill you…or the Lord will.
And if he doesn't, he makes sure no one leaves.
The Lord aside, since you apparently know so much about me, and I
little of you, may I have the pleasure of learning your name?
Please write back, or I will be miserable.

Yours truly,
Ro

<div align="center">~~~~~~~~~~~</div>

  She sure isn't the romantic sort, I thought as I grabbed ink and paper from my bags. *Still, she asked for me to write back. That's something, I suppose.*

  I nibbled on my tongue as I wrote, careful to be steadier with my letters and careful to be less careful on what I said to her. Why be careful when I'd already sounded like a fool? She'd asked me to write her back, right? Maybe my writing wasn't as repulsive as she had let on.

I thought about her calling Lord Monté 'the Lord,' as if there were no other lords on the earth. *I suppose if I was trapped in one place by such a man and in such fear, I might say it as well.*

If I wrote hastily enough and sent it off immediately, she could receive my reply tonight, though she wouldn't be able to reply until tomorrow night. I was sure she had realized by now she couldn't be caught sending me messages. If she was caught, well, that was why I had been discreet in my wording. The Lord would know little of my intentions once I arrived.

Pigeon messengers were fast. Legends say they could cover a horse's five-day journey in a matter of hours. Then again, they weren't burdened with cargo and riders. If that wasn't so, maybe a horse's reputation could fall closely behind a pigeon messenger.

I'm sure Julius would think so.

I returned to my writing and finished minutes later. I glanced back over the message, satisfied. I then began shoving the pieces of the letter into the cylinders when there was suddenly a knock, and someone stepped from around the corner. A wooden wall separated me from my comrades. *"Built for privacy,"* Endres had said. **So much for that,** I thought.

It was Arthur.

Great, I thought sarcastically. Smiling, I kept my composure. *"Hello, Arthur."* He glanced at the cylinders on the wood floor. I waited for him to ask the obvious question.

Instead, he said, *"Writing to your old man, I see. There's nothing you can keep from me, Dust. You aren't all sobby over leaving him for this journey, eh?"*

Relieved the boy was too naïve to pry, I raised my brows. *"Good heavens, no. I'm simply giving him a report is all. You're not all 'sobby' — as you call it — over your old man, are you?"*

Arthur shook his head, moving his curls into quite a frenzy. I didn't buy the denial, but I didn't say anything.

"Dagny made breakfast," he said, gesturing across his body to his right, pointing towards the kitchen.

It was early for breakfast, but the Black Warriors and I wanted to get a head start today. Plus, I'd told them we'd be on our way early. *Sweet of her to think of us,* I thought. I then noticed Arthur's wistful expression. *"That's **Mrs. Dagny** to you, Arthur. Try not to get too interested. I don't want to have to give you over to Endres as a peace offering because you couldn't stop staring at his Häschen,"* I said, using the unfamiliar word with humor.

He flushed. *"**Mrs.** Dagny. Of course. **Mrs.** Dagny. That's what I meant. I'm off to breakfast,"* he said, musing and scolding himself as he walked along the hall.

I grinned and turned my attention back to the pigeons. When I finished latching the cylinders to their claws, I opened the window and whistled them off.

I hadn't been able to recall if Ro had learned pigeon speaking, leaving me unsure if she could send the birds back to me. To be safe, I told them if she wrote a message back, they were to fly it back to me with or without her consent.

I then pulled off my nightshirt in exchange for a tunic, then threw my cloak over that—making sure my hood properly masked my face as I walked from my room to the kitchen, which was alive with hushed chatter. The children must've still been asleep.

"I'd hate for you boys to grow weak out on the road eating stale, week-old bread and dried meat. It's the least I can do for you," Dagny was saying to my companions. Only the men were around here, sitting in chairs they'd moved from the table as she cooked. Ocean was by the table we'd ate at last night, shoving on gloves and muttering something under her breath.

"It's not a week old yet," I said, walking into the room.

My companions turned to look at me, throwing me looks suggesting I hush up. It was my first sign of folly. The second was the twinkling in Woodruff's eyes. I swear: That man can't hold a smile in, even when he tries.

"But your friends told me—"

*"My **friends** just want good food. They're a greedy bunch, Dagny. I would agree it would be much more civil if they'd just said it outright."*

Dagny smiled. *"So, you haven't been on this journey for weeks?"* She directed the question at Silas, who must've spoken the lie.

"Heavens, no!" he proclaimed. *"Did I say that l-lads?"*

There was a full round of, *"I didn't hear a bloody thing!"* and *"You said that? When?"* and, of course, the *"I swear on my life, I didn't hear that!"*

I grinned. *"There. You've lied in front of a lady — two actually — twice. You've made yourselves the biggest fools in the region. Go run a lap!"*

Woodruff looked at himself and shook his head. *"I've just eaten. Besides, I haven't run one of those lap things in years."*

*"About time you did, **idiot**,"* Egon snapped, which led to a hushed argument between the two.

Dagny fondly glanced at Ocean. *"Do they always go on like this?"*

Ocean shrugged. *"Except when they're sleeping. Then, they snore everyone's ears off like a pack of overgrown pigs."* The two were too busy bickering to hear Ocean's statement, however, and they didn't stop until Endres walked into the room with a wide grin on his face.

"Hello, my Häschen. Smells good." He smiled. *"You seven will be leaving within the hour, ja?"* I confirmed, and the man passed me and thumped down onto one of the chairs next to the table to the left of Ocean. *"Good, 'cause you are a noisy gruppe."*

I laughed, just as we all heard a knock on the front door. Almost as quickly as the knock came, a cloud seemed to cover the moonlight, sending rays of light through the windows. The room grew darker and cold.

"Could this be the friend you spoke of?" I whispered.

Endres set his jaw and walked toward the door. *"Nein,"* he said firmly. *"This is not a friend. Hide."*

The Black Warriors hesitated. They were unaccustomed to the word. Hiding was not what they were trained to do or built for. It went against every ounce of their being.

Endres turned to face us. *"Hide, I said. Dagny, stay in the kitchen."*

The second time he instructed us to hide, I hid behind a shelf of books to make sure I was close enough to the door to see who it was that knocked.

Endres approached the door, and I glanced at Dagny. She was cooking over the pot all the same, but I noticed her hands shook with worry. Cursing to myself, I realized this was out of the ordinary for both of them, which meant **danger**. I peeked through two books far enough apart to leave a crack of open air that I could see through.

Endres opened the door. Cold air and the aura of the figure standing on the opposite side of the door drifted in. The man stood there, grinning. He had black hair — quite the unruly bunch of it, I might add. It wasn't curly as much as it was untamed. Untamed, almost as much as his eyes. They were wild eyes — grey with hints of blue, almost as if the grey had taken over with the insanity. The man had a patch of beard on his chin…probably the only thing he'd taken care of. There were streaks of white in it. Streaks of age. His trousers and tunic were dirty enough to have been passed off as rags. He was also barefoot. Hie yellow toenails were visible to all who could bear the sight of them.

"Why hold me at the door, Endres? Hiding something?" His voice was like a gurgling sound in his own throat, as if he were always choking and on the verge of a coughing fit.

"You are not supposed to be here. You know that. Would you upset the woods by disobeying the Law?"

The man at the door patted Endres' shoulder as if to console him. *"No,"* he said quietly. His face then turned into a pained snarl, sending the hair on my back spine straight up in the air. *"I think some friends of yours might've hurt one of my…"* He paused, then smiled endearingly. *"Children."*

All I could see was Endres' back, but his posture spoke his disgust. *"Don't be a fool, Conrad,"* he said, moving his shoulder away so the man was no longer touching him. *"I have no **friends** beside William, and I haven't seen him since yesterday morning. He hasn't been near these parts of the forest since then."*

I attempted to follow along. The man — Conrad — must be the one I spotted in the bushes. The leader of the Reapers. The other — William — was Endres' friend who'd spotted us near the same time. He'd been the one I hadn't seen, much to my great displeasure.

Conrad looked over Endres' shoulder into the house and set his eyes on Dagny. She hadn't glanced towards the conversation since Endres had opened the door. Then, Conrad's eyes fell, and I found his pupils had suddenly darkened and were boring into mine.

Could he see me through the cracks of books? He was staring straight at me, not just at the bookshelf but through the bookshelf. If he did see me, he showed no sign. His face was blank.

When he next addressed Endres, he said rather accusatorily, *"**Lies!** Your friends are here with your wife — **your Häschen.**"* He said the latter mockingly then grinned just before he went too far. *"You're a **rat.**"*

Endres hit him in the face. Hard. Conrad went down. When he looked back up from the ground, his nose was bleeding, but he only smiled. *"Tell them this, **freund**."* He spat the last word I came to learn meant 'friend.' He stood nose-to-nose with Endres. *"Never touch one of my children again. They'll already be out with the permission to kill them all. If my children are hurt again, I'll send them all to hunt those fools down. Do you understand?"* As he spoke the last three words, he spat in Endres' face on purpose. In response to the threat and onslaught of spittle, Endres just nodded.

How could the man I'd come to befriend be so calm one second and enraged the next?

Conrad turned away and walked down the stairs. He didn't look back, and I expected Endres to shut the door, but he didn't. Instead, he called out, *"When did the Gummies ever care for your **permission**? You are not their father; you're the only fool who thinks you are."*

That got Conrad's attention. He turned, and the crazed, angry look on his face didn't even seem human anymore. His eyes held no more hints of blue or grey. What were they now…yellow? The man screeched at Endres. It was the most unnatural sound I'd ever heard come from a person. It sounded much like an angry bat or the scream of a frightened dog. He then turned and ran. In a flash, he disappeared into the darkness.

Endres finally closed the door. He stood with his back against the door and stared at Dagny. She stared back at him in shock. Everything was pin-drop silent. Even the Black Warriors didn't move.

"What the – ?" I heard Egon say quietly, which eventually broke the silence.

Dagny spoke up. *"Why would he come here and risk the wrath of the forest just to threaten them? Why didn't he wait? He hasn't been here in years!"* Endres walked forward and wrapped her in his arms. She gave in to the sobs I didn't understand the full meaning of.

Coming out from behind the shelf, I asked Endres, *"Is that true? The man – Conrad – hasn't been to your house in years?"*

Endres nodded, letting Dagny continue to cry into his shoulder. *"If Conrad was willing to break the law in coming here, he could do it again and attack the house."*

*"For u-u-**us**?"* Silas asked.

Endres nodded again.

"Well, that's just fine. We're leaving anyway. He can't attack you if we're not here," Egon stated.

Endres shook his head. *"He won't know for sure. It's fine. I can protect my family. You guys go. You cannot be here when he returns."*

Ocean spoke. *"Nor can we leave you."*

I felt her pain. Not with the children here. Not after we led them to Endres and put his family in danger. The Black Warriors could handle the Reapers.

"Go. Pack your things. Wherever you're headed, don't look back," Endres instructed with finality.

I glanced at Egon, who shook his head. Cederic seemed reluctant.

Endres saw the gestures, and his tone grew impatient. *"Black Warriors aren't invincible. Yes, you are trained to fight large groups of people and there are six of you, but this is an army of maniacs who won't die from a fatal wound. **They're monsters.** Monsters that never die."*

I hesitated and then moved towards my six companions. Egon cursed, and I put up my hand to stop him from speaking. *"He's right. We must think of our destination now. Staying here won't help anything. Maybe if we leave, they'll stop attacking Endres and chase us..."*

Endres heard me and shook his head in disbelief. *"You **want** that?"*

Cederic clenched a firm jaw. *"Life rarely gives us what we want, Kraus."*

Endres nodded thoughtfully, and Dagny finally pulled away from him to speak. *"Please ready your horses. I would be happy to pack some food into your bags."*

I cocked my head towards the stable, and the Black Warriors followed me. The cold air wasn't inviting. I felt I deeply wanted the sun to lift above the horizon, even though it was hours before that would happen.

I couldn't get Conrad's contorted screech out of my head.

14: ARCHIE COCKBURN

The human race longs for a sense of leadership.
Now, here comes the dreaded
And most doomful 'consequence.'
And when it arrives, we squirm under
The weight of guilt and pleasure,
And we blame it on the one who
Truly, truly knows what's better.

Mallory thought me silly when I said I had goodbyes to say the night we murdered our parents.

"Who even cares enough to wanna tell you goodbye, brother?" he'd said to me jeeringly.

I know he thinks of me as a weak idiot. No matter how hard I tried to seem indifferent about our parents' demise, I couldn't. **"They deserved it,"** hate would say. Most times, I agreed, but I couldn't bring myself to Mallory's level. I never can. I never will. Even now, I write in my father's journal we'd found next to his bed.

The first few pages were lined with words; my Pa's words. I'd wanted desperately to read the pages, but Mallory had scorned me for it. He then tore the pages out and threw them into the dying flames of the fire.

Something in me wonders, though: Did our Pa have any regrets about how he raised us? How he spoke to us?

My mind towards my parents, who were now gone from this life — never to return — had changed drastically in the last couple of hours. I learned much like me, Pa liked to write. We'd found tons of journals filled with hundreds of entries. It was hard trying to picture my Pa sitting still long enough to write in a journal. It was even more difficult picturing him pouring his soul into anything.

Hours ago, I wasn't even sure my father had a soul. Now, I find myself wondering how much of his soul I truly missed…

What Mallory didn't know was I needed to say goodbye to Cecil. I found parting without seeing her one last time would hurt too much. As I made my way to her cottage in the night, I felt naked. I'd just killed my parents and now walked to my friend's house. It was a walk I took daily, but it was different now and would never be the same. Somehow, in a matter of a couple of hours, I'd sabotaged my life worse than it had already been.

At least I couldn't control my parents. Beatings were out of my hands. I could always deny I was part of the family I was born into, even when things were painful. Now, with what I did, I played their way. I'd made them both suffer. I was finally victorious over the ones who had ruined my life.

Why, then, did victory make me feel like a monster? I was a monster. A weak and cowardly **monster**.

As I approached Cecil's cottage, I grew hesitant. Cecil shouldn't see me like this.

I noticed there was light coming from the glass window to the right of the wooden front door. I moved over to it quietly, trying not to step on the plants in their small garden. Peeking in, I noticed a cozy room lit by a raging fire. Next to the fire was a massive chair with a mat underneath. Sitting in the chair was a large man with a blonde beard and hair that crawled down his neck and over the collar of his tunic. He sat with an open book resting on his right thigh, reading aloud to Cecil, who sat properly on his left. No doubt the man was her father, for she had inherited his blonde locks. As she leaned her head against his chest, she looked tired.

Relaxed. Happy. Safe.

I turned away. Perhaps my coming had been a mistake. I glanced back at the window one last time and noticed Cecil getting down from the man's lap. She was coming towards the front door.

She spotted me, I thought. I turned and attempted to take off running, but my foot caught in some weeds, and I went face down into the dirt. I heard the front door open. I breathed softly but didn't move. The voices in my head were making enough noise for me.

Weak. Stupid. Monster.

Those words repeated again and again until my head began to hurt.

"Archie?"

I gritted my teeth.

"I see you. What on earth are you doing in the mud? It's late. Are you okay?"

Seeing no point in staying still any longer, I stood. Like looking through the window of another person's house was normal. Like lying face down in the dirt was nothing. Slowly, I brushed myself off. There she stood. The moonlight shone brightly off her white nightgown. I realized her father hadn't followed her outside. He must not have seen me.

I collected a little more dignity before I said, *"Sorry to bother you. Didn't know you were spending time with your father."* I stepped past her to leave, and she followed me. I'd expected her to do just that.

"Hold on. Didn't you wanna tell me something?" She matched my strides.

The village was eerily silent. It seemed every person in every home was watching me, shaking their heads in disgust, waiting to jump out and give me what I rightfully deserved: a gruesome death.

I shivered, cutting down between two cottages and out of plain sight. *"Not anymore. I…"*

Cecil grabbed my arm and stopped me. *"You stay in your head too much, Archie. If you don't tell someone your problems, you're going to do something drastic that's not going to make any good sense."*

You have no idea.

"You wouldn't understand, Cecil. I did something horrible…" My words fell off.

"Whatever it is, we'll fix it," she said assuredly.

I sighed. Mallory wouldn't have gotten himself into this. He would've backed out and shut up. He would've stopped — stopped, thought, and not made another stupid mistake.

I am not Mallory. Oh, how I wish I were.

"I killed someone." The words rolled off my tongue like boulders banging and breaking as they descended a mountain.

What made me say those wretched words? *Cecilly was all I had. I couldn't lose her.*

She started to smile. I think she thought I was pranking her. When she looked into my eyes, she frowned. Her brow furrowed when she asked, *"What?"*

I paused.

Weak. Stupid. Monster.

"I killed my parents."

Her reaction was so real, so right, so heartbreaking. She backed away from me slowly. *"Archie, stop **playing** with me."*

I took a step towards her. *"I'm not playing, Cecil. I killed them both. Go to my place if you don't believe me. Their bodies are still there. I had to do it. Can't you see that? I **had** to."*

The shock hit her then, and she looked around to see if anyone else had heard. *"How could you? **Why** did you?"* she whispered harshly.

"Didn't you just hear me?" I spoke at the highest level of volume while still passing it off as a whisper. *"I **had** to. They beat me, Cecil. They would've beaten me to death. I swear it."*

Cecil's eyes widened, and she turned to run. I grabbed her arm firmly, causing her to cry out. I then yanked her towards me and began shaking her. My hands trembled all the while. I was so angry.

"Don't you run away from me. Everything I know I am about to run away from. Don't you run!" I spat. Then, I threw her to the dirt where she laid trembling and sobbing. My heart twisted. *"Cecil, please… Understand me."*

She didn't look up at me; she just continued to sob.

I cursed then realized I'd never done so in front of her before. I felt ashamed, but I couldn't afford to embrace that emotion at the moment. Instead, I jeered at her.

"Of course, you don't understand. You've got it made. Good food, nice home. Your brother has the ear of Sans Défaut's king. You have the type of parents who cook for you and read you bloody bedtime stories." I laughed dryly. *"They **love** you, so of course, you don't understand. You don't understand a thing."*

She finally glanced up at me with tears spilling over her eyelashes. *"No, I don't understand,"* she said brokenly. *"I can't."* She shook her head. *"You should've told me…"*

*"Told you what? About the **beatings**?"* I asked through gritted teeth. *"Do you understand what a man like my father would do to me if I told anyone? I wouldn't live for a moment after he'd heard I'd told!"*

Cecilly swallowed hard. I could see how much she trembled. I knew I was the one responsible for it, and it nearly made me choke.

"Do you still think we can fix it?" I asked in a small voice.

She stared at me. Her expression spoke of something so distinct, I couldn't mistake it. **Disappointment.** Cecil was disappointed in me.

Weak. Stupid. Monster.

Despite her expression, she nodded. *"Yes."* She sighed and stood. *"It could be messy, though."* She placed a hand on my shoulder. I shrugged it off.

"Forget it. Mallory and I are leaving. I just came to say goodbye."

Her face dropped. *"If you run away, you'll forever soil your reputation here. They'll think you two are mad!"*

"I know, but I can't be forever remembered as a murderer. Not by Souffrance. Not by your family and Geoff, your legendary big brother. Not by… Not by you."

She sniffled. *"It's cold, Archie. Please come inside and tell my father. He'll understand. Even if he's angry, he will not have you punished too harshly…I think. I know for sure it wouldn't be as bad as if you ended up in the hands of The Rank of Souffrance. They won't care how young you are; they'll punish you like a grown man."*

I laughed indifferently. *"I doubt anything they do to me will shock me, Cecil."* I lifted my dark hair, revealing The Fork marks.

She grimaced. *"I'm sorry, Archie."*

*"Are you? 'Cause you'll be the **only** one. Didn't you just say it? The people of Souffrance will still think ill of me, even if your father were to lessen my punishment. No, no. I have to go. I must get away from here. I'm sorry."*

She nodded, trying to be strong. *"My father has some horses. If you want two of them, you can have them."* She gestured toward the stables.

I hesitated. *"Cecil, I won't be the one to get you in trouble,"* I said firmly.

She glanced up at me, pulled my head down lightly, and pressed her lips to mine. Yesterday, she wouldn't have done that. Even today, she couldn't have kissed me on the lips because she would've been too scared. I think we both knew **this** kiss was goodbye— *forever.* I could never return to Souffrance after an error like this. After running away, returning would mean my death.

I had never been kissed before, but I was sure this was the sweetest it could ever get. It was over too quickly. The cold air hit my lips as we separated. There was a stab of regret in my stomach. I regretted this had to be our end in the first place.

"I want you to stay safe," she said, a sob in her throat. *"Please promise me you'll never do anything like this again. **Please**."*

I tried to clear my mind. *"I – "*

"Cecil!" It came from the cottage we'd walked away from. I realized quickly it was her father calling out in the darkness for her. *"Cecilly! Where are you?"*

She locked eyes with me. *"Go. Please take a horse."*

I nodded, unable to do anything else.

She ran off to her father. After a couple of moments of hesitance, I ran off into the darkness.

I didn't take Cecil's horses, and I never told Mallory about them. Can you blame me? I think it was the only choice I could be proud of at the moment. At least I hadn't gotten her too involved.

Mallory and I carried the bags we'd packed with personal belongings on our backs. We walked all night. I was terrified someone would find the bodies in our home and come searching for us, but Mallory didn't seem too worried.

"They won't know which direction we went or how far we've traveled. Therefore, their search will be halfhearted and won't last long," he stated confidently.

I began to trust my brother deeply during those days.

After all, he was all I had.

15: ROSETTA KELLINA MABEL

Birds of a feather,
They all flock together
With secrets hidden in their talons.
Birds of a feather,
Never ever heed the weather.
They fly to the heart of the challenge.

I opened my eyes and cursed, bolting upright, causing the pillow on my head to fly off and me to fall off the bed. I wasn't accustomed to the two beady eyes that stared back at me when I awoke. I had a feeling that when the pigeon that scared me didn't move at my fright, it was used to getting that reaction. My mind un-fogged, and I scrambled up on the bed.

"Did you bring me a letter? Please say you brought me a letter." I checked its talons and noticed the full cylinder. My heart felt an inexplicable flare of joy. I climbed off the bed and

noticed the sun was just now peeking over the trees. How long had the pigeons been here? Maybe a couple of hours?

I hadn't gotten a lot of sleep. Peter had been so excited to be inside the castle. I had to lie to Aldus at the gate about Peter, and I had a rough time keeping his presence unknown to Margery.

It was late when I went to bed. Even then, I wasn't tired. I read the journal I'd found in the library and rolled restlessly around in my bed for hours. Archie's story was disturbing. It made me think too much. I found it hard not to sympathize with the boy, even though he had a disturbing mindset that seemed to get worse.

I detached the cylinders and spread them around on the floor quickly. As soon as they were in order, I began to read the letter.

<div align="center">~~~~~~~~~~~</div>

Dearest Ro,
I wish I could answer all your questions now. I am elated you wrote
back to me. I hope the pigeons didn't give you a difficult time of it.
Also, you may address me as Geoff, if it makes you more comfortable.
I know your name quite familiarly, for where I come from, it is often
used. Though Ro is not your name and only an abbreviation for it,
I'd like to think I'm the only one who uses this abbreviation.
I am not afraid of Lord Monté as Jocunders are,
for I know his weaknesses far too well.
That is why I am coming for you.
You have been under his power far too long.
Jocund, in its current state, is no place to live.
Boring and serious things aside, I do have a couple of questions
myself. Do you still sleep with the pillow over your head and bite
your lip when you're nervous?

Lord Monté: The Journey from Nothing to the Throne

What does the view look like outside your window?

Your Curious One and Only, Geoff

P.S. Does my penmanship look any better?

~~~~~~~~~~

I laughed aloud. Indeed, it did look better. I found that even though his words were strange and confusing, I was comforted by them. Unfortunately, I couldn't send a response until tonight. It drove me crazy.

I had no work today, other than meeting with the man who was in charge of arranging the Battle of Bloodshed. I had also planned on dropping by Peter's home. I'd escorted him home last night—showing Ferrando just how much I **cared** for other people.

I glanced over the letter again and frowned. *Geoff? The name sounded familiar.* I knitted my brows together in confusion. Then, it hit me. *Geoffrey* was Cecilly's older brother in the journal. I knew it sounded familiar!

I shook my head from where I sat in my nightgown on the cold floor. Surely, it was simply coincidence he would choose that name. If not, then I was speaking to a man who not only knew Archie but was also his best friend's brother.

So, why would he be trying to rescue me?

I felt goosebumps rise on my arm as I skimmed over the last bit again. How did he know I slept with a pillow over my head? How did he know I bit my lip? The latter, I tried desperately not to do. The first one, no one was around to know about...or I **thought** no one was around to know about. The
~~~~~~~~~~

man had to have known me at some time or another and known me well. Better than anyone in the castle, as a matter of fact.

Wait. I'd never left the castle—or at least as far back as I could remember.

I laid down on the floor, my head throbbing with question after question.

One of the pigeons squawked in my ear, and I jumped. **"Bloody raindrops!"** I exclaimed, glancing at him angrily. *"A tad unnecessary, don't you think?"* It cocked its head unnaturally quickly, and I sighed. *"Bloody animals,"* I muttered under my breath, but I think it heard me, for I was given one last squawk before it flew to perch on my drawer. Unfortunately, I truly loved birds. I admired their freedom. I suppose I wasn't a good actor. *"Yeah, good riddance!"* I said, smiling as I approached the drawer and removed a bright blue dress with gold trimmings.

The bliauts were long, just the way I liked them. After all, it was me who had done the business of making the dress. I had fancied the idea of the light blue on my skin tone. I fancied it all the more when I'd tried it on.

I finished dressing and looked up to an even more exaggerated cocked head. *"What? You could have looked away, you know,"* I said to it. He gave me a blank stare.

I sighed, sliding the letter underneath my bed. **How was I going to keep someone from coming into my room and seeing seven loud pigeons?** I flashed a dirty look to the one perched on my drawer. I then searched my wooden chest at the end of my bed for a snack I might've smuggled in a few days ago.

"You guys better be thankful I'm so darn busy and so darn messy," I said, pulling out some day-old bread from yesterday's

breakfast. The one on the drawer squawked. I decided 'Squawk' was a good name for him. I opened the door to my wardrobe and tossed the bread inside. All the pigeons began to talk loudly, waddling and flying into the wardrobe. I lost track of Squawk, which wasn't so bad. *If he stayed as loud as he was today, it wouldn't be the least bit hard to find him again.* I shut the door after them. Now, I just had to hope they wouldn't be too noisy for the rest of the day.

Turning, I picked up a black shawl, just in case it grew too chilly. I drew it around my shoulders as I walked to the door. I was too busy making sure it was on correctly to see Kenneth standing outside my door. I ran, most abruptly, into the poor man.

"Mercy!" I breathed as I pulled away. *"Have you been standing here this whole time?!"*

"No, no. Of course not," he said quickly. A bit too quickly for my taste. I couldn't tell if it was because he was lying to me or he was so flustered. His cheeks bloomed.

The silence stretched on too long. I remembered our last discussion ended rather awkwardly, only I couldn't recall all the details. Not many at all. I did remember Lydia had been listening and told me to… ***Apologize?*** My mouth went dry.

"You left the Battle early last night," he stated.

You noticed? Oh, yes. You stared at me for half the night, didn't you? How flattering?

"I didn't think it necessary to listen to the Lord's statements. I felt most of what he said was quite pointedly declared in the way he went about putting the bloody Battle together."

Kenneth's face became pinched. *"Yes, the poor old man in the beginning went down rather quickly."* I shuddered and mentally cursed the man for helping me remember the killing.

"Yes. Eric…" I mused quietly, remembering the woman who grabbed my dress as I'd left from the horrid Battle.

"Ah." Kenneth raised a brow. *"Eric, is it? You were well acquainted with the man?"*

*If I were, would you think me disgusting for knowing someone so **low**? Would it turn your interest from me?*

"I stumbled upon a close relation of his…"

He nodded his understanding. *"I'm sorry you were put through such a disturbing situation."*

What's disturbing to you? My having to talk to such a nasty thing as a weeping woman in dirty clothing? Or perhaps the untimely and unnerving situation of having to tell someone they'd lost a loved one?

I was itching more and more to get this conversation over with. *"So, what brings you to my door?"*

"Your health, among other things. I was worried as to if you felt ill after last night's events."

I nodded. *"As you can see, I'm quite fine. What 'among other things' are on your mind?"*

He dropped his eyes, careful this time not to speak too quickly. *"I am sorry if I offended you the last time we spoke. Sometimes, I'm a bit too hasty."*

"It's fine. Apology accepted. I…" I hesitated. *"I am sorry for telling you that you had the opinion of an Arming Squire. I shouldn't have said that."*

"Yes, I suppose we were both angry," he said, sighing and nodding simultaneously while he spoke. *"We're fine, then? The two of us?"*

If it clears your conscience…

"Yes," I said simply. The statement seemed to please him.

"Indeed. I'm off now. I'll see you for breakfast, Rosetta?"

If it makes you happy…

"Of course." I lied through my teeth. I had no intention of attending breakfast or lunch. I watched as he retreated and then let out a breath to ease the knot in my chest.

How long had he been standing at my door? Had he heard the pigeons or me talking to them? What if the arrival of the pigeons reached the Lord's ear? Somehow, even though I knew nothing of Geoff's plans, I knew the Lord couldn't figure it out. If so, it wouldn't be just Geoff's neck getting strung up on a rope; it would be mine as well.

I let out a huff of air and looked both ways down the hall. I took the way to my left. Both ways eventually led to stairwells, but Kenneth had traveled to the right. I wasn't the least bit eager to run into and converse with him again.

The Forge was on the lowest level. The lower, the colder. It didn't need to be any hotter in the Forge than it already was — at least that's what James had told me years ago.

James was a funny man—far too wild for me, though I suppose Héloise didn't think so. She'd been forcing the man to love her for nearly two years, and he was finally starting to do so…I think. I planned to use that to my advantage today in a place I never went, even when I was ordered to.

I reached the front gate and let Aldus see the document Margery had signed as proof of my day off. I couldn't help wondering if Aldus was gone, would anyone have to sign the bloody thing.

"Mmm," he hummed in his throat. *"You don't often leave the castle on your day off."*

"People change. Besides, I need fresh air."

He gave me the document back and lowered his dark brows. *"You left the Battle early…"*

I rolled my eyes. *"Was **everyone** watching me?"*

Aldus' face grew serious. Too serious. He leaned into my face, and I tried my best not to flinch. His eyes had veins of red in them as if he hadn't slept in a while or cried a lot just minutes before. The latter seemed ridiculous. *"No, Rosetta. You **draw** too much attention."* A chill went down my spine and lingered at the bottom.

What did he mean? Was this a warning of some sort? Did he know about something? The pigeons…the letters…the journal?

I swallowed before responding so my voice wouldn't quiver. *"Sorry, Aldus. You lost me."* I stepped away from him. *"Until next time!"* I called out as I continued on my way.

I passed the Eighth Garden and noticed the gardeners were hard at work. They'd managed to plant seven massive gardens since the Lord had taken over. I was told there was supposed to be 17 in total, each representing one of the 17 flags that flew atop the castle. I wasn't sure what the meaning of that number was, as it was relevant even before Lord Monté took over Jocund. Frankly, it didn't matter now.

I spotted Lydia on her knees next to a blue flower, shovel in dirt-stained hands, filling a hole with soil. The gardeners typically started their day early and ended early. No one liked to work in a garden once the sun was at its peak. Nevertheless, Lydia still looked sleepy. I sought to wake her up and make her smile.

"Lydia!" Her head swiveled around to look at me. *"Where is your lover? What was his name? **Mack?**"* My voice echoed off the cobblestones of the castle's exterior. Lydia blushed, shooting me a dirty look and quickly putting her head down to avoid the stares from the other gardeners.

Mack, who stood nearly 15 feet away from Lydia, turned to see who'd made the comment. I made sure to stand in place to let him get a good look at the culprit. I gave him a nod and laughed.

For all the pain Lydia had put me through with Kenneth—a man I despised—my jest was a lenient punishment. It was one that would undoubtedly earn me some respectable prank in the end. Just add it to the long list of pranks between Lydia and me.

The castle where the king of the land was supposed to reside was massive. The walls were exceptionally strong, made with the reliable cobblestone and limestone. The hint of limestone made the castle less dreary to view. The colors—blue and gold, representing the land of Jocund — were shown off in banners on each side of the front gate, while the 17 flags above waved in a persistent wind. Visible to the eyes of all the Jocunders below, it all served as reminders that their kingdom stood. Now, however, that fact was laughable.

Their kingdom stood under another ruler. A tyrant. A man who had taken — no, **stolen** — what was rightfully theirs. To them, the flags were a bad joke that grew more and more bitter as the days passed. I'd been out enough in the city's main marketplaces to know the people never looked up at them anymore.

Now that I think about it, Jocunders spent a considerable amount of time looking down…

I reached the Forge a little too quickly, though my thoughts had compelled me to walk fast. I could hear the sound of metal being hit by different types of hammers. It was a quaint little place on the outside and might've passed as cottage, had I not been familiar with the architecture. The back of the Forge was open, the roof sustained by wooden columns so that air could flow through the cursed place. Little good it did.

I took a deep breath then ducked inside. The noise erupted. Metal slapping metal became the only thing I could hear. Two tables stood in the middle of the room that was laden with stools pretty much in all the corners and next to them. Two men in the middle of the space were responsible for the racket. I knew both men — James and Drek — but I was only there to see one of them.

Drek, who wore a cloth around his head, had patches of beard and yellow teeth. He stopped long enough to nod at me. James, who either hadn't heard me come in or didn't care, kept plunging his hammer down into the sword on his anvil. His beard was full and falling off his chin in sweat. His shirt was open, revealing a drenched bit of brown chest hair.

I approached James and cleared my throat. *"May I have the pleasure of speaking with you?"* I asked over his continued clanking.

"Huh?" he grunted. He never stopped bringing the strange-looking hammer down on the sword.

"May I speak with you on an important matter?" I repeated louder.

Beads of sweat dribbled down his head into his beard. The place was too hot and too smelly, and these two sweaty men just added to the catastrophe. *"Huh?"* he asked again before banging the hammer down.

My patience evaporated. **"I have something to ask of you. Now, would you do me the honor of putting your bloody hammer down?"** I shouted.

He stopped, turned, and raised a burly brow at me. *"What are ya shoutin' for, lass? No need to get angry and blow me ears off!"*

I sighed. *"My apologies."*

He gestured towards a chair. *"Take a deep breath, then. Been in here for a mite three seconds, and ya already blown yer head up!"*

I wasn't quite sure what that meant, but I was in no position to argue with the massive man. I climbed onto a stool that was too big for me and let my feet dangle. I felt like a child consulting my parents—an uncomfortable picture for one who'd lost their parents young.

James gave me a long, hard look…long enough to make me think about squirming. He then broke the stare, grabbed a cloth, wiped his black-stained hands, and pulled over a stool to sit on. He sat with his legs spread as he cracked his knuckles. *"Alright, tell this old man what's on yer mind."*

I couldn't. Not now while I felt like a fool…

I crossed my legs, trying my best to cover up my embarrassment, and raised an uncharacteristically flustered brow at the man. *"I have a friend named Peter."* I made sure to throw in a closer word than 'acquaintance,' which I had a habit of calling everyone besides Lydia.

James looked me up and down openly and cut in. "No doubt you do, lass. This is about a man, then?"

"A boy," I said quickly. James merely raised a brow. It wasn't an encouraging gesture, but I kept going. *"Peter is maybe nine or ten years of age, but he's been required to compete in the Battle the Lord has set up. He has no other family to do so."*

"Aye. I saw him." This came from Drek. He'd stopped banging to wipe his brow. *"Last night. Short and scrawny. Blue insignia."*

I recalled the color of Peter's insignia, which had seemed unimportant at the time he'd nearly been killed. I unreasonably felt responsible. I nodded. *"He needs a special set of armor and a lighter but sharper sword. He is the youngest in the fight and the most ill-equipped."* James' face wasn't sympathetic. As a matter of fact, it showed absolutely nothing.

He turned in his seat to look at Drek, who, besides recognizing the boy, hadn't given me much reaction. Drek glanced at me, though, then said to his friend, *"Doesn't sound too appealing."*

James looked at me. *"Me hands are blistered, I'm hot, and if I don't add on extra projects like yours, I can get a good night's sleep into tomorrow's day off. Fancy that. Now, tell me why I should do this? Why **you** want me to do it…"*

"I just gave you all the facts about the boy," I said irritably.

*"Then you didn't listen closely enough, lass. I asked about **you**."*

*How do I tell him I don't know how to answer his question verbally? I show I care because I'm **challenged** to do so. Plus, I love challenges.*

This armor thing was different, though. I'd come up with it on my own. I somehow knew the boy would die without it the next time he went to the Battle. I couldn't just stand by and watch it happen.

Who was this newfound me?

"I don't know what you want me to say. If you do it for me, I'll work overtime tomorrow so Héloise can get a day off with you," I said finally.

James' cheeks colored. *"Aah. That's who ya are then. The Rosetta girl from work she talks about."* He winked. *"You're not half bad as she says ya are, though ya do got some serious anger issues, kid."*

I carefully made my way off the tall stool and stood. *"Does that mean you'll do it?"* I tried not to sound overly anxious.

James nodded. *"Aye. I will. Drek?"*

Drek shrugged. *"What's a few more swings with this hammer gonna do to me?"*

I felt proud to have done something like this, even at the expense of having to work overtime tomorrow. More time working meant less time talking to people I hated, with Chancellor Kenneth being a brilliant example.

I turned away and called thanks over my shoulder.

"Where ya off to now, lass?" James asked.

I turned slightly to address him but never stopped walking. *"To prove somebody wrong."* I then headed out the door.

16: DUSTIN ELRIC CARPENTER

A shadow comes, a shadow dies.
When it does, do not look back.
Press forward, press forward with open eyes.
A stranger's got your back.

I must confess: My energy level is close to buggin' nothing in the mornings. I never was much of a morning person. It started when I was young. I always loved sleep over schooling, but my father didn't encourage laziness. So, when I grew to be a young man, and he could control me less, my sleeping habits grew worse. Now, I found that even though I loved what came with the mornings—the sunrise, cool dirt, breakfast, and an early start to the day—I still could not rise for it.

Of course, the journey had fixed the condition insurmountably. I was already suffering from sleep deprivation and kept finding I could hardly sit upright in my saddle. My butt hurt. My legs hurt. My feet hurt.

The Black Warriors and I had much more of it to look forward to. For miles and miles, there was nothing but trees, which only led me to think. I couldn't forget my conversation with Kraus by the fire. What it meant… I leaned forward and noticed Arthur perking up.

It'd been three hours since we left Endres and his family, with no sign of any Reapers at all. I was starting to worry. Better they were on our backs than Endres' back. With our current pace, they should be behind us right now.

Egon scratched behind his ear, sitting terribly upright in the saddle next to me on the left. His stallion never showed much emotion—at least compared to Julius—but trotted restlessly, as if doing so would tell his rider they should pick up the pace. Julius just glared at his counterpart warily from time to time.

On my right, Cederic was quiet as usual, but I made sure to glance at him often. He'd most likely be the first to spot the Reapers—if they ever appeared. Less talkative than the rest, he was the most attentive. Ocean was also quick to notice her surroundings, and Arthur, as an archer, also had a good eye.

"Y-you think they'll come?" Silas asked from out in front of us.

"You know what I think, Silas? I think we're only a day out, and we've already murdered an entire family," Egon replied, obviously concerned about the fate of Endres, Dagny, and the little ones.

Silas, who'd been glancing back at us, winced. *"Endres would've kept his children safe…"* He didn't sound as confident as the statement was intended.

Egon snorted. *"Wishful thinking that."* His tone was too dead for anyone to take him seriously. He believed — they **all** believed — the Reapers were still coming…eventually. Plus, we couldn't go back now. We'd just have to hope the family of five survived.

"Y'know, you could do with an authority figure in your life, Egon," Woodruff said to him. Cederic chuckled.

"Oh? Why is that, creature?"

"To tell you to smile. Your resting face — a rather revolting glower — makes you appear horribly unattractive, in my mandate."

Egon gave him his best glower. *"Check your mandate for holes instead of checking my face for them. At least then, you'll find something ugly."* The comment made Arthur laugh.

"Boys, not now," Ocean cut in. *"I've got the worst headache."*

Silas glanced up at her from his book but didn't say anything. The book was a different one from yesterday morning.

Arthur spoke up. *"Perhaps the best way to shut them up is to stuff a rag in their mouths."*

"Can't we b-b-be the least bit c-c-civil?" Silas asked.

People had a bad habit of assuming who Silas was when they heard his speech impediment. They often related the disability to meekness. If I must say, he did a good job playing that role in the group. However, people were often built to hide something. I've seen Silas with his knives and Requisite. He could kill a person walking in a market in broad daylight, and no one would know who did it. As a matter of fact, I'd seen him do it before. I'd seen him do a lot of things before that he will never speak of openly.

His stutter, though? I didn't know from where it came. As long as I'd known him—a little less than a decade—I never heard the story. None of us had. It was something to do with a traumatic experience in his youth, but no one knew the specifics. In this group, each was entitled to their secrets.

Well, unless you were the prince, and they thought it safe to know your secrets in order to protect you from serious harm. As a result, they might just get a peek when it's least expected because of their paranoia. That's when you hide certain secrets.

Hence, my letters, although I trusted my friends far more than my father did. He says that when a secret such as this mission is concerned, the less the ears know, the less mouths will tell. That response honestly surprised me, for my father liked my friends well enough. This journey had, in fact, been an exception.

"All I'm saying is that you're liable to lose a bit of life, Egon, if you don't learn how to put a grin on your face," Woodruff was saying.

Egon grunted, and I laughed. *"Well, as Egon likes to say: 'Bloody nuisance that.'"* I cast Egon a wink.

The shift to my right made me tense. I glanced towards Cederic, who had perked up considerably.

"Do you hear it, Dustin?" he rasped.

I listened. I heard it. Horrid sounds. Familiar sounds… It was the sound of **thousands** of screeches. *Those* screeches. Inhuman ones. Direct repeats of Conrad's.

I turned just in time to see them: thousands running over the hill we'd descended, like ugly little ants. They were too far to make out their details, leaving them to look like quickly-moving black specks. Unnaturally quick.

"They're fast, but we should be able to outrun them!" I shouted over the bone-chilling noise.

The next comment came from Arthur, who was doing his best impression of being brave. *"Shouldn't we be off then?!"*

Cederic gave me an indistinct nod. He already understood what I was going to do.

"The farther we draw them away from Endres, the more unlikely it is they'll go back to his house!" I yelled.

Arthur looked at me like I was crazy. *"You **want** them to reach us?!"* Everyone else lifted their weapon. I didn't answer him.

The things grew closer, giving me a better look at them. They were strange things. They didn't bleed, even though their skin was falling off their bones. Most of them had lost every trace of their hair, but some — like the one we'd run into at camp that night — had thin strands that remained. So thin, you were scared if you blew hard enough, you could blow it out of their head. The lack of eyebrows was odd. The lack of clothing was perfectly atrocious. It revealed their sunken ribs that a worn-out skin couldn't cover, leaving the bones of their ribs open and visible.

I waited 'til the nasty things were mere steps away before calling, ***"Black Warriors, let's ride!"***

Ride, we did, though it didn't do much good as far as escaping the Reapers was concerned. They had momentum on their side, and our horses were just getting their feet under them after a complete stop. Undoubtedly, the Reapers would reach us…which was the point. I needed to give them a taste of blood to get them to follow long enough for me to be comfortable knowing they wouldn't return to Endres.

They reached Woodruff—next to Cederic on my right and slightly behind me—first. They jumped onto the side of the horse with a firm grip and then climbed up like madmen, scratching with their rotting fingernails at Woodruff's legs. Woodruff took the reins with one hand and punched one of the Reapers with the other so hard, it dropped to the ground like a rock. It was trampled by the back legs of Woodruff's horse.

I had no time to keep staring at Woodruff, for now, the ugly things were upon me. Focusing on anything else could cost me some ugly gashes in **my** legs.

A Reaper jumped and caught on my right side. My left hand was my dominant one, so I had to shift the sword over. I did so quickly, swinging it wide and away from my own legs but enough to slice through the thing's useless neck. When it fell, its head and neck separated halfway to the ground. Yet another was near and on my left before I could even finish lifting my sword. I didn't even bother switching my weapon back to the left. Instead, when the thing poked its head up, I sent an unmerciful elbow, causing a loud crack of bone. The thing went sprawling to the ground.

"C'mon, Julius! Push it!" I grunted, grabbing the reins with my left hand and urging him forward. Two more Reapers lunged at Julius on either side. One of them began to scratch its way up towards me, cutting Julius in the process and causing him to whine angrily. I thrust my sword into the Reaper on my right, stabbing him thoroughly through the heart. Finding the beast surprisingly light, I flipped the ugly thing over my head while it was still hanging from my sword and used the corpse to knock the other Reaper off my horse. I then firmly propped the first body up on Julius' side — which took a moment at our swift pace — and yanked my sword free.

Air whizzed past me, the chill from it deafening my ears. I decided 'Gummies' was too funny a word for the ghastly things. They were disturbing enough to send shivers up a **grown** man's spine.

I took a glance behind me and saw I was clear of the demons. I'd outrun them and highly doubted the ones further back could catch up again.

I looked around me. Woodruff, Cederic, and Ocean were on my right and faring wonderfully. Each had only one Reaper left and wasn't necessarily struggling with it. When I glanced over at Arthur, I noticed he was out of arrows. He kept using the same one and yanking it out of fallen Reapers. He'd somehow managed to attract **three** of the little devils.

I whistled and pushed my calf against Julius' side. ***"C'mon, boy!"*** We burst ahead to run in pace next to Arthur. ***"Arthur!"*** I called. ***"Sword!"*** I barely waited for him to turn to catch it, hoisting the weapon towards him.

He caught it and, in one fluid motion, sliced an arm off one of the Reapers. The downward strike was followed by a sideways swipe. The second motion cut off two heads at once, but the bodies hung on. Their ugly yellow nails remained stuck in the horse's side. Arthur pushed the headless beasts down with a grunt, which was when I noticed how badly his hands shook. He gripped the reins hard as if he were afraid he would drop them.

To be honest, I was afraid he would, too…

I swung my head back to check on my companions. All six Black Warriors had disposed of their enemies and were riding freely from the horde that continued to advance roughly eight feet behind them.

*My plan ought to work…if the Reapers chased us a **little** longer.*

My head began to hurt from the steady screeches. Instead of dwelling on the pain, I leaned forward in my saddle and hollered, ***"Onward, Warriors!"*** Then, I let out a laugh. It was good for Arthur to see me laughing. The rest, well, they didn't need any moral support after a battle. They'd seen plenty. Perhaps they were also familiar with the thrill I was experiencing.

We ran at a speedy quip for a long time. The demons were persistent. I remember the sun reaching its peak and wondering how far into the afternoon it was. 1:00? 2:00? I pushed the Warriors and our horses on until the sound of footsteps and screeching were gone. Completely gone.

I reined Julius into a complete stop and turned to face the Warriors, who'd followed suit.

"So," I said between breaths, *"how about a water break?"*

17: ROSETTA KELLINA MABEL

Kindness is underappreciated,
Overappreciated,
And nearly never done right.

The village's atmosphere was so gloomy, it made me want to appear as miserable as it seemed. Eyes followed me down every strip of pathway. Hateful, condemning eyes. Suddenly, I realized why Edmund and the Lord's personal attendants hated their jobs.

Everyone wants to kill the messenger. No one thinks of who might've caused the whole problem. Everyone wants to blame what's in front of them, instead of just looking a little deeper within. The hatred I was getting from the Jocunders was no different. Bad news? Kill the messenger! What a wonderful solution.

I think the only reason I hadn't been killed already was that most of these people had enough sense to know killing me could end their own lives, especially if my dear admirer — Chancellor Kenneth — figured out who it was. I smiled to myself, thinking about life after my death.

Kenneth searching for those who murdered me.

Eyes of hot coals.

Kicking down doors for me.

Even as I smiled, I realized the thought was utterly ridiculous.

I stopped next to the small hut Peter had shown me last night. I hadn't entered, but the exterior told me enough about the place. It was barely big enough for two people. Consisting of nothing but wood and dirt floor, Peter's family was the epitome of poor. The front door, which I suppose was once a firm, wooden one, was now a creaky spook of a thing, hardly capable of standing fully.

There was a small garden, untamed from being unattended. I clutched the warm pot I carried closer to me and ambled towards the door. I wasn't sure what I was supposed to do. I knocked hesitantly, and the unreliable door creaked open a crack from the gentle rapping force of my knuckles.

I stood there, frozen in place.

C'mon, Rose. It's just Peter. If he is mad about you showing up, the worst thing he could do was tell you to get lost.

That's not what I was worried about, though. It's just what I wanted myself to **believe** I was worried about.

No. That wasn't it, either. I couldn't help thinking of my reputation. I never did things like this. Why did I do it now? To prove a silly man wrong? Ferrando didn't matter one iota to me, so why had I let his comment bother me? Never mind. It didn't matter now.

I'll just drop off the pot, say hi to Peter, and le —

The door pulled open. A disgruntled Ferrando stood on the other side. *"What are **you** doing here?"* he asked sharply.

Somehow, I knew my cheeks were blooming with color. I could feel the heat spring up and slap me in the face. *"I didn't know you were here…"* was all my startled mind could think to say. I cursed myself inwardly.

He grunted. *"Didn't expect me, huh? Who did you expect? Peter? Gonna whisk him off back to the castle or something, 'Miss Magical'?"*

Now, I felt even more ridiculous. I supposed no matter what I said, Ferrando would want me gone. Still, I'd trekked all the way here, and I wasn't going to trek back with the pot still full without me at least trying to sway the cursed man otherwise.

"I brought him soup," I said more firmly. *"You'd be a fool not to take it."*

He narrowed his eyes. *"I don't need 'noble soup.'"* He then turned his head away as if to indicate the conversation was over.

I spoke before he could begin shutting the door. *"You need **food**. Don't let your bloody pride kill the boy, too."*

He paused and looked at me intensely. *"Here I am, getting told off for **my** pride by a noblewoman. My friends would surely laugh at me."*

"Yes, I'm quite the hypocrite, am I not? So, what is your decision?" My tone was bitter, my patience short.

He stared at me for a couple of moments. The silence wasn't disturbing, but it was a little confusing. Then, he laughed at me. Pointed his finger and **laughed** at me! I didn't know how to interpret what was happening.

"You're a fool, woman! A fascinating one, I must admit." He opened the door widely, turned, and walked further into the house without another word. I suppose it meant, 'Come in'?

That was the greatest compliment of the day, I thought, as I stepped through the threshold.

The hut was one room. A decent-sized one, I suppose. It was also utterly disgusting. Between the dirt floor and the unpolished wooden walls that were too thin in some places not to let sunlight in, the home was dreadful. I found myself wondering just how sturdy this place was. A creaking sound floated to my ears every few seconds from somewhere in the kitchen to the left of me.

A woman was lying on a grass mattress in the middle of the room's floor. Peter sat with his knees pulled up to his chin, reading to the woman, though it appeared she was in no way listening. I guessed it was the mother he had spoken of after the Battle. The sight made my heart sore. A small ache grew in my chest.

I forced a smile before offering my greeting. *"Hey, Peter!"*

He glanced up at me, narrowed his eyes, and went back to his reading. I raised a brow. Ferrando snorted and moved slightly to the left into the small kitchen.

When Peter finished his story, he shut the book and gave me a dark look. *"What do **you** want?"*

"I just took you through the castle as you asked. Why am I getting this treatment?" I asked the question with humor, though I was truly embarrassed and confused.

"I know why you're here. You wanted to see for yourself what a poor person looked like. Wanted to see how sick my mom was. That's why you took me to the castle. You thought I'd invite you inside my home so you could 'have a look around,'" he spat accusingly.

I just scoffed. To take him seriously when things were already so solemn would only add to my growing issues.

"How is your mom?"

Peter looked back at her and shrugged. *"Well, how does she look to you? Up, well, and happy?"* His sarcasm was not lost on me.

I stared at her long and hard. *"She looks dead."* His head came up sharply to look at me. I continued. *"She's not, though. I can see she's still breathing. There's always something worse which could be, I suppose."* He wrinkled his nose. *"I brought you soup,"* lifting the pot so he'd notice it. I saw his brows rise slightly, though he tried to hide his interest.

"Like pottage?" he asked.

I smiled. Pottage was peasant food and terribly overrated in the villages around The Main of Jocund. It was a soup made with nothing but bland vegetables. No salt, for that simple seasoning was far too expensive. I had never tasted pottage, of course; only heard of it. I did hear about the time one of the cooks in the castle had tasted it nearly a fortnight ago. She said it tasted like water, especially with the famine complicating everything, and that even with the addition of the vegetables, it was a shameful meal. I believed her. After all, what would food taste like without a dash of salt?

"No, Peter. This is lentil soup." I'd been disappointed at the time. Still was. I wanted to give him something he'd never had before. He'd undoubtedly had lentil soup before. Unfortunately, the cooks weren't willing to give me any of our dinner we'd be having tonight. 'Chike Endored,' a common dish among the nobles and workers in the castle, was roasted chicken covered in a delicious batter. I'm sure it would've served as a better treat…

Peter glanced at Ferrando. *"Can we have it for lunch? Please?"*

"A-ha! Now we're all polite," said the gruff man as he pulled out four bowls from a cabinet. *"Just last night, you didn't want to hear a word I said about going to the castle."*

"Well, he must've gotten his manners from somewhere," I stated in a hinting manner. I placed the stew on a table with room for only one thing that was next to the kitchen area. *"I do believe this pot should've been taken from me at the door, considering the circumstances."* I made eye-contact with Ferrando as he looked up.

He snorted. *"Forgive me. I forgot all my manners when I saw* **you** *standing there."*

I smiled but said nothing. I decided I wouldn't encourage his dry behavior. I addressed Peter. *"Let's get your mother something to eat."*

As I was finishing the statement, Ferrando pushed a bowl into my stomach and turned away. As much as I wanted to shoot a nasty comment at the man, I placed my focus on the pot and ladled soup into the bowl. I ignored Ferrando's brash mood.

"Has Merek bothered you much since last night?" I made sure to obviously direct my question to Peter.

He rolled his eyes. *"I don't pay him no mind. He doesn't think I'm gonna make it out alive next time. I'm not even worried. I'm ready."* I would've felt better, had Peter not shivered after making that statement, and if his brows hadn't knitted together so closely in such a solemn way.

I thought Peter was watching me, until I glanced up from the pot and noticed him staring at Ferrando's back.

"What?" I mouthed to him, spooning a little more soup into the bowl.

Peter glanced at me, then back at his friend. To himself more than me, he said, *"Ferrando doesn't like you."* Ferrando didn't turn around or stop whatever he was doing.

"I know," I said quietly. I placed the ladle back in the pot.

*"You remind him of his wife. She acted **just** like you."*

My head shot up. I heard Ferrando pause behind me. *"Peter, hold your tongue..."* I said slowly.

"Why?" Ferrando asked, turning to face me. *"Isn't that what **all** noblewomen do? Pry? Go ahead. Ask as your heart desires! Ask about my **wife**. Ask about his **sick mother**. Ask away! Why would we stop you?"*

I parted my lips, prepared to say something, thought better of it, and placed the bowl next to the pot. My knuckles whitened. Peter looked slightly afraid.

Ferrando continued, yelling into my face now. ***"Why so civil? Why don't you tell me what you truly want to know, woman? Let's have a real conversation!"*** He was inches from my face when he finished yelling.

My heart was in my throat. I had never played a role such as this. Typically, I was the one delivering the blows, not receiving them. It took everything inside of me not to send a blow or two back.

"I think…I'll just leave now." I stepped towards the front door, which wasn't far away from where I stood. I reached for the door and heard Peter groan in annoyance.

"She just got here, Ferrando!"

Silence.

I don't know what occurred in the silence. I didn't turn around. I swung the door open and stepped outside.

*"I'd let her stay if she'd give me a reason to. The woman won't even defend herself! She's worse than **most** of the nobles back in The Main — and **that's** saying something!"*

Ferrando's words made me stop. I turned and saw that Peter stood closer to the door, as if he'd chased me slightly as I left. He looked angry. In fact, he trembled with it. Ferrando hadn't moved since I'd turned and walked away. He stood, arms crossed, ready for me. Perhaps he thought I'd make a fool of myself. Frankly, I didn't care if I did. I would say what I felt needed to be said and never return. I'd made a fool of myself coming here in the first place. As Ferrando noted, this was not where I belonged, even if his words made it seem as if nobles had **nowhere** they belonged.

The voice that left my body was firm yet quiet. *"My dear man, you haven't given me the chance to be anything other than what you've already told me I am. You know me from head to foot. Therefore, what is there left to show you?"* I inwardly cursed the weakness in my voice, though my point was sound.

Uneager for his answer — and too vulnerable to listen to Peter's pleas for me to come back — I turned on my heels and left before either happened and stepped into the sunlight. My thoughts took over as I made my way back to the castle.

As I walked, some of the people in the village gave me a pat on the back. However, I found most of them were angry at me. I felt a pang of loneliness to confirm the latter's point of view.

Lydia was my only friend, and it'd been that way for a bit. I never had many people in my life I truly enjoyed being around. Somehow, someway, even though I'd known them for less than a day, I was growing attached to Peter and Ferrando.

"Miss!" someone shouted from behind me. I turned to see Ferrando. He looked a bit flustered as he stood outside of the home. He wore a light brown tunic and black trousers. The first button of his tunic underneath his chin was loose, leaving him to look terribly disheveled. *"You never told me your name."*

I gave him a hard look, commanding he not play games with me.

"Peter wants you back for lunch," he continued.

I crossed my arms and raised a waiting brow.

"I would like you back for lunch," he admitted, giving me a smile that seemed only a bit forced.

I nodded slightly and walked back over to him. *"Well, then. My name is Rosetta. Rosetta Kellina. My **friends** call me Rose."*

He stared at me intently. *"You have won over Peter. I love the boy. Couldn't dare see him hurt more than he already is."* He paused and sighed. *"So, I guess I'm going to have to make things work between you and me."*

I smiled. *"Indeed."* Remembering what Peter said about me reminding Ferrando of his wife should've made me uncomfortable. Instead, I felt confused and despondent. How could **he** have married someone like **me**? He **hated** me! Any other person—other than these two—and I would've shouted back at them, told them off, and never came back. Was there something different about them, or was it **me**?

I was brought back to the present by a gesture from Ferrando, signifying I walk back inside. *"After you?"*

Peter looked so forlorn sitting next to his mother on the floor, reading to her, I nearly shed a tear. Nearly. Perhaps I would have if I hadn't also been so overcome with anger and animosity towards the Lord or any person who inflicted the poor boy in such a way.

The three of us ate together in silence and then retired to casual conversation.

"You read well," I said as he finished yet another chapter. I sat on a stool, patching a hole in Peter's mittens with a needle and thread.

"My mother taught me. Ferrando thinks I should keep up the skill while she's ill, but I think it's wretched to read to mother in this state. She can't even lecture me when I mispronounce a word."

Ferrando was sitting on a stool in the corner being miserably silent, having already decided to disagree with anything in the world which might present itself agreeable. He had lit a pipe in defiance and was smoking up the room with it. The room was far too small for his smoking. Neither could it be good for Peter's mother's health, but I didn't dare say a word.

"You need to keep up all your studies so you're not an imbecile like most of the children in the village," Ferrando felt the need to imply.

"Plus," I added, in a softer tone, *"how would your mother feel when she wakes up to you having abandoned your learning?"*

A dark shadow flashed over Peter's face. ***"If** she wakes up."*

"Stop talking like that," Ferrando snapped.

Peter huffed but thankfully said no more on the subject. Instead, he stood, turned to me, and asked, *"Rose, where are your parents? Do they live in the castle?"*

I stiffened. *"No. They died when I was young."*

"How young?"

"Nine."

He paused. Lifting the left side of his mouth just a tad, he asked, *"Were you sad?"*

It was the stupidest question, yet how could I scold him for it? I was trying to ignore Ferrando's eyes on me while thinking up a proper answer and continuing to sew Peter's mittens at the same time.

"Yes. Very. I still am."

Peter stared at me pensively. *"No wonder you're such a boring and serious old woman! I bet I would be a boring little boy if my mother dies, too…"*

Ferrando began scolding him again on his depressing outlook. All I could do was engage in my bad habit: I bit my lip.

No wonder you're such a boring and serious old woman! Indeed, what a boring old woman I'd become. I felt a little dejected and angry for reasons I didn't understand.

"Well, maybe if you were better at making me laugh, I wouldn't be so boring." I managed to cut through their bickering.

Peter shrugged. *"I am not a funny boy. My friend, Samuel, is funny. He knows jokes."*

*"Samuel is **not** funny. He's dull,"* Ferrando stated.

Peter ignored the comment — something he was excellent at doing.

"There are other ways to make a person laugh, you know. Do you know any stories?" I asked Peter.

"What kinds of stories?"

"Hmm… Funny ones," I mused.

Peter appeared to think earnestly for a moment but came to the same conclusion. *"I am not a funny boy. Do **you** know any funny stories?"*

I smiled, remembering one my mother had told me. *"Actually, I do."*

*"Great! I want to hear **your** story!"* He sat down cross-legged and waited patiently while I collected my thoughts.

I began without raising my eyes from the sewing needle:

"There was a hunter in the forest, armed with
quiver, bow, and arrow – "

I was interrupted when Ferrando stood so abruptly, he knocked over his stool, causing both Peter and me to jump. He cast me a dark look, swore something under his breath, and left the house, sulking.

After a moment's silence, I continued:

"He'd been out hunting for hours when he was suddenly overcome with hunger. 'I'd better eat,' he said, 'while things are quiet.' He sat down, opened his bag, and withdrew his lunch. He gorged himself on bread and cheese until he heard a noise. The man turned around, and lo and behold! If there wasn't a large bear staring back at him not too far away. 'Please don't eat me!' he cried, alarmed. 'I've got bread and cheese to share.' The bear opened his mouth and said, 'I did not think

*you meant to share by the way you stuffed it down. Besides, you forgot to pray for it. What a shameful man you are!' So, he ate the man, without remorse. On his way back home, he was shot and killed by another hunter wandering through the forest. When he had lifted all the way to Heaven, he had just one question for God: 'How could you let me die like that? I was always such a good bear!' 'Really?' God asked, smiling. He shook his head and laughed before saying, 'Because I do believe **you** forgot to pray before you ate that man.'"*

Peter grinned at my conclusion. *"Bears don't go to Heaven,"* he stated matter-of-factly.

"Well, how do you know? Have you ever been there?" I asked in a scolding tone.

"Bears don't talk, either."

"Yes, and people do not negotiate with them. I know. I do believe you are thinking too much, Peter."

"I like it," he said finally. *"I think I'll tell Samuel **I** came up with it. He'll think I'm funny then!"*

I laughed. *"Very well. Tell Samuel it is yours."* I glanced up at him, noticing his knitted brow as if something was troubling him. *"What's wrong?"*

"I'm not sure I will remember it."

"Get me some ink and paper, and I will write it down for you."

He sprung up and ran to the kitchen. *A funny place for ink and paper.* I was too amused to dwell on it much. Peter's youthful excitement warmed me more than I'd anticipated. I watched him scramble around through the cupboards, fish for what he needed, and bring it back to me.

I laid his mittens aside—along with the thread and needle—and welcomed another task. I took the ink and paper and wrote in silence, with Peter overseeing my scribbling.

"Isn't it funny that the bear did exactly as he had condemned the man for immediately after he pointed it out?" he proclaimed.

I pulled myself out of my writing for a moment and managed a thoughtful *"Hmm…"*

I returned to writing. **Forest?** Check. **Man?** Check. **Bear?** Check.

Again, Peter broke in. This time, he mused to himself, *"It's just like what the Lord did."*

My blood went cold, and I froze. I looked up at him, hard. *"How do you mean?"*

He blushed a little at my having heard him but regained confidence in moments. *"Well, he says all the time in his speeches what a naïve country we were before he got here. How we were ignorant, weak, and vulnerable. He says he has fixed it."*

I waited with bated breath for him to go on. He took a moment to form the exact words to describe what he was feeling.

"But he didn't, right? Jocund's more vulnerable than ever. It was weak, but now it has been pointed out. It has been mocked. Exposed. It is broken. It's his fault, but he won't admit it."

I stared at him, and he fidgeted underneath my gaze, his large eyes downcast and shifty.

"At least," he said, shrugging away the statement, *"that's what my mom says."*

There was nothing but the creaking to be heard and the quiet, steady breathing of Peter's mother on the mattress.

Goodness, I hadn't thought of it that way.

*"You probably… No. You **better** not repeat what you just said to anyone else,"* I told him in a low voice.

"Oh, I know. That's why I told you. I can't tell anyone else the truth, or they'll be cross," he admitted.

I bit my lip and went back to writing. Peter returned to his mother's bedside and sat next to her on the floor. I wrote the rest of the story, all while being plagued with thoughts. Another question came to mind, which I asked just as I finished. I handed him the paper, ink, and quill and picked up the mittens to begin sewing again.

"Peter, why did you approach me after I read Lord Monté's message?" I asked carefully.

Peter blushed. *"I don't want to tell you."*

I didn't push and continued to sew the patch into his mittens. *"Okay. That's fine."*

A silence followed. I began to feel it was less awkward for me than it was for him.

"Okay, I'll tell you," he blurted out.

I paused my sewing and looked up at him.

He blew air out of his colored cheeks and pulled his knees to his chest for comfort. *"I thought you were really pretty. I wasn't going to speak to you — I wouldn't dare. I just wanted to get a closer look."* He halted for only a moment and then rushed on at my skeptical expression. *"That's an awfully hard thing for a boy my age to admit, so do **not** laugh."*

"I wasn't going to."

"You wanted to."

"No, I didn't."

Ferrando returned home, and the carefree atmosphere drifted out the door to make room for a circumspect one. Peter hardly noticed, saying, *"When can you take me to the castle again?"*

I didn't bother answering, for I knew I would only be interrupted by the man who liked to answer for me.

As if on cue, he said, *"She's not."* He passed by me and jerked up his stool to sit on again. The pipe was gone. *"People are already talking. I don't want to give them more reasons to."*

I didn't meet his eyes. I knew what I would see there. I kept sewing.

"You're only concerned about others' opinions when it's convenient for you," I heard Peter snap at him.

*"I notice people's **opinions** when they matter. Wait. Are you ignoring me?"*

"Yes."

"Why?"

"Because I think you're being a pain in the rear end. I am not being a brat to point it out, so don't you dare say it."

Ferrando fell silent at Peter's demand for silence. Peter went back to reading to his mother. Finally, I could feel a bit of peace in Ferrando's presence.

It remained that way for half an hour. Peter read stories to his unresponsive mother. Ferrando brooded and occasionally watched me from the corner. I, sewing the patch into one mitten and then the other. The creak resounded, becoming a relaxing rhythm…a comforting pattern. I began to hum an old tune that put me at ease.

Peter stopped reading to listen, then rested his head on his mother's shoulder. She woke up enough then to place her hand on his head. He fell asleep in the comfort of her motherly touch.

I hardly realized the change in the atmosphere until I looked up to say something to Peter. He was snoring softly. Just as I noticed, I also became aware of Ferrando's eyes on me again — and the lit pipe. The former soothing creak now seemed scattered and annoying. Having finished sewing Peter's mittens and having nothing else to occupy my time, I decided to leave. With Peter asleep, there was nothing more to keep me here, and I was growing uneasy.

I stood.

"Sit down," Ferrando barked.

I thought about leaving anyway, thought better of it, and sat. After all, Peter and his mother were right there. They were only sleeping. I wasn't truly alone with this man.

"*Your mother and father died?*"

"*Yes.*"

"*How?*"

"*The Theft.*"

"*In the castle or elsewhere?*"

I scoffed. "*In the castle. Why?*"

"*So, they worked in the castle? Servants?*"

"*I suppose.*"

He leaned forward. "*What do you mean, 'I suppose'? Don't you know what your parents did for a living?*"

"*I was nine last I saw them. I was supposed to know things I didn't care to know about.*"

"*Hardly an excuse for it.*"

"*It isn't an **excuse**; it's a **fact**. Why are you asking these questions?*"

"*To get to know you a little better. I thought it **proper**.*"

I raised my chin in hidden annoyance. "*Then, I am sure you will **properly** deal with my asking you some things as well.*"

He leaned back again and blew some smoke into the air. "*As you please.*"

"*Where did you learn to fight like that?*"

"Like what?" he asked, flashing a knowing grin.

I pressed my lips together. **Such an impossible man.** *"You're stalling. You know exactly what I mean."*

"Not at all."

"The Battle. Last night. You fought off Merek like a trained soldier — like you held a sword before. I want to know why."

"Perhaps I have trained as a soldier."

*"Ha! That answer will **not** do."*

He knitted his brows. *"Why ever not?"*

"It is not an answer at all, and you know it."

*"Very well. I **have** trained as a soldier."*

"When? How?" I wanted to know. No. I **needed** to know.

He put up a finger to stop me. *"That'll do,"* he said while puffing on his pipe.

I held my hands, squeezing each finger occasionally. *"Am I allowed to leave now?"*

"No."

*"I can't sit here **all day**,"* I said, exasperated.

"Then talk. You do it very well with Peter."

I turned away from him and mumbled, *"**Peter** does not glare at me as you do."*

*"Which is to be expected. He is **eleven**. I, however, am nearly **thirty**."*

"I don't care."

"What do you think about Lord Monté? He killed your parents, so you must hate him."

"What kind of question is that?"

*"Seeing as I'm holding this conversation by myself, **I** ask the questions, and **you** answer them."*

I flushed. I don't think I'd ever been so angry in all my life.

"If you are wondering whether I will defend the Lord like any other noble in the castle, you are mistaken. I hate him nearly as much as I hate you at the moment. I will not pretend otherwise to satisfy another. I am only who I am behind closed doors, Ferrando. So, yes: I hate him with all of my being." Tears formed in my eyes. I stood in disgust—disgust with him, myself, and the rest of the world who looked upon Jocund's plight and did nothing. *"I am leaving. It will take the power of **God** to stop me."*

I left the house with Ferrando smirking at my back, Peter sleeping, and something in the kitchen still creaking.

18: ARCHIE COCKBURN

I speak of my accomplishments
And weave 'round sense like a whirlpool.
I participate in reckless sin.
I am a fool…

I don't know how one strikes out on their own as well as Mallory and I did, especially considering our ages and how terribly frightened I was. I know I couldn't have made it without my brother. I wish I could say the same for him. He was so composed, so put-together. I was of little help to his emotional state. Or anything for that matter. He started our fires when it got dark, fixed our food, and kept me from giving up and going back home. For his sake, I decided not to whine so much, so our days were mostly quiet.

Mallory was a quiet person, rarely stressing his thoughts. We've always had a decent relationship forged by a bond of our indistinguishable and rather unfortunate situation with our parents. Yet now that the situation had been most abruptly finished, I had no words for the strong young man beside me—words which would fit snugly enough into the silence. He was quite extraordinarily content with it and letting nature do the talking, rather than us. I tried to match his maturity, but, of course, I couldn't get that right either.

As we crested a hill filled with trees losing their leaves and Fall tickling the air, I broke the silence.

*"So… Mal… Do we know **exactly** where we are off to?"*

He didn't look at me. Instead, he looked down the incline of the hill, as if my question wasn't worth turning one's head for. His tone further implied it.

"No. We're running into oblivion. Hopefully, we'll find some help there," he replied sarcastically. I waited for him to drop the joke. As he took his first steps down the hill, he called back to me, *"Haestingas. The city to the north. They'll be looking for us soon. Word will reach the surrounding cities eventually. Haestingas is big, so it's a good place to blend in."*

I nodded, realized he couldn't see me, and hastened after him down the hill.

The last of the birds flew overhead, heading south to where we'd just left. A chill dulled the atmosphere and bit at my bare neck, whipping my unkempt hair into a terrible mess. The farther we walked down the hill, the more and more I thought of Cecilly. Surely, she would've liked to see such a city as big as Haestingas—a place I could've taken her in the next couple of years. If my parents were alive, maybe they would have consented. They were cruel, heartless even, but they weren't stupid. Maybe I'd have been better off letting them live.

If only I'd pushed through the horror…

Just thinking about it made my Fork marks hurt. I reached behind my ear to rub the sensitive spot.

Weak. Stupid. Monster.

"**You're** *the weak, stupid monster,*" I said to the voice, like an idiot. "*All you do is repeat the same words. You're a* **fool.**"

Weak. Stupid. Monster.

"*You're weak.* **You** *are,*" I muttered. I tripped and regained my footing.

Stupid. Stupid. Stupid.

"*No, I'm* **not!** *No, I'm* **not!**" I blubbered.

"*Who are you talking to?*" Mallory asked.

I realized he'd stopped and turned around to stare at me questionably. I put my hand up in front of me to block the afternoon sun and shook my head. "*Nobody.*"

He peered at me. "*Well,* **that** *sure as heck ain't comforting! I'd rather you be talking to a voice in your own head than* **nothing.** *Never nothing. Talk to someone — or* **something** *— that talks back to you, not to people or* **things** *without opinions. That's what you talk for, isn't it? Knowledge?*"

"*I suppose so.*" I was quite startled at his statement and flustered tone.

*"Then make up your mind. Do you want **knowledge**, or do you want **silence**? 'Cause silence lets you do whatever you want and pays no mind to where it leads you."*

"I guess I would like knowledge," I replied bleakly.

*"Because that's what you **want** or what you think **sounds** right?"*

"The former, Mal, of course!" It came out rather hurriedly.

He turned back around, continued down the hill, and called to me, *"Then listen to the bloody knowledge-led voice and follow it wherever it takes you. **Never** listen to nothing. **Never nothing**."*

I was perturbed by this Mallory and followed him most cautiously. He said nothing more and didn't turn around. I lost my edge and continued on. Mallory rarely spoke out of hand. I tried to find the reason he had spoken so sharply to me, but I couldn't conjecture much of a rationale for it. I couldn't decide what bugged him so, enough to open his mouth to say it.

We reached the bottom of the hill in excellent time. I must have appeared tired because Mal said we'd take a 15-minute break. If I were him, I likely would have said, *"No. Of course not,"* while denying I was tired and suggesting we keep moving. Instead, I fell onto the grass and stretched my legs.

"Water…pouch…" I said between breaths. Mallory threw it to me. I thought I saw a bit of amusement on his face, though I couldn't be sure. I whipped the pouch open, placed it to my lips, and swallowed twice, savoring the coldness. It felt nearly like the water was bringing instant energy to my body. *"We've kept up like this all day for three days, Mal,"* I said as I handed the pouch back to him. *"Is this necessary?"*

He exhaled roughly through his nose, took a swig from the pouch, and glanced out at the trees. I asked for the water pouch again, and he tossed it back to me. *"No,"* he said, *"but we're two little boys, walking these woods by ourselves. I just want to be careful."*

I wanted to point out he was hardly a little boy and couldn't rightfully throw himself in the same category as me, but he probably wouldn't have listened. Plus, I heard a sound coming from a-ways off from the north — the same direction we were headed. Mallory must've heard it, too. We made eye contact for a brief moment before he ushered me off the path and up into a tree. I stepped on branch after branch as my legs cried out for me to stop.

The voices grew louder.

"Stop," Mallory whispered from below. *"We're high enough now. Any more climbing, and they'll hear us."*

I straddled a branch and stilled myself against the sway of leaves. All was silent for a moment, besides the thundering of my heart against my rib cage. After climbing, it became a bit of a struggle to let out air slowly versus all at once. My breathing was labored. I looked down and saw a dirt floor covered in leaves...**and the pouch!** I'd dropped it during my haste to get up the tree. I'd left it to be found. *Oh, no...*

I whispered a curse, triggering a response from Mallory. *"What?"* he asked me. I pointed down. I saw his face fall when he saw it — no doubt considering what we were going to do without it. It still held half a pouch worth of water and would've lasted us the next three days' journey to Haestingas.

Weak. Stupid. Monster.

Just as I prepared to curse the stupid voice, I remembered what Mallory had said and hesitated. I settled on not saying anything at all back to it, and it was just as well because it was then I heard shuffling as two blonde heads come into view.

"What's this?" a strained voice said. The person knelt next to the pouch and picked it up. Both wore a set of shiny armor, which led me to believe they were of the Watch Guard of Haestingas, considering the direction they'd come from. *"Water pouch."* He sniffed through a runny nose and addressed his companion. *"They've been through here alright, and not long ago either."*

It didn't take much digging to know who they spoke of.

His companion scanned the forest, looking everywhere but up. *"It doesn't make sense. We would've seen them coming through here. The man said they were headed **toward** the city. Wouldn't we have met them on our path from it?"* he said, only after careful thought and consideration.

The one with the strained voice stood with our pouch in hand and finally scanned his surroundings.

They should have looked around when they first arrived, I thought. *We probably could've killed the two fools and gotten our pouch back before they looked around.* The last thought came unbidden and disturbed me to great lengths.

The one with the strained voice shrugged. *"Never know; something could've happened to 'em, Vic. Something terrible. After all, they're young and traveling all alone with the Curse."*

Vic didn't seem convinced. The mention of a curse seemed to darken his mood further. *"What use are dead bodies to us? If it is as you say, and the Curse has taken the lads, then might we be on our way?"*

"Alas, the king has ordered us to search."

"The king need not know we didn't search thoroughly. Come on now, man," said the nervous Vic. *"Or do you want it to take us, too?"*

I was forced to believe Vic held little honor in the kingdom.

The still-unnamed dumb one thought about it for a moment. He knelt in the dirt and shrugged. *"Bloody waste of my time anyway."* He stood and dropped the water pouch, much to my great delight.

"Wait. Keep it, Earl. Indeed, we might get some kind of buggin' promotion if we bring it. Proof that we searched."

Earl picked up the pouch again, and the two men bustled off the way they'd come, whistling like typical cowards and laughing like fools.

I was disgusted, cramped, discouraged, and weary as I moved back down the tree. Mallory quickly put his hand up, stopping me. He mouthed for me to wait. I didn't know what for. For a while, maybe a little over 15 minutes, we sat in the tree. We didn't speak. We didn't move. We sat terribly still and quiet.

When Mallory chose to speak, he said, *"Alright. Now."*

I tried to look as calm as he, but I realistically **scrambled** down the tree. *"Well, that went surprisingly well,"* I said when I reached the bottom and dusted myself off. *"First of all, they* *didn't find us, and even though they took the pouch, they think we're dead. We might not run into any more Watch Guards on our pa —"*

Mallory grabbed the front of my tunic at the collar, lifted me off the ground, and slammed me into the tree trunk of the oak we'd just descended. I had barely oriented myself enough to recognize him, much less the reason for his outrage.

"Dang it, boy! Don't you ever listen?" he said angrily, his eyes ablaze. ***"I give you restrictions, and you spit on 'em?"***

I never had a reason to be frightened of my brother…until now. As I stared into his eyes, they looked familiar. They looked the spitting image of Pa's.

"W-w-what?" I stuttered incoherently.

"You told her, didn't you? You told the blasted girl!" His rage seemed to swell.

I shook my head, even though I didn't understand what he was saying. Surely, it hadn't been me who'd offended him so. He slammed me harder into the tree, causing me to groan.

"Did. You. Tell. Cecilly? Tell me!" The irate emphasis he placed on each word was no mistake.

I began to cry and hated myself for it, more than I'd hated myself before. Even my parents' deaths had been an act of courage, but this was an act of cowardice. Even knowing this, I couldn't stop myself. Tears flowed uncontrollably. Disgusted, my brother threw me to the forest floor, where I continued to weep.

The voice returned and had grown deeper and deeper, the more it spoke.

Weak. Stupid. Monster.

Weak. Stupid. Monster.

Weak. Stupid. Monster.

I choked on my own tears as my brother paced. *"You've got to understand something,"* he said through my sobs. *"Survival is not a game you get up from…"* I quieted, and he turned to look at me. *"It's not a game one should play with, to tug at another's emotions, or to risk it all to see if one might win. Winners of the game of survival don't come from daring oneself, but from fierce determination."* He shook his head in aggravation. *"If you continue to play the game as **you** are playing it, you will lose. We both will."*

Part of me—a scary part—wanted to spit in his face. He'd needed me to kill our parents. He'd always needed me. Now, I was the reason the patrols were out earlier than we thought they'd be, all because Cecil ratted on me. I couldn't fathom it. What would make her tell where I was? What would make her betray me?

Mallory must've read my mind. *"She has a family, brother. She won't ever lean on someone like you will. She has a family to lean on when she needs a buggin' hug. I tried to tell you…"* he finished, turning away.

I looked ahead of me, sort of in a daze. *"I didn't tell her where we were going."*

He turned back to me and raised his brows in scorned excitement. ***"Oh, good for you!"*** he said sarcastically. *"You kept your cool, especially since you didn't even know where we were going in the first place,"* he mocked.

I cursed at him, and he snorted in response.

"Come on — unless you're going to lay there and cry all day…"

There are moments when you feel so in power, everything you say comes to pass, and everything you do turns to gold. Then, there are times when you want to do something terribly bad, and the pieces won't move together. This was one of the latter moments. I wanted to hit my brother hard for no real reason besides my hurt pride, but I was too scared to do it. I couldn't will myself to go through with it. He was bigger, stronger, and smarter — much more capable of leading than I. So, I couldn't hit him; I had to play my role because I **needed** him.

For the first time in my life, I despised my older brother and the way I had leaned on him for so long. Was I so weak? So stupid? So useless?

You always were. You always will be.

The voice had spoken different words. It was not just a chant. It meant that **some** of what Mal had said was right. It meant I did, in fact, have a friend, even if this one was a bit discouraging. He was **my** friend and no one else's.

In reality, I stood; however, my tears, my hopes, and my innocence remained there on the forest floor. What's funnier is I'd had those three things all my life and didn't even notice I'd lost them.

"Well, let's bloody go, then," I said, my voice betraying me with a slight quiver.

Mal managed to raise one brow in an amused but unimpressed smirk. He then turned around without a word and started walking away.

We ran into two more patrols that day, each time hiding behind whatever nature laid the closest. Stress made me weary. After dinner—cold biscuits and some dried meat—I found a comfortable place to sleep: leaves I would soon discover were infested with spiders.

My brother cursed from behind me, where he'd just put out the fire. The curse was quiet, as if he hadn't wanted me to hear it.

I rolled over and addressed him. *"What is it?"*

He gave me a leveled look. *"It would seem we haven't rationed well at all. I thought there was more in the bag than there was. Did my adding wrong. We are out of food."*

Earlier in the day, I wouldn't have worried too much. We'd be hungry, sure, but only for two-and-a-half days. Now, however, the patrols had shown up and slowed us to nearly a snail's pace. We wouldn't arrive for a long time; five or six days easy. Not to mention our bodies, already struggling to understand the shortage of food we consumed the last few days, might not even make it—especially without water.

I cursed under my breath, right there in the darkness, and squinted at my bigger brother. "Well, I guess we're even," I said dryly. I rolled back over and closed my eyes.

It was then that I heard a voice on the wind faintly say: **Strong. Persistent. Leader.**

A smile graced my face in the ever-pressing dark.

19: DUSTIN ELRIC CARPENTER

The Or'geth's breath blows away
The small and steady men.
But if they raise a frightened hand,
They'll live another day.
These are the rules of survival…

In the early evening, we climbed off our horses to give them a break from the constant weight. We walked beside them, slightly ahead, pulling them along behind us by a lead rope. We kept at a decent pace, even off the horses. Hours later, my legs began to ache.

Julius seemed to be giving me a sideways look as if to say, *"See? That's how I always feel, you jerk."*

I gave him a lopsided grin. *"Play nice. No one likes a sour apple."*

*"Well, except Egon. He **is** one."* It came from Arthur, who was walking beside me. Everyone else was well behind, enough to probably not have heard me speaking to Julius.

"Shh." I hushed him. *"We don't want Julius to think ill of Egon."*

Arthur shrugged, grinning. *"Too late for that, I think. How are your legs? Did the aging get to you?"*

I shrugged. *"To be honest, I hardly got a scratch."*

"Woodruff wasn't as fortunate."

"Well, that's why we put him in the back."

Arthur laughed a little. *"I suppose,"* he said. His face grew serious. *"Do you think some of us won't make it? On the journey, I mean?"*

I shook my head. *"I don't know, Arthur."*

He sighed and let silence stretch between us. I heard the bickering of Woodruff and Egon behind me. It seems they never stopped.

"I'll die first. I'm the worst Warrior out of all of us," Arthur said quietly.

I glanced at him. *"That rarely means anything in war, Arthur. There's always someone else controlling our fate. If it were just fact and skill that determined one's story, a lot of people would be dead."*

"I know that, Dustin." His voice still sounded troubled. *"That's the catch, though. We don't know for sure. Going into this, I'm the most ill-equipped to survive. It's been my history ever since I was brought to the Academy. I am not the Warrior I should be — the Warrior Ocean credits me to be. It's terrifying, Dustin. It's like going against the best archer in the kingdom while not knowing how to draw the string of your bow back or like facing a horde of monsters and not being strong enough to lift your sword. I'm scared, Dust. Unlike the other Warriors, I have a Mum waiting for me to come home and a sister I..."* He choked and looked away. Though he knew I could hear the tears in his voice, seeing them would be different. It was proof he was terrified. Proof he was younger than his companions. Proof he was weak.

I didn't see him that way. No. Arthur was untainted by war or hate — the only one from the six Warriors who had any kind of normal background. After all, he was still young — 15 years old — but expected to behave as a man twice his age.

"Only the innocent consider themselves inexperienced. Everyone else considers them privileged." Arthur looked at me, and I offered him a smile.

"Figured you'd say that, but it means I will die. Tell me: Is it a **privilege** *to fall while your friends stand?"*

"Arthur, it is a privilege to be where you're supposed to be. If it means falling for your country, your kingdom, and your king, so be it. Not even your worst enemy can fault that. Anyway, you ought not worry. If any danger comes, we will be by your side to see to it you get back to your Mum."

Arthur sighed and shook his head. *"How can you say it so easily? Neither of us has faced war, yet you're still better prepared for it."*

"Am I?" I asked, longing to lighten the course of the conversation.

Arthur raised a dark brow.

"When I stop moving, my knees shake."

Arthur paused then laughed at that. *"Aye, mine as well. Evelina would laugh at me."*

"On the contrary, Evelina would be terribly proud of you, and you know it. My only regret with leaving so secretly was she didn't get to know where you were going."

Arthur shrugged. *"Well, sisters tend to just **know**. I figured she knew something was happening. She held me a little tighter before I left."*

I smiled. *"You're lucky to have her."*

He glanced back at the Warriors and smiled. *"I'm lucky to have you, Dust. You're good company for this kind of stuff, y'know?"*

I snorted. *"Now, would anyone **else** in this group agree with that?"*

"I think they would, wholeheartedly. We're such a terrible group of misfits. You bring us all together. Without you... Well, I guess we'd all part ways. Cederic would go back to his mindless training to forget his mother's death. Egon, to his group of bandits. Woodruff would pick up his confounded pranks again, losing favor with our teachers at the Academy. Ocean would search on and on for the father who never loved her. Silas would pop back into his ever-silent shell and never speak for fear someone would notice his stutter and ask questions. As for me, I... Well, Dust... I would sit back in the

comfort of my home and never engage with the real world. Unfortunately, that's what being spoiled can do to a person." He sighed and took a breath. *"But with you, we are a company — not a random group of individuals, but a team. I believe you have the influence of a king before you've even become one."*

I stifled a blush after the compliment. It was too much praise for me to be comfortable, even from a friend. *"There is nothing left to do but thank you for such positive evaluations."* I smiled uncomfortably, and he laughed.

*"Oh, that's no bloody good. **I've** seen your face when the others haven't. Ocean and Woodruff believed you couldn't even blush. Now you have, and they're not here to see!"*

I suppose I could've found some humor in it, but you must remember I had been pushed and tricked into the base of the waterfall just yesterday. I was still nursing my pride. *"Oh, hush! If ever **they** hear about it, I shall never hear the end of it."*

"You certainly shall not!" Arthur cried with laughter.

I busied myself with looking ahead of us while he heaved a hearty laugh from his lungs. Ocean chimed in, after looking at the rain clouds. *"Looks like you lads will be getting a bath whether you want one or not."*

Arthur flipped around to plead his case. ***"I bathe!"***

Woodruff and Cederic laughed at that.

"Good for you," Egon spoke from behind. *"I suppose you're expecting a prize?"*

"She was j-j-just joking, Arthur," Silas said, looking up from his book and smiling.

"Aye," she said. *"We all could use another one, if you ask* me.*"*

"Well…" Woodruff spoke up, *"I project we can all go a whole three days more before we cause all the forest plants to die off from our smell."*

Ocean scoffed. *"You're disgusting!"*

"Yes," Cederic said. *"A bit uncalled for, don't you think?"*

"What are you reading now?" Arthur asked Silas.

Just as he opened his mouth to reply, Egon cut him off, commenting rather dryly: *"Don't ask."*

Arthur became annoyed and knitted his brows together in sudden passion. ***"Good heavens, Egon! Why ever not? I have already asked him. If you don't like it, you have the freedom to stop up your ears!"*** he bellowed.

Before Egon could conduct a proper retort, Silas answered him. *"It's about an orphan boy l-living on the streets of some southern city. It is a-a-amazing what these poor p-people must endure!"* He sighed. *"Reading is the only t-t-true way to experience things distant f-f-from you."*

"That's why I always tell Woodruff to read those love stories," Cederic said quietly, but we heard all the same.

I choked and believed everyone fell into a fit of laughter at my reaction.

"It's not true in the slightest!" Woodruff protested earnestly. Little good it did. His cheeks were flushed. *"I was fond of a certain librarian for a time,"* he added.

Although no one but I heard him, Egon found a way to say, *"Indeed, I have never seen an uglier person in **all** my existence."*

Woodruff had reached the end of his tolerance for such teasing. His head snapped up at full attention. He whistled his horse to a full run to catch up to Egon, who, upon hearing the rapid footsteps of four hooves behind him — and knowing who the rider may be and his temperament — took off ahead as well.

"They're going to wake the dead!" Ocean laughed.

*"And the **living**,"* I added. They were already too far ahead to be stopped, fading from view behind perhaps trees or brush. It was getting too dark to tell.

"I'm hungry," Arthur whined.

"We just ate," Silas reminded him, *"You m-more than a-a-anyone."*

"No, he's right." Ocean glanced at the sky. *"It's been some hours since we last stopped to eat. It's getting harder and harder to tell the passing of time the deeper we get into the forest."*

"We'll stop in a bit," I said distantly.

Cederic hummed his agreement. He'd noticed it, too.

"There's a lot of strange things about this forest. You get the feeling…" I paused. *"It's a bit unnatural."* I looked around me, aware of the wind and the chill it carried. The sky was covered by grey clouds. It was evening, but there was no telling just how late in the evening it was.

"Or you're all just paranoid and thinking like chil — "

"Hush." Cederic demanded, cutting Arthur short. *"Do you hear that?"*

It took a minute for my ears to hear anything but wind and the ring of Cederic's voice. After those things had cleared, the sound of moving water floated in.

A river. Somewhere ahead.

There was a steady clop of hooves as Woodruff and Egon rushed back onto the scene.

"Mates! Looks as if we're going to collide with a river!" Woodruff bellowed.

"Is it shallow enough to cross?" I asked as they reached us.

"Sure. It's mighty strong, though," Egon informed.

"You think the horses will have trouble?" Arthur looked anxious.

*"We're worried-we're worried about **you** being th-thrown downstream, my dear Arthur,"* Silas joked.

"I am worried about this cut those monsters gave me," I mused. *"Won't stop bleeding…"* It had opened again, sending red streaks down my arm.

"Here. Take this." Cederic threw a roll of cloth to bandage it.

I had run out of mine, bandaging cuts that probably weren't important. However, I had been a bit paranoid when we started. I caught the roll and thanked him.

It was such a pleasant evening—the kind you wished you could enjoy were it not for some other pressing matter which had to be dealt with immediately. As the river came in view through the grey tree trunks, I was sieged with the urge to slow down.

"Let's buggin' eat before we cross the river, eh?" Nobody grumbled, which I assumed was just as good as a "yes."

Eventually, we broke from the covering of the trees. There was finally nothing above but the sky. Ahead of us, the river roared its greeting. The openness of the riverbank was relieving. I even spotted a yellow flower hanging onto life in the chilly weather.

The horses were a bit closer to the forest than we were. I wanted us to be closer to the river because, on the bank, I could pretend we were next to an ocean and not simply about to cross a river into more woods. I had sailed an ocean only once. I'd never experienced something more frightening and beautiful at the same time.

"I wish we had music," Cederic admitted as I handed out the food.

"Indeed. It's so quiet out here," Silas added.

It occurred to me that the silence had been the very thing I was enjoying.

"Dust, did you bring your chalemeau?" Arthur asked.

He was sitting in the dirt along with Woodruff and me. Ocean was stroking her horse closer to the forest but still within earshot. Silas, Egon, and Cederic had chosen to stand.

"I forgot," I said as I bit into a cold biscuit. Besides, its shrill sound in this forest may create problems for us.

"Oy. Well, if we can't hear Dustin play, we might as well hear one of Woodruff's stories, should we not?" Arthur suggested.

*"Ohhh, let's **not**,"* Ocean protested.

We all shushed her, and Woodruff stood—his red hair the only thing clearly visible in the dark. He started as if he'd simply been waiting for one of us to ask.

"Once upon a time…"

Egon snorted. *"What kind of bloody introduction is **that**?"*

"Shut it, Egon. It's b-b-beautiful, Woodruff. Go on," Silas encouraged.

Woodruff began again, perhaps to irritate Egon a tad.

"Once upon a time, there was an elderly man named Simon who decided being stuffed up in one's home as long as he had been was rather unhealthy for the soul. So, he left the house to take on some exercise in a brief stroll. Upon taking a couple of steps outside his home, he was hit with such a chill, he wondered vehemently, "Why, it is freezing! I shall surely die out here!" Simon meant to head back towards his door, but just then, a snowstorm overtook him, and he couldn't find what was where. He stumbled along like a drunken man in the night…"

Snickering among the group had to be quieted before Woodruff could continue.

"Simon began to weep, and his wailing grew so loud, the neighbors could no longer ignore him. The ones to the right of him came out

and tried to console him. 'Snow! Snow is everywhere!' Simon cried. 'Can you not see it, my friends?' 'Nonsense, nonsense,' they said. 'It's the middle of July!' When they could do nothing to console him, they left him to his wailing. He took one step after another, all alone. The snow fell with more anger than ever. Meanwhile, the occupants of the house on the left stood watching from the windows as Simon stood wailing in fear — right outside his own door. They were silent until one of the lads spoke up. 'Should we tell him he's sleepwalking again, father?'"

Woodruff's accents and voices made the whole thing so much more wonderful. I **had** to laugh along with the rest of the group — Ocean excluded. I never knew how Ocean never found much humor in these stories.

"You try so hard to be funny. You're not funny," Cederic chuckled.

Woodruff pretended to be hurt.

"That's what's so funny about it, mate," Arthur said.

Ocean was still by her horse. *"It's not funny."*

"How's that, Ocean? Give us some explanation as to why you hate it, or we will be convinced you are jealous for attention," Egon teased.

I stood, hearing Ocean start up behind me.

"What's so funny about an elderly man being made a fool for sleepwalking?" she pressed.

I walked away towards the river. Egon was right about it being strong. I underestimated it by gingerly putting my hand in. The water slapped hard against it. *It's not too deep. It should be okay to cross, though it is strong. Perhaps there was a waterfall nearby…* The trees on the other side of the river awaited us, looking the same as the ones behind. We were trapped in a never-ending forest, on our way to a dead city. That idea kept hitting me in waves.

My delight with Rosetta answering my letter came back with force. She seemed so calm, yet I knew how hard it must be to live in her world. **Any** world with Lord Monté was a difficult one, indeed.

Suddenly, Cederic was at my side. I hadn't heard him approach. *"If I may ask, what are you thinking about, Prince Dustin?"*

"A woman." Through my peripheral vision, I saw a slight smile cross the man's face. The other Warriors would have laughed or made a scene of it, but this man seemed to know things before they were said and reacted as such.

*"They **do** demand space in our thoughts, don't they?"*

I smiled. *"Yes."*

"Any second thoughts about this?" he asked knowingly.

"Many." I let out a half-laugh. *"I must, though. If I do **anything** in life, it must be this."*

"So, you are resigned?"

"Pretty much."

It was his turn to laugh. *"Hard decisions are often the most fruitful ones."*

"I hope so, my friend."

"What about this river?" he asked, hunkering down and feeling the flow. *"Ha! This is far too deep to cross. I do not know what Woodruff and Egon were thinking."* He called to them. As they neared, he said, *"You two are **insane**, thinking we can cross here! We'll need to go down the bank a-ways!"*

"Really? I just felt it and thought it would be alright," I said, crouching and feeling the same as he had. It **was** deep. In fact, **much deeper** than it had been just moments before.

Something in the water caught my eye. A white object floated slowly beneath where my hand was. It was the color of milk or bone. Such an unnatural color. A chill went up my spine.

It was an eye.

As I yanked my hand out of the water, something cold and slimy grabbed hold of me. Crouched as I was, I had little balance to speak of and plunged headfirst into the freezing water.

Something—some **thing**—had me. I wanted to scream but knew I couldn't. I jerked against the slimy thing's hold to pull it off my arm, but its grip was too firm. My mouth opened in a panic, and water began to fill my lungs. It was the worst kind of claustrophobia, and I was quickly losing my mind. Kicking was useless, but I tried, nonetheless. I tried so desperately until all my strength was gone. My lungs were burning with the foreign liquid taking up space.

Something else grabbed my other arm, jerking me upwards. The thing in the water still had its hold on me, though, and a tug-of-war ensued, inciting pain in both arms. I needed to breathe bloody air, or I was going to pass out. Something dark passed in front of me and advanced towards my face. It looked like a tentacle or limb of some sort. It darted at me, and I wanted to stop it, but my arms were continuing to be yanked…

I was fading to black.

Three seconds…

Two seconds…

One…

The thing in the water let go. It jerked back as if it'd been hurt. Whatever was pulling my other arm heaved me up, and I suddenly felt cool air on my skin. It began to cut through the water in my lungs, causing me to gasp violently.

Ocean had my arm. I could hear Ego shouting somewhere off to my left.

I was coughing and wheezing, yet through it all, I'd managed to weakly say — through rather erroneous thinking — "Or'geth. It's an Or'geth."

"Yep," Ocean confirmed.

The danger had already shifted to the Warriors. Storytime over, smiles gone. I spotted Egon, Woodruff, and Silas on the bank to my left, Requisites in hand. Just then, the monster burst from the water. My whole back got sprayed, and I quickly turned.

White eyes without pupils scanned the bank where we tiny people stood. Twelve — maybe 15 feet into the air it rose, and some of it was still in the water. Its teeth were black needles that held a constant snarl. Its tentacles swung about, the same type of needles on the ends of them.

Goodness! Had that been coming for my face?!

"Prince Dustin, it would be wise to head further up the bank," Ocean suggested.

"Yeah. Don't look it in the eye," I said while still staring at the Or'geth. I tore my gaze away. Heading up the bank, I watched as Silas ducked underneath a tentacle, slicing with one of his knives as it came back across. It came to me then. Or'geths were merely legend. There was only **one** known way to injure them.

"Give Arthur a clear shot at it!" Cederic shouted, stabbing two shurikens into a tentacle and backing away from it. He had read my mind.

Woodruff cut through an entire tentacle with his ax. The Or'geth seemed to quiver when he did that. The beast roared, swinging its head down at Egon. He managed to jump back from it.

"It's low! It's low! Sh-shoot it now, Arthur!" Silas screamed.

Arthur was ten or so paces to my right. He held his readied bow and arrow in shaking hands. He then pulled back on the string, aimed, and prepared to shoot.

"Shoot now, Arthur!" Cederic cried.

I saw Arthur's trembling hands. I saw how big his eyes were — how they were glazed over. It seemed like hours, but it was only seconds that passed without event. He wasn't going to shoot. Right now, when we **needed** his talents, fear had its grip on him.

"Cederic!" I called to him. *"It's got to be you!"*

Cederic muttered something under his breath. Woodruff looked quickly at Arthur—no doubt to see why no shot was coming—got knocked down by the beast. Ocean made it to him just in time to cut back the tentacle that tried to sting him.

Cederic backed up a couple of steps and yelled an order to his companions. *"Get his head down again!"* He closed one eye, estimating the distance and angle. He extracted not one, but three shurikens from his case.

Ambitious little bugger, I thought. A shuriken was too small to affect this massive creature, but Arthur was incapacitated at the moment.

"Get its head down!" I cried impatiently to the others. I knew they were trying. I had to resist the urge to run out there with them.

Woodruff regained his footing, only to be knocked over again. Silas was tied up with fighting back a tentacle, and Egon was shouting something to Ocean from across the bank, but Ocean did not respond.

A tentacle from the right blindsided Silas, knocking him down and forcing him to fight from the ground. Water sprayed everywhere, splashing up and onto the bank. It was as if the tentacles simply appeared from thin air, from every direction. Ocean kept moving closer to it, and I heard Egon shouting something at her again. She charged straight at its body.

"What on earth…?" I moaned, heart throbbing.

She ran straight at its heart. No less than four tentacles dashed in to stop her. They would be too late.

The creature brought its head down. At the same time, Cederic released his shurikens. Ocean made eye contact with the Or'geth and froze for just a fraction of a second. Two tentacles came rushing in, shocking her. She went limp just as the shurikens lodged in the creature's right eye, the space between, and the left eye. She fell just as the Or'geth let out a gurgled scream.

Thankfully, I was wrong: the shurikens did enough damage. I threw my hands up, covered my ears, fell to the bank's ground, and screamed at the pain the ringing sound was doing to my eardrums.

Then, the earth shook. Just as quickly as it had come, the creature slunk back into the water. His presence—though still very much occupying our thoughts—faded into the evening dusk.

"Ocean!" I spotted her, still unconscious near the river's edge.

Silas and Egon made it to her first, followed by Woodruff, Cederic, and I.

"She's breathing, right?" I asked Egon when I reached them.

"Well, how should I know? Silas is checking!" he snapped from on his knees.

Silas lifted Ocean's head and placed two fingers on her neck. *"Yeah,"* he said, letting out a huge sigh of relief. *"She's still b-b-b-bloody b-b-b-breathing."*

We all took a moment to calm ourselves and began to breathe normally again.

*"I told her we should go **together**!"* Egon was angry.

"Who even c- even cares?"

"Besides, you were too far away to help," Cederic added with a hint of irritation.

Ocean stirred. Her eyes twitched and then snapped open. Feeling so many people around her, she impulsively shoved her forearm into Silas' throat. Jerking back, he found his voice quickly. *"It's just m-me!"*

She winced at him, looking guilty. *"Oh…"* She then squeezed her eyes shut.

"You got stung," I said. Not because it was at all intelligent or informative. I just felt the need — after such overwhelming relief — to say **something** to her.

Sitting up, she rightfully asked, *"Is it gone?"*

"Yeah," I said.

She tried to stand, but it was obvious she was holding back a cry of pain. Cederic ordered her to be still. Silas agreed, and she sat back down. She closed her eyes, focusing on her breathing so intently, I was sure she was going to stop breathing altogether.

When she opened her eyes, she immediately asked, *"Where's Arthur?"*

The memory of the scene moments earlier slapped me like the tide coming in. I realized Arthur wasn't standing around Ocean with the rest of us. He was higher up the bank, still in the same spot he'd been in during the fight. His bow was dropped at his side, and he was staring at it like it had let him down. *Like it had betrayed him somehow…*

He sensed our stares, and his head came up. At the very sight of us, he went red around the ears. He dropped his head again. For just a moment, I thought he might cry.

"Come over here with us, Arthur," Cederic gently coaxed.

He looked like he just might do so until he seemed to buckle as he bit his lip and shook his head.

"Now," Cederic said sharply. The hair on the back of my neck stood at his tone. Obviously, Arthur could not refuse him this time. He muttered something to himself under his breath and walked towards us.

I was still worried about Ocean. She winced virtually every time she blinked, but Silas was at her side and seemed attentive. I found my eyes inexplicably drawn to Cederic and the posture he had taken: hands behind his back, watching the sky, and then watching Arthur approach.

When Arthur reached us, Cederic stared at him for a solid minute. We all watched the scene before us intently. I thought he was deciding what to say, but once he started, it seemed he had little doubt.

"Draw your arrow back on your string," he commanded.

Arthur pressed his lips together. *"It's no use,"* he muttered.

Cederic ignored him. *"Draw your arrow back on the string,"* he repeated a bit more firmly.

With a careless attitude, Arthur did as Cederic said.

"Shoot that tree trunk over there."

Arthur followed Cederic's pointing finger, lifted his bow, and, with the arrow already nocked, aimed, pulled, and released it. In the dead silence, it whistled through the air, embedding itself in the selected tree trunk with a 'thunk.' He dropped his bow to his side again, but Cederic wasn't done.

"Shoot one of its branches."

Arthur gritted his teeth but lifted his bow anyway and did it again, lodging an arrow in a skinny branch closer to the top of the tree.

"I'm going to throw a shuriken," Cederic continued before the last arrow had even hit its mark. *"Shoot it out of the air."*

"Why?"

"Because I told you to." He threw it when Arthur wasn't even ready.

Arthur raised his bow, barely aimed, and shot the shuriken out of the air. The heavy metal halted its flight up and sideways, falling hastily and heavily to the ground.

Cederic then extracted three more and showed them to Arthur. *"I'm going to throw three now — "*

"It doesn't matter how many you throw, they aren't living targets," Arthur exploded, face red. *"Everybody who saw what happened now knows I'm bloody useless when it comes to those!"*

Cederic threw all three anyway. Cursing, Arthur reacted quickly. He extracted three arrows at once from his quiver with speed I couldn't understand. All three flew through the air and clattered — one against each of Cederic's shurikens. The arrows fell to the ground with more grace than the shurikens, which slammed into the bank like rocks.

"Nobody thinks you're useless. Not one of these Warriors is surprised by what you did, so don't blame us. Blame yourself."

"I can't shoot when it matters," he almost whined.

"Then climb on your ruddy horse and leave."

Arthur hesitated. *"What?!"*

Cederic was one who despised repeating himself. *"You heard me. Climb on your ruddy horse and **leave**."*

Again, Arthur hesitated.

"The only person you're letting down by not shooting is yourself, Arthur."

"What if it doesn't work? What if I miss? What if I let everybody down?

*"People remember **effort**. They remember **attempts**. They remember people who **tried**, whether they succeeded or not. They don't remember ideas, dreams, or intentions that never turn into*

something else." Finished with what he needed to say, he turned to **me**. *"Dustin?"*

I perked up. After that speech, how could I not? *"Yes?"*

"We cannot stay here. Though powerful weapons, shurikens cannot kill an Or'geth. It will be back, and it will be angry."

"Right," I said. It was time to take some action. *"Come on, lads. Help Ocean onto your horse, Silas, and let's cross this river."* As we did, Arthur was as quiet as I had ever seen him. We made it across without meeting the cursed Or'geth again. Was it luck? I had a hard time believing that.

I had no hand on the reins in this forest. Whatever magic bewitched it was in full control. I had an uncomfortable feeling that if the monster hadn't appeared, there would've been some other incident the forest had in mind for its visitors. 'Luck' was a useless word here.

By the time it was dark and time for us to stop, I was damp and exhausted. Cederic instructed me to stay back while the others got wood for a fire. Ocean stayed with me, and I told her to sit while I got her cot from the bundle of her horse.

She watched me without saying a word for a little while. I glanced at her after a couple of minutes and seen she was trying not to wince in pain.

"Still hurts?" I asked in the dark. I laid out her cot and blanket.

She sighed. *"A little. My head still stings a bit. It's not bad. It'll wear off."* I laughed at her, causing her to lower her black brows. *"What's funny?"*

*"I don't know if spending this much time with the boys is good for you, Ocean. What kind of answer is **that**?"*

She smiled. *"No use whining when you're traveling with a bunch of taciturn dimwits!"*

I raised my blonde brows in mock surprise. *"'Taciturn dimwits,' you say? We should have thrown you in the river while we had the chance."*

She laughed as I went to start grabbing the others' cots. She then sat on hers. *"Anyway, I'm glad I'm here with you guys and not back there."* She said the words to my back because I was turned away, trying to get Woodruff's cot off his horse.

The statement made me stop and answer seriously. *"This journey was not designed as a means of escape for you, Ocean."*

"I know...but it is."

Holding the cot in my hands, I walked over and laid it next to hers. *"You need to stop running from your childhood."*

"Yeah, sure," she said distantly.

I stopped what I was doing to look at her. *"No. I'm **serious**, Ocean. Don't let the past change who you are."*

"I'm not," she denied quietly.

*"You most certainly are, Miss Bravo, and it's my job to stop you from doing it. If you need a hug, I'll give you one. If you need to cry, fine. Do **something** instead of just hiding behind those walls of yours. Deal?"*

She sighed and shrugged. *"Deal."* She pulled her blanket up and laid down.

We stretched the silence to let nature speak. I jumped at the snapping of a branch, then realized I'd stepped on it.

"Do you mind if I ask you something?" I asked on my third trip for the third cot.

"That's what I love about you, Dust. You go from being as nosy as a newsmonger to a polite little gentleman." Her voice was muffled by her blanket and the cloak she used as a pillow. *"'Do you mind if I ask you something?'"* she repeated humorously. *"It seems as if I have no choice but to answer in the affirmative."*

I shrugged shyly and laid down another cot. *"So… I was going to ask… When did you and Silas… Y'know… When did **this** happen?"*

She sat back up. ***"Excuse me?"***

I blushed. *"The thing you said yesterday…Silas' blushing. When did it start?"*

I suppose it was now Ocean's turn to laugh at me, which she did thoroughly. She only stopped because it made her wince when she laughed too hard. *"What on **earth** do you mean by that?!"*

"Well, it just looked like… I thought the two of you were… It seemed…" The more I rambled almost incoherently, the more she laughed. I blushed because I sounded ridiculous. *"Never mind, then. Fine. Keep your secrets. I just thought there was something there,"* I said, finally piecing together a sentence that didn't sound preposterous.

*"No, Dustin. I'm afraid it isn't **that**. My, my, my…Nothing quite so **funny**!"* she said between laughs.

I waited for her to quiet. Waited for things to grow serious. *"Then, what is it?"*

She sighed and shook her head slowly. *"Silas told me how he got his stutter."*

I paused. We'd known Silas for years. None of us knew what happened to him to cause his stuttering. He would never tell, as it was a sore spot for him, so we didn't push. He never told…but **now** he had.

"Honest to God?" I needed to know she wasn't pulling me a stiff one.

She nodded the affirmative.

"Egon owes me."

"What?!"

"Egon owes me. I told him if Silas told anyone about his stutter, it'd be you. Females just have the right touch. He didn't believe me."

*"So, you **betted** on it?"* she asked.

I nodded, and she rolled her eyes.

"So… Was it like a secret thing, or can you tell?"

*"I think he meant for me **not** to tell."*

"Oh. Okay. That's understandable." I set my cot down and had a seat.

She laid back down, and things grew quiet. I tapped my finger against my calf, counting the seconds…minutes… My curiosity got the best of me.

I broke through the silence. *"Is it like **secret-secret,** or is it just…secret?"*

Ocean didn't even move. She kept staring up at the night sky. *"Yeah, it's pretty **secret-secret.**"* I heard the smile in her voice.

"Oh. Okay." Point made. She wasn't telling.

The guys returned a couple of minutes later, leaving me to wonder what the secret was.

20: ROSETTA KELLINA MABEL

Unsafe are the sewn-closed lips
Which never speak a word.
Not to poverty, not to plenty,
Not too little, not too many.
The same consequences befall the passive
As they do the outspoken.

I was excited to write the mystery person—the self-proclaimed 'Geoff'—again. His words excited me. He fascinated me to no end, almost as if I liked him simply because I didn't know who he was. My interest seemed to grow more and more with each letter I sent.

As I entered the castle, I decided I would tell Geoff about Ferrando and Peter. As far as I knew, the man behind the letters was either playing a cruel joke or meant what he said. If it was the former, I doubt he'd take much interest in my acquaintance with peasants. If it was, indeed, the latter, it might be time I told someone about the two…even if it was someone quite the distance away.

Initially, the visit with Peter was intended to be a "drop-off." I'd hand over the pot of soup, exchange a few pleasantries, and then leave. That was not to be. Although his overprotective, hard-headed bodyguard, Ferrando, tried to prove difficult, in the end, Peter enjoyed the soup, but he enjoyed giving some to his mother even more.

When his mother moved, moaned, and rolled in response to the yummy goodness of the soup, Peter's expression made the moment well worth it. After that, Ferrando didn't look at me like I was a witch meant to be burned at the stake.

I was still raw about having to stoop so low. Befriending two peasants was not my original plan, but I had no choice but to swallow my pride. Peter needed help. Whether he liked it or not, he couldn't get that help from Ferrando. I satisfied myself with the thought that it was simply my duty to do so and lingered no more on the matter.

I made it to my bedroom door without disturbing a soul. I placed my ear against it and noticed it was terribly quiet on the other side. I opened the door cautiously…

Squawks of all sorts erupted from my bedroom wardrobe, where I'd stuffed the lot earlier.

"Shh! Shut up!" I whispered harshly as I threw open the door. My berating did little to quiet them. They continued their squawking until they had fully stretched their cramped wings. They then turned to look at me, each cocking their head from side-to-side in wonder.

"Of course, I'm going to write him!" I proclaimed—rather idiotically, I must add. *"I have to ask him how, in anyone's name, he knew I slept with a pillow over my head. It's kinda alarming he would know such things."*

Why am I having full-blown, one-sided conversations with pigeons? Did I expect them to vocalize, "Okay. We'll wait"? I laughed at myself.

I removed my ink and paper from underneath my bed and took to writing about the day's events and asking way too many questions than was polite. Who cared? Frankly, I didn't know him well enough to be concerned about his feelings, nor he concerned about mine—though he seemed to know **me** well enough...

I finished the letter and was putting the last cylinder in the last pair of talons when someone knocked on my door. Before I could do much, the door to my bedroom flew open, and in came Kip.

*"Where have **you** been all day? I've been trying desperately to find you. I needed to tell you how much of an **imbecile** you are for talking about Lydia and Mack in such a manner!"*

Now was not the time to look startled. Too late.

*"What on earth are all these **birds** doing in here? I mean, I know you like them well enough, but they've always stayed on the terrace as far as I was concerned,"* Kip stated matter-of-factly.

I stood, commanding my body not to shake. *"It's good to try new things. The birds need company as well as Lydia. What is it that's bothering you?"*

"You haven't heard?"

*"About bloody **what**?"* I asked irritably.

"The Lord Monté you speak so wonderfully of has taken note of you. Chancellor Kenneth says it's not a rumor. You prance around the castle like you own it. Don't you think it would've drawn attention?"

My stomach twisted until it hurt. *"I wasn't aware I was doing anything wrong,"* I said cautiously — willing her not to look too closely at the pigeons…willing her not to notice the cylinders.

"Well, Chancellor Kenneth has…'spoken' of you in the Lord's presence. If I were you, I'd tread carefully on what I said from this point forward."

I lowered my brows at her. *"I'll make sure to thank the Chancellor when I see him,"* I stated dryly. *"When did the Lord take any note of others, anyway?"*

"Starting now. As well, the Chancellor has drawn a card, so you can no longer disgrace him as you did in the library. If you misbehave, he has the power to bring it up before the Lord. The Lord may not be as pleased with your behavior as you are."

*"You know about **that**?"* I asked — referring to the events in the library.

"Yes, and if you're not careful, the Lord Monté will hear of this, too. Please, for all our sakes, accept Kenneth's attention and keep your mouth shut about the Lord for once. You may want to be seen, but I do not," she said hurriedly and quietly.

I was shocked into silence. For once, I had no retort.

Kip shook her head quickly and backed away. *"I just wanted you to know for **your** sake. We all wanted you to know."*

After she left, I was left to ponder nervously well into the night about what it all meant.

How in the world was I going to shut my mouth?

21: DUSTIN ELRIC CARPENTER

I rode a softer horse;
You rode a hard one.
I try, but not so hard…
You travel farther.

I could tell by the frequent flapping of wings overhead that the pigeons wanted to deliver something. I was delighted to know she had written me back again. Honestly, I was such a dunce in my first letter, I thought she wouldn't write me back at all. I suppose I have a little charm somewhere in me…

It's always hard to step away from the group. This time, however, it was near impossible. As much as the Warriors wanted to guarantee my safety, **I** wanted to read a love letter in private.

"Egon, I'll be back in a minute. I've got to walk my horse a bit and get him stretched. I'd also like to relieve myself before the morning's through." My tone was frustrated because I was, indeed, just that. Ocean seemed to notice.

"Let him go," she said. *"At least if he dies, we'll all rest well knowing it was in the pleasure of him relieving himself."*

If I hadn't been so excited about getting away, I would've told her to shut her little pie hole. The reality was quite the contrary. I smiled and walked Julius away from the group and on towards the enchanted woods. "Should've known she'd try to get me back for last night." I shook my head. "I should've known."

I welcomed the pigeons as they swooped down. *"Well, hello to you, mates! Pleasure seeing you again!"* I rubbed the back of my neck. *"A **real** pleasure."*

As I unhooked their cylinders, each seemingly squawked an appreciative, *"Thank you!"* I grinned and shook my head. Almost in unison, they took flight, and I settled on opening each cylinder, preparing to organize the papers. Once that task was complete, I read the following words:

<div align="center">~~~~~~~~~~</div>

Geoff,
Thank you for giving me your name, or most likely a name to call
you by while I do not know your real one. Do you write often?
Writing me a letter at such a random time is strange.
I know you can't answer this confusion, so I won't press.
Stranger still is the way you speak. To not fear the Lord, whether
you are Jocunder or not, is foolish. (Forgive me for being so harsh.)
He does not allow rebels or much of anything else,
and he is quite ferocious.

N.D.M.

I do not know him personally,
but I have seen him and heard the tales.
I suppose I haven't told you about the Battle. The Lord's cruel joke
on us. A battle for food. Can you imagine that? Children fighting for
food? I could pretend it wasn't concerning
(if I hadn't had to watch it for myself).
I have a friend named Lydia, and I met a boy at the Battle yesterday,
whose name is Peter. He is eleven. He still had to fight, and he would
be dead were it not for his guardian. Peter's sweet, though I cannot
say the same for his guardian, Ferrando.
I can see the arena they built from my balcony. I'm glad I sleep with
the pillow over my head (how on earth did you know that?), as the
ring of hammer to nail has been deafening the last few days.
The arena is my and all of Jocund's view.
As of late, there have been no clouds in sight, no rain. The 17 flags of
Jocund don't fly; they hang limp. Nobody cares, as no one has looked
at them in years. People in Jocund are broken. They all stand outside
the arena with candles lit while the people within fight. When
someone dies, it is reported, and the loved ones of the dead blow out
their candle. The Battle of Bloodshed (such a sick name by a sick
man) will be held again in a couple of days.
I know I told you not to come, but I hope you're not foolish and just
incredibly brave. If you're coming, please come soon.

Your Dearest Ro
P.S. I'm praying this is not a prank of some sort.
I find you very agreeable.

<div align="center">~~~~~~~~~~</div>

There was no way to describe the way I felt, other than **absolutely thrilled!** Although Rosetta still seemed pretty antsy about my resolve to save her, it was of little concern at the moment. Simply her continuing to write, ask me questions, and tell me thing goings-on in Jocund was enough. I quickly wrote another letter to send later tonight because daylight was approaching, and then headed back towards the group.

254

I stumbled into camp unaware and certainly without caution. My mistake was being too comfortable with my companions. They were nowhere to be found.

The horses stood lazily, chewing what little grass was close, kicking up dust for entertainment periodically. Nothing moved. The fire had long since been extinguished. The forest was silent. I knew better than to call out the Warriors' names, yet their disappearance meant danger. Surely, I was in the thick of it now.

Should've known the Or'geth was setting us up, I mused darkly. I approached Julius slowly and grabbed my sword.

I only had myself to blame. Had I been paying any mind early on, I would've noticed the oddities from afar and found a safe way to approach. Since I hadn't, if what the Warriors had hidden from was nearby — which it most likely was — it and my companions would've already seen me.

"Bloody rosebushes," I muttered.

The first one came from the sky…

22: ARCHIE COCKBURN

Cling to it too much,
And destiny will take it away…

I despise walking. It drives me utterly insane — not because of the loss of stamina after being at it for four hours, but rather its pattern. Patterns make me sick, yet **most** things consist of them.

Walking is one foot in front, then the other.

Smiling is a lift of both ends of your lips.

Relationships are letting another speak before you. Consideration.

You see? Those things don't change. Ever. No matter how you do them, when you do them, or who you do them with, they stay the same. Why am I telling you this? Because right now, I'm sick of them **all**.

The cold wind was a constant reminder, making sure to slap me in the face every so often with a whispered, *"You're not going to make it."*

"Well, you're bloody right," I would mutter to it deliriously. *"Maybe you should help."*

The wind wouldn't say anything then, as if it didn't like the idea of helping me survive long enough to get to Haestingas. Perhaps it didn't know how. Whatever the reason, it wouldn't answer, and I refused to address its silence. When it blew, I shivered. When it was still, I thrived.

The line of communication between Mallory and me had failed. Whenever we did speak, it was laden with bitter words and curses. Neither of us wanted to be reminded that we were probably going to die. So, instead, we reminded ourselves of nothing at all. We were quiet so as not to rub our inner toxic moods on one another and cause what was sure to be a brutal, to-the-death fight between two brothers.

Still, I made sure to point out the slip-up with not keeping track of the food at every given opportunity. It was only a fair share of what he'd given me all my life.

What's funny is Mallory didn't make any moves to defend himself. Perhaps he felt he shouldn't have to, given my track record. Either way, it infuriated me even more, and we resolved to basically ignore each other's existence…although it didn't work well.

Suddenly, Mal stopped dead in his tracks a couple steps ahead of me. *"Did you hear that?"* he asked — looking around like a man who'd been scared half to death.

"Nobody can hear a thing over your stomping."

He paid my newest bitter statement little mind. *"Get down. Hide."* He scrambled off and away from the area where we'd been standing. He took to hiding behind the thickest tree trunk he could find.

I followed his movements with my eyes but didn't budge. I strained my ears to hear whatever it was that caused Mal to freak out. *"I don't hear a thing,"* I said with an attitude.

Without peeking around the trunk of the tree, he called to me in a harsh whisper, ***"Move your bloody feet, brother!"***

I nonchalantly moved towards him and had just made it around a different tree trunk when someone's footsteps became perfectly audible. As a matter of fact, it was several pairs of footsteps.

"It would help if you told us something, sweetie," a deep voice said. A familiar one. *"Do you have **any** idea where they're headed?"*

"No," came the response with a sniffle. That voice, I knew well.

"Cecilly?" I mouthed in silent shock. Peeking around the tree trunk — to Mallory's apparent dismay — I saw her walking where we had just been, next to her father.

He was a big man who looked frustrated with her. *"Geoff said you talked to him before he left…"*

I cursed under my breath.

"I did, father. He never told me where he was headed," she answered, paying her father little mind.

"If he had, would you tell me?"

I clenched my fists at the question.

The answer came quickly, without any form of hesitation: *"No."*

Her father sighed and stopped walking. As he looked down at his stubborn daughter, he said, *"We can't help them, Cecilly, if you do not tell us where they went."*

She met his eyes, saying confidently (for her age), *"You cannot help them at all. Not anymore. They're safer out here somewhere than they are with you. I know you think Archie was insane to do what he did, but he was only mad **after** what he'd done."* Tears sprung to her eyes. *"If I could just see him again, tell him everything is alright..."*

*"It would be a **lie**!"* her father cut in sharply. *"A bloody lie, at that. I love Archie same as you, but he didn't think this through. You were wrong to keep this from me, and Geoff was right to tell me. The best thing you can do for Archie now is pray The Rank doesn't find him before I do. The **worst** punishment I'd give him is the **best** they would."*

Cecil let a tear roll down her cheek. Her father saw and put his arms around her in a loving, fatherly embrace. *"Don't cry. We'll find them. C'mon."*

Then, they were gone.

Not realizing I had held them in place so long, I unclenched my fists and felt pain where my nails had bit into my palm. Cecil had been so close, and now, she was gone. Why did I have to see her again? I'd actually grown to dislike the mere mention of her name in my head after her betrayal. Then, she shows up, and I learn it wasn't **her** betrayal at all.

I cursed Geoff thoroughly. Thanks to him, Mallory and I were probably going to die of starvation soon. *I truly owed him one…*

Mal moved out from behind his tree after a couple of minutes, and so did I. We moved on in silence until he broke it. *"Good seeing your bloody lover, I would guess. I'm just glad the little twit can keep a secret,"* he mocked.

I balled my fist and thought about hitting him. How sweet it would feel to land one good blow. Yes, it would be wonderful!

Either he read my thoughts or somehow saw my balled-up fist. *"Don't do it, boy. I've had hard enough a day as it is."*

***"Yours? Yours** has been hard? **You're** the one who got us here, you rodent! **You** set our destination. **You** called the shots. As far as I'm concerned, you're leading us straight to Hell!"*

"Oh well, that's just lovely. You apparently had no choice, huh? You're here because I dragged you by your hair, eh? Tell it to the devil, you hideous murderer. Tell it to the devil." He looked me over with such disgust, you would've thought we weren't related or even acquainted in the slightest.

"I never wanted to kill our parents! It was your idea! Yours!" I screamed.

"Having second thoughts, aren't you? Don't come crying to me like a bloody baby."

My anger knew no bounds at that point. ***"You're the bloody baby! You couldn't even kill them without me!"*** I yelled angrily.

Mallory shushed me and looked around. *"Do you want your girl to hear you screaming like the fool you are? If you've got any sense left at all, you'd stop now and shut up."*

*"Just tell me this: Why did **you** need **me**?"*

He turned and shot me a dirty look. *"I didn't **need** you; I **wanted** you."*

I stared at his back as he walked ahead.

*"You wanted me to have **murder** hanging over my head?!"*

I heard him snort loudly. *"Just tell **me** this: How does Cecilly deal with you and your questions?"*

"She loves me," I bragged.

"'Cause she didn't tell on you? 'Cause she cried about you? No one loves a murderer, brother. Nobody."

*"No, Mallory. No one loves **you**."*

He paid me little mind and just kept walking. Could I ever get under his skin? I began to shake with what I thought was just anger. I soon realized it was a mixture of that and hunger.

"If we make it to Haestingas, brother, I am leaving you. I would be better on my own than stuck with you," I chided.

"Ha! You think you'd survive without me?" he asked simply, knowing I would know better than to verbalize the word 'yes.' Mal had always been the one I truly leaned on. I could threaten him all day, but whether I'd go through with it was the real question.

I wanted to say something. I grasped for straws, but fate didn't want me to give voice to my thoughts. Instead, I felt a ripping in my stomach, which can only be described as severe hunger pains. It'd been two full days without food, and my body couldn't disguise its need any longer. I cried out where I stood and bent over.

Mallory was at my side in seconds. *"What the heck is the matter?"*

"My…stomach…feels…horrible." I dry-heaved into the dirt, unable to bring up anything. When I stopped, Mal patted my back in the most compassionate way he could.

"Probably for the best, nothing came up. Someone would've smelt it and discovered where we'd been."

Was that his way of saying we were starving, yet even **that** wasn't our biggest problem? Hooray.

The hunger pains didn't stop; they went on all day. If Mallory was feeling them, too, he made no outward sign.

I dry-heaved my way to Haestingas. I dry-heaved myself to sleep. Even my dreams depressed me because even there, the hunger pains continued and served as a vague but pressing reminder of my sorry life. At least in my dream, the pains were just a dream. It wasn't to be the same when I awoke.

There are times when the comforting smell of bliss cannot last long enough—when the beautiful thing called 'silence' presses ever softly and for a moment…just a moment…all is well. Somewhere during that stage of sleep and consciousness, the latter made an important point.

Wait. Shouldn't Mallory have awakened me by now? He always had… Maybe my mood towards him had changed his mind. Maybe he let me sleep late in an attempt not to have to speak to me.

When I opened my eyes fully, the world seemed brighter, as did my thoughts. I had a positive attitude about making it to Haestingas because I knew if I didn't, we weren't going to make it. If I didn't try, we would die of starvation out here in the middle of nowhere. The horrid sense of determination fueled me to sit up and address my brother, who turned out to be an **empty** spot beside me.

Confused, I stood shakily and looked around. I rubbed my sleep-deprived eyes ferociously and searched madly for what was not there.

Where could he have gone? Had he left me? Would he do that to me?

Cursing repeatedly, I looked all around me until my neck hurt from swiveling. I saw nothing but bloody tree after bloody tree.

Slowly at first, I ran through the trees. My eyes searched every inch of the forest before me. I grew scared. No, not scared; **frightened beyond comprehension.** The kind of frightened that can't believe it is in this situation, minutes to hours after it's happened.

He left me. He left me. He left me.

The words were a cursed drumbeat in my head. I felt the saltiness of tears fall into my mouth. Trees passed me. No: I passed them, but it didn't feel like it. It felt like everything in the world was moving but me. I was terribly still.

Sleep had robbed me from hearing Mallory leave. Sleep had robbed me of my awareness. I wished then that sleep was tangible so I could break it in half. I wished I could…

I wished…

I felt a branch slap me, somewhere in another place. Somewhere in another lifetime. I was so completely lost to this life, I tripped over a twig I should have seen and fell. I almost swallowed a broken leaf, spitting it out before I erroneously consumed it. My eyes burned. My soul burned. I still hadn't seen the worst of it.

Fate wanted me to slow down. To **look**. To see…

I saw feet. They hung limply in the air next to a tree. Above them were legs which didn't kick, a waist which didn't twist, a stomach which had ceased from grumbling. Above it was dead shoulders holding a snapped neck—a neck no longer capable of holding up a head anymore, so the head sadly decided to hang, chin against chest, and stare at the ground forever. Never again would it look up at the rope, which was its demise.

The rope.

It was tied too tightly around a welcoming neck. Did the neck want to feel breath at the last minute, when it was too late?

Mallory? No! Not my brother!

Yes, your brother, you bloody fool. All good things end. He was a burden anyway. Dead weight. An unreachable itch on your back. I got him off of you, kid. Never to breathe again. Never to speak again. Never to haunt you again.

The words lifted the hair on the back of my neck. The words of someone else.

I walked towards the corpse slowly, trying to see if it moved. Was it all just a joke? Was this suicide a mere illusion like my dreams?

"No," I whispered. *"No. That's not my brother. He's not dead..."*

"I'll save you," I muttered incoherently. *"You're choking, that's all..."* I clawed my way up the tree like a madman and untied the rope from the branch it clung to. Mallory's body fell from its hanging position and onto the forest floor with a thud. I quickly descended, crouched down near his body, and clawed at the rope around his neck. As I untied it, I cared little about the deep scratch made in the process.

It didn't matter, anyway. He couldn't feel it.

"See? Now, you can breathe. Now, you can speak. Now, you can haunt me." I stared at him, my eyes filling with fire that burned away tears and left smoke trailing its way down my cheeks. **"Speak! Please!"** I said angrily. Angrily, but mannerly. *"Speak, Mal! I can't go on with life until you speak!"*

Silence was a cruel orator. It spoke so loudly, I couldn't hear Mallory speak to me at all. Silence swallowed his whisper.

*"Don't you realize you're leaving me behind?! How **dare** you! How **dare** you do this!"* I mumbled that last bit, stood, and kicked my brother's body in the ribs.

"It's unfair!" I shouted to whoever was listening.

I'd hoped Mallory was listening from somewhere and could take it back. Could take it all back. I spoke directly to the corpse:

"You can't just leave and go somewhere else where I'll never reach you! You can't just leave me with nothing! There's no note. No last words. Nobody to look after me. I can't survive! Not without you!"

I was hysterical! I kicked his body over and over again. Call me a monster. Call me insane. I was so broken, I didn't care what I appeared to be to others.

"You can't control this! It's not fair!" I shouted at the trees, the dirt, and the sky. *"I'm going with him,"* I resolved, grabbing the rope and climbing the tree.

I tied one end of the rope tightly to the same branch from which he'd hung, then the other end tightly around my neck as I looked down at the ground. If I jumped, the branch should catch me abruptly and snap my neck, a lot like what Mallory had done.

I'd be with Mal then. I'd be with the brother who'd helped me in our crime. The brother who knew my dirty secrets but ignored them because he'd done them, too. With him was where I belonged.

I readied myself to jump.

Was it? Was with him where I was supposed to be? Would I even go where my brother went? Death was a black void I knew nothing about, and if death was Hell, I couldn't go back to earth if I wanted to. I'd be stuck in Hell forever.

I can't do it.

You're not strong enough.

I leaned back to where the trunk met the branch, covered my face, and wept.

You're not Mallory, you fool. You're just his brother. You were never Archie Cockburn — the boy you pretended to be. You were always Monté.

With the benefit of hindsight, I asked myself, *"Why did I weep?"*

My brother's death was the **best** thing to **ever** happen to me.

23: ROSETTA KELLINA MABEL

Hmm…
Yes, you can be poor
And prideful, too.

The thing about being a seamstress is people know clothing is a need, and rich people think **beautiful** clothing is a need. They demand it. When it is given, they do not thank their givers. As far as the nobles were concerned, they were undoubtedly entitled to it. My unfortunate fate was being one of the poor fools who worked for them.

Ferrando was wrong: I hate the stench of rank. In one place, it put me on top of the world, while in the other, I was a footstool. Today, it would seem I would play the footstool.

I hastily condemned my confounded luck when I heard who I'd be fitting: Lady Camilla Dickenson of Haestingas. I could tell by the looks of my coworkers how relieved they were that it wasn't them.

"It's so terribly unfortunate you'd get Camilla, Rosetta," Héloise said as she happily examined a halfway-done dress.

I didn't even look up from my loom. Why pay the woman any mind? She wasn't even attempting to sound genuine.

"I'm sure you'll do well," she continued. *"Just don't freeze up or anything…"*

Kip completed Héloise's sentence. *"…or give one of your darn opinions."*

Faye spoke quietly from the corner. With the noise of the machines, it was hard to hear when she said, *"There's nothing wrong with opinions."*

"Unless they're against the Lord Monté. Then, they're unwelcome." Kip gave me a warning glare.

She and I hadn't spoken much since the scary conversation in my room. After she'd left, I'd been so relieved she hadn't noticed the cylinders, I'd collapsed on my bed after sending the birds off and went fast asleep. Only this morning had the message Kip's words contained hit me.

The Lord has taken note of you.

What did that even mean? Had he been watching me? Do me a favor. Don't laugh. I have no idea what to expect of the Lord. I'd only seen him a handful of times at best, and those times, he'd been so far away, it was hard for me to tell anything about him.

The last time I'd seen him was at the Battle. *Had he been looking at **me**?* I shivered where I sat.

The girls were still talking…

"I was not lying. It is unfortunate Rose would have to do it," Héloise said.

"She's lying," Kip said to Faye.

Héloise had lost the will to defend herself and simply stated, *"Well, Rosetta is probably better suited to do it than me, anyway. She's probably better suited than all of us."*

Kip scoffed. *"Oh? And why is that?"*

"Rosetta's got more head then you and Faye put together."

Well, that didn't go over well.

*"What does **that** mean?"* Faye asked, obviously hurt by the comment. She'd finally spoken up for herself.

"It means exactly what I said! Sometimes, it's absolutely impossible working with you lasses. I think just maybe I'd have a better chance working with James in the Forge than sewing clothes with two old hags."

Faye gasped, and Kip faltered.

"Hags?!" Kip asked, shocked. *"Well, I never…!"*

I cursed my ability to start an argument all about me without ever uttering a word.

"Well, darn it! Aren't all of you supportive? Bickering like it's the end of the world — right before I have to fight the devil." My annoyance was not to be mistaken. Perhaps referring to Lady Camilla as 'the devil' wasn't smart, but it sure had a heck of a lot of truth in it.

The girls glanced guiltily at each other, just as someone entered our mess: a dark man with telling eyebrows and eyes of stone. He must've been one of Lady Camilla's many servants. He looked disgusted at the state of the room, although the mess was simply clothing we would give to the people **he** served. It didn't seem to matter much to him. Only Lady Camilla could have servants as spoiled as she was.

"I was sent to fetch the clothier by the name of Rosetta Kellina Mabel."

I nearly gagged. **Fetch** *me?* How disgusting one word could be.

"I'm here," I said, standing. **I wish I weren't.**

The man looked me up and down openly. *"A bit young for a reputation like you have,"* he said in disapproval.

I couldn't help it. I hated being looked over like a piece of meat. *"Aren't you a bit old for having no reputation at all?"*

I heard the girls behind me suck air in through their gritted teeth in obvious shock, but the man just raised a comical eyebrow and turned away.

"Follow me," he tossed over his shoulder.

~~~~~~~~~~
~~~~~~~~~~

The room was far too big for a fitting. It stretched far both ways and held absolutely nothing but chairs and places to lounge. *What a waste of space,* I thought. Above us were three chandeliers. The walls were full of artwork, largely composed of naked bodies.

I felt the need to throw up my breakfast. Instead, I busied myself by pulling out the material I needed and some darts.

In walked Lady Camilla Dickinson of Haestingas, her blonde hair of locks and curls bouncing in satisfaction. She was trailed by three other ladies.

For the sake of understanding, I will mention their names.

The woman to Lady Camilla's left was stunning in her black dress of silk. She managed to hold her head up well and wore bright jewelry, looking expensive enough to equal the same amount as every fruit in the center market — and then some. Her name, for the record, was Lady Vivian Beaumont.

Behind her and still to the left of Camilla was the red-headed Antonietta Paulina, Princess of some eastern land. She walked with confidence, as long as she thought one was looking in her direction. She looked perfect in her pink dress with beautiful ribbons. She even wore makeup, making it obvious with too-rosy cheeks.

Lastly, and to the right of Camilla, was Illaria Threston. She was of no importance, other than her relationship with Antonietta. It was rumored they were inseparable best friends. She wore a linen gown with a gold brooch and one lonely necklace. Her skin was pale in comparison to the rest.

Not only had I looked pale; I was. I felt like the smallest person in the room. To be fairly honest, I, in fact, was.

Camilla looked around the room. Everywhere but the corner in which I stood, that is.

"Jacob!" she called, and the man with the stone eyes who'd brought me here was back. She slapped him. It was so unexpected, I jumped slightly and winced for him. He didn't even move his feet. His neck, however, turned sideways. *Had he expected it?* He did not even flinch. ***"Where is the tailor I told you to bring?"*** she barked.

"Forgive me, m'Lady. She is in the corner there." He pointed a ridiculously long finger my way.

Camilla turned and looked at me as if she'd just realized I was there. *Are you blind, woman?!*

*"This imbecile is a **tailor**?"*

"I thought women weren't allowed as tailors, only seamstresses," Antonietta chimed in. Illaria nodded like she, too, knew that bit of information before it had been said.

I bet she didn't.

"I am here to fit you, my lady," I said as submissively as I could.

"I doubt she could even do this job," Camilla said, choosing not to talk directly to me. *"I was expecting a handsome **man**, not an ugly **woman**!"* Her girls laughed at that. *"Fine, then. If you are who they sent for, I suppose we have to suffer with you."* She came towards me in the dress that needed some touch-ups.

Her last statement was the best thing to have exited her mouth so far. At least this time, she had addressed me and not the women beside her. I also noticed the servant left the room stoically.

The other women took seats in the chairs around the room. Silently, they watched me as I worked. Silently, they judged.

*It was **almost** worse than —*

"I heard the Lord plans to throw a party. A masquerade, maybe? It would be lovely," Antonietta said happily.

*"**Wonderful, indeed!**"* Illaria said a little too brightly. *"Vivian, will you be attending?"*

"Only if the Lord himself attends. I have much desired to see the man who obtained such a kingdom."

*Obtained, she says? Only Heaven knows why she harbored that desire! He is **horrid**!* Not only did he kill the previous king, queen, and their children — one of them being a good friend of mine — he also killed that which had made up Jocund. He cut the joy out of every conversation. Only nobility loved him. Just ask anyone on the bloody streets! You could even ask a bloody fool! They'd all say the same thing: Darn Lord Monté and his sieging success!

"I imagine he's wonderfully handsome. You've seen him, haven't you Camilla?" Antonietta asked.

Camilla stood, arms out, while I loosened the bust area of her dress. *"I haven't had the chance of speaking to him often. He's such a mysterious man. It's hard to tell if he's handsome or not."*

Antonietta raised a brow. *"Well, I've never associated one's ways with whether they were handsome or not. That's all in the color of their eyes."*

Vivian laughed at her. *"You're young. Nothing is as important as a man's ways, though from what I can tell, the Lord's ways are quite umm… Let's just say 'efficient.'"*

*"If all you want is handsome, you ought to talk to the Chancellor like I do, Antonietta. He's always standing beside the Lord with such a beautiful smile. It tickles **every** part of me,"* Illaria said to her friend.

Camilla raised a brow at Illaria's crude admission. *"I heard he fancies someone,"* she stabbed nonchalantly, receiving the reaction she wanted from Illaria.

"No!"

"Ah, but it is true. A servant in the castle. I do believe she is a seamstress."

Everyone's eyes fell on me again, and I grew uneasy. *It isn't me,* I wanted to say. *I don't know who it is… Well, I don't **want** to know.*

*"I'm sure it isn't **serious**,"* Vivian said to break the silence. *"The man will get over that little affair and turn to a more stable love interest."*

To my relief, the subject was dropped after that was said.

"I cannot wait until the next Battle. They're so wonderfully frightening. They excite me," Antonietta said, playing with a curl of red hair.

"It doesn't take much to excite you, Antonietta," Camilla stated cynically.

"You're right! I've been like this from birth," she said while trying to shrug off the insult.

"Oh, yes. I enjoyed it, as well. Quite frankly, it didn't last long enough. I think the Lord likes building suspense," Vivian laughed.

*"Well, I, for one, wish he **wouldn't**,"* Illaria interjected.

Camilla watched my work closely before saying, *"I hope they find a way to quiet the noise outside. The wails coming from outside the Battle arena were perfectly **horrendous**! Honestly. Jocunders are savages and terribly useless."*

I wanted badly to stab her with a needle, but the action would have been savage of me. I continued pricking at a dress I was tasked to make beautiful.

"Well, no wonder. They've been through hell if I've ever seen it," Illaria said.

Hearing the compassion in her tone, I decided that even though she was certainly not the brightest, she made sense. I wished I could make sense of everything as quickly as I had worked Illaria out.

"Oh, please," Camilla said, irritated. *"Those fools are fine. They should be happy they have healthy family members who can fight for their food! Besides, some of those idiots have relations working in the castle, like this poor tailor right here. She probably gets a nice bed and good food to send to her family."*

I clenched my teeth.

"Since you seem quite certain your assumption is correct, let's put it to the test and ask her, then," Antonietta said, standing up for her friend.

"I do not care what you ask the wretch. She probably can't speak well, though." She shot a look at the top of my head as I stooped at the bottom of her dress.

I'm right here. You can talk to me.

When Antonietta spoke directly to me, it felt so good to be addressed. *"What is your name?"*

I looked up from what I was doing, but only slightly. *"Rosetta Kellina Mabel,"* I spoke clearly, without restraint. Why be reserved when they already considered me such a nuisance?

"What a royal name for a hired hand," Vivian stated. I cringed.

"Well, then, Rosetta. Do you get a decent meal to send back to your family?"

At first, I considered not even answering the stupid question. Whatever I said would just be laughed at, and I was standing on unforgiving grounds.

"I don't have any family, my lady." I made it appear my working hard on Camilla's dress was my excuse for not looking up when I addressed her. They couldn't lock me up for working, could they?

Camilla laughed, making her dress shiver, and my hands grow unsteady. *"What a **joke**! Are you trying to make us feel **bad** for you?"* She continued laughing at me, and, again, I had a mental struggle: Should I stab her with a needle or not?

"I'm sure she was only telling the truth, Camilla."

*"Truth? About her 'many hardships'? Don't lie to me, girl. She's got a warm bed in a castle and doesn't deserve it. Just **look** at her!"* She laughed harder.

I found little humor in her ignorance.

"Besides," the wretched woman continued, *"it's better you have no family anyway. You have no one who could possibly be killed in the Battle."*

You have no idea, woman.

"Let the girl speak for herself," Antonietta said. *"You can't expect people to simply grow accustomed to murder so easily. Surely, it will take time."*

No amount of time will fix that.

"Oh, I'm sure they haven't grown accustomed to it, Antonietta. I bet they hate it. I have little reason to care."

She'd snapped the last civilized part of me.

POKE!

"Do you mind being a little more careful with your needle, fool?" I tried not to laugh.

"Of course, my lady."

"What ever happened to your family?" Illaria asked.

It took me many moments to realize she was speaking to me. The silence was loud in my ears. *"My parents were killed during the Lord's arrival, along with my best friend. I had no other relatives close to me; no brothers, no sisters."*

She sighed. *"What a shame…"*

"See? Even her story shows how wonderfully compassionate and efficient the Lord is, for this lady is with a job and a place to sleep," Vivian said. Why she was so infatuated with the Lord, I do not know. What I **did** know was the Lord was not compassionate. He showed little virtue and seemed to be profoundly familiar with selfishness.

If the Lord were compassionate at all, he would've left Jocund alone.

The Lord probably looked like the devil. He surely didn't share the same emotions with normal human beings. He probably talked like a dimwit and carried himself like a fool. He was likely insane and laughed at things that appeared cruel to most. I'm most certain he had the ugliest eyes on the full scale of the globe.

Of course, had I verbalized any of that, I would've been sent to be hung.

Instead, I wished I were anywhere else but in this room with these women of utmost importance. They were fools—fools with money, rank, status, and reputation. When you have those things, you can **afford** to be a fool.

*"How is your **husband**, Vivian?"* Camilla asked, perhaps trying to get her mind off the whimsical Lord she imagined.

Vivian did **not** appreciate the gesture. *"The old croak will always be fine as long as he's alive and I must suffer him."*

"That is what happens when you marry for status without first falling in love with his eyes," Antonietta mumbled.

"Pardon?" Vivian asked, pretending she did not hear correctly. The comment was not repeated.

I hated how Camilla was able to control a conversation or simply stir it into what she wanted. She asked questions for hidden answers within the one you'd given. She spoke haughtily without the slightest restraint, and, when she took aim at a person, she usually hit her mark. Most times, words hurt more than a physical wound. Although I was aware of how much I spoke, surely, I wasn't nearly as bad as this…**woman**. She gave me a cruel headache.

Antonietta seemed to think of something, her eyes growing wide with excitement. *"If the Lord throws a party, do you think he'd invite the men from the Battle? I would love to speak with the blonde one."*

Merek? Eww! I nearly threw up again.

Camilla made a 'tsk' sound with her tongue. *"Antonietta, my dear, you always fall in love with the barbaric and savage men. You ought to have better footing when it comes to this."* She shook her head. *"Did you see the way he chased the young boy? It's a shame he did not kill him. Why survive, when next time, he might have an even worse fate?"*

Illaria's expression showed pity. *"Poor boy."*

*"Yes, poor boy — and probably a poor family as well. What kind of **parent** would allow their child to fight to support their family? This proves my point. **Savages.**"*

I felt my face growing hotter with every word Camilla spoke and could no longer control myself.

POKE!

I'd kept my mouth shut the entire time — and would continue to do so. Lydia would have been proud of me.

"Ow! Are you done, you scum?" Camilla asked upon feeling yet another hard prick from a goal-driven needle.

"Yes, my lady. I think you're quite ready," I replied sweetly. I added a slight bow at my waist for good measure.

Camilla glared at me and huffed as if she didn't care. As if I wasn't worth enough to even care about. *"Well, then. Come along, girls!"* she said, steeling herself ever gracefully out of the room, with her host of girls trailing behind.

When they had disappeared down the corridor and around the corner, I was alone in the big room and began to laugh. When I started, I couldn't stop myself! It was the kind of laughter I needed. Sometimes, things like these are too hard or harsh, I believe, for the human brain to handle. When things are incomprehensible, you might be compelled to laugh instead of cry. I do believe laughter is sometimes better than tears. This time, I could not stop laughing.

"It is funny, isn't it?" A voice behind me said.

I did stop then, in a terrible hurry, and turned to see the servant who had escorted me to the room. He'd entered through another corridor behind me. His eyes were no longer just 'stone.' There was an unmistaken hint of light at the top; a bright white in his eyes making the stone sparkle.

I was at a loss for words, wondering if I should apologize. Had my behavior towards his mistress made him angry?

"I'd say the woman deserved far more than a couple of needle pricks. I was hoping you'd open your darn mouth and say one of those pretty sentences like you used with me. I suppose, though, you could have damaged a lot more than a man's pride had you said those types of things to Lady Camilla."

I was startled by the change of events and began to smile. *"My friends would've been proud of me for holding my tongue."*

He shook his head. *"Actions speak, too, Miss Rosetta. I think you spoke just fine."*

24: DUSTIN ELRIC CARPENTER

*Not all those who wander are lost…
But most are.*

Whatever it was, it swung down and knocked me off my feet. I should've undoubtedly been ready for something but hadn't expected it to come from the sky.

There were swarms of them. Hundreds and hundreds came from everywhere. Behind the trees. In the trees. Some even seemed to come from the ground, climbing their way up like bugs pouring into a campsite. It didn't take long for the hundreds to overwhelm me. I'd managed to cut down a mere five before they beat me down to the ground.

I tried to get up and felt a kick in my ribs. *Stay down*, I tried to tell myself. *You're beat. At least for now.* My face was in the cool dirt.

"WHAT ARE YA DOIN' IN MY FOREST?!" my attacker shouted maniacally.

My brain was stuck, trying to figure out why he was so angry and what I had done to receive such a heated question.

Where were the Warriors???

"ANSWER ME!" he shouted something awful before kicking me repeatedly. How did he plan on me answering him when he continued to throw his foot into my side? Sharp stabs of pain kept flooding in.

The last kick was to my head. I moaned, letting out a strained, *"Darn it, man. Let me speak."*

I then looked up at him. The man had blackened teeth from something he must have chewed over the years, coupled with a lack of care. His hair was cut down to his scalp, maybe because, like the unruly hair on his chest, he wouldn't have been able to keep up with it.

He was surrounded by people who looked just like him. Women, more men, and an occasional child. They all had hacked-cut hair. They all were covered in soot.

"Why is it so buggin' illegal to pass through a forest?" I asked, squinting at him.

A long stick—much like a walking cane—came down and slammed against the top of my head. The impact jarred my neck down into my shoulders, and I grew dizzy and nauseated.

"I ask the questions! I sure as heck ain't letting ya pass through here, ya dirty foreigner!" the man spat. Half his spittle sprayed on me.

That's when I heard it all occur: scuffles, groans, and a familiar cry. It was Woodruff's! It was the Black Warriors! When I moved to stand, the same man kicked me in the back of my head.

"Don't move another step, Warriors, or I'll kill your king," I heard him snarl. I felt a pointed end of metal gently rest against my temple. The stick I was being jarred with had a blade.

The hair on my neck stood on end. I lifted my head just a little and glanced at the Warriors. They'd formed a circle.

Goodness! These 'people' made up an entire army and were everywhere, surrounding us. They just might be a threat…

*"You don't want that, **do ya**?"* The man spat on the ground again, missing me this time.

"A-an you taking your last breath t-today? I don't think we-we want that, either," Silas said quickly.

Egon wasn't having anything to do with negotiations. *"If you're wise, you will not make me angry, mate."*

The man pushed the blade a little harder against my skull. I groaned, losing sight of the Warriors as my face fell back into the dirt. *"Oh, there's no doubt in my mind whether ya can kill me or not, fool. It's whether I want the trouble of the Prince of Sans Défaut tramping around in my forest!"*

There was an uneasy silence. The man above me then broke it with a belly laugh. Even the sound of it was harsh and uninviting.

*"Everyone knows who ya are! Word travels fast in Precursory. Now, on your knees! **All of ya!**"*

None of the Warriors were quick to give in. The man flipped the spear around to the stick's end and cracked me in the head again.

"Alright! Hold it!" Cederic shouted. The Warriors dropped to their knees. It was a humbling, unforgettable sight.

"Drop your weapons out in front of ya! NOW!" the man screamed.

Grudgingly, the Black Warriors did what he said. Each threw their weapon just beyond their reach. As soon as that was done, the dirty men and women were upon the Warriors, tying them up with rope and the like.

"Make sure the knots are thick. These Black Warriors are sly dogs," the man over me said. I would have to assume he was the leader. He had to be in his late-40s — maybe early 50s — with greying, stubbly hair. No doubt about it, he was strong. His blows had sent me into a steady state of confusion and left me weak.

I felt bad for being the reason the Warriors were in captivity. Mostly, I felt bad for Arthur.

A woman approached the crazy man and me. She was young; my age, maybe. It was difficult to make out her features through all the dirt. Her eyes were like salt crystals or fogged glass, grey and unmoving. Like the rest of the filthy clan, her hair was cut short, too.

I felt a wave of further discomfort as the realization that we may be at the mercy of these beggers gripped me.

"The forest is safe again, Longsigh," she said.

The man looked at her with indifference, almost as if he hadn't heard her. *"As it should be."*

The woman glanced at me. It struck me how young she was. Again, I tried to smile. The man caught my gesture and kicked me in the side again. *"What are ya smiling at her for?"*

I rolled from my stomach to my back, writhing in pain and wheezing. *"Force...of...habit,"* I said between breaths and growing rage. My simple statement couldn't have been the cause of the darkness that came over his face, could it?

The answer to that thought came with force. I didn't even see the butt-end of the spear coming for my head again. Light, trees, and voices were there for a moment. Then, there was blackness. *Terrible* **blackness**.

<div align="center">~~~~~~~~~~</div>

I heard distant voices, none at all familiar—although with them being so distant, it was hard to tell. Faint murmuring, slowly growing louder. There was the sound of running water slapping a bank, and the eerie silence of night. How long had I been in the dark? Why did my head hurt so much? *Something must've happened, Dustin. Think, darn it! Think! The beggars. That's it. They caught you and your friends. The mean one with the ugly teeth knocked you into oblivion. Nice going, Dustin. Well done. Who is speaking?*

Finally, the words being spoken outside of my head became clear. My thoughts fell quiet so I could listen…

"You see how they march? Determined faces. Full of attitude. I know what they've come for. I hope Longsigh knows, too," a gruff voice said.

There was a loud swallow, followed by another voice saying, *"Old Longsigh will handle it like old Longsigh does. Don't ya worry. I're bettin' those dirty scoundrels will be dead by're tomorrow."* Then, another content and nasty swallow.

I could tell my throat was dry. I was experiencing an unpleasant, scratchy feeling before I had even opened my eyes. I was uncomfortable because I was standing with my hands tied above my head next to a tree. Oddly enough, my arms didn't hurt. As a matter of fact, I couldn't feel them whatsoever—confirming I'd been standing in this spot for a long time.

I must've been terribly unconscious to sleep like this, I thought.

I managed a look around. I saw a camp—quite a large one—with an army of people. Dirty people. I couldn't understand their filth, considering they were all next to a river. I heard the sound of water, after all. It ran behind me. I wondered if it was the same river we had crossed earlier, and I wondered where we were. There were also lots of tents pitched and people buzzing around, engaged in all sorts of things.

My head still hurt and was having a hard time settling down so that I could focus and think clearly.

There were two men in front of me—both with their backs to me and too far ahead for me to attack. The one on the left kept swallowing as if he were dying of thirst, but he wasn't drinking anything. His cropped hair was short and without reason. The other on the right had a stocky build: a thick back and broad shoulder blades. His dark hair was also hacked away to nothing. It seemed to be the way of things here.

"Hey. You two," I managed to say weakly.

They turned at my call and glared at me.

"Can you direct me to the skunk they call Longsigh? I would like a word."

The leaner one with the bad swallowing habit laughed at me, and spittle flew everywhere near. *"Longsigh'l see ya, boy, but it ain't gonna be now."* He swallowed.

The stocky one grinned. *"Looks like we're your company,* **filth***. So, you just hold your horses and wait, big boy."*

I nearly cursed. *"I need to talk to him* **now**. *Surely, you're not so savage here as to deny a prince an audience?"*

"Hold your tongue, fool! The only person around here who gets whatever **audience** *he wants is Longsigh."* A slurp-sounding swallow. An angry, twitching brow.

Anger shot through me. *"Well, in that case…"* I gathered as much saliva in my mouth as possible and sent it flying in the wind to land on the swallowing man's shoe. *"There. Would you send that to him for me?"*

The stocky one growled. *"Why, you little…"* He came at me, and a punch landed on my face. A knee caved in my torso time and again.

"What is going on?" A voice cut through the whistling air, prompting my assaulter to stop.

I tasted blood on my lip and tongue, and my ribs ached—not just from the stocky man's knees, but from the blows that landed me here in the first place.

The voice had come from the same woman who'd gotten me knocked out. Now, she'd come through the bustling camp to see what was going on. Her eyes were still dead. It seemed to me they were incapable of change.

"Saraid!" the swallowing man said in surprise. *"We were just giving the man a warm welcome."*

She stared at him blankly. *"The problem is that is not what you were stationed here to do, Rian."* She pulled a knife from the sheath on her belt and cut the ropes holding my hands. *"Fall back to your routines. Try not to trip over your own feet."* As she turned to walk away, she gestured for me to follow her.

I grinned at Rian, and he glared at me. Once I caught up with the Saraid, I asked, *"You know who I am, right?"*

"Yes." I then noticed she had a slight accent; a familiar one I couldn't put my finger to.

I looked around the camp, studying its layout. *"Then, you know you can't hold me here forever without putting yourself in danger."*

We passed two men who were betting on some dead animal with playing cards.

*"I know **you**, Prince Dustin. You will not leave your friends."* She glanced at me with those dead eyes, seemingly satisfied

with what she saw in mine. I couldn't read hers. Not yet, anyway.

I grew exasperated. *"You know, I'm not playing games. I'm responsible for those men. If **any** harm comes to them —"*

She turned slightly. *"Trust me, Prince Dustin. I am the last person you need to worry about."*

I dropped the subject right there because I didn't know what she meant. Did she mean she wasn't capable of killing them or something else? Whatever the meaning, my exasperation ceased when I noticed she wasn't as uptight and uninformed as the two men I'd met when I woke up. Neither was she as angry as Longsigh. I was moved to ask her some questions.

"The monster in this river — the Or'geth. You can't bathe because of him, right?"

I thought she didn't hear me because of her prolonged silence. *"Yes."*

My eyes widened. *"You've encountered him, too, then?"*

"We lost 50 people to that thing the first week we came to this forest. We've lost about half of that since then."

"When did you get here? Who are you?"

We reached a tent, and Saraid looked at it reluctantly. *"I'm sure Longsigh will answer those questions for you."* She gestured for me to follow and ducked into the tent.

"What if I don't want him to?" I muttered to no one in particular as I looked around. I thought about running for it. I

had a good chance of getting away, but finding my friends and getting them away, too, was pushing the odds a bit. I sighed and ducked under the tent's flap.

No one was inside, save for Saraid. There was a small cot and underneath, a worn-down mat. A crude, rough-edged and tiny table was set to the right side of the bed. Several books laid open on the table. There was a container of ink, which was obviously used for quick scribbles. *That's a good sign. At least these dirty barbarians had the decency to write,* I thought.

As I prepared to ask Saraid where Longsigh was, she put a finger to her lips—a quick gesture telling me to hush—and motioned me towards the corner of the tent. Nothing magical happened. I stood there confused, until she lifted the mat.

Beneath, there was a sliver of a hole in the dirt ground. A person could barely get their body through, but I knew that's what was expected of me. I saw the crooked, jagged ladder, and knew Saraid wanted me to climb down.

I looked at her questionably. She glared back. I gave in. I wasn't about to tell her how terrified I was of the dark. I squeezed down the hole and onto the ladder.

You know, it's often at the least humorous time when you think of the funniest things. I began to picture Woodruff trying to squeeze down the hole and snickered. It echoed.

Saraid, who'd just started down, must've not heard or chose not to address my stupidity. By her level of focus, I suppose it was the latter.

They better be okay, I thought, growing grim again. *They better not have a scratch on them, or these people will see just how unmerciful I can be. They'll wish they hadn't triggered such madness.*

I had a schedule to keep: seven days. I'd given myself seven, and we were already at the end of the third. Here I was, stuck in a camp full of weirdos. I couldn't afford to remain stuck here, especially since I'd already lost hours' worth of time.

Dang it, I thought when I hit the bottom of the hole that stretched deep into the ground. *How does she expect me to see in this darkness?* I waited for Saraid to arrive and then jumped when I felt her hand touch my elbow. *Why hadn't I heard her reach the bottom?*

"Follow me," she whispered. Goosebumps raised on my arms.

"Oh, sure…sure," I said, in spite of myself. *"Just follow the creepy lady into the dark. How do you expect me to follow when I can't* **see** *you?"*

I felt her move past me. *"I would hold your hand, but I thought it might embarrass you."* I assumed she was mocking me, then second-guessed myself. Her tone hadn't sounded mocking.

I stared at what I thought was her back moving away and muttered, *"God, help me."*

She made no sign of listening to me, though I hadn't meant for her to hear. I followed in the direction she'd left and tried to listen to footsteps to keep up. She was quiet as she moved. I couldn't tell which way she was going nor which way she had been. I should've been scared, but my adrenaline told me to focus. Several times, I felt completely lost until I felt her hand brush my arm or heard a gentle call under her breath, which I assumed was her signal to get me back on the right path—wherever the 'path' was.

The dark warps time. It seemed like we walked for an eternity. I would soon know it was just a matter of minutes. Nevertheless, I was happy to see a small hint of light ahead from where the empty cavern met a smaller nook in the rock (or what I could only assume was rock).

This nook of a room was lit by two eerie candles on a misplaced and uncomfortable wooden table. At the table were two men sitting in expensive chairs belonging more—in appearances—to a manor of some sort, not in a cave. Both chairs sat at both heads of the table.

The person on the left was a young man who could only be a few years older than I. His hair was—not surprisingly—cut down to his head by a shrewd and unforgiving blade. His eyes were familiarly dead, except for a hint of anger lit like a fire atop the left side of his pupil. He wore a chiseled jaw, which virtually mirrored the man who sat with him to my left. That man I recognized. It was Longsigh—the man who pinned me to the ground with his spear and knocked me over the head a billion times. He also had my friends only **God** knew where. I hated him the minute I laid eyes on him again.

The two sat together, but oddly, they didn't speak. As a matter of fact, I hadn't heard them speaking since I'd been in the cave. Surely, we would have heard them, with the cave walls being the perfect rebound for echoes. It was strange to think of them just **sitting** here in total silence. The idea of it while standing in a dark cave was spooky and made my muscles grow tense to keep from shivering.

"Are you wondering where your friends are?" Longsigh asked gruffly. His voice echoed—as I knew it would—in the darkness.

I stared at him. I wouldn't dare tell him I was, indeed, wondering about their fate. I wouldn't dare give this man what he wanted. He reeked of evil. *"Longsigh,"* I said in greeting, letting him know I now knew him.

"Prince."

"Y'know, I respect you on certain terms. You hit me on my head, knocked me out, and took my friends. You're a proper piece of trash, aren't you? However, my respect will surely diminish if you've laid even **one** *harmful hand on my company."*

"Oh, I wouldn't sweat my boots too much, butterhead," the younger man said. *"You're gonna be here for a long time, so I suggest we get off on the right foot."*

"I will **be here** *until my father doesn't get word from me. Then, you all will be six feet under,"* I said through clenched teeth.

Longsigh stood quickly, pointing a jagged and calloused finger at me. ***"SHUT UP!"***

"No! I want to know what you've done with my companions!" When I made the demand, I'd completely forgotten about Saraid on my right. In no way did I think she would be particularly harmful. She seemed to be the sensible, quiet one of the lot—the last person I expected to strike me. However, she wasted little time in slamming my head into her knee and busting my nose. I fell over, dizzy. Angry. Trying to think. *"Okay, okay,"* I said, wobbling to my knees defiantly. *"Who are you? That's a good place to start."*

"I'm glad you're finally being civil. Get up," the young man said shrewdly, lacking a drip of emotion.

Longsigh was still standing from when I'd stirred his anger a moment ago. He walked towards me, pointing that gross finger in my face. *"We feel right proud ya' don't know who the heck we are. We're the **Forgotten Ones**. We wouldn't be, but where was bloody San Défaut when we needed them, eh?"* He smiled and then laughed in my face—his hot breath reeked of rotten food, nearly making me vomit. *"I'll tell ya where ya were! Sitting with your thumbs up your bums, **laughin'** at us!"* He shook his head. *"Yeah, they sure got a good kick out of seeing us squirm…"*

"Excuse me? Who is 'us'?"

*"Jocund, boy! The **real** Jocund. The old one! Before the cursed Lord and his band. You can't begin to understand how beautiful it was…"* His voice broke—a feat I thought was impossible until it happened.

The young man at the table grew grim. *"Father…"* he started but didn't finish.

Longsigh turned towards his boy, his son, his flesh and blood. *I **knew** it, especially since I could now see their shared features a bit clearer.* **"Westeros, hush!"** he growled at him. The young man fell silent.

"I'm sorry," I said quickly, genuinely sympathetic. I was sorry for calling them beggars because they weren't begging for anything but their home back.

Longsigh spat in my face. It took all my willpower not to reach up and wipe the dirty saliva off with haste. Instead, I held his gaze. I hadn't expected him to say, *"Oh, yeah. I forgive ya, mate!"* anyway.

*"You're lucky I haven't already **killed** your bloody friends. The dark-haired one tried to bite me."* He turned away to sit back in his chair.

"Shame he didn't," I said to the angry man's back. An angrier fist swung around quickly to hit me over my head. My head snapped to the side, but I immediately lined it back up and glared at him. I couldn't figure out why he enraged me so. I didn't know the man, but I knew his type. He infuriated me to no end. *"What's your point in beating me? You don't want Sans Défaut on your tail,"* I threatened.

"Of course not," said the young man as he stood. *"We just want to know some answers to a couple of questions. Now, be a good boy."*

I narrowed my eyes. *"You haven't promised me anything. Why should I do a thing for you?"*

"Well, you know the answer to that, my friend," Westeros said with a smile. *"Let's start with those horses. You're obviously in a hurry and need them to get to your destination. I'm not sure you'd like my plan of cutting out their eyes for sport and throwing them in the river for the Or'geth. Then, there's your friends…"*

I flinched.

"We thought not." Longsigh laughed. *"My blessing to ya is this: The longer ya stay, the longer ya friends live. I ain't as mean as they say, ya know."*

"Are you promising to let us go unharmed?"

*"**I SAID NO SUCH THING, BOY!**"* Longsigh exploded. *"Ya had better focus on telling me what I need to know. It will do wonders for yar getting out 'unharmed.'"*

"Fine. I'm resigned, then. What the devil do you want to know?" I just wanted it all to be over with. I had no quarrel with these people. If anything, I was trying to make things easier for them.

Longsigh leaned closer. I caught a whiff of not just his breath, but also the ragged coat he wore over his torn and filthy tunic. I smelt smoke, soot, sweat, and ale of the worst kind because it was mixed with everything that came before it. I tried not to scowl at the repugnant odor, but I probably did.

"Where are ya headed in such a hurry, eh?"

Dang it. I would have liked anything but that question. *"You know I can't answer that,"* I said dryly.

"Oh, I think you can," Westeros said. *"Eventually."* He walked past me, and Longsigh whispered in Saraid's ear. I saw her flinch slightly but answer coldly. The answer was clear as crystal.

"You know the way, Westeros. Show him yourself."

Westeros stared at her, hard. I'd seen that look before. I grew tense because I thought he was going to hit her. Instead, he laughed. *"You've been raised well, sister. Just don't grind your teeth too hard!"*

Sister?!

The more I thought about it, the more it made sense to tell the men where we were going. Wouldn't they be happy we were going to take Jocund from the hands of Lord Monté? What danger could there be in them knowing? I wished my father had told me differently. I wished I had the right amount of rebellious courage to disobey him.

Still... How else was I going to get out of here with everyone? We were in the middle of a camp of people who were as savage as they were insane!

All I could do for now was milk time while trying to devise an escape plan and hope our captors were too undecided and nervous to kill my company.

"Follow me, prince." Westeros walked handsomely off.

I remained glued in place, wondering if I should follow him. *As if I had a choice.*

The deeper we went, the more I grew sick to my stomach. I knew better than to ask where he was taking me and realized Saraid's trip down should've been far more appreciated. Westeros' journey was much worse, and he was no help whatsoever with directions—or anything else, for that matter.

I grew aversive of the underground walls, and they grew aversive of me. I suppose it was only fair they disliked me. I'd been shooting them dirty looks since I stepped into this horrid, damp place. They stared at me coldly, chilling me properly.

As far as one could tell in the dark, it was an assortment of tunnels. Tunnels, tunnels, and more tunnels. We approached the end of one, and, as things cleared out in front of me, I saw the shadows of six bodies lying dead-still on the cave's ground. Their hands were bound to chains buried in the floor, and their faces were smashed quite uncomfortably into the dirt and rock. It didn't take a rocket scientist to know who they were.

Chains jingled as we approached.

"Well, well, well. If it isn't the young and ugly one come to behead the lot of us," a muffled and dry voice—surely Egon's—said. Because of the way they were splayed on the ground with their arms stretched to terrible lengths, they were unable to lift their heads much and could not see me walking towards them with Westeros.

"You **must** *know I wouldn't allow that,"* I said. Egon coughed at the sound of my voice.

"Dustin?" Cederic croaked. *"Tell these fools we have no quarrel with them."*

"We know you don't," Westeros replied. *"I doubt that's going to help much."*

"D-Dustin? Are you alright?" Silas asked.

"I'll be better when you're all on your own two feet, after Westeros hears me out."

"Don't think we'll hesitate killing your friends, prince. Longsigh thinks he has an idea of where you're going, and we know someone who'd pay a hefty price for your heads. I brought you here so you'd see it's impossible to rescue them, so don't even try."

He spoke of Lord Monté. How could they **bargain** with that horrid man?

"What good is money to you out here?" Ocean asked angrily.

Westeros clenched an unsettled jaw. *"Money is always good."*

*"I know something **better**,"* I said. A plan began to form in my mind. There were many risks involved, but what was I to do?

Westeros glared at me, but I could tell he was interested.

*"**Food**. You need it. Bad. Your people are starving. With the famine raging, there's no way you can continue to survive out here. Money will run out. You will have to use it to leave here, and you'd lose more of your people to illness that way. So, you're stuck here."*

*"We're not **stuck** anywhere,"* he growled at me a bit too defensively. He knew I was right.

"There's a hidden hut belonging to Sans Défaut somewhere near the forest that contains enough food to last you the journey from here to Mystérieux. All you bloody need is the location, and I can give it to you..."

Westeros remained quiet.

"Only if you let my companions go and allow us to leave."

"Liar."

"Truth. I give my word."

*"Your word means **nothing** to me,"* he spat. *"Bloody **nothing**!"*

*"Okay. Then let's up the stakes for me. You get to keep my company down here, except for Egon. He will play your best man in a game of Karnöffel. If **he** wins, we get to leave. If **your man** wins, we're at your disposal, **and** you get the location of the hut. How's that?"*

Westeros licked his lips. At the same time, his stomach growled. *"You're being funny."*

"Not at all."

*"We must play **six** games of Karnöffel. One for each member of your company. Your man must win all bloody six to win freedom for all."*

I hesitated. I could practically hear the foreboding of my companions. Not to mention Kraus, who was undoubtedly using that storage hut for food. I hadn't asked him, but I had an idea. He wouldn't have any for his family if Egon lost the card games…

"Fine," I agreed.

Arthur moaned. *"Dustin, **please** no. How can we trust them?"*

Westeros laughed. I guessed his thoughts. He knew I wouldn't leave a single Black Warrior behind. All his guy had to do was win one, and he'd have us all. *"You're a fool, boy. I respect your idiocy."*

Ocean spoke up again. *"So, it's settled?"*

Westeros laughed wildly, then grew serious. *"I will have to pass it through Longsigh. See if he's in the mood for a little entertainment. Until then, continue to enjoy smelling the dirt down here."* He laughed again and walked off, expecting me to follow, which I did.

~~~~~~~~~~
~~~~~~~~~~

I could not rest knowing my friends were still in the cave, uncomfortable and worried for their lives. Some of it also had to do with me being in the weird position of having to sleep while standing, with arms stretched over my head. My head was hot, and my arms ached terribly. Half the time, I stood and stared at whoever was passing. My guards, Rian and Richard, despised me more than they already had because of our little 'exchange.' Either they would glare at me for long periods or would doze off. The latter was the case now. They slept quite obnoxiously, both snoring like pigs.

As the night stretched on, I grew tired. One of the worst things is feeling tired to the bone but unable to drift into peaceful slumber. My eyes darted around me, trying to find Saraid. I'd need her help if Longsigh and Westeros didn't keep their word. Just as I was getting tired of searching for her, the sun sprang up, rising from the dead like a surprised Lazarus wondering why the devil he was here.

I lazily looked through my sleep-deprived eyes at the camp. It was still quiet but started to slowly come alive. People passed by without so much as a glance. Others peeked, snorted at what they saw, and moved quickly towards an unknown destination. Soon, I spotted Saraid moving towards me.

She reached my lonely tree and popped her knuckles on the back of Richard's neck, which hung waiting to be noticed as he snored the camp into agony. He whimpered and bolted to his feet, looking at Saraid in a slightly disoriented way. He called to his companion, *"Rian! Wake up!"*

Rian, much more alert, jumped up quickly and stood, awaiting his punishment.

Saraid just shook her head. *"Night shift's over. Go get breakfast."*

They nodded quickly and bolted, recognizing they'd dodged some serious discipline and not wanting to stick around to see if she would change her mind.

She looked at me, then turned to go.

"You're gonna leave me here, unguarded?"

She stopped and looked over her shoulder at me, her expression blank. It often was. *"You saw where your friends are. You're not getting them out, which means you're not leaving, prince. I was just told not to let you get to them. In the meantime, I don't care **what** you do."* She turned to leave again, and I felt something rise inside of me.

"Wait!" I called.

She paused and turned fully.

"What did your father say to the bet? Westeros told you about it, didn't he?

She raised a brow. *"You won't win."*

"Does this mean he accepted?"

She shook her head at me. *"I respect your determination, prince, but if you'd risk your friends' lives on six silly card games, you're a fool."*

"Dustin. My name is Dustin," I said quickly, mildly annoyed. *"Prince **Dustin** Elric Carpenter, the fool. Thanks for telling me what I already know. When's the card game?"*

"After breakfast. The sooner you guys are dead, the better — according to Longsigh."

*"You mean your **father**."*

I saw the shiny blade too late. It lodged into the trunk behind me, an inch away from my head. I jerked to the side, luckily not enough for it to connect with my skull. It was an accurate throw meant to miss me. I met her glare.

*"Watch your tongue, **prince**. You look much better when you keep your mouth shut."*

I hadn't realized I was holding my breath until I let it all out. *"You don't agree with all that your father says, do you? You know I'm your best shot at getting Jocund back. If I don't do it, no one else is ever going to try."*

Her eyes flashed — the first sign of emotion she'd shown since the knife she threw that was embedded in the tree trunk. What was it that I saw? Anger? Fear?

"My father tells me what to do," was all she said.

"Does he hit you? Does he hurt you?"

Unmistakably this time, I saw a flash of anger. I threw up my hands before she could do anything rash, such as throw another knife.

"I'm not trying to pry… I just… I have people in Jocund I love, too. I want it to be restored just as much as anybody," I pleaded.

That caused her to pause. *"If it's my help you want, I cannot give it."*

"You can give anything. Your help is yours to offer. Nobody else's." I couldn't tell if I was getting through her wall, but I had to try.

She stared at me. *"Good luck with your card game, **Prince Dustin**."* She then left, leaving the knife lodged next to my head as a reminder of just how close to death I was.

I tried to use the edge of the knife to cut my bonds, but it was a perfect throw. Too close to my outstretched arms to reach with either hand and too far to grab with my mouth. I was forced to wait.

~~~~~~~~~~

Richard led me through a silent camp. There were less people wandering around. I could tell from the noise ahead it was because they were all in one place. Fires had been dashed. Breakfast had been consumed.

Fortunately for them, there was a little entertainment planned for today.

Even the trees seemed to mock the idea of me placing my friends' lives on six card games. I knew that's not what they were truly mocking, so I shrugged it off.

We continued on, moving past several tents. Once past them, the scene opened up to me clear as day. There was a crowd of nearly a hundred around a campfire. Next to that was two boxes across from each other and a shabby, almost crude table in the middle. I assumed that was where Egon and their proud champion, Ralph, would play their noble game.

Two big chairs were on the inner edge of the crowd's circle. One held Longsigh; the other, Westeros. They looked on as if this was a puppet show. A joke. A waste of time…and humans.
~~~~~~~~~~

The clearing was manmade, with no trees nearby. I could clearly see the blue sky and lack of clouds in the early morning. I cursed inwardly. *We'd lost a lot of time already…*

Westeros smirked at me, and I held his eyes without reaction. Longsigh looked on with amusement and confidence. I couldn't find Saraid as I searched with my eyes, and it bugged me. I liked knowing where everyone was.

I then spotted Egon—and only Egon. The rest of my friends were being held below so as not to cause any 'mischief.' Egon was led by two big men to the table in the center of the chaos.

I also saw who I assumed was to be his competitor walking behind him…unguarded, of course. He was a man of little individuality. He wasn't big or small. His teeth were crooked, his nose pointy. His eyes were dark; his hair cropped to his head. The only thing about the poor man's face even worth noting was the scar just below his left eye, running a little past the left corner of his mouth. It was an older injury. Perhaps one he'd received during Lord Monté's Theft.

I was led to stand directly in front of Longsigh and Westeros. With steady eyes, I assessed them, not minding much else.

The boos, as Egon took his seat, gained volume. A couple of people spat at him in disgust. He might've spat back, but I caught his eye. Judging my expression, he held his tongue respectively. When it came to things involving this man, that was unheard of.

My heart was flipping, making me queasy and nervous. My palms were sweaty. With no other way to get out of the camp, the Warriors needed Egon to win—and do so expeditiously—before we lost more time.

*I have to hope the men will keep their word if—no, **when**—Egon won all six games.*

As the chant grew in Ralph's favor, Longsigh's did as well. He was thoroughly amused. After listening to his clan for a while, he stood quickly, silencing the group of rowdy devils.

He pointed an accusing finger at me. *"We found this man—this **prince**—yesterday, did we not? Well, ya'd think he'd show us some respect for it, eh? No. **This** man thinks his friend can beat Ralph in a game of bloody cards! I think he's a bloody fool!"* he bellowed.

The crowd roared their approval. **Of course, they did.**

*"**This** man,"* he said while pointing at Egon, *"thinks he can win all six card games for his six friends' lives. Ya know what I think?"* He held still for a moment until his clan was hanging on every breath he breathed. *"**I** think a lotta people are dyin' this morning! **I** think it's gonna be those seven cowards!"*

The crowd went wild. Longsigh turned toward me again and spat a big wad of saliva at me before taking his seat.

I raised a golden brow at him. *Such a repulsive man…*

A man with a beard that had grown down to his chest stepped out from the crowd and announced what hadn't been said. *"Six games of Kärnoffel will be played. The stranger must win all six to have his and his friends' freedom granted. The contrary is death. Let's begin."*

I grew annoyed when yet another man approached to shuffle the cards. I couldn't trust these barbarians to play fair. I did, however, trust Egon. He was familiar with the cheats, tricks, and cards in general. I'd put my money on the guy every time.

Or, in this case, my life.

The shuffler was also the dealer. He dealt the customary five cards, glanced at Ralph, and nodded his support to the lad. Perhaps it could have **also** been confirmation that something phony was going on.

I then noticed Saraid sneak up next to Longsigh and Westeros as if she'd always been there. She hadn't, though. Where had she been? My thoughts were interrupted by the dealer.

He cleared his throat to announce: *"It has been agreed Ralph will go first."*

Agreed to by whom? No one asked **me** anything. Oh, well. I'd asked for this when I'd posed the idea of a card game, so what was the point in arguing when outnumbered?

The game of Kärnoffel required Egon to win three tricks to win the game, and he'd have to win six games to save all six friends. I think we both knew if he lost even one, we'd have to try to muscle our way out. Neither of us wanted to do that.

Ralph smiled, drawing a card face down from his hand and slamming it on the table face up as confidently as one doing something a hundred times.

Ralph looked down at it. Egon looked down at it. Everyone strained their necks for a look.

Ralph frowned. The card was a four. Also known as the Unterstecher, it was known as one of the worst cards to be thrown—better only than the Farbenstecher, which was a five.

Egon grinned and placed a Pope—a number six card—on the table. He won the trick.

The crowd moaned. Surely, Ralph just had a minor slack-off. No one was perfect. Maybe he'd underestimated his opponent. Ralph would bounce back.

Ralph then smugly threw a Kaiser—a number two card—and stared at Egon, who thoughtfully rubbed his beard at the Kaiser. He placed another Pope atop and won that trick, too.

I heard a man behind me mutter, *"Well, what d'ya know?"* The crowd was abuzz and anxious.

Ralph knitted his brows in confusion. With a slight bit of hesitance and less confidence, he slowly placed down an Oberstecher—a number three. That was quickly beaten by a Devil—a number seven.

Egon had won the first game! He'd saved one of his companions without breaking a sweat.

Ralph's face was beet red. He was embarrassed, and his nostrils flared in a fury. I knew then he had been trying to cheat, but the cheater was beaten by a calmer Egon, who had leaned back on his box to look up at the sky.

I glanced over at the father-son team. Westeros' face was mildly annoyed. I guess he supposed it was only one loss out of six; Ralph could still win. Longsigh, however, looked ready to blow a blood vessel.

I noticed Saraid was giving the game little attention, if any. She watched Egon and the crowd with interest.

The next game started a little differently, with Ralph beating Egon with Karnöffel and winning the first trick. *"Two more, and the fools will bloody die,"* I heard Westeros say from behind me.

*Two more was **a lot** more with Egon…*

Ralph grinned and threw another card down on the table after the dealer had shuffled. He was shocked to discover he'd thrown a measly eight, which Egon easily beat with a three.

Egon won two more tricks in quick succession — and the freedom of another one of my companions. The crowd grew uneasy.

Four more, I thought. *Four more wins. Was I bonkers? Hardly so.*

The next three cards played were Karnöffels. Even though I was relieved Egon had won that game — his third — as well, the crowd was now **livid** and began crying foul.

"He's a bloody trickster, he is!"

"Goodness me. Three in a row? That's not in the slightest bit right!"

"Cheater!"

The cries were endless. I would've laughed, had I not thought the mob would've stoned me to death right where I stood. As a matter of fact, I was trying to stand as still as possible so as not to draw attention to myself.

The crowd drew nearer to where I stood, attempting to get a better look at the game. I was surrounded by shouts of disdain, leaving me unable to hear anything clearly. Despite the crowd's rage, the game continued.

I wondered if it would ever finish…

Game four played for our fourth companion began with Egon stoning Ralph with a Devil to his Oberstecher. Ralph made some adjustments and won the next trick. Then, to my dismay, he won the next as well.

Westeros laughed boisterously behind me. *"I **knew** he couldn't beat him in all six games."*

I calmed myself. Ralph still needed one more trick to win.

Egon ended up winning the next one with a lucky Kaiser. The game was tied: two tricks each. A win for Egon would mean we gained our fourth companion. On the contrary, a win for Ralph would mean Egon, and I would have to get our friends out of here by brute force — a feat just as spectacular as it was nearly impossible, especially with all the bodies around us, hogging airspace.

"Win it, you old fool," I said under my breath. I couldn't help but glance at the mysterious Saraid again. She'd taken note of the game and was watching now, rather intently.

At the start of the next game, my heart was pained when Ralph threw a Devil — the second-best trump card of the game.

He was confident and smiled with triumph. It was too early but seemed final, anyway.

Egon had a sly smile on his face as well. My blood went cold. He'd bested him in whatever cheating match must've been going on under the surface. I nearly laughed when Egon slid his card across the table: a bloody Karnöffel Jack—the only card with enough value to beat a Devil **and** the best card in the game. The crowd roared with anger, as did Westeros.

Longsigh stood, stopped the game, and said, *"I'd like to examine those cards!"*

I couldn't help but protest. *"My lad never touched the deck! It's **your** man doing all the shuffling and dealing!"*

Longsigh turned a red and veined head in my direction. ***"YOU! SHUT YOUR MOUTH!"***

*"What's wrong? Scared of **losing**?"* I taunted, causing the crowd to roar even louder. I probably wasn't helping my popularity with these people much, but it hadn't been generous to begin with.

The dealer was given a new deck for the next game, much to my disgust. *If Egon lost this one because of this…*

Longsigh wasn't the only one red-faced; I was about to have a conniption! Westeros laughed at me, and even Saraid raised a brow in apparent amusement. I couldn't see what was so funny to them.

A new deck and fresh shuffle were far from comforting. Egon watched the dealer intently as he laid each of their cards on the table, leaning forward in a focused trance. The men picked up their cards, and game five began.

The crowd breathed. I didn't.

Egon drew a card and laid it on the table. We all craned our neck to see what he threw. A Pope: number six. It seemed to radiate on the table. Ralph nearly winced at the sight of his number two—the card valued one step beneath a Pope.

It was remarkable to me how Egon managed after the decks were switched. I was surprised, although I'd known Egon's cheating techniques were rather efficient. The surprise felt good, far better than the other way around. Egon won two more tricks for the win.

Five down. One to go.

Suddenly, winning six games in a row against Ralph didn't sound farfetched to me or anyone else standing there who witnessed the slaughter.

I heard Westeros whisper, *"Something's going on here…"* I'm sure he hadn't expected me to hear.

I turned to address him. *"Then, call it off. Are you a man of your word or not?"* I made sure to speak loudly. I wanted everyone to hear me and know that if their leader **did** call it off, it was merely out of fear that Egon would win the next game — and the freedom of all our companions.

Westeros' face darkened. Longsigh ordered me to shut up again. I felt a man step close to me on my right. He wanted me to feel his presence, reminding me that Longsigh and his lunatic band were still the ones in control.

The sixth and final game started with Egon throwing out an irritably low Unterstecher. Ralph easily beat it with a Pope. The next bout swung in Egon's favor when he won the trick with a Kaiser. The next was won by Ralph, and the crowd cheered. As fate would have it, Egon won the next trick. The formerly rowdy crowd fell silent.

Game six. Two tricks to two tricks. *I held my breath, as did everyone else in the crowd, I believe.*

Egon threw a Devil and smiled widely. Westeros was growing angry, and he was just about to say as much when Ralph threw down his card: the Karnöffel Jack The crowd erupted before I could lay an eye on the final trick. I felt the energy, though. It wasn't a good sign.

The first thing I noticed was not the card, but Egon's face. Perfectly flummoxed. Perfectly still.

Perfectly defeated.

I started looking around for a way out, but there was none.

The crowd shoved me mercilessly as they moved in to congratulate Ralph on his miraculous win.

*Think, Dustin! You have to **think**! How do you get seven people out of here?*

I felt the ominous man next to me get closer, perhaps to seize and kill me. I moved away as fast I could — as fast as the crowd would allow. Thankfully, the momentum of their shoving pushed me farther away from my captor in no time. *Pushing…pushing…* I could see the edge of the crowd coming closer. One or two more steps, and I'd run to get a weapon. Any weapon. I'd rescue my companions and return for Egon, hoping he was still alive when I did.

I glanced back to see if the big man was still behind me. I felt relieved when I didn't see him. *Now, I just have to push the rest of the way out of here*, I thought, swinging my head back around. I ran hard into someone, each of us regaining our balance almost simultaneously. There stood Saraid.

"Where are you going?"

"To save my friends! You won't stop me," I said, pushing her to the side.

She smiled in a sardonic manner. *"You'll never save them. Someone will reach you before you get down there."* She then turned to her right, glanced at a tent next to the clearing, and leaned her head that way. *"I'm glad I thought of that."*

What did **that** *mean?*

Suddenly, I heard Woodruff's battle cry. The whole crowd did. Five Warriors ran into the crowd with weapons: their weapons. A fight began — one I was sure would lead to our slaughter. In a panic, the crowd ran to get their own weapons…or anything they could use to defend themselves. They hadn't been ready for this.

My jaw went slack slightly. I turned to look Saraid in her eyes. *"You did this?"*

"You'd better run along now and help your friends before I change my mind." She handed me my sword.

Without a second to waste, I took off towards the crowd — and into the heart of the fight.

25: THE BOY

To be all alone is to be lonely.
To be lonely is to be all alone.

I don't know how many branches cut me as I ran. I lost count. All I knew was my arms stung, my feet burned, and my throat throbbed angrily. I couldn't breathe. I hardly swallowed. I forgot to blink. I forgot to think. I just took one step after the other, and even that notion was proving difficult.

I did occasionally stop to hurl. I hated it because I felt as if I'd already hurled every bit of my guts out onto the forest floor. I was so empty physically and emotionally, I was nearly numb.

If I'd had a way to tell time, I would've realized I'd been running full sprint for over half an hour without stopping. I never thought I could run so long, but then again, I hadn't thought I would've killed my parents or that my brother would've…done what he did.

I heard my blood coursing in my ears, and my heart was pounding too loud to hear the approaching danger. Not that there was much to hear.

An arrow whizzed over my head, taking a bit of my hair with it, and thumping into a tree to my left. I froze. It was an inappropriate but understandable move. My heart raced, but I didn't budge. My mind cursed at me, scolding me to move my feet and take cover.

Even if I had, it wouldn't have done any good. I was hastily grabbed by the ear by someone from behind who cursed at me. I yelped and held still.

"Do ya reckon this fool boy is worth any money?" I heard a man ask another.

Through my blinding pain, I saw a couple of figures pop out from behind the trees. By their dress, I assumed they were bandits. The kind every parent tells their children to run away from.

Great, I thought. ***Look what you've gotten yourself into.***

"Tell me who ya are, boy, or I'll cut off yer ear. Where do ya come from?" The man continued to hold tightly to my ear. A cold blade lifted the hair behind my ear and rested on the tender place behind it. He applied pressure, which hurt more than he probably anticipated.

"Honest to God, sir, I am nobody. Just a boy from a village south of here," I said hurriedly.

*"**What** village?"* he growled.

Ow! Ow! Ow! My ear!

"Souffrance!" I exclaimed.

"This boy isn't worth anything," the man said.

One of the other bandits approached the man who still held the knife at my ear. He was dressed similarly as the rest: a hood and short cape. Only his face was visible from behind it. *"Should we move farther west, Uzzah?"*

"No. We're done for the day," Uzzah replied.

"What to do about the boy?"

Uzzah twisted my ear, inflicting more pain. He got down on one knee so that he was level to my face. The man had a good bit of whiskers covering an unattended face. His grey eyes were steel, and steel was emotionless. *"Ya don't tell anyone about us boy, ya hear?"*

I was tired of this man calling me a boy. I was sick of grown people pushing me around. *"I've met people like you before. I'm not doing you **any** favors."* I then spat on his boot.

I saw a flash of silver and felt a sudden blinding pain on my cheek. I yelped and drew back from him, but he held me in a firm grip by my arm. I could feel the hot blood dripping down my cheek in droves, but I dared not reach up to touch the wound he'd given me with his knife.

He laughed at the fright in my eyes. *"Well, well, well. Ya have some fire in ya', boy. I think I'll adopt ya. How would ya like to be my assistant?"* He threw his head back and howled a laugh.

I nodded quickly at the offer, not sure if he was joking or serious. If he wasn't serious before, he grew taciturn in little time.

"Obedient now, aren't ya? Well, just so ya remember what I think of little brats…" He punched me in the jaw, and I fell to the ground. All of a sudden, my Pa's beatings weren't so bad. Pa's fist was made of wood; Uzzah's was made of metal. It was vicious, too. It enjoyed preying on a kid who had just overstepped his boundaries. It enjoyed preying on whatever it could. That fist was heartless.

A horde of blows took me after that, one after the other until I was condensed to lying on the ground with my knees tucked under my chin. I sobbed, waiting for the hellacious beating to stop.

I was a boy who couldn't be a boy.

I think I passed out at some point. I lost feeling, and things went black. I remember being thrown onto the back of a horse like a sack of grain as Uzzah laughed mockingly.

Most importantly, I heard a strongly-accented and intimidating voice with hot breath whisper into my sore ear, *"Hold yer horses, little man. Things will get better when we reach Clover Nest."*

26: DUSTIN ELRIC CARPENTER

There are friends everywhere,
If you wish to make them.

Ultimately, as much as I enjoy being a prince, I was relieved I knew nothing of what was going on. Saraid and Cederic had taken to calling all the shots, and I was looking around for Westeros. *How nice would it be to stab him in the gut?* Unfortunately, I didn't get the opportunity. Saraid and Woodruff were pushing us out of it all, and I felt someone tugging at my tunic while I ran. The bottom edge ripped from under my belt. I kept running without looking back.

We ran relentlessly through the camp to a nook between a smaller tent and a campfire. I breathed a sigh of relief when I saw our horses were there unharmed, waiting for their masters.

Conversely, Julius looked none too happy with me. When was the last time he had?

I jumped into the saddle and spoke my version of the simpler 'giddy-up': ***"C'mon, Julius! Get! Let's go!"*** With a whistle and a click, Julius got the message. He veered hard to the right, jerked me to the left, and jolted forward with a burst. Each action threatened to nearly throw me off the beast.

Looking back, I saw my six companions were behind me. Behind them was another group of horses led by Longsigh, with Westeros right beside him.

Julius felt my panic and pulled longer strides. I forced myself to breathe steadily, so as not to scare him. We ran out of the camp clearing and into thick woods. Branches stung our skin as they slapped their crooked fingers against our bare faces.

How were we to ever lose our pursuers? Longsigh and Westeros were bound to know the woods better than we did. Plus, they had faster, fresher horses. Not to mention, there was a herd of them and only seven of us. Yes, we were the world's brightest lads and lasses who would fight in vain any stronger and better-numbered group, but we were worn and beatdown.

I had barely thought those things through when Saraid was by my side then quickly taking the lead. ***"See you in a minute, prince,"*** she shouted. She took off to my right into the thick woods, disappearing and leaving me with a string of harsh words I desperately wanted to say but didn't have the energy to put together.

Why save us just to abandon us? I thought as I looked over my left shoulder at the party drawing closer to us.

"Dustin!" I heard Cederic shout. His tone was a warning.

I turned around and jerked Julius' reins, barely dodging a tree. We shifted left, and Julius' legs got caught and tangled in the underbrush. Gravity pulled us down to a floor of leaves with spiders in hiding, both mocking us with bites and scratches. I struggled to get up. The Warriors had stopped on their horses and closed in around fallen Julius and me.

"We can still outrun them! Keep going! I'm right behind you!" I yelled to the others. They didn't budge. I tried urging Julius to rise, but he wouldn't move. It was then I noticed a laceration on his leg that was large and bleeding profusely. The Warriors saw it, too. They formed a semi-circle around us just as the band of Forgotten Ones rode up to us.

I drew my sword from its sheath and stood.

"Congratulations. You succeeded in making us look like fools for a moment. I'll give it to you: I wasn't expecting my sister to fall in love with you, prince," Westeros mocked, looking us over.

I counted their numbers in my head. Forty? Fifty? As worn as we were, we couldn't beat this many. It was physically and mathematically impossible.

"Maybe there's several in your camp who aren't as loyal as you believe."

"SHUT UP!" Longsigh cut in. *"YOU WILL NOT GET ANY FARTHER, YOU FOOL! YOUR CARD GAMES AND WITCHCRAFT CAN'T SAVE YOUR LIFE!"*

"Now, hold on a minute," Egon said, hurt. *"There are a lot of ways to win a game of cards, but witchcraft and sorcery I would consider a tad farfetched."*

"SILENCE!"

I stepped forward. *"There are other ways to end this without anyone dying."*

Westeros scoffed. *"There is no future where your lot doesn't die, **prince**. None."*

"W-well, then. I'll die on the g-g-ground with my prince," Silas said. He threw his right leg over his horse and jumped to the ground. All the Warriors did the same, sending their horses off into the woods to find them later. They wouldn't last long in the middle of this unavoidable bloodbath, anyway. Julius couldn't move much, and he whinnied to tell me so. We'd somehow have to keep him in the center of our circle.

Longsigh called his men forward. They moved quickly, overrunning our smaller group. I gripped my sword handle tighter and called for the Warriors to stay close-knit. Being separated at a time like this would surely be our downfall.

The first wave was baffling and almost fatal. I barely withstood the slicing above my head and the wave of utter momentum. The Warriors fared better than I, though. Nearly every one of them had downed a foe. Even Arthur, who was shaking madly, shot an arrow into the heart of one foolish enough to come near. Woodruff had downed two.

None of the Warriors appeared too hurt, which was of little comfort because more of our enemies were on the way.

This time, I felt a sting to my right arm. A new sword had sliced a nice-looking beauty into it. I used my sword to slice along that rider's abdomen. Unfortunately for him, **my** strike was fatal.

"Cut their horses down!" Cederic shouted.

The next time, I attempted to do so but missed. Seemingly out of nowhere, one of Cederic's shurikens penetrated the rider's neck, and, after screaming in agony, he toppled off his horse limp and dead. I threw my sword hard at the next horse's legs, slicing one all the way through. The horse fell quickly, as did the rider whose head was quickly detached from his shoulders by Ocean's blade.

I felt Arthur back up on my left and jerked around to see a rider coming too close for him to clear a shot with his arrow. I stepped in front of him and cast a flashing sword in a 180-degree motion, straight down and cutting nearly all the way through one of the man's arms. It got stuck in the arm of the wailing attacker! His horse continued running blindly with his rider. I lurched forward a bit, trying to get the sword to break free but failed. **Dang it!** I liked that sword.

I yanked the sword up from the now-headless man Ocean had decapitated. *I'd have to find my sword for sure — if we* survived, of course.

A dozen more assailants moved in on horseback. One of them was Westeros. I felt Arthur move a step backward to my left. I knew he was scared. Understandable.

This wave was the hardest yet. I was knocked into Arthur and down to the ground. In a split second, the Warriors' huddle was broken. Several enemy-clad horses bolted through the spot Arthur and I used to be. We were separated from the rest. I scrambled up in time to duck underneath a flashing sword. I swung at the rider's back. It connected, but I didn't have time to look back and see the damage done. Instead, I offered my hand to help Arthur stand.

Once on his two good legs, his eyes widened as he looked just past my right shoulder. ***"Duck!"*** When I did, he pulled back his arrow on a tensed string and aimed, letting go quickly but accurately. He'd shot a man who'd been running at me from behind. His expression showed his exhaustion. *"It feels like we've been through a whole lot, but we've barely done damage to them!"*

I glanced around quickly. *"Actually, I think we've killed all their horses."* I was about to brace for another wave of them when I spotted a trembling Westeros limping towards me. I recalled seeing him move to my right towards Silas right before the wave hit, but it seemed he got the worst of it.

Below his knee was a huge gash the width of his thigh. He was bleeding profusely from the wound. The scarlet liquid built up around the nasty cut. He gritted his teeth as he approached. I couldn't tell if his trembling was the result of the loss of blood, anger, or a combination of both.

"Curse you, prince! You and your friends have been nothing but trouble!" Spittle sprayed from the irate man's mouth, and his veins were strained taut.

I gritted my teeth as I spoke. *"We didn't ask to be bothered."*

Suddenly, he moved forward, leaving me little time to raise my sword to block his reckless, unsteady strike. He swung the other way, and I turned my sword nearly straight downwards to block his. I pushed hard against his sword to knock it away, using the momentum to swing for an unguarded neck. He did well to get his sword around and in the way of the attack. He swung again. I moved slightly left and dodged his attempt, much to his irritation. He was relentless, though. He moved in again, and again, I did not pull back, content to analyze the pattern of his strikes. He made one final attempt to kill me, and I countered with a quick move that ended our duel. He had passed out after the blow to his chest. I wasn't ready to end his life just yet.

I heard the clanking of swords behind me and knew there were more waves coming. I also noticed a blur in my peripheral vision, telling me Arthur was engaging another attacker.

I was alone on this one.

I noticed the approaching man's right leg was hurt. His dominant leg. He couldn't lean on it when he edged forward without the pain being unbearable. The man was weak when he swung his weapon and could easily be countered if he wasn't careful.

He wasn't.

As I sat back and toyed with the injured man, he grew more agitated. More anxious. More reckless. I used that time to observe that the faster he swung, the more gingerly he stepped forward. His leg was letting him down. Any other day, I would've felt sorry for him. Frustrated with my blocking another of his strikes, he drew back his right fist and yelled, ***"Fight me, pig!"***

I raised a brow, tickled with amusement. *"I'm not exactly the one who's angry here. Please, do the honors,"* I said with obvious laughter in my tone. I had tired of playing with this man and was ready to end him.

Just as predicted, he lunged at me, fist still raised. I sidestepped away from his intended blow. As I'd hoped, the man had committed fully to the punch and couldn't quite recover in time. I flipped my sword and cracked the hilt onto the back of his skull. His knees buckled, and he fell to the ground, his body dead and unmoving.

I returned to Westeros' injured body. To be sure of his demise, I pointed the sharp edge of my sword at his neck, hesitated, then moved to cut into his jugular.

"Stop it!" I was shoved from my left before my blade reached his neck and was sent sprawling to the ground. It took a second to get my feet under me so I could look at the person who'd put me to the ground.

It was Saraid. With a sword.

"Well, look who it is," I mocked over the faint sound of clanking swords. The battle had thinned out considerably. *"Decided to come back after all the action was over, huh?"*

She snorted. Looking away from me and down at Westeros, she kicked his limp leg. *"He's sleeping. He won't awaken for a while. He's no more trouble to you, so do not kill him."*

*"He's a **murderer**."*

*"He's my **brother**!"* she responded angrily. It occurred to me that was the most emotion I'd ever seen from her.

"Fine. Here you are, back to order me about."

*"I am not ordering you. You may do whatever you'd like, **prince**."* She stepped past me and caught the end of a strike meant to pierce my back. Throwing the man's sword back at

him, she stabbed his with hers, yanked it from his dead body, and turned back to me. *"We need to move back a little. Can you get your companions to do that?"* she asked, annoyed. Or perhaps just tired.

I stood there, confused. *"Just what game are you playing?"*

She looked irritated. *"I wouldn't play a game costing so many lives. Move your people back.* **NOW!***"*

For some uncanny reason, I decided to trust her. After all, she had gotten us this far. ***"Move back! Get back! Now!"*** I shouted to the Warriors. When they responded, it was then I realized they'd fought off nearly all the Forgotten Ones. To my dismay, however, there were at least 20 more standing with Longsigh, ready to attack with a fresh wave. The chances were slim we'd make it, especially if Saraid was a liar and I, the fool.

I chose to run with Saraid and the Warriors, away from Longsigh and his men. I was about to ask why we were running away when I heard a thunderous snap, crack, and thud — the latter shaking the earth.

I turned to see a massive branch had fallen on an unlikely place: atop Longsigh and his men. I could only stare at the gruesome sight of crushed limbs and bones for so long before I grew nauseated and had to look away. Saraid stared at the scene with an expression I could not read, though I was getting used to that about her.

"You did this?" I asked, tilting my head towards the carnage without looking at it again.

Reluctantly, she looked at me and nodded slowly. *"It was intended for the hostages who'd escaped."* She scanned the area, briefly settling her eyes on the Warriors. *"I was supposed to be in charge of letting it down on your company if you won."*

Totally shocked, I felt the need to ask, *"You saved your brother from the end a **sword**, but you crushed your father underneath a massive **tree**?"*

"A branch," she corrected. *"My brother is a result of being my father's son. My **father**, however, made a choice to be the man he is…well, was. My grandfather was nothing like him."*

"That's…terrible," I muttered.

"Call it whatever you'd like. I'm sorry I had to leave you to fight them alone. The trap had to be set."

"Apology accepted, I guess." I slid my sword into the sheath attached to my belt.

"Why do you sound uncertain, prince?"

"You tend to when you've just been captured then rescued by the same person." A small chuckle found its way up from my belly.

As she prepared to reply, I heard someone approaching from behind me.

"Drop your sword! Do it now!"

Saraid didn't move a muscle.

I turned to the sound of the very familiar voices. Arthur and Woodruff were approaching fast, with the rest of my team close behind them. Arthur had an arrow nocked on an eager string. They all looked at Saraid with a hint of confused animosity, which could only be associated with a betraying acquaintance.

Woodruff impatiently shouted his order again. *"Drop the sword, or he'll put an arrow in you!"*

"I have no doubt you will let loose the arrow. I'm not quite sure, though, where it will end up. I wouldn't trust an archer with a trembling hand," Saraid stated.

"You may doubt anything else about me, Miss, but do not doubt my aim," Arthur retorted.

Woodruff cast me a questioning look, to which I nodded and went on to explain. *"Saraid is who triggered the branch to make it fall on her father and his men. She's fine."* I motioned for my friends to relax.

Arthur lowered his bow. *"Thank you, Saraid. We would be dead without you."*

Egon cocked a flustered head. *"Well, y'know if they hadn't* **cheated***, I would've won the card game."*

"That is left to be determined," she replied to him. She then turned and asked me, *"You are going to Jocund, yes?"*

I nodded.

*"You all deserve the chance. It was a beautiful kingdom, not so long ago. I'd be honored to see it ruled by **anyone** other than Monté."*

I grinned. *"We'll try our best to take it back."*

"*But wh-where will* **you** *go?*" Silas asked with concern. "*Your camp will n-not take you b-b-back.*"

Saraid looked thoughtfully around at the Forest of Many Enchantments. She seemed to consider the question intently before responding. "*I will do what my mother always wanted to do. Leave this place.*"

No sooner had those words left her mouth than I suggested, "*You can come with us.*" It seemed the best thing. After all, she'd sacrificed everything to help us and —

"*No,*" she said quickly. "*Jocund is not my home anymore. I won't hold on to it. There is much more of the world to see.*" She moved her gaze to me and looked me in the eyes. "*If you take Jocund, you will see me again. I would like to visit the kingdom when it's alive, not dead. Alive like it used to be…*"

I held her eyes for a solemn moment, then said assuredly, "*I'll take it. Or I'll die trying.*"

27: ROSETTA KELLINA MABEL

*We're going to be wrong
A lot in our lives.
We might as well get used to it.*

I felt movement by my bed and wondered quite excitedly if the messenger pigeons had returned. I was awake in a heartbeat and had already sat up to rub the sleepiness from my eyes when I was startled to near-death by a chorus of, **"Surprise!"**

I blinked several times and saw Lydia next to my bed, along with Héloise, Faye, and Kip. They stood nearby, with Kip holding a… Was it a coat of armor?

"What the heck is going on?" I croaked in my sleepy voice.

Lydia laughed. *"You've been working hard lately, so we thought we'd surprise you!"*

At my still bewildered expression, Faye giggled softly. *"My goodness, Rose! Have you forgotten your own birthday?"*

My eyes widened. *"My God! I have! It's bloody today, isn't it?"*

Kip rolled her eyes in a playful motion. *"I wouldn't be holding this armor if it wasn't."*

"Who's the armor for?"

"James told us to give it to you. You asked him to make it, didn't you?" Héloise asked.

"Oh!" I blushed. *"He told you that?"*

"Please, Rosetta," Kip said with a smile written between her words. *"We were happy to see you have at least **some** heart."*

"Oh, hush!" I proclaimed as I threw the covers off myself. *"It's beautiful. I'm so happy with it! Peter will love it, too. No longer will he have to shrug around in armor too big for him."* My words ran together excitedly.

Just then, I noticed out the corner of my eye the pigeons had gathered in the early morning darkness on the balcony of my bedroom. Another message! I grew excited. *"Let me meet you ladies outside the room after I've changed. We can have breakfast together if no one's busy."*

Faye shrugged. *"I'm not. Sounds like fun!"*

I smiled, pleased by not only their thoughtfulness but also about what awaited me on the balcony. I hurriedly took the armor from Kip's hands. Lydia noticed—as only a best friend could—my excited expression and glanced inconspicuously at the birds. When she saw them, she let out a small shriek and then ushered the girls out quickly, making sure to toss me a wink on the way out.

No sooner than the door shut, I ran across the room like an elated puppy. In my excitement, I practically ripped the cylinders from the birds' talons. One cast me a warning look, to which I thoroughly apologized to. I then laughed at myself for talking to a bird.

I hummed to myself while I worked to place the papers into a comprehensive order.

<div align="center">~~~~~~~~~~</div>

Dear Ro,

By the time you get this, it ought to be your birthday, so I wish you a happy and relaxing day. I'm glad you are in need of company. I am as well! It is a terrible thing, indeed, to have unequal levels of happiness in a relationship.

I do write often! I enjoy writing stories the most, as it helps the uneasiness and constant demands of what is life. However, writing letters is such a romantic thing. I'd hate to waste it on idle chatter with a stranger, which is the reason you are the first person I have written to in my free time.

I shouldn't have said that, with how awkward our situation is, me knowing so much of you, and you so little of me. I will refrain from acting so strange so as not to throw you into confusion, making you resent me. My apologies!

The Lord Monté is a brute. I have heard many stories of him. His devastation to the land of Jocund, the Theft, is known well where I *come from. The Battle… He conjures up those things to keep you under his control, his fear. I wish I could spare you that pain. Your friends sound bright. I'm glad you have them. I hope they will keep you safe until I get there. I will arrive as quickly as I can. I promise. You are important to me. You'll understand this soon.*

Love,
Geoff

~~~~~~~~~~

My cheeks were red hot by the time I finished. I huffed a satisfied ad flustered breath. *Love?* I pretended to myself that I hated the idea, though it'd managed to excite me for absolutely ridiculous reasons.

Why do you have to be so complicated, Rose? How can you love a man you've never known?

Maybe I had known but don't remember. How could I struggle so intensely with what was right in front of me and accept what was far away? How could I run away with feelings so wrong and misguided?

Yet, this so-called stranger knew my birthday. The exact day. How could I possibly not be stirred? How could I avoid the inevitable intrigue that comes with mystery and conversation such as this? Cursing, I glanced at the sky.

"Do you realize how much trouble I could be in if someone discovers me writing to you, Geoff? I'll tell you: Way more than I bargained for. Maybe you knew that. You seem to have a firm grip on what's going on here," I muttered.

I desperately tried to think of anybody I knew who could have possibly sent this to me. I had never been romantically
~~~~~~~~~~

involved with anyone and tried to stay far from it. It was nearly impossible to think who it could be.

Except Chancellor Kenneth. *What if he was my mysterious love interest?* The thought made me nothing short of miserable. I moved to get dressed and forget about **that** idea.

Did the mystery man have a link to my parents? Calling me Ro could be a clue...

The thought brought chill bumps to my arms. The thought of my parents was never an invited one. I missed them tremendously, almost to the point of going numb with it. I thought I had, until the man used my parents' pet name for me.

But how? How would he know such a thing without knowing both my parents? There must've been a link there... I shivered. He practically haunted me. I couldn't sleep without thinking of him. I wondered if that's what he wanted.

I put on a simple dress and tied an apron with a pocket to hold my sewing tools in. Glancing at myself in the mirror, I found myself wondering what Geoff would think of me. Seeing he seemed to have known me, he must know how I looked or used to look. Did he think me beautiful then? I'd always hated my dark hair and freckles—light freckles sprinkling my face with no intention of letting go. They reminded me of my age and how young I was.

"Rose" was a red flower. A beauty. A standout. None of the definitions reminded me of me. Quite frankly, they reminded me of the opposite: A sweet-tempered, well-mannered girl who held her pretty hands in a submissive manner and held her tongue. I couldn't hold my tongue if the world depended on it. A young boy who'd loved me deeply told me once it'd be the reason I burned in Hell.

Maybe it would. It hadn't stopped me from telling **him** to burn in Hell. What a mess I was, indeed! Geoff was sure to hate me. At least the present me, anyway.

I combed through my hair almost angrily. *Seventeen years old today and no better for it. If I'd cared to make any difference with my tongue, I'd march to the top floor of this atrocious castle and tell the Lord what I thought of him to his bloody face!*

There were, however, limits to how far even my tongue would go. Oh, what a grip death had on someone's soul! I was as afraid of the cursed man as I despised him. He had my marks for that.

My mind lingered on the Lord and what he was doing at this moment. *Probably burning incense to some stupid god. Plotting the annihilation of the kingdom he had stolen.* Of course, it was a prejudiced assessment, seeing I had no clue what he was doing. Maybe he was thinking about the next Battle of Bloodshed happening in two days. Two dreadful days before the worst one of all.

I wondered what Geoff's definition of "quickly" was. If he did mean to save the kingdom — *if he could* — then right before the Battle would be an idealistic time for a hero to step onto the scene.

Not just for me, but Jocund as well.

Before meeting the girls, I pulled out my ink and paper from my drawer by the bed, wrote a quick letter to Geoff, and slid the paper-filled cylinders into the birds' talons. Watching them fly away in the dark, I tried to tell the direction they were headed. They seemed to head east towards Precursory Wood, but it was hard to tell in the dark if they veered north or south on their course towards it.

Were the birds smart enough to trick me in the direction of my writing companion? Messenger pigeons were smarter than any beast I knew of. Maybe the man was coming from the bloody west. Maybe he wasn't coming at all. After all, I could finally be going insane. A man writing me letters from Precursory. How stupid could I get?

Still, I believed. **Still**, I shuddered. Surely, Geoff wasn't coming through *there*. Was he going around it instead?

I heard someone behind me and turned.

"Rose? Are you alright?" Héloise had peeked in to check on me. I realized then I had taken far too long for the excuse of my getting dressed.

"Oh. Yes. I was —"

"Looking at the birds?" She smiled. *"I'm okay with you loving the creatures. Just don't throw yourself off the balcony trying to fly."* She turned to leave, and I caught up with her.

"Nonsense," I said as we left my room. *"If I killed myself, you girls would have no one to lead you and would throw yourselves recklessly off the balcony as well. While I can be responsible for my own death, I will not have any more than my blood on my hands. Is that clear?"*

She wrinkled her nose at my statement. *"I suppose."* As we approached the rest of the group in the corridor, she turned as if she'd just heard me say it and asked me, *"Wait. What did you say about us throwing ourselves off the balcony?"*

I smiled at the other two girls as we reached them. *"We should be off, then."* We made our way to the stairwell.

"I'm just curious, Rosetta," Héloise whispered to me in a hushed voice. *"Did you happen to befriend the man who saved the boy?*

"Peter?"

"His name's Peter, then?"

I rolled my eyes. *"No. Peter is the boy. Ferrando is the man."*

Héloise widened her eyes. *"Then you **do** know him?"*

"Sort of." I watched her expression. *"Does James know you're asking about him?"*

She blushed and grew defensive. *"Oh, for God's sake, Rose. I was only asking about him. It's not important if I'm only asking."*

I grinned. *"Well, let's leave it at **that**, then."*

She scoffed. *"If I didn't know better, I'd say you're attempting to keep him all to yourself."*

"Nothing could be further from the truth. Hats off to you for changing the subject, though."

Before a mildly offended Héloise could answer, Faye announced from the front of our little group, *"Almássy is cooking today, so don't expect anything good at breakfast."*

"Almássy?" Lydia sounded dismayed. *"I thought they executed her for poisoning the Chief Official."*

"Apparently not. I was told she was spared because someone of rank liked her pies," Faye informed us.

"I'll make sure to check my meal for poison, then," I mumbled.

Kip turned to me as we went down the last bit of steps and into the last corridor leading into the Great Room. *"Don't mumble, Rose. It's so unladylike."*

"Oh? Who on earth cares, Kip? The air in the stairwell? Perhaps I should lift the hem of my dress while I walk the stairs, too," I said sarcastically.

"Now, don't put words in my mouth Rosett – "

Faye cut in. *"Hush. Here's the Chancellor."*

I froze at the mention of him. There he was, in front of the large entryway to the Great Room. He was beaming as if he'd just hunted a large elk or ended the victor. I glanced over his white suit, forever untouched. Clean and making a statement. His curls a busy mess on a full head. His smile making me dread even coming to breakfast.

"Hello, girls. It's a nice day, is it not?"

We all nodded. Héloise giggled. *"Yes, it is. Are you here for breakfast?"* she asked.

"Precisely so. I was made aware it was Rosetta's birthday."

To my great annoyance, the group parted like the Red Sea so I would be visible to the man. I noticed his eyes softened when he saw me. I was also aware mine had gone dead.

"Thank you, Chancellor Kenneth. I appreciate you taking the time to acknowledge it." My words fell out like dry sand, tasting like nothing.

"It's your day, and I'd hate to interrupt it. However, I do have something for you…" He looked at the girls as if expecting something. It was Kip who caught the hint.

"We'll check what's for breakfast. Come along, girls." As they followed Kip into the Great Room, Lydia shot me a comforting look of sympathy. *Hang in there,* it seemed to say.

Well, in the end, it didn't matter. I would let Kenneth do the talking and remain quiet as a mouse. *Oh, if **only** I could believe that.*

Kenneth was smiling wretchedly, and I was obliged to play the game or hang for it. *I should've never thought of breakfast. I should've gone straight to work. God! Why couldn't I ever just enjoy myself?!*

"Rosetta, would you like to join me on the balcony?"

Nooo. *Why are you even **asking**? You know what I **have** to say, I wanted to scream.*

"Of course." I moved with him to the end of the corridor, where two massive doors led to a large balcony. I had never been on this balcony, or at least not since the Lord had taken over.

There was a couple on it now, sharing intimate conversation next to the balcony's stone wall. When they saw Kenneth and me, they moved to leave quickly. He seemed to hardly notice them in the first place.

He led me to where the balcony wall was. I could view the courtyard and village beyond from over the wall. The sun was barely breaking the horizon. I couldn't see it, but it cast a warm glow on the castle, leaving shadows to dance around in places. The air was still damp from the early morning dew, my hair layered with the fine mist.

We stopped. The Chancellor in front of me and I in front of him.

"Close your eyes, Rose." It wasn't a demand as much as it was a request.

I hesitated then obeyed, counting the seconds that seemed to last days, months, and years all at the same time. I felt his hands brush my neck. They were cold, but they didn't tremble. Why was he touching me? I resisted the urge to let my eyes snap open and punch him in his handsome nose. Something cold fell and touched the skin beneath my throat. Was he holding a sword there? Maybe he knew about the pigeons? Maybe the hidden journal? My palms started sweating.

"Open them."

He'd whispered the words into my hair. I felt his breath there and nearly screamed. My eyes snapped open, expecting to see whatever cruelty awaited me. I saw nothing. He stood behind me until I looked down at the cold object still touching my skin. I inhaled sharply.

It was a necklace. A silver chain with a golden bird and diamonds adorned it. I had never seen anything quite like it. It was possibly the most expensive thing I'd ever beheld.

"Who is this for?" I asked breathlessly, though I wasn't foolish enough not to know the answer. The shock of it had made me ask.

"You, of course. Just a birthday present for my lover," he said, taking my hand and coming around to face me.

I was so taken aback by the sheer beauty of the jewel, I managed not to hear the last bit of his statement. I stared, amazed by its beauty. *"How could I even wear such a thing?"*

He laughed at me. *"What do you mean? You wear it like a bloody queen! Or is that too vulgar a word for you?"*

Somewhere in my mind, I knew he was teasing me, but I couldn't collect my wits in time to counter it. Instead, I lifted the bird from off my breasts and gazed at it. Never in my life had I owned anything close to it. It was truly magnificent.

"Do you like it?" he asked, perhaps to tear my eyes away from it and back to him.

I did no such thing. I kept gazing at it and said, *"Never in my life did I imagine receiving anything like it."*

"Well, now you have, thanks to me," Chancellor Kenneth said, rather pleased with himself.

I finally looked up at him. *"Thank you."*

It occurred to me then that he held each of my hands in his own. He looked down at them as if he were admiring a trophy he'd won. I studied his face. He made me uncomfortable—like a mere object he needed to obtain.

"Chancellor, why have you given me this?"

He looked up then and smiled at me. *"Please, it would bring me joy if you would call me Kenneth. Calling me Chancellor just won't do."*

"'Won't do'? What do you mean?"

"I love you, Rose. To death. I cannot express it more. You and I were made to be together. You must understand that…"

No, I wasn't sure I did. *"Please tell me why you have chosen me, then."*

He withdrew and wrinkled his face. *"What kind of question is **that**? We love one another. I would assume that's enough."* He leaned against the balcony wall and looked out.

"Not at all," I ventured to say, trying desperately not to offend the man. After all, I'd already overstepped my boundaries. Any decent woman would have told the man she loved him, too, accepted the necklace with joy, and moved on. It was inevitable. *"You've told me you love me, but I know little of what attracts you to me."*

Still leaning on the balcony wall, he turned to look at me again. *"Ah, I see. You want a bit of **flattery**."* He moved from the wall and cupped my face with his hands. *"I never thought you to be the least bit vain, Rose. I suppose all women need a man's assurance at some point in time."*

I closed my eyes to shut the man out. He knew what he was doing. Charming me was a hopeless cause, and he was half-hearted because he knew he was my only option.

Or so he **thought**. He wasn't, right? There was someone out there coming for me. I **had** to hope because I had no love whatsoever for this man.

"I appreciate your gift…Kenneth."

He scoffed. *"Is that all you have to say to someone who's professing his love to you?"*

"It is all one says when she feels nothing back." It rolled off my tongue like a boulder. I hadn't meant to say it. It was in my head, and then it was out in the cold morning air with the dew-sewn wind.

He looked slightly hurt. *"I'm going to pretend you didn't say that."*

"I suppose I shouldn't have," I mumbled.

His eyes narrowed. *"You **suppose**? It is a privilege, Rose, to be loved by a man such as I. I thought you'd understand that."*

"Who's privilege?"

"Watch your tongue!"

"Why? Will you strike me? Am I to submit to your love like an animal? Who do you think I am?" My voice rose with each word spoken.

Chancellor Kenneth's face grew hot. *"An intelligent and beautiful woman who needs to think things through before bashing a man such as I! That's who! You are without parents. You're lucky to still be alive. You live by the whim of the Lord and speak ever too quickly about matters you don't understand. I am your **only** chance at stability, Rosetta. **Your one chance to secure your bloody happiness!**"*

"Happiness is overrated. Hardly any of us achieve such a thing. I am not after happiness. I am after truth."

"This is the truth, Rose. The unavoidable truth," he said softly. *"I am a man of success. I'll grant you whatever you need."*

"I have no feelings for you, Chancell – "

"Kenneth," he corrected irritably. *"Feelings aren't love, Rose. You are not a child waiting for a bloody hero anymore. You're a grown woman. Think about what you're doing."*

What if my hero is talking to me through love letters? What if he truly does exist?

A tear tore its way to the surface and fell down my right cheek. *"Please don't make me do this,"* I whispered. *"If you love me, please let this go."*

Kenneth laughed then, almost cruelly. *"Are you asking me not to love you? Are you so foolish, Rose? Many girls would give* **anything** *for me to tell them what I've admitted to you. I put my heart out there, and you're trying to crush it?"*

"I wouldn't dare. I swear to God, I am not. I am only telling you how I feel. I'm not ready for this, Kenneth." It appeared he wasn't even listening to me, as he was too pleased with my usage of his name.

He touched my cheek gingerly, leaned down, and kissed me on my cheek close to the corner of my mouth. His lips seemed so sharp, they felt like they cut me on the inside.

"You'll grow into it and me, my darling Rose. You'll see I'm the best thing to ever happen to you." He smiled and, without another word, left me standing on the balcony, alone and cold inside…with the most splendid piece of jewelry I'd likely ever own.

I leaned over the wall and bit my lip, trying not to cry. *"God, why?"* I breathed brokenly. *"I don't want this man. I don't want any of this. Please take it away,"* I sobbed brokenly. *"Please. I just want my parents back. My friends. My soul. It's all been taken from me."* I stared through watery eyes into the courtyard and out at a waking village. *"Kill the Lord, please. **Please** kill him."*

It took me a while to collect myself and enter the Great Room for breakfast. When I did, people stared. I wondered why and lowered my head. I then remembered the jewel around my neck and nearly cursed. Confound it, even Kenneth, who had taken a table with several burly men, was watching me.

I made my way across the room as best I could and sat with my friends—curious friends who wasted no time asking me what went on. They wouldn't let it drop in the slightest, and Héloise wanted to know where I'd gotten the jewel.

I lowered my voice so no one at the next table over could hear the few words I said. *"Ask me again, and I'll throw myself off the palace balcony onto the stone below. Would you like that?"*

No one asked again.

28: DUSTIN ELRIC CARPENTER

To let wisdom leave
Is to surely doom yourself.

"I see it through the blur of tears.
I see straight through your heart.
I see your broken beauty, lass.
I know you long for love."

Arthur and Ocean sang, loud enough to wake the dead. Egon was huffing curses at the pair who'd just reached the 30th verse.

"But this soul of mine is taken, lass.
My heart is not to buy.
I've lent it to another lass
Who never asks me why."

"I wonder why," Egon muttered with sarcastic curiosity. *"Will you two be quiet? You're hurting my ears, for God's sake. We've got **too** long a journey for me to hold my patience."*

Arthur finally turned to look back and address him. *"There are 70 verses, Egon. Can we at least do half? That's barely five more,"* he pleaded.

*"Yes, I'm quite aware how to add my numbers, **Arthur**,"* Egon said through gritted teeth.

Woodruff and Silas laughed, while Cederic watched the sky.

"Well, can we?" Arthur asked Egon politely.

Ocean didn't wait for an answer. She started the next verse:

"I'd write a different story, too,
Our love the core within it.
I'd write the words in mountain runes
In stone, they won't forget it."

As she sang, Arthur joined in again for the chorus:

"But this soul of mine is taken, lass.
My heart is not to buy.
I've lent it to another lass
Who never asks me why."

Egon snorted. *"Spare me."*

I laughed at his irritation and joined in for the last three verses:

"I'm weary from the dusty road
And broken from the deaths.
I'm just a man of funny whims,
Who's gone and lost his head.

"So, don't give me your angry eye
If life treats you so poor.
It can't be me; I'm just a man
Who's torn apart your soul."

Silas and Woodruff joined in for the last bit, to make Egon's dismay even more enjoyable:

"I never meant to hurt you, lass,
Or make your life so ill.
I just meant to tell you, lass,
I'm married to Lucille."

At that, we burst out laughing until our sides hurt.

"As much as I enjoyed that, I think we'd better be a bit quieter," Cederic said with a half-smile on his face.

Egon groaned. *"It can't be healthy to busy myself with befriending so many fools."* He addressed Ocean next. *"You sing so bloody well! You should sing the choruses at some church."*

"She should, shouldn't she, Silas?" Woodruff chimed in.

"Most-Most definitely!" he stuttered and smiled.

Egon snorted again because his statement had been sarcastic. He shook his head. *"I think I've had enough tom-foolery for one day."*

"*Oh please, Egon. We just escaped a band of revengeful Jocunders. You ought to be over the moon,*" I reminded him.

"*No thanks to your horrible card skills,*" Woodruff added.

If getting under Egon's skin was easy, then he was **terribly** vulnerable about his niftiness with cards. The latter statement made his face hot. "*Well, bless **you**, Woodruff!*" he exclaimed. "*I'd like to see you win five straight games of Karnöffel! Even better with all our heads at stake!*"

Woodruff laughed at him and provoked him further while we rode through the thick forest. "*You're right; I would lose. I can't say I'd be unhappy to see you go, though.*"

"*You'd go, too, you **idiot**!*" Egon said, throwing his bread at Woodruff's head with laser-beam accuracy.

"*There went your late lunch,*" Woodruff said amused, wiping the crumbs out of his hair.

Egon grumbled. "*I'm tired of bread, anyway.*"

I grinned and turned back to him. "*You know what I'm tired of? This **journey**. We're halfway through, at least. No point in giving up now.*"

Silas crept up next to me as the group fell into one of their thoughtful silences. "*I know you've st-studied the castle-the castle, Dust, but I still feel as if we're riding with our h-h-heads down. How do you plan on getting to Monté without anyone n-noticing us? The castle's huge. I've been there-been there several times. Before the Theft, of course. I c-ca-can tell you now it won't be as easy a-a-as you might be thinking.*"

I turned to him and noticed he wouldn't look at me. He was looking straight ahead as he spoke. I know he hated doubting me. Hated questioning what I had decided to do. These Warriors were close to me—closer than anyone I'd ever met. Even then, they struggled with speaking to me like any sort of equal at times.

"My father thought this would be the perfect time. I do, too. I'm not the best at taking kingdoms from evils lords, but I might not need to be. Maybe if we stick together and trust one another, we could best him."

Silas smiled at that and nodded. *"I think s-so, too."*

He and I fell silent, and I was left with my thoughts.

Honestly, I was a bit nervous. Traveling with six to take a castle full of thousands? Monté had done it, though. Why couldn't I? I'd heard, too, Lord Monté was about my age when he took it. Was he nervous? Did he care at all? From the stories I'd heard about him, caring wasn't in his blood. Neither was compassion. He was a brute who was quite unpleasant to hold conversations with. My father didn't even talk about him—and my father spoke to me about nearly **everything**.

To murder a king, his queen, their officials, an entire staff, and many guards didn't sound at all like your normal massacre. Once you'd eliminated the king, queen, and officials, why kill the staff? The people? Was he afraid they would turn on him or was it just bloodlust?

Rose was lucky she'd survived, yet it almost worried me. There had to be **some** reason she was spared. Not knowing what the Lord Monté had planned is what scared me the most. I prayed every day he wouldn't hurt her, and he hadn't. I just wanted the chance to see her again.

"So," I said to Silas. He perked up a bit. *"Ocean told me you told her how you got your stutter."* I said it casually because I knew it was a bit of a touchy subject. I didn't want him to feel like I was questioning him at all.

"She told you-told you about that?"

"Yeah. Well, I mean, she didn't tell me what happened. She was pretty secretive about that part, if saying so eases some of your anxiety." I saw him glance over at her humming figure, and I grinned. *"You two have been getting along just fine."*

He tore his eyes away from her and looked down. *"I knew how I felt about her a long-long time ago. She took a while to f-f-feel the same."*

"Always seems that way," I replied thoughtfully. *"Takes the lady far more time than the man to make up her mind,"* I said jokingly. I watched as his unsure eyes roamed back over to the subject of our conversation. *"She does feel something for you. I know,"* I said confidently. It was enough to make him swing his head in my direction.

"How?"

"Well, her eyes light up whenever she's talking to you or when we talk about you. She stares at you too long, also. If you turn around in your saddle right now, you will see she's doing so," I said, amused and in a hushed tone.

Silas blinked and then turned slowly to find a nonchalant Ocean looking straight ahead. Not at him at all. *"No, she's n-n-not."*

"You were too slow. I swear she was looking at you just a near second ago," I said honestly. *"If you'd just turned around quicker, you would have seen her."*

*"If I had t-turned around any quicker, it would have m-m-made me look like I was sitting-sitting in my saddle, blatantly **watching** her."*

*"Isn't that **exactly** what you're doing?"*

His face was red as a pepper. He whispered to me rather harshly, ***"You kn-know what I meant-what I meant, D-Dustin!"*** Obviously flustered, he pulled a book from one of his bags on the back of his horse, Idla, and started thumbing through the pages quickly, as if he had to find a spot to be interested in before I addressed him again.

"I'm joking," I admitted, laughing.

He continued thumbing through pages without looking at me, cheeks still hot. *"Well, i-it wasn't fun-funny,"* he retorted.

I laughed aloud until Egon and Cederic hushed me.

"Someone's coming," I heard Cederic's deep voice muse. Indeed, now that it had been so blatantly pointed out, I could hear it, too. A person who was distinctly uncareful was disturbing the brush and making noise as loud as a trumpet.

"I'm going to be honest," I said, swinging my leg over and jumping off Julius. *"I'm getting tired of people trying to creep up on me."* I pulled my sword from its sheath and moved towards the noise. Something broke out from around a tree and ran towards me. Instinctively, I grabbed it hard by its shoulders and realized what it was right before it went limp.

A child. With strawberry-blonde hair, freckles, and everything.

Shocked, I felt her pulse. It was there. Faint, but there. **"Bring water!"** I called out to the Warriors who were still on their horses. They got off them quickly to see our new arrival. Woodruff reached me first with the water. I took the flask and let a few drops fall into her open mouth.

"That's Ilse! Isn't it?" Arthur asked. *"Endres' little girl…"*

I nodded as I grew sick to the stomach. If she was out alone without her father, mother, or brothers, there was definitely some ill news. *"Please wake up,"* I pleaded with an edge of guilt.

Her eyelids lifted like weights had held them shut. She seemed so frightened. *"Where's my daddy?"* she mumbled.

"I was hoping you'd know that, little one," I said.

"I'm supposed to tell you something… Something about the bad man… I forgot. I forgot." She started to cry. I grew increasingly uncomfortable because I had no clue how to comfort a sad, little girl.

Ocean knelt beside her. *"Hey, hey. It's okay."* Ilse stopped crying and looked at her through tears. Ocean continued. *"It's okay if you can't remember. Let's start from the beginning."* The little girl nodded. *"Your dad told you something, right?"*

She nodded again.

"But you don't remember what he told you?"

Again, the nod.

"He told you to tell us…? Did he tell you to go quickly to tell us?"

Her eyes widened because she'd remembered something. *"They hurt daddy, so he told me to go get you…"*

"Who hurt him?" Egon asked harshly. Ocean shot him a displeased look, and the girl started sniffing.

"I can't remember," she mumbled. *"Es tut mir leid."* That was mumbled as well.

"It's okay," I said softly, collecting my wits. I was usually good with kids, at least when my mind wasn't on bands of forgotten people and things of similar nature. *"Just try as hard as you can."* It hit me just how young she was. Five, **maybe**?

"The boys and daddy and mum are trapped in the dark place." She shook her head, dissatisfied. *"The cellar. That's where they are. Daddy can't fight them anymore. They hurt my daddy. Mum was crying, too."* Her eyes teared up again, and Ocean rubbed her back soothingly. *"They're trying to get through the door. The door to the cellar. I had to go through the top window. It's the only window in the cellar. I was the only one small enough to fit through. There isn't a lot of them, but daddy can't fight at all anymore. He's hurt, and mum is scared."*

"Who's hurt your father?" Woodruff asked.

She sputtered. *"The…bad…guys. They're going to hurt him. Please help us."*

Woodruff grew thoughtful. *"Did they have yellow wrinkly skin, girlie? And no teeth?"*

She nodded ferociously, and I grew grave.

*"**Reapers**. Darn it."* I turned to the girl again. *"You said there wasn't a lot?"*

*"Daddy stopped a lot of them, but daddy's really hurt. He was… He was **bleeding**."* She said it like it was the worst word ever uttered. She began to cry softly.

I left Ocean to tend to her and stepped away from the tedious situation right into another.

Egon cursed as the six of us men grouped together. ***"We can't backtrack. We're on a schedule,"*** he said angrily.

"But we can't j-just leave them, Egon. They helped us. Don't you-you have a compassionate bone i-i-in your body?"

Arthur pinched the bridge of his nose thoughtfully and then raised a finger. *"I got it, mates. It's not too many, right? Let's send just **one** of us back. The rest of us could move on, and the one could catch up. They'd make a quicker pace traveling alone, anyway."*

"Aye. Good thinking, man," Woodruff mused. He stroked his red goatee and wrinkled his freckled face. *"The girl ought to go back, too. It's not many of the Reapers. She won't be hurt, and we can deliver her back to her family."*

*"What if something happens to whichever one we send back, eh? Is anyone thinking about **that**?"* Egon butted in.

*"Well, at l-l-least we're thinking of **something**,"* Silas muttered.

"Good, then." I ignored the two bickerers. *"Who's going back to help Kraus?"*

"I will go," Cederic said without hesitation.

"Oh, bless your heart, Cederic. Forever brave when duty calls," Egon said, though I knew he would've volunteered if he could bear the presence of a child for as long as would be required.

Arthur piped up, his voice offended. *"I would've done it, too…"*

Egon looked sharply at him. *"'I would've' doesn't mean a thing when you're a Warrior, Arthur."*

Arthur stared at the ground.

"It's settled, then," I said quickly. *"Cederic, might I have a word?"*

His light eyes moved towards mine. Two pearls inside of dark skin. *"Of course, Prince Dustin."*

I turned and saw Ocean had calmed Ilse, obviously making her feel safe. I walked over to the girl who was giggling at something Ocean had said.

"Hey," I said as I bent down to her level. *"Do you want to see your daddy?"*

She nodded.

"Sir Cederic is over there," I gestured toward the man, and he smiled on cue through his beard. He even gave her a little wave. *"He's going to help your dad and take you home, okay? No more bad guys."* She nodded but seemed a little reluctant to approach the strange man. I smiled and whispered to her, *"I heard he's ticklish on the right side of his neck."*

She looked at me, eyes wide, and then back at Cederic a little less afraid. *"Is it true?"*

I had to swallow a laugh. Her face was so disbelieving. How could such a strong man possibly be *ticklish*?

"I guess you'll have to figure it out," I said. I picked her up gently, walked to Cederic, and placed her on the horse he'd received from Kraus.

Cederic smiled up at her then mounted his horse, in front of Ilse. He looked back at her. *"Do you have a dolly at home?"* he asked — the word 'dolly' sounding out of place in his deep and rough voice.

She nodded.

"Good. Wrap your arms around me like I'm one of your dollies, and don't let go. Hold on tight, okay?"

For strange and childish reasons, the statement made her giggle. Cederic smiled like I'd never seen before as he whistle-clicked his horse forward in a brisk walk.

I followed his horse on foot while throwing over my shoulder to the rest of the group, *"I'll be back in a moment."*

I heard Egon call to me, *"Just don't go getting lost!"*

We continued on, away from the group. When we were out of earshot and nearly out of view, I spoke to Cederic. *"Give Kraus a hearty thanks. Don't let him give anything to you, either. He's done more for us than we did for him, endangering himself like this."*

"Indeed."

"Stay overnight if you can. I would like to see the Krauses stay safe and be assured of it."

He nodded, but it was Ilse who spoke from behind while still hugging his waist. *"Who are the Krauses?"*

I laughed. *"You. You're Ilse **Kraus**, and your dad is Endres* **Kraus***."* I could tell this was new information. It occurred to me how insanely refreshing it was to talk to a child.

"Well, off you go. Hurry back tomorrow, Cederic. I fear we'll all be lonely without you."

He cracked a smile and then urged his horse into a trot until they were gone, and I was alone in the woods. I turned to return to the group when I noticed the birds ahead.

"Good to see you, buggers! What have you brought me from her?" I moved farther from the group so they couldn't see me before I called the creatures to the ground. I sat in the dirt like a little boy and pulled the letters from the containers, impatiently organizing them.

<div align="center">~~~~~~~~~~</div>

Geoff,

If you want my honesty, I have no idea what you would find so interesting about my companionship. I lack romance, and my acquaintances say I lack heart as well. What I really lack is hope, Geoff. I fear losing people. It's why I don't get close to them anymore. Are you afraid of anything?

There's a book I discovered in the castle library. It's a journal of a boy who struggled through much turmoil as a child. I feel I'm not supposed to have it. I know I'm not supposed to send you letters — whoever you are. Most certainly, I shouldn't be telling you about the journal, but I can't help myself. I need to be careful, but I'm too busy

*being curious. You've changed my life as well as ruined it. I'm
angry with you (if you didn't sense it).
However, do not stop responding.
I am growing restless. Jocund's growing restless, too. I can feel it. I
imagine the Lord is as well. I'd love to tell you more, but I'm in quite
the hurry. I'm supposed to accompany my friends to breakfast.
Which reminds me of your birthday wishes. It is something I
appreciate more than you could ever know!
Thank you for knowing. For caring.
I trust you. I know it's a funny thing to say so early after meeting
you, but I do. I feel the statement will make you happier
than I can imagine.*

*Your Friend,
Ro*

~~~~~~~~~~

I was grinning rather stupidly at the pages and didn't
even care. Her aches, her worries, her emotions… She was
sharing them with me — a start I never could have imagined.

To my disappointment, there was no use writing her
back, as it was too bright outside. I'd have to wait until tonight,
though for all the progress I'd made with Rose, I didn't even
mind.
~~~~~~~~~~

29: THE BOY

Trickle, dimple, fickle, simple.
If there's a God above, He must think me mental.

I opened my eyes and saw a rack of dirty teeth. I punched whoever it was and jerked to get away but was slapped in the face...slapped into stillness. A thickly-accented voice told me to stay down. I did. I heard a trickle of water, the sound driving my head insane. I was sitting against something jagged and hard. Most certainly, it was stone. Had I lost my sight, or was it just dark? Where was I?

"Stop taking my stuff, you big lummox!"

The voice came from my left. My head jerked to see two men pushing each other in irritation. The one on the right was trying to take a belt from the man on the left, and they were pretty open to risking a broken nose for it, too. There was some serious aggression occurring between the shoves.

At their feet laid a dead body. Completely naked and motionless on a stone floor. I realized then the men standing over him had probably killed the man and took his clothes.

"Don't mind them, bru. They're just whining each other's ears off, that's all."

*Over a **dead** body,* I thought. *Is that so normal?*

My cheek burned, and I remembered the man I'd spoke to before I was knocked unconscious. The mean man. Where was he? Had I been rescued from him? I looked around again and hissed when the accented man put a wet cloth to my hurting cheek. *"Where's the man who beat me up?"* I asked through clenched teeth.

"Oh. Uzzah." The man, who I realized was the one who whispered to me before I passed out, laughed. *"Wherever he **wants** to be, I assume."*

I huffed. *"Yeah, because men like him think they can do whatever, huh?"*

The man looked at me, puzzled. *"That's a rather bitter statement, but I suppose it's true enough."*

I stared at the man as he went back over to his tin bucket of water to wet the rag again.

Upon further examination, I found I couldn't rightly call him a man. Sure, he was several years my elder, but he was much younger than his voice suggested. Or his stature.

I always knew I was tall for my age. The accent man was only a couple inches taller, so he must've been short for his age. No matter, he had more muscle in his arms than my father had. With the man's skin almost black, you would've thought he was a person to fear if his eyes didn't give him away.

I laughed. I couldn't help myself. *"You're just a kid."* I felt his open palm slap me on my cheek. I was shocked he had done such a thing. He didn't look like someone who'd resort to violence.

"Sorry," he said. He flashed me a smile of his dirt-infested teeth. I noticed — through the throbbing from my cheek — that he had a deep dimple on the left side of his face. *"You ought not say things like that. It'll get you into trouble with the other members."*

That was a warning, not necessarily an angry outburst. The accented man was punishing me softly now, so I wouldn't say anything like that to maybe the two men still over there fighting. I nodded slowly. He watched and nodded in response, as if he realized I'd understood.

"Members?" I asked carefully.

"Yes." The man grinned proudly. *"Welcome to our band of Wolf Head. Thieves and bandits, they call us. We're the Scavengers."*

I made an impressed humming sound, and he continued.

"Uzzah Keres, widely known as Anonymous, is our sole leader. This is our lengthily sought hideout. We call it the Clover Nest. It's underground."

"Clover Nest? What do bandits have to do with clovers?" I asked.

He eyed me warily and shrugged. *"Not much. I think Uzzah picked it because there are three core leaders, like the three petals on a clover. He's the first and highest in command. Then, it's Of. Of is second, of course. You'll recognize him because he's a bit bigger than the other men. Then, it's Tomas over there."* He gestured to the two fighting men.

I glanced over there and raised a brow. *"Which one is Tomas?"*

Accent man laughed. *"Flat nose. Scarred eye. That's Tomas. The other is Steven, the prettiest of all of us, you might say — and the first one Uzzah would murder, given any good chance."*

"Has he done it before? Murdered someone?"

"Plenty," he said. I grunted.

"So, what's your name?"

"Aldus. What's yours?"

I shifted. *"Nothing."*

He laughed. *"Okay, Nothing. Let's see if you can stand without falling over now."*

The statement made one of the men who had won the brutal battle for the prized possession look over at Aldus and me and grin.

"What have we here? Another child that's going to get killed in the next few months?"

I stood, drawing up to my full height, trying to look brave and much older. I felt pain everywhere and tried hard not to wince and give my façade away. I could tell it was Steven—the pretty one—as he moved towards us. He had a skinny nose and dark eyes below a mess of dark hair that was a lot darker than mine. His mouth seemed to twitch constantly, as if he always wanted to laugh at someone whenever he got the chance. He had signs of a bit more than just a stubble, which was an indication that these bandits didn't have time to shave, let alone the resources.

I think Aldus could tell the statement left me steaming. He moved in quickly to answer.

"This bru is different. You ought not mess with Steven."

"Oh, shut up, Aldus," Steven jeered, stuffing the hard-won belt in his pocket for safekeeping or for wearing later. *"I want to know if the boy can talk. Just a little. Just say one word, kid. Let's start with your name."* He leaned into my face. *"Try saying 'cox comb.'"* He burst out laughing. *"That's your name, isn't it? Cox comb?"* He grinned with a set of teeth much cleaner than Aldus'.

I realized then bad people had to have some cover for themselves to be slightly effective in the world. A lot of times, they came in handsomer packages.

I paused and then smiled to myself, causing him to drop his. *"You must be the cook, then. You're too soft to be a bandit."*

He punched me in the gut. I groaned and doubled over. Just as he walked away, I winked at a concerned Aldus and called to Steven from on my butt next to the stone wall of whatever cave we were in. *"Hey! **Steven**, is it? I meant to give this back when we finished talking."* I pulled the rolled-up belt from my pocket and smiled at him. *"Couldn't be bothered thieving on my first chance of meeting bandits. How dreadfully rude of me."*

Steven narrowed his eyes and growled as he stepped forward, jerked the belt away from me, and kicked me in the side. It hurt, but I wanted him to think I'd never been kicked before. Maybe staying with this band would do me good. None of them could possibly know what I'd been through.

A boy, indeed, I was. Weak, I certainly wasn't.

As Aldus offered me a hand to stand, Steven crossed the cave again and began digging in a pile of nasty clothing.

He winked at me, dimple flashing. *"Darn it, Nothing. I just knew you weren't like the others. Now, follow me so I can show you off."* He winked again, and I followed him because he seemed to know how to be a friend.

We moved through a dark and skinny tunnel I could barely breathe in, into a cavern. The cavern was considerably prettier than the other. On the right side, the stone wall broke off completely to a waterfall running on the other side. It created an amazing illusion of water pouring from nowhere and sent light and shadows dancing inside the cave. It wasn't a big area or full of much.

There were several men in the cavern talking or eating. Two, I noted, were sitting on saddles they'd placed on the hard, cold ground. They played a game of cards with a deck looking older than its time.

There was a girl, too, who was maybe Mallory's age. She was wearing cuts and bruises and stirring a pot full of something hot. Steam drifted from it like a yawn, lingering only for a moment before dashing off towards the waterfall. The waterfall made the space feel slightly damp, beautiful, and brilliant.

I found myself liking it…until everyone in the cavern paused what they were doing to look at me.

"Well, will you lookie here? Uzzah's prized possession!" one of them laughed.

"Bah," said another one holding a crooked spoon full of something hot midway to his mouth. *"He had one of those last week. This one ain't gonna last much longer."*

I let them throw me around with their words, remembering Aldus' warning. It was him who spoke next. *"This here's my bru. His name is Nothing, and he's the newest addition to the band."*

They all snorted as if it was the funniest thing he could've said. Some of them even went back to what they were doing in pure disgust.

"Gonna die before the end of the day," I heard a man grumble.

Aldus smiled at me. *"You're probably hungry, aren't you?"*

As if he'd awoken it from hibernation, my stomach twisted painfully. I nodded. I must've looked a beautiful sight after not eating for several days.

He led me to the girl who was still stirring the mixture. The closer I got to her, I saw she wasn't using a pot for cooking. It was, in fact, an upside-down helmet.

Aldus picked up a bowl for each of us and handed me one. *"Aalez, give me and Nothing a bowl of gruel."*

She spooned some gruel into my bowl without ever making eye contact and did the same for Aldus in the exact same manner. I smiled at her, trying to make a connection, but she just stared at her feet.

Aldus then led me to a corner where we sat down on the floor with our bowls of gruel. I watched as he spooned his into his mouth greedily. As hungry as I was, I was a bit suspicious. I put a spoonful to my mouth and found it tasted just like water — something I hadn't had in two days as well. I gave in and 'ate' the bowl of gruel without further examination.

Midway between swallows, I glanced at Aldus. *"Hey. Aalez, you called her? What does she do here?"*

He looked up at me, mouth full of gruel. *"Aalez? Well, her rightful place is the crew cook, but as long as she's been here, I suppose she's used for much more. This just ain't no place for a girl."*

I nodded and lowered my head, only raising it to stare at her for a bit. From the looks of it, she might have been beautiful behind all the soot, weariness, and fear. I felt bad for her. Life just wasn't fair to some. Period.

Just as I was staring, the man who said 'Bah' shouted at her to fix him another bowl. She fumbled to do so. He knocked the spoon out of her hand and slapped her. None of the other bandits paid it any mind, but a fire kindled inside of me. I moved to stand.

"I wouldn't do it, my friend." The voice came from one of the guys playing cards. He had a curled 'stache and burly

eyebrows. He was perhaps just too heavy to be of much use to the bandits, yet too small to be kicked out for it.

I turned to him and noticed he wasn't even looking at me. He was wholly absorbed in his game, but the warning had undoubtedly been aimed at my direction. *"Excuse me?"* I asked him.

He threw down one of his cards without looking at me. *"Plenty a fool has done it. I've seen 'em all get themselves beat to mush."*

"So?"

He chose then to look at me. *"Everything you do on your first day is important. It sets the bloody tone."* He lowered his eyes back to his game. *"Besides,"* he continued, *"you look bloody awful. You can't be saving a damsel lookin' like **that**."* His card-playing partner chuckled.

I lowered my brows, deciding right then to stay put. I was a bit more self-conscious of myself now, as well. I turned to Aldus and whispered, *"Who is he?"*

"That's Of. Always remember: The only person more important than him is Uzzah."

"Yeah. Okay. Where is he?"

"Hold off, bru. I'm trying to eat."

"Oh," I said awkwardly.

"Bloody heck, Nothing! I already told you," he continued like there had never been a moment of silence between us.

"Uzzah comes and goes as he pleases, though I suppose he's looking around outside, scouting for another ambush."

"We've been in here for a while now. The others won't talk to you. Why?" It was something else I'd noticed. People intentionally acted as if Aldus wasn't there.

"I have no idea. Maybe it's my hair, my eyes, or, more likely, the color of my skin. People filled with hatred will always find something about you to hate. I'm in no mood to figure it out, bru. The fact is Uzzah accepted me here, so this is home. This is family."

Lousy family. Then again, what was **family**?

I nodded, and he narrowed one eye at me. *"You're a curious one, aren't you? Still, curiosity is better than fear."*

I looked away from him and back at Aalez. She was just picking herself up after the man who assaulted her had left.

"The world is just a rotten piece of filthy fear, anyway. I'm going to expose it someday. I'm not afraid to do so."

I said it too loud, and Of's card-game partner glanced up to address me. *"What does a boy know of the world? Your mum and dad's always fed you the good part of the meat and sheltered you from harm."*

This man obviously knew nothing about me… **Nothing**. He wouldn't understand that my parents knew less than me about the world. Not all children were sheltered. Not all adults were well-informed.

I laughed at him openly, which I suppose was not a smart thing to do. *"You're right,"* I proclaimed between laughs. The man seemed confused. I'd taken so much humor in his so-called life assessment. Of course, I took humor in it! The man was positively mad! My agreement was simply a way not to ruffle any other feathers.

Inside, however, it was also because I didn't want anyone to know about the fire that burned in my belly. The fire was burning every bit of my spirit and leaving behind piles of ashes. My broken mess of a past was making me stronger. For the first time in my life — in my entire young life — I wasn't the least bit scared.

Uzzah plays a game of fists, while you play a game of lies, the voice told me. ***Your father played the game of fists, too. He fell. Uzzah could, too.***

I smiled crookedly at the beautiful thought, and Aldus gave me a warning glance. *"Better watch your tongue,"* he said, voice lowered. *"Don't give the crew anything to spit on you for."*

"Of course." The thing was, though, that I wasn't scared of being spat on.

Not at all.

30: DUSTIN ELRIC CARPENTER

Grey hairs falling.
Love is calling.

It was getting late in the day. The sun was beginning to rest on the edge of the horizon, shining bright yellow rays through the trees. Woodruff had ridden out ahead only a half hour ago to see where we could stop for the night. I had expected him to return with news, just maybe not with so much enthusiasm.

"*What is it?*"

"**It's huge! It's so big!**" Woodruff exclaimed.

"*Oh, yeah. That's definitely answering the question,*" Egon grumbled.

Woodruff shot him a smile. *"My poor and miserable man, I guess you don't want to hear about the **manor**?"*

"The manor?" Ocean asked, interested. *"How is there a manor in Precursory? No one can live here, and certainly not lavishly."*

Those were my exact thoughts. I lowered a brow in curiosity.

*"I bloody saw it, I did, mates! It's humongous...and **abandoned**!"*

"This is ju-just great. Let's all run into-into a h-h-haunted mansion and hope we c-come out."

"Oh, don't be a wuss, Silas," Woodruff teased. *"At least it'll shelter us from the blasted rain that's sure to come."*

Yes, that **had** become a problem. The skies were grey, and the clouds were full. At any moment, they would burst open and drown us all into misery. I wasn't afraid of water, but no one liked getting rained on. Plus, Julius would be livid.

"We might as well check it out. The person who built it probably ran away a long time ago," I surmised.

I heard Silas mumble to himself, *"Or g-got killed."*

Egon swung on his horse and looked back at the man. *"Oh, hush. You read too much. You're buggin' paranoid!"*

"This is an enchanted forest! A d-dark p-p-power is upon it! This isn't something we sh-should take lightly."

I nodded my agreement. *"Silas has a point."*

Woodruff grumbled. *"How about the **point** where we find somewhere to rest and eat?"*

"Yeah. Somewhere where our food won't get soggy," Egon said crossly.

Arthur, who had been silent for a while, smiled. *"Maybe we should check it out, Silas. Endres had a safe house. Perhaps this person was trying to do the same."*

"Before h-he was viciously killed by m-m-monsters…"

Egon groaned loudly. *"Oh, for the love of God! Spare me!"*

I rubbed the back of my neck, thinking. I could understand Silas' desire to pass the manor, but there were opportunities he hadn't considered. After all, **I** was the leader of this entire journey. It was never **their** job to figure this stuff out.

Yes, we could possibly make enemies, but if the manor was still inhabited, we might befriend someone. Of course, if it wasn't inhabited and was indeed abandoned — as Woodruff claimed — we didn't know how long it's been sitting that way. It could still be packed with food, clothing…anything. Useful things we could use later. Heck, even matches.

How could I simply say no and walk away from the potential bounty? Plus, I had five Black Warriors in my company. Danger was their breakfast.

"Well, then. We'll check it out. I wouldn't raise my hopes, though, Egon."

~~~~~~~~~~
~~~~~~~~~~

The manor was, indeed, big. I think the word Woodruff had been looking for was ginormous! A lot of trees would've been cleared for it to be built. A lot of gold must've been invested in it, too.

*"Who would abandon **this**?"* I found myself whispering.

Its towers were tanned stone underneath a Romanesque red roof. The edge was lined with corbels. Windows blotted the walls of stone, each with a half-circle curved at the top. There were also lancets—windows with pointed tops. I marveled at how many different windows there were. The designs were ornate and magnificent. The entrance's welcoming gate awaited us.

Ocean shook her head. *"To leave this, you must be bloody mad!"*

"The front gate's open, mates. Let's go," Woodruff said, climbing off his horse.

I hesitated at the idea of going inside. As I did, I heard a rumble of thunder like nothing I'd heard before. *"Yes. Come, my friends. Let's go inside and have a look around."*

I heard Silas grunt in dismay, but he obeyed as quickly as the rest. He dismounted his horse and tied its lead rope to the gate.

I found it odd the manor's gate was open, as if some man scared by whatever followed hadn't the time or courage to close it. I glanced up and saw a raven staring down at me. *What a lofty-looking thing it was, with its beady and black untrustworthy eyes...*

I grew uneasy.

Inside, though, was an entirely different matter. It took on quite the normal appearance of a manor. I swept the grand room with my eyes. The dining area had an expansive table lined with chairs. I opened a cabinet that creaked loudly as if telling me, ***"Shut the door, mate!"*** Within, cobwebs lined old bowls and plates. There were even dry spices left untouched.

"Search for matches to light the manor when it gets dark," I told the rest.

"S-s-so we're staying?"

I nodded. *"Whoever lived here definitely doesn't anymore. I think it was a lack of food that drove him out. Who builds a manor in Precursory? There's no game to catch. Hardly any edible plants…"* My voice trailed off as I thought deeply about my own assessment of the situation.

"Endres makes it," Arthur pointed out.

"Yes, he has. Aided by my father, I presume."

The sun peeked over the horizon and cast a yellow stream into the manor.

"I found some matches," I heard Egon call out.

I searched the rooms for any sign of life. I moved down every hall, but we were definitely alone. I was content to scour the house for the rest of the time light shone through the windows.

As I roamed the manor, I thought about Rosetta and Jocund. I had been concerned about the kingdom for many years. News of Jocund's fate became terribly difficult to come by. Rumors spoke of their years of suffering. My father had been hesitant to stretch his hand to aid—not because he hadn't been a friend of the former king, but because Lord Monté was a shrewd one. No doubt, he would defend his new kingdom well. With so little news to scout the place, sending an army so ill-informed would surely be begging for their deaths.

Conversely, with so few of us, not only would the Lord be surprised, but he would be without the advantage of knowing where or how we would strike. He wouldn't even know we were there. We'd be like a whisper in a shadow. A blink in the dark.

It was being king someday that threw me off my rhythm. I trained for a long time for this moment. I was supposed to be ready, but a noble kingship was something one could never truly be ready for. My only hope was that not only was my mind properly trained, but also my instinct. I hoped beyond all hope that being a king was ingrained in my blood and heart. My opportunity was on the horizon.

I glanced up, realizing it was now dark. The sun had lowered, and the moon now shined. The sky was still blue, but I knew it wouldn't be for much longer.

I had checked enough rooms. There was nothing for anyone to live off of for any length of time, so I backtracked and paused when I heard the laughter of my friends coming from a room to the right of me. I stepped inside.

Moonlight showed me it was large room made to perhaps be a dance hall. Lots of objects lined the wall, now covered in sheets. I wondered how any men in Precursory could have a dance hall, when no one wanted to visit your home. Whatever the reasons **were**, dancing was exactly what Egon and Ocean were doing at the moment in the middle of the dance floor. Or more like Ocean was guiding a confused and miserable man down a floor he didn't desire to move down. Arthur, Woodruff, and Silas were getting a kick out of it, though.

"No, don't jump like a buffoon, Egon. Take long and graceful steps," Woodruff teased.

Egon shot the laughing group a glare as he tried to keep up with Ocean's lead.

I laughed, too. I couldn't help myself. *"What's going on in here?"* I asked with a smile in my voice.

"We thought we'd put the dance hall to good use — and gracious me, are we not doing just that?" Woodruff replied as he continued watching the spectacle before us.

I doubt Egon is the perfect dancer for these quality floors," I mused.

Ocean spun once. As they grew closer to us, she began to laugh.

Egon's brow furrowed. *"What? What am I doing?"*

"You're just lovely, darling. I just need to rest a bit." She sat next to Arthur, still laughing.

I thought Woodruff was going to bust his gut laughing. Even Silas was having conniptions.

Egon gathered his hurt pride and smiled. *"Dancing's for fools, anyway. Not Warriors. I pride myself on how fast I swing my staff, not how well I can lead a woman across one of these accursed floors."*

Arthur grinned. *"Well, the Good Lord in Heaven knew what He was doing when He gave you other talents!"*

Egon narrowed his eyes. *"You have five seconds…"*

Arthur squeaked and jumped to his feet, dashing across the hall Egon was hot on his heels.

I laughed. *"It's dark in here. Light one of those matches, will you? I found an unlit torch in another room and brought it back with me."*

Woodruff picked up a match one of them had laid out on the floor and scraped it hard against the floor repeatedly until it lit. He then set the torch I was holding ablaze. *"What do you need light for? If you ask me, it's time to sleep,"* he said as he stretched and yawned.

"I just want to see what's under all these sheets." I walked toward a large, square object. I slid the sheet off slowly, cautious of what might be behind. From the light of the torch, I could see it was a painted portrait of a small boy smiling in a garden. *"Hmm… Maybe a relative of the owner?"*

"Most likely," I heard Silas clearly say.

I stared at the painting. The child looked like such a kind boy, with his dark hair neatly parted in the middle and his dark eyes. I wondered where exactly the image had been made, knowing full well I would never get the answer.

I walked down the line of sheet-covered objects, removing each to reveal portrait after portrait. Each told its own story under my flickering light. The first, a boy. The second, a girl nearly Rosetta's age. The third, an elderly man. The latter looked back at me in an inviting way, as if he were my grandfather begging for one more hug from his grandson.

I loved history. Something about someone living a story before mine was captivating. *Who were these people?* **Where** *were these people?*

"Dust, you might want to check out this darned thing," Woodruff shouted at me.

In unison, several of the others asked him, *"What?"*

I ran over to see what it was.

Almost breathlessly, Woodruff pointed a shaky finger at the first portrait of the boy in the garden.

"Yeah. Okay. The boy has to be — " I suddenly felt as if the wind was knocked out of me from some invisible giant. I had seen the impossible. The cursed, darned **impossible**.

The boy in the picture had blinked.

Egon and Arthur took notice of the confusion and joined us at the portrait.

"Did anyone else see…?" I asked, my mouth agape.

Woodruff nodded slowly, as did Ocean.

Right before our eyes, the boy in the portrait began to grow. Taller. Broader. Older. We watched the boy's life transition from a wee boy, to a man, to elderly. He didn't die, though. As an old man, he continued to age until his skin sagged, and he was far older than any human in modern history. He became ugly beyond repair.

We watched the man's teeth rot and fall out in quick succession.

We watched as his bones tried to break free from their skin's outer shell.

We watched as his hair thinned, and his fingernails grew long, yellow, and rotten.

We watched as his eyes went from dark and playful to bloodshot red, almost protruding from his face.

He became unbearable to look at, so I turned away in disgust. I looked down the room at all the portraits I'd uncovered.

They all had aged.

"What kind of witchcraft is this?" Egon spoke softly to the darkness of the room.

"I don't know," I said, my voice shaky. *"I don't like it. Let's get out of here."* I grabbed someone's bag they'd brought in and tossed Woodruff his ax that he'd laid on the ground. I turned to leave, knowing the Warriors would follow me.

That's when I heard it: A faint tapping on glass.

It made me turn back around to face the former boy's portrait. The rotted man's eyes bulged out of his skull, and he was banging his forearm on the portrait's surface as if to break it. The rest of the figures in the paintings began to do the same, but my eyes rested on this one — the first one.

The Warriors grabbed their stuff quickly and moved away from the thing as if it would break free from the portrait's glassy finish.

It cracked.

My stomach knotted up. *"Let's go! NOW!"* I ran, my sword bouncing against my hip.

Where was the bloody door? Why couldn't I remember the way? If Cederic has been here, would we even be in this manor?

"Where's the door?!" I shouted anxiously.

Silas jerked his head. *"R-r-right! It's t-t-to your bloody r-right!"* he shouted back.

We ran out of the room and into a corridor. My torch was the only light, guiding the way like an angel.

I heard glass shatter and knew what it was. Dread loomed over me, and sweat dripped down my back. They all had looked so familiar. I was only just realizing the boy in the portrait had turned not only into a monster, but one I had encountered.

A Reaper.

That wasn't the right name for them. They were horrifying creatures. My mind was blank as I tried to recall what Endres had called them. It had been hard enough to kill just one of them. How many bloody portraits had I uncovered again? Ten? Twenty? Fifty?

The sound of footsteps like rolling thunder was behind us. Groans of every sort drifted down the corridor like a stench.

I did two things: I ran as fast as my years of merely 17 would allow, and I did not look back.

We made it to the stairs. Someone — something — was close behind me. I could feel their heat. I tripped over my own two feet and fell a couple of steps before my companions tripped over me. I shook my head, trying to determine what had caused the terror. It hit me like lighting hits the sky.

My torch had burnt out. We were lying in pitch-black darkness.

I never told anyone how deathly afraid I am of the dark, ever since I was little. I certainly didn't need Woodruff knowing. It's such a strange thing because I hadn't been a paranoid child. I didn't imagine monsters crawling out from under my bed or my closet door cracking open to reveal some strange being behind it. Even now, I wasn't scared because there might've been something standing in the dark I couldn't see; it was the blackness. It pushed me into a box where I couldn't move, think, or speak. The blackness overwhelmed me.

Now, I had the horde of Hell on my tail, and my torch had burnt out to nothing.

How humorous, I thought.

"What happened?!" Egon shouted.

"Torch went out," I said in a small voice.

"Leave it! We have to go," Woodruff said. *"Everyone still here?"*

There was a collective yes, but I noticed Silas' voice wasn't one of them.

*"Where's Silas? **Silas!!!**"* I squeaked, the panic in my voice apparent.

Everyone felt around and up and down the stairs, madly searching for him.

"Here he is!" Arthur called. *"He's unconscious. I think he knocked his head on one of the stairs."*

I could hear the monsters upstairs approaching the stairwell.

I heard Woodruff move towards Arthur's voice. He grunted, picking up Silas, and said, ***"Let's go."***

"You first," I called out into the darkness. *"You'll be the slowest."*

Woodruff led us down the stairs, just as the monsters entered the stairwell. I heard their chilling groans echo, and I breathed quick, uneasy breaths. I cursed as something grabbed me roughly from behind. Nails scratched all the way down my arm, trying to find a grip. I pushed the thing I couldn't see off of me and rushed down the stairs. Blood dribbled like a stream down my arm, hot and wet.

I saw light ahead. It wasn't much, but my eyes had adjusted to the darkness. I could see now that Woodruff had reached the bottom of the stairs and was moving into the lowest level.

"I see the bloody door! Follow me!" he shouted gruffly, and then disappeared from my view.

I looked back. It was too hard to tell how many of those gross things were following us, but I did notice the glint of what seemed to be a million eyes rushing my way, fixated on me and…Ocean? I think it was Ocean behind me. I could hear her steady breathing.

The beasts were quickly advancing. I knew they would reach us before we reached the bottom. Ocean did, too.

"Run, Dust! Please don't stop!" I heard her say as she unsheathed her Requisite.

There was a screech from one of the buggers behind me. I debated turning around and helping Ocean. I knew it was a dumb idea. With two of us trying to fight our way through those things on a bloody staircase, neither of us would ever make it down. I ran down the last few steps and out of the stairwell, calling over my shoulder that I'd made it and that she'd better hurry.

I waited for her at the doorway. Moments later, she emerged. Three marks looking like the work of the beasts' nasty fingernails had ripped the skin above her right eyebrow, and her left hand was bloody.

She pushed me from my stationary trance. ***"Go! Go!"***

I took off running. It was a good thing I did because the ugly things that poured out after us had taken several steps our way.

Woodruff — supporting a shaky Silas — Egon, and Arthur were waiting for us at the front door. It was Egon who shouted to me as I reached them.

"We'll hold them off! You get on a buggin' horse and get out of here! We'll be right behind you!"

I cursed but did what they said. I made it out the front door into the darkness of night. It was too dark for comfort, but at least I had the Warriors with me and could get away from this darned placed

Julius was at the gate, waiting patiently. He looked spooked. I should've noticed his reaction to this place before I went inside. I should've been paying attention. I heard the blood rushing through my ears as I took the final steps to Julius.

Something hissed, like the sound of a snake. I froze, looking for the culprit. *Where was the animal? Or was it one of those old, rotten things from inside?* At first, I didn't see anything. Then, I saw a figure creep out from behind Julius. The shape did not match that of the monsters I had awoken in the manor.

This was more…*human?*

"My children! You're hurting them!" It shrieked.

I suddenly matched the figure standing before me to a name. **Conrad.** I was certain I understood that Endres said this *"man"* was the leader of the monsters behind me.

"Tell them to leave us alone, and we will do the same," I said viciously, gripping my sword tighter and willing my wrist not to cramp.

His eyes gleamed — wilder than I remembered — in the darkness and cold of the night. *"My children have been hurt tonight. You will not leave with all your companions. You must promise us one."*

I noticed his wrinkles. They were beyond what was considered normal. He was perfectly old, though his voice was young. Right before my eyes, he began to turn into one of those **things**.

He stepped forward, stroking Julius' mane with his repulsive yellow nails, making Julius uncomfortable. *"They're Reapers. They're my **children**. You sowed the seed when you lifted the sheets, and they will be the ones to reap from it."*

There was no reasoning with him. He was practically one of them.

I shook my head. *"I'm actually getting sick of you."*

He hissed, inhuman-like, and lunged at me. I hadn't noticed he had a blade — a knife, to be exact — in his right hand, so I moved to stab him with my sword. His blade slashed my side, just as my sword plunged deep into his flesh. His face contorted, and he screeched something horrible. The blow should have ended him. Instead, he dug his teeth into my shoulder like a savage and bit me — hard.

Cursing, I twisted my body, throwing his off. With my bloody arm and shoulder, I felt like a weakened, battered zombie. Somehow, however, I was fully alive. My blood grew hot. I went for Conrad head-on. He lunged towards me with his knife again. He was so reckless, I knew I could beat him — as long as I kept my eye on his weapon. He was unpredictable and wild, though. I moved out of the way of his next strike and kneed him in the mouth, sending him tumbling into the dirt. I followed, meeting him as he regained his footing.

He thrust his knife forward for a stab. I sidestepped it. I then swung downward with my glimmering sword. It didn't go through his arm, to my dismay. It lodged itself halfway through. I cursed as he screamed in agony and dropped his knife.

Neither of us had our respective weapon now. He surely had an advantage because of his savageness. He tackled me before I'd collected my wits.

He had me straddled on the ground and wrapped his long fingers around my neck, choking me. His nails bit into my flesh. I moved my hips, trying to get him out of his darned straddle position, then threw a sidearm blow at his head. It landed, and he loosened his grip for only a moment. That was all I needed. I hit him in the side and threw him off. He scrambled to his feet.

I scrambled for the knife. **Where was it?** I found it and pointed it upward, turning just in time to be tackled back to the ground. He straddled me yet again, but this time, I had a knife he hadn't seen in my right hand. He threw a punch at my face. Everything around me blurred. I stabbed blindly, not knowing where it would land. Wherever it landed, he shrieked like he was dying and then fell over, limp.

As my vision cleared, I threw him off. Standing, I glanced down at his corpse and saw where the knife had pierced: his left eye. The blade was still lodged there, and blood oozed out of it. I turned away from his grotesque face and grabbed the handle of my sword, yanking it from the man's arm. I sheathed it and ran to Julius.

Climbing into the saddle, I glanced towards the entrance of the manor and saw my companions fighting, their backs to me. If not so heavily devoted to me, they would've run on ahead. I know I'd be dead without them. I owed them my life, 30 times over. They knew that, though. Nevertheless, they kept protecting me, which is partly why I'd befriended them. I wished I could repay them somehow. I wished I could get down and fight with them…

I nearly did, against my better judgment, but Silas saw me and screamed, ***"Get out of here, Dustin!"***

I turned Julius, gave the command to ride, and took off into the woods…all while praying they would all make it out alive to follow me.

31: ROSETTA KELLINA MABEL

Rose Red.
Red Rose.

"How *ow many shillings?"* I asked. Behind me, a goat bleated. People passed by in streams, despite the fact the sun hadn't broken over the horizon yet. The morning fog was terribly thick today.

This was the villager's center market—an unfriendly environment where people bullied and ran over others while shopping for goods. You wouldn't usually find me here, but I was dying for fresh air before going to work. Plus, Lydia said it would do me some good.

"One pound," the lady said stubbornly.

My head snapped up. I looked at her like she was insane. I could feel Lydia beside me just about to tell me to just give the lady the money.

"**A pound**? For **this**? I could buy this whole crummy market with a **pound**!" I said angrily.

Lydia laughed. "*Come on, Rosetta. Give the lady a pound, and let's be off.*"

"*I have a husband back home who's got to eat well 'fore tomorrow. Nearly killed he was in the last Battle. I can't have my son out there fighting, neither. **I'd** fight before I'd let 'im,*" the woman said despondently.

Thinking of Peter, I handed the coins to her begrudgingly, grabbed the linen fabric I'd just purchased, and tucked it under my arm. I wouldn't buy it for a pound if I was burning in Hell, yet I had just done so. **Was I growing soft?**

"*You know, it's impolite to tell someone the goods they're selling are crummy,*" Lydia informed me as we moved on through the marketplace.

I snorted. "*Darn it. Is that so? Well, it's impolite to sell such a fabric for a pound, so who was impolite first?*"

She laughed at my remark, and I broke a slight smile.

"*I suppose you're still bent on not telling me about the necklace?*" she asked between strides.

Chancellor Kenneth's necklace had become a burden chained around my neck. Yes, I was fond of the jewel, but jewels carried stories. I wasn't proud of mine. All around the castle, they asked where I had gotten it. It either earned them a blank stare, a cough, or a change of subject. I was ill-prepared to tell my best friend about it, although she at least knew from whom I'd received it.

*"He's mad, you know? **That** man. There's no getting through to him,"* was what I came up with.

*"By **that** man, I suppose you mean the Chancellor?"*

"Would you hush? I would prefer no one else knew."

"Rose, you're wearing the jewel he gave you around your neck like a bloody trophy. Everyone and their mothers have put the pieces together by now."

*"Darn it! You're right, Lydia. What am I going to **do**?!"* I asked with a hint of despair.

As only a best friend could get away with, she laughed. *"You don't have to make a decision now, right? If you despise him so, you ought to stall for more time."*

Just as she said that, I recognized two people ahead of me and smiled.

Peter was holding a single carrot in one hand, and Ferrando was arguing with a man selling oats. *"I'll buy it,"* I said, walking up to them. Peter turned and beamed when he saw me. To my utter astonishment, he threw his arms around my waist.

Ferrando turned and arched a brow, either at the amusing sight of me in the marketplace or Peter's reaction to me. Perhaps it was both.

It occurred to me then I hadn't been hugged in years. I couldn't find the strength to hug him back, though I did ruffle his hair as he pulled away.

"Rose!" Peter shouted unnecessarily in the busy market. ***"You smell good!"***

I laughed at the compliment, as did Lydia. Ferrando's eyes flickered as they rested on my friend.

"Who is this?" he asked.

*"Someone I **care** about,"* I said sharply.

He raised a knowing brow at me.

"Hello. I'm Rose's friend, Lydia. You must be…Ferrando?" she asked politely while introducing herself.

Peter wrinkled his nose at me. *"You **talk** about us?"*

I felt heat rise to my cheeks. *Why would such a thing be embarrassing,* I wondered.

"I sure do. Why wouldn't I?"

"You're such a busy woman, I just never thought you'd get around to it," Peter replied as he shrugged.

"Nonsense." I moved the conversation in a different direction. *"Did you get my gift last night?"* I asked, referring to the armor James had made for Peter.

His eyes lit up as he nodded profusely. *"I thought I was dead meat, but I think I just might make it tomorrow, thanks to you!"*

"Ahem." The vendor at the oat stall cleared his throat. *"I've got people behind you. Are you gonna buy it or not?"*

"How much?" I asked, stepping towards him.

"Two shillings and 12 pence for one quarter, ma'am."

Ferrando started to protest. I gave the man the money with little heed to him.

We moved to the right of the stall as I gave the bag of oats to a disgruntled Ferrando. I laughed at his expression and teased him because his dissatisfaction pleased me. *"Even nosy, ranking women can give a couple of shillings to a friend."*

He huffed. *"I'm sure. You seem to always have the best intentions."*

"Do you know Rosetta well?" Peter asked Lydia.

She bent her knees slightly to get down to his eye level. *"I do! We're good friends, actually. Do you want to hear a story about her?"*

"Sure!" he said excitedly.

"I'm not sure we have time for that," I said hurriedly, not quite sure if a story about me is something I wanted a smirking Ferrando to hold over my head.

"Darn it! I wanted to hear a silly story about Rosetta," Peter whined. *"By the way, Rose, where did you get your necklace?"*

An ice-cold stare wouldn't work on this kid. I smiled. *"It was just a birthday present, actually. From a friend."*

"Oh, yes. I heard about that," Ferrando cut in. *"I'm happy for you and the Chancellor,"* he said mockingly.

My head snapped up dreadfully quick. ***"Excuse me?"***

"The listing on the church door. Did you not know?" he asked, almost apologetically at my deathly white expression.

Without excusing myself, I lifted the hem of my dress and ran past Ferrando. I dipped in between two stalls, through two people holding an intense conversation, and into a man pushing a cart full of leather. The latter cursed at me. I apologized and continued on my way, down the dirty market and to the end of the strip of stalls.

I reached the bottom of the church stairs and climbed them desperately, speaking to myself under my breath madly and cursing myself for not being prepared. I saw the poster on the church doors, speedily scanning the list of names — willing myself not to see mine and muttering the names I read to myself. I read the whole list through without seeing my name and then went back through a bit more carefully.

There it was:

Chancellor Kenneth and Rosetta Kellina Mabel To Be Married Saturday At Noon

I'm sure my heart stopped beating at that moment. I stared at the 12 unfair words. One of them held so much power, my knees grew weak. I turned and fell to a sitting position against the church door in complete astonishment.

Married?!

Peter came bounding up the steps, followed by Ferrando and an out-of-breath Lydia.

She looked over the list and stilled. *"Oh, Rosetta. I'm so sorry,"* she said as she sat next to me.

Peter sat on the other side of me to my right and gently patted my back.

I recalled the Chancellor's words yesterday as he breathed on my skin:

"It won't do you calling me Chancellor."

Suddenly, it made sense. *It won't do because I'm going to be marrying you Saturday.* Maybe he should've finished the rest of the cursed sentence!

My eyes burned, but no tears came. *"I'm not marrying that man,"* I said dryly…defeated.

"I'm afraid you are. It's posted everywhere. When something is posted, it will be done." Ferrando's tone was gentle. He wasn't trying to hurt me this time; it was just the truth.

"I'm not marrying him," I said in defiance. I stood, walked down the steps, and paced the ground in front of the church. Peter and Lydia remained seated in front of the doors. *"This shouldn't be fair! He shouldn't be allowed to post this without my consent. What if I **don't** want to marry him? What if I **won't**?"*

"It's just the way things are, Rose," Lydia said quietly.

I spun on her. *"Just the way things are? You say that as if I have no power at all!"*

"You don't. I think the Lord is behind this marriage. If he is, then by God, it's going to happen," Ferrando said with bitterness in his tone.

That was not the name I wanted to hear. The very thought of the Lord sent me into hysterics.

*"So, we all just **bow** to the man? We don't even try to change things. He kills our families and takes over our kingdom, and we just let him do it? We adopt his thinking. We adopt his ways. We worship him as if he's our king. Well, he's not **my** king!"*

"Rose..." Ferrando said warningly.

I knew what I said was treasonous. I just didn't care. *"Why do we call him 'The Lord'? After all, he's just a lord and certainly not anything to worship. He bloody isn't! I'm not going to marry the Chancellor just because he wishes it. I don't care **what** he wishes!"*

All was silent around me. I felt the need to repeat myself. I was hysterical. I knew it because of the near-trench I'd made from pacing back and forth during my rant.

"I won't marry him. I won't! I swear to all: It will never happen! I hate the Chancellor! I hate him!" I shouted to the entire marketplace.

All while I yelled, Lydia, Peter, and Ferrando tried to hush me. Ferrando, who was closest, grabbed me firmly and looked me in the eyes. *"Shut up, Rosetta! You can't say those things aloud!"*

"Please, Rose. Listen to him. You can't get yourself killed. I need you, my friend!" Lydia pleaded. She descended the steps,

grabbed my left hand, and squeezed it, trying to calm and comfort me.

I had yet to calm all the way down, despite their best efforts. *"You can't make me love him! I hate him! I wish he were dead! I wish he'd take the Lord down to Hell with him!"*

Ferrando shook me roughly and shouted in my face, but I couldn't make out a thing he said.

"I won't marry him."

"You don't have to, Rose," I heard Peter say.

In a snap and at the sound of **his** voice, I came back to myself. I looked at the three of them. My tears had gotten lost somewhere on their journey to my eyes, never appearing. The rock in my throat, however, remained. It seemed to serve as a barrier, preventing me from speaking another angry word.

"I'm sorry." I turned my back to them and climbed the stairs again, trying to grab control of my crazy mind with each step. *"How long has this notice been posted?"*

"Just this morning," Ferrando replied.

"You'll grow into it, my darling Rose. You'll see I'm the best thing to ever happen to you," **the man** said just yesterday morning. It was ironic and perhaps almost humorous that he was the **worst** thing to ever happen to me…in my entire existence.

~~~~~~~~~~

After seeing the notice, I didn't want to work. My stomach felt ripped open, gutted, and void. How was I
~~~~~~~~~~

supposed to work like the day was a normal one when, in nearly four days, I was expected to marry the only man on God's green earth who had an ego as large as his ignorance?

Héloise, Faye, and Kip all started talking at once when Lydia and I arrived. After seeing my face, they stopped and grew silent.

"You ought to be happier, Rose. He's a good man," Héloise scolded.

"Oh yeah? Just what is a good man these days?" I retorted as I took my place by the loom to work.

"Don't bother, Rose. I got it." Faye moved towards me. *"There's a man outside whose master needs to be fitted."*

I stood and grabbed the bag full of needles, thread, and other items needed for the fitting. *"Did he mention who his master is?"* I asked over my shoulder as I made my way out of the room.

"I suppose you'd be ill-pressed if it were Kenneth," Kip teased.

I cast her a wary look. *"The more you say his confounded name, the closer I get to my deathbed. Now, if you'll excuse me."* I hastened out the door then paused to look down the corridor I had just walked through to get in the factory.

There hadn't been anybody outside when I entered, and nobody was there now. I turned to go back inside to ask Faye where the man had gone off to, when someone came running up the stairwell. He was drenched in a cold sweat and in an ill mood.

"Were you in need of a tailor, perhaps?" I asked, biting my lip to keep from laughing at his blood-red face.

He cursed at me first, then bent over slightly to place his hands on his knees as he heaved long, exaggerated breaths. *"Darn it, woman! I thought you'd **never** come!"* He stood and exhaled sharply. He looked poorly tended to for a noble's servant. Scars lined his face, and his eyes were hollow. His beard was patchy, like it hadn't been groomed in ages.

After the events of my morning, I wanted to laugh at him but couldn't quite make myself do so. *"I report to work at 6:30 every morning, not before. I had no idea I was needed before then,"* I stated. *"Before coming to work, I went to the marketplace to purchase supplies."*

He glared at me. *"That's all well and good, but I doubt my master cares any about your schedule. We need to hurry along now. I'm already late,"* he said, wincing before turning to the stairwell.

We headed up the stairs. In the castle, height determined rank. The higher, the wealthier.

"Who is your master, anyway?" I asked as we climbed, my voice echoing off the stones.

"The Lord Monté."

Surely, he was joking. **Surely**, he had a dry sense of humor. I actually laughed aloud at his jesting.

The man turned and looked at me as if I were the dumbest human on the planet. *"You mustn't laugh around him, you hear? This is **not** the time for humor."*

Only then did I realize he was quite serious. My knees turned to water, and I felt my body — not just my face — drain of its color. I somehow managed to follow the man…albeit weakly.

How could I — of **all** people — be called to this task? This was the wrong morning. This was terrible timing. I hated the man with a burning passion, yet now, I had to fit him. God above must be laughing at me. *Is it His laughter I hear?*

Coming face-to-face with the man was supposed to be impossible. It was happening, though. I wasn't ready. Would he even speak to me? Would it be nearly half an hour or more of silence? This wouldn't be so bad if I weren't sending those letters to Geoff…

How could my life spiral out of control so quickly? A minute ago, I believed I could hardly work at all, knowing I was to be married soon. Now, I was preparing to fit the man who'd ordered the death of my parents, friends, and a once-joyful kingdom.

I breathed quick and sharp breaths, but they did nothing to satisfy my lungs. Sweat tickled my forehead, though the air in the castle was cool. I was experiencing a different kind of sweat.

A nervous sweat.

I continued to be led down a corridor, through a door, up some more stairs, up some more secluded stairs, and then to another door. The man stopped and looked me over like I was the scum of the earth with the question in his eyes that asked, ***"How could I possibly present her to my Lord?"***

"Is there something wrong?" I asked. I was out of breath, but not because of the walk.

*"Aye. Everything's wrong. **You're** wrong."* He sighed and continued in a hushed voice so as not to be overheard. *"To keep your life, you must bow to him, you hear? If he smiles, you must **not** do the same. He's a peculiar fellow. Just because he seems lighthearted does not mean he is. You mustn't ask him questions unless he asks you to. Lastly, keep your bloody head down."* He then turned away briskly, and I shivered next to the door.

"Wait," I called with a harsh whisper. He turned at the top of the stairs he was preparing to descend. *"How will I ever make conversation with him? What in Heaven's name should I say?"*

*"Say **nothing**. Get in there, do your work, and get out. If you value your life, you will do as I say. Now, go!"*

I glanced ahead of me and then back towards the man who'd led me there. He was gone.

There — in front of me — stood that **ghastly** door.

ABOUT THE AUTHOR

Naomi D. Moore is an 18-year-old first-time author who presently resides in the Great Smoky Mountains of North Carolina. Her passion and inspiration for writing came from reading similar stories in the young adult fiction genre.

Lord Monté had humble beginnings as Naomi's high school senior project. During that same year, other memorable moments included: purchasing a piano keyboard, wearing a yellow prom dress, and buying her first car with cash.

To learn more about Naomi, visit:
www.MooreJoyinFamily.com

CITY OF JOCUND: MONTÉ'S MASQUERADE

Lord Monté's Story Continues...

1: THE BOY

Patience take your precious time.
It always pays off to wait.
What it costs to begin with, though,
Most souls will not pay.

*ore of the same today… Uzzah's let me use a knife he gave me, and we robbed a passerby. Uzzah made me punch the man just for sport. I pretended I was afraid to hit the man, though. It was funny because I **wanted** to hit the poor, innocent man who was on his way to Haestingas. I wanted to hit him **harder** than I actually did.*

Innocence makes me sick.

I got into a fight today with Steven — one he started. He's so much bigger than I, so he beat me good. Still, it was worth it because I got a few hits on him. His jaw felt so good under my fist. I even cracked his nose. Uzzah, however, was mad that we fought. He beat me good, too. I don't know why 'cause Steven already had.

*I suppose Uzzah just enjoys beating people. How could I blame him? Given a chance, I'd beat him. When I have the chance, I'm going to **kill** him.*

Someone cracked Aalez's rib last week. They didn't mean to, I'm sure. The Scavengers like to beat her, but never to the point where she can't cook for them. As it is, she's our only cook. I've visited her several time this week, fed her from a bowl, and kept her company. I work to keep her healthy 'cause I'm gonna need her help to kill Uzzah. The last time I saw her, she kissed me on the mouth. I scolded her for it, even though I'd enjoyed it.

*Cecilly kissed me on the mouth, too. I wanted to remember **her**, not Aalez.*

~~~~~~~~~~~

Aldus caught me writing in this journal — Pa's journal. He don't care too much. He said, "When someone's in as bad a place as this, it don't matter what they do to cope, as long as they're coping." *I liked it when he said that. It sounds like something Mal would have said. Such wisdom…*

*I would have to say Aldus is the best friend I ever had 'cause he never says anything mean to me. He never touches me, either. I don't mind him calling me **bru** so much. Not at all, hardly.*

~~~~~~~~~~~

The weeks seem to fly by when you're a bandit. We have to move a lot, even though I really liked the cave with the waterfall. I even said as much to Uzzah, just to sound weak. He laughed and punched me square in the face. I then pretended I couldn't get back up, although I hardly felt any pain at all.

*It's been three months since I was forced to join the Scavengers. I can't say I'm happy with living a bandit's life. They are a group of intelligent **cowards** who pick on one or two people and then run off with the prize. I can't help but think we're wasting our time and that we could be doing much bigger and better things.*

I still have a yearning to see Haestingas — the place all these travelers are journeying to see. I've heard it's a beautiful city.

~~~~~~~~~~~

Three days ago, Uzzah killed Steven. He's been wanting to do that for a while. I don't know why it took him so long…

*Last week, Steven beat him at cards, and I thought for sure he'd kill him right then, but he didn't. The day after, Steven made fun of Uzzah, calling him a yellow-bellied coward. I thought for **sure** that'd be the end of Steven.*

The day Steven was killed, he was playing cards with Aldus. I was watching while chewing on some dried meat. Tomas was there, too, but he was sleeping on a blanket he's stolen from some idiotic traveler. Aalez was hugging herself in the corner, muttering something incoherently.

Uzzah suddenly burst into the cave, stormed over to the men playing cards, and punched Steven right in his face without saying a word. He beat him to the ground with his calloused fists until Steven was a whimpering mess. After a hearty laugh at the damage he'd done, Uzaah stabbed one of Tomas' arrows straight through Steven's chest.

Aalez screamed. What I considered an innocent crime turned out to be horrendous for her because Uzzah turned around and beat her, too.
~~~~~~~~~~~

*I didn't utter a word in her defense. I couldn't **afford** to.*

~~~~~~~~~~~

I have been upgraded from a knife to a bow and arrow. The tips of the arrows are razor sharp. I understand now how Uzzah easily stabbed one into Steven's chest, though I can tell it still would've taken a lot of strength to do so.

I'm almost taller than Uzzah now. Of told me to be careful not to draw up too much around him. After all, it doesn't take much to get Uzzah to snap. I guess I could say I learned from Steven that it doesn't take much at all. Just because we are spared doesn't mean we are forgiven.

*What does **forgiveness** look and feel like, anyway?*

~~~~~~~~~~~

It's been a year now. I feel so worn out. I know it'll all be worth it when it's over, but I am so tired of letting Uzzah tell me what to do. I've never wanted to hit someone this bad before. Not even my parents.

*He's getting older, though. I can tell. He's getting tired, too. I'm glad he is. Heck, I'm glad **anytime** he suffers 'cause it's rare he does at all.*

~~~~~~~~~~~

I killed somebody today. It's the first time I've killed since my Pa and Ma.

I let off an arrow that went straight through the traveler's head, causing him to fall off his horse. He never even saw it coming.
~~~~~~~~~~~

Afterward, I pretended to cry. I pretended it was hard to do. This time, though, I didn't even get sick. I just stood on my own two feet, walked over to the dead man, and checked his pockets for anything worth keeping.

*I pretended his death mattered. I pretended I was trying not to **let** it matter.*

Uzzah saw me and laughed 'cause he thought I was the weakest boy he's ever known.

Mallory would have been proud of me. I was proud of my acting.

~~~~~~~~~~

Those lawmen from Haestingas are persistent. We've been raiding more, which means we've been hunted more. We've had to move a lot recently. Much more than before. From cave to cave to cave to cave…

Aalez is nearly sick as a rabid dog, yet Uzzah keeps making her cook anyway 'cause she's still the only bloody cook we have. Surely, it can't be healthy to have the person preparing our food coughing all over it the entire time, but hey… Half the time, I don't even know what it is we're eating.

*One of those lawmen caught Tomas. As far as I know, getting caught means we are not going to rescue you. I'm pretty sure Aldus is mad about it 'cause Tomas and he have known each other for quite a while. Aldus didn't say anything to Uzzah, though. He **never** does. For such a strong guy, Aldus sure is good at being submissive.*

Tomas was one of the head authorities of the Scavengers. He was quickly replaced with a man named Gale — the one who'd first spoke to me when I'd walked into the waterfall cave over a year ago.
~~~~~~~~~~

"Will you lookie here?" *Gale had said.* "Uzzah's prized possession." *To keep it brief: I don't think he likes me.*

~~~~~~~~~~

I'm taller than Uzzah now. **Much** *taller. I don't know how tall I am exactly, but I'm taller than everyone in the Scavengers. I'm feeling long and gangly – too big for my own dang self. Too tall and lanky to be me. Seems that's what I've evolved into.*

I think the color of my eyes has gotten lighter. I wonder if eyes are supposed to get lighter…

The Fork brand scars behind my ear itch a lot. I try not to scratch at it 'cause the skin's so raw there from so many brands over the years from my Pa. It don't feel soothing whatsoever to scratch there.

~~~~~~~~~~

I don't think about Mallory much anymore. I don't think about much of anything anymore except killing Uzzah and taking my place as leader over the Scavengers.

Once I kill him, I can think of other things.

Once I kill him, I might not have to think about killing so much anymore…

Stay tuned for
Author N.D.M.'s
jaw-dropping conclusion—
coming in 2021!

N.D.M.